BATHING
BEAUTY

BATHING BEAUTY

A NOVEL OF MARIE PREVOST

LAINI GILES

ALSO BY LAINI GILES:

Love Lies Bleeding

The Forgotten Flapper

The It Girl and Me

*For Bob Demunbrun and Connie O'Hearne, English
teachers extraordinaire, with fondest admiration and
gratitude*

NO DEPRESSION
IN HEAVEN

PROLOGUE

AFTONIAN APARTMENTS 6230 AFTON PLACE, HOLLYWOOD, CALIFORNIA *January 23, 1937*

"First thing we need to do is shut that dog up so I can think," Sanderson said. "We've got to get him out of there. Filkas, grab that houseboy, will ya?"

Officers LeRoy Sanderson and Joe Filkas had arrived at the Aftonian that morning after dispatch took a phone call from a Mister Jenks, who said he was the building's landlord.

"One of my tenants is dead," Jenks said when he met them in the hallway outside apartment 10. "We hadn't seen her for a while, and her dog, Max, has been barking non-stop for three days. She... well, she drinks a bit. I finally got worried enough that I sent our houseboy to check on her. I don't know how long she's been lying there."

Filkas nodded. He and Sanderson were close to the same age, but Sanderson's slight bit of seniority put him in charge. He noted the hand-written sign tacked up by the apartment's door:

Please do not knock on this door more than once. It makes my dog bark. If I am in, I will hear you, as I am not deaf.

Bill Bogle, the colored houseboy, hovered in the hallway, clearly still shaken by his discovery.

"Hey, do you know anything about this dog?" Filkas asked him. "Every time we try to get near her, he snaps at us."

"Yessuh. Let me try to get him for you. He knows me a lil' bit."

Sanderson cracked the door, and the little dachshund instinctively backed up against his owner's body, barking even more frantically than he had been.

Bogle slipped in and approached slowly, letting Max sniff his hand.

"Sure, tha's right. You know me, dontcha boy? You're jes' a mite scared, ain't ya? Don't worry, ole Bill's not here to hurt you. Ain't nothin' to worry about, Mist' Max." He petted the velvety ears, and the dog whimpered. "Come on, fella. Let's let these policemens do their work. I'll take care of ya. My ma always talkin' 'bout gettin' a dog."

Max let Bogle pick him up, but he continued to whine for his mistress. "Mist' Jenks? Ima take this here dog home with me, but can Miz Jenks watch him while I make my rounds? I'll come back by 'fore I leave."

"Sure. Henrietta will like the company." He opened the door to his own apartment, and Bogle handed the dog to Mrs. Jenks. "Honey, Bill's going to take Maxie. Keep an eye on him until he heads home, will you?"

"Okay. Come on, Max," she said. "I've got a big ham bone you can gnaw on."

Mr. Jenks and the houseboy stood outside as Filkas and Sanderson explored.

"What's the tenant's name?" Sanderson called through the open door.

"Marie Prevost," Jenks said, moving into the vestibule of the apartment.

"Marie Prevost?!" Sanderson said, doing a double-take. "Not that Marie Prevost. The actress?!"

"Yes sir, she's an actress," Jenks answered.

"Jesus," Filkas said, looking around the room. A single iron bed dominated the space. The only real decoration were some blue ribbons from what appeared to be dog shows. A few framed photographs of the woman in 1910s and 1920s-era clothing hung on the walls. "I had such a crush on her years ago."

"Me too," Sanderson said. "Any sign of the bus yet?"

Filkas peered out the window. "They're pulling up now."

The ambulance braked to a stop out front, and two attendants pulled a stretcher out of the back, then hurried up the front walk, followed closely by the staff medical doctor.

When Doc Harris arrived upstairs, they made notes of the scene, while he analyzed the dead woman on the bed.

"I'd say she's been dead about three days, judging by the body temperature."

"And look at the scratch marks," Sanderson said. "Her dog's been trying to wake her that whole time. Poor little fella."

"Any idea what it was, Doc?" said Filkas.

"Offhand, I'd say heart attack, but no telling until I get her back to the morgue."

Filkas took note of the four bottles of Old Crow in the kitchen sink. He shook his head, remembering the beauty with the pretty pout who'd entranced him in *Heroes of the Street*. It was right before Christmas of 1922 at the Liberty Theater in Lewiston, Idaho. He'd sat in the dark mooning over her and imagining the charmed life she must lead. "Evidently, she's been celebrating the end of Prohibition a little longer than the rest of us," he noted, picking up one of the bottles.

"She's had a run of bad luck the last few years," Mr. Jenks said. "But I guess none of us knew quite how bad."

"Looks like Joan Crawford gave her some money recently," Sanderson said, holding up a receipt of some kind with the actress's name on it.

"Hard to believe, ain't it?" said Filkas. "She used to be a god-damned millionaire, didn't she? I mean... look at this place."

I LOVE THE
NAME OF MARY

CHAPTER ONE

GRAND AVENUE, BUNKER HILL NEIGHBORHOOD,
LOS ANGELES, CALIFORNIA *April 1, 1912*

NO DOGS, JEWS, OR ACTORS said the sign in the window. It was hand-printed in big block letters.

"Whae de ye think of this one, medears?" Mum said in her Canadian-flavored Scottish burr as we approached the big pink Victorian two-story with gingerbread trim. She knocked on the door, and the older gray-haired woman who answered peered at us through round, wire-frame spectacles.

"Hello," Mum said. "I'm Hughina Prevost, and these are my daughters, Mary and Peg. We've come about yeer room to rent."

"Oh yes. Please come in," the woman said, her face brightening with a welcoming smile. "I'm Ellen Taggart. Welcome to my home." She ushered us into the parlor, which was papered with fading floral wallpaper. A divan of midnight blue velvet dominated the room, surrounded by occasional tables and several elaborately carved armchairs. Crocheted lace antimacassars covered all the upholstery arms and backs.

"Where are you ladies from?" Mrs. Taggart asked.

"Ontario, Canada," Mum said. "But we've lived out west for several years."

"And your husband? Will he be following later?"

Mum saw Peg ready to open her mouth and beat her to the punch.

"I'm a widow," Mum said. Peg's mouth drooped closed and she and I both watched Mum for direction.

"I'm so sorry," Mrs. Taggart said.

"He was...killed in a mining accident," Mum said.

Mrs. Taggart clucked sympathetically. What she didn't know was that my sweet, unassuming mother was determined to erase the existence of my stepfather, Frank, from our lives. Fully and permanently.

To hear Mum tell it, my real father, Teddy Dunn, had been a complete prince—funny, handsome, and a good provider. We lost him when I was only a baby. He'd been a conductor for the Grand Trunk Railroad, and on his shift one cold November night, gas leaked into the St. Clair Tunnel on his #34 eastbound route between Port Huron, Michigan, and Sarnia, Ontario, where we lived. He and the other men never stood a chance.

After Papa's death, we lived with my grandparents, Angus and Mary McDonald. Other than my mother, my favorite person in the world was my grandmother. I was named after her. No one ever called her Mary. Her entire life, she was Wee Mae. Wee Mae had come from Scotland to Canada with my grandfather after they were married. She was all of four foot ten inches tall, smoked cigars, and had her dram at breakfast.

I was only about two and a half when Frank Prevost came

sniffing around. He'd been a friend of my father's, and he'd gone out west to prospect. It would have taken a far stronger woman than my mother to resist Frank's dashing good looks, his diamond pinkie ring, his ivory-topped walking stick, and his tales of riches. He proposed and moved us out west to his home in Ouray, Colorado. It was there that my half-sister Marjorie arrived. They called her Peg.

Frank proceeded to move us nearly once a year for the next twelve years, always in search of the next big strike, whether lead, copper, gold, or silver. Mum did this without complaint until August of 1906. Frank had made a respectable sum from a strike, and was headed to Denver to invest it. He had filled our heads with dreams of moving someplace civilized, buying a little house, and having a nice life together. Then, somewhere between the hotel and the bathhouse, the $42,000 disappeared, and so did our fantasy. Frank came home with his tail between his legs, and Mum filed for divorce not long after.

She told us stories of southern California—the ocean, the oranges, and the bright sunshine, and now, here we were in Los Angeles. But Mum's biggest fear was anyone discovering the divorce and the shame of it. Although I'd loathed Frank and wanted to keep my birth name of Dunn, she insisted I had to be a Prevost to hide it all.

"I'm a widow now. No one need be the wiser, pet," she'd said.

"The room is my largest one upstairs," Mrs. Taggart said, bringing me back to the present. "It's quite spacious, even for the three of you. It has a larger double bed and a Murphy bed too. Plus there's a bathroom down the hall with a tub. It's right over the porch, and you get lovely light in the mornings. We all share the dining room, and Eva—she's my maid—makes a scrumptious breakfast for me every day. I'd love the company. I also have another tenant in my first floor room, Mr. Howe. He's a salesman, so he's often out of town. Do you work?"

"I'm looking for employment right now," Mum said. Realizing her blunder, she corrected herself. "But Ah've income from me husband's estate." She smiled in that charming way my mother did, and soon, we were moving our things into the large bedroom upstairs. Peg and I shared the large bed, and Mum took the Murphy.

I'd realized years before that Peg would always be my half-sister and never my real sister. In looks and temperament, there seemed to be no Mum in her at all. She was Frank's daughter, completely—the shiftlessness and the constant excuses when she couldn't or wouldn't do something. Not wanting to admit that Peg didn't take after her at all, Mum made excuses for her. I had grown to resent my sister for many reasons, but mostly for her ability to wrap anyone around her little finger. Peg was allergic to any kind of work, and was perfectly happy to let others do her chores for her. Usually, that ended up being me.

Mum got a job as a cleaning lady to make ends meet, and when September arrived, Peg and I started school. I attended classes at Manual Arts High School. My inconvenient November birthday already put me a year behind my peers, but because of my spotty education, I lagged behind the rest of the class by two whole grades. Peg and I had both gone to school—if you could call the one-room affairs we attended throughout the west and southwest "school"—but I was only too aware that my education had huge gaps, and so was Mum.

She was determined that her girls were going to be more educated than she had been, and we were going to make better choices.

The first day, I took a seat halfway to the back of the room in algebra. A pretty blonde in a sailor blouse and long navy skirt plopped down in the seat behind me.

"Do me a favor," she said. "Lean to your left a little."

"Why?" I asked, glancing over my shoulder.

"Because this is my morning nap time. The teacher can't call on you if she can't see you."

I turned in my seat. "Don't you like math?" I said.

"Do you?" She looked at me as if I had two heads.

"Well, no but we should try to learn *something* while we're here. Shouldn't we?"

"Math is boring. My favorite class is lunch. And art. I don't hate art. What's your name, Smarty Pants?" she asked.

"Mary Prevost."

"Mary what?"

"Pree-vost. It's Swiss."

She shrugged. "Okay, if you say so. I'm Phyllis. Phyllis O'Haver. Where you from?" She pinched her cheeks and fluffed up her hair as some of the boys filed in.

"How do you know I'm not from here?" I said.

"Your accent. Besides, nobody's from California. Everybody just moves here. My family moved here from Kansas when I was little."

"Oh. I've lived all over the last few years. Colorado, South Dakota, Utah, Arizona, Nevada. But I was born in Ontario, Canada."

"I've never met a real live Canadian before."

"Well, you have now," I said.

Phyllis was flighty, but she was fun. We endured algebra together and shared a table at lunch. Mine was rarely anything more than a hard-boiled egg or a mustard sandwich. For a splurge, we'd sneak off to the Del Mar Café around the corner on Vermont and split a black cow. Phyllis' stepfather was a demonstrator for John Deere, and he made decent money, so she got an allowance. She treated because she felt bad for me.

We talked about the boys we liked and the teachers we hated and our dreams for the future. I wasn't sure I had any, other than never marrying a miner. "I want to settle down and have a pretty little house with a garden and a dog. Maybe a couple of dogs," I said.

"You don't care about a husband, but you want a dog?"

"I could never have a dog because we've moved so much," I said, sipping the chocolate ice cream soda she'd bought me. After seeing what Mum had gone through with Frank, I was in no hurry to marry. "I want to stay in the same place for a while and be happy. If I find the right fella, that'd be wonderful, but I *know* dogs are faithful. What about you?"

"I'm going to be a famous actress, like Maude Fealy," Phyllis said. "She's so beautiful and graceful. I check plays out of the library and pantomime in front of the mirror at night so I can get the movements right."

"Really?"

"That was my favorite thing back in Kansas. There's nothing else to do there but watch the corn grow. Mama and Daddy would take us to tent shows, and I'd go home and try to imitate the ingénues."

"It would be very glamorous, wouldn't it?" I said.

"Thrillllling," she said, enunciating like she was playing Lady Macbeth.

"But no tent shows for me," I pronounced. "I'm done moving. Done."

For two years, Phyl and I did everything together...seeing the latest flickers at the Woodley or the Superba downtown and spending hours at the beach in Santa Monica.

The day of graduation, we hugged and promised we'd keep in touch. But Phyl met a boy over the summer, and ended up spending all her time with him. We grew apart, even though I tried to keep our friendship going. When three letters of mine went unanswered, I figured maybe she had married him or moved away.

One of my teachers, Mrs. Horne, had taken me under her wing and told me she thought I'd make a good secretary. She showed me how to use a typewriting machine, and let me practice on the one she had at home. Then she negotiated an interview for me at a law firm, Goodman, MacKenzie, and Blatter on Spring Street, tucked among the big banks. Lucky me, I got the job, with a salary even higher than Mum's.

CHAPTER TWO

LAW FIRM OF GOODMAN, MACKENZIE, AND BLATTER,
LOS ANGELES, CALIFORNIA *January 1916*

"**M**iss Prevost, I have an errand for you," Mr. MacKenzie said, pausing beside my desk. "I need you to go to the Keystone lot in Edendale. The address is 1712 Alessandro. You can hop the streetcar to get there. Ask for Mr. Sennett. I've marked the pages he needs to sign."

Mack Sennett was a well-known figure around Los Angeles. His Keystone Kops flickers were good fun and entertained the masses, but their film shoots made a chaotic mess of city streets. No respectable rooming house or café would allow him or his employees inside.

I pushed my chair back from my desk, and Mr. MacKenzie handed me the sheaf of papers. I took them and waited at the streetcar stop until the next one came by. From downtown, the tracks veered north to the studio, past orange groves and looming hills.

The Sennett lot lay on either side of Alessandro at the intersection with Effie Street. It was composed of a series of lightweight sheds and open-air stages in various stages of completion, with lengths of muslin draped over the tops to deflect the sunlight. One roof read "Mack Sennett Studios," and another, "Comedies Mack Sennett Comedies." Peeping out at strange angles were a tower and a large number of buildings with false fronts. Catercorner from the main lot, a giant carousel painted with scenery spun behind a group of actors doing a chase scene. I watched them for a few minutes after the streetcar dropped me off, laughing as they performed athletic-looking falls. Caleche dust blew up from the ground as they ran, along with the herbal scent of eucalyptus from the trees across the block. I turned toward the main building and gate, where a striped awning flapped in the breeze and a sign proclaimed:

Keystone Film Company

"Excuse me, could you tell me where I might find Mr. Sennett?" I asked the attendant at the front gate. "I'm from the law firm of Goodman, MacKenzie, and Blatter. I have something that needs his signature."

"He's around," the man said with a shrug. "Probably in the tub. Go on in. Somebody'll find him for you."

The tub? At a flicker studio?

I had just passed buildings marked Wardrobe on my right, and Projecting Room on my left when a man dashed up to me. He wore a goatee and a fake mustache, little round glasses, and a crumpled stovepipe hat. His eyes were like agate—dark and intense.

"You!" he said, grabbing my hand.

"Who, me?"

"Yeah, you," he said, pointing. "When I give you the signal, run to that table over there and sit down in the chair next to it."

I shook my hand loose. "But I'm not…"

"No time to argue! Hurry! You'll ruin the shot!"

Reluctantly, I trotted over to the chair and sat down. As soon as I did, it collapsed, tossing me on my caboose. My legs went flying, along with my skirts. Mortified, I gathered them around me and brushed myself off.

"Damned actors and their trick chairs," I muttered under my breath.

"Perfect! Cut!" A voice called.

I coughed from all the dust I'd kicked up, then seeing the animated gazes of cast and crew members eyeing me in amusement, I summoned all the dignity and gumption I had left.

"I'm here from the law firm of Goodman, MacKenzie and Blatter, and I have some important papers for Mr. Sennett to sign. I'd appreciate being able to do that without starring in any more scenes!" I yelled. "Where is he?"

A funny-looking man with a perfectly square face, prominent nose and cauliflower ears pointed up to the tower with a sheepish grin.

"Thank you," I said, dusting myself off. The administration building was two floors, and the tower stretched up from one side, like the neck of an awkward giraffe. I climbed the stairs, then opened the door to an office. In one corner was a desk covered with papers and folders. In the opposite corner was a huge marble bathtub with silver fixtures that was in the process of draining.

In the tub! He wasn't kidding.

On the far side of the room, a long table was set up for a massage. The man on the table was still relatively young—mid-30s,

I guessed—but his hair was already white, with only a few streaks of dark still remaining. His eyes were the hard blue-gray of a winter sky in Ouray. Beneath the small towel around his middle, he was nude. Standing over him, a taller, dark-complected Mussulman worked out the knots in his muscles with an earthy-smelling oil.

"Whaddya want?" the white-haired man asked.

"Are you Mr. Sennett?" I asked, averting my eyes.

"Well, I ain't the gosh-darned Kaiser," he said.

"I'm sorry, sir. I'm here from the law firm of Goodman, MacKenzie, and Blatter. I've brought some paperwork the partners need you to sign, from KB Pictures. Mr. MacKenzie would have come himself, but he has several huge cases on his plate right now."

"I'm a little busy, Miss..."

"Miss Prevost. I realize that, Mr. Sennett. If you sign, I can leave as quickly as possible, and you can get back to enjoying your massage."

"All right. Give it here."

He gestured impatiently at me. I handed him a fountain pen from my bag and lay the pages in front of him. He made an illegible scrawl on the line at the bottom of each where I indicated. I hoped Mr. MacKenzie wouldn't be too annoyed by the greasy massage oil spots now dotting the page.

"Say," he said, looking up and meeting my eyes for the first time. He craned his neck over the edge of the table for a better glimpse of me. "Lemme see your knees."

"My what?" I asked, thinking I'd heard him wrong.

"Pull your skirt up a little so I can see your knees."

"I beg your pardon!" I said. *The absolute cheek of this man!*

"Good day, Mr. Sennett."

I stalked away with the signed papers hugged to my chest, shoved them into my bag, and descended the stairs. Although I'd once thought flickers might have been fun, my experiences at the lot had now convinced me otherwise. I'd never been so happy to get back to my typewriter.

The next morning, Mr. MacKenzie called me into his office. I clutched my steno pad, shut his office door behind me and took a seat.

"Miss Prevost, I'm not sure what happened at the Sennett lot yesterday, but whatever it was, you need to get back down to Edendale right away."

Maybe I got him to sign the wrong line?

"I had Mr. Sennett sign the paperwork, Mr. MacKenzie. That's all," I protested, leaving out the part about my big scene and the viewing of my legs.

Is that Sennett fellow trying to get me fired because he couldn't see my knees?

"He's insisted that I send the girl with the contract back to the lot. And he's a very good client of ours. So please give him what he wants."

Good heavens. I've blown it but good. I'm going to lose this job.

Filled with dread, I stepped off the streetcar and approached the man at the front gate again. This time, he directed me into the administrative offices. The dark-haired man from the previous day hovered outside. When he saw me, he ushered me in with an exaggerated bow. Then he closed the door behind us and stood there with a silly grin on his face.

"Hiya, doll. Good to see you again," said Mr. Sennett from

behind the desk. He worked a hunk of tobacco jammed in his cheek, and aimed a wad at the spittoon in the corner.

"Is it?" I asked nervously. I shifted my weight, trying to find a comfortable position.

"Of course it is! You're the girl from the law firm. The one that Ford there finagled into our scene, right?" The dark-haired man gave me a little wave.

"I...yes, sir," I said.

"Sorry if I was a little rough on you yesterday." Mr. Sennett continued. "I liked your look so much I needed to get you back here. Please, sit down."

This was unexpected. I sat and listened.

"You know what I do here?" Mr. Sennett said.

"Yes, sir. You make flickers."

"Correction. I make a *lot* of flickers. And I need a gal like you for some bit parts—when we need a pretty girl to stroll by, minor walk-on roles like maids—that sort of thing. I have an idea for a group I plan to promote here at the lot. Real smick-smack girls in bathing suits. And I want lots of beach photos of them to promote the studio. I'd like you to join us."

"Thank you for thinking of me, Mr. Sennett, but I'm not interested," I said. "I have a job I like, and I've been there over a year. Soon, I'll be making ten dollars a week."

"Ten? Honey, I'm offering you fifteen right off the bat."

"Fifteen dollars a week? For standing around in a bathing suit?"

"There's a little more to it than *that*," he said, looking offended. "A few stunts here and there, publicity photos, public appearances, maybe a beauty contest or two. Whaddya say? Wanna come work for me?"

"I'm not sure..." I said. I didn't know how I would explain this to Mum. Or more importantly, to our movie-hating landlady, Mrs. Taggart.

"What's your name again?" he asked.

"Mary Prevost," I said.

"Is that a Frog name?"

"It's Swiss," I clarified.

"Close enough. We can tell the fans you're French and call you Marie. Sounds more exotic," Mr. Sennett said.

"But I love my name..." I began, thinking of the bond I'd always shared with Wee Mae because of it.

"It's boring. It's conventional. You're going to be *un*conventional!" Mr. Sennett said, ignoring me.

The dark-haired man nodded with enthusiasm for the name change. "Where you from?" he asked.

"I've lived all over out west, but I was born in Sarnia, Ontario," I said.

"You're Canadian?" Mr. Sennett said, blinking at me in surprise. His face lit up. "Well whaddya know! I'm from Danville, Quebec!"

"Small world," I said with laugh. At least we had something in common. And the extra cash could sure come in handy.

"Do we have a deal?" he asked. He held out his hand.

After a little more consideration, I shook it and smiled. "All right."

"Then go quit your job and show up here Monday morning at 8:00 a.m. sharp." He passed a one-dollar bill across the desk. "Here's a little advance to get yourself a humdinger of a new suit. Something spare—none of those Old Mother Hubbard things. And buy a new hat or some slippers to go with it. Make it look good."

I nodded and turned to leave.

"Oh, Miss Prevost!" he called.

"Yes?" I slowly turned back.

"I don't suppose you know how to swim, do you?"

"Like a mackerel," I said. All that time in Santa Monica with Phyl appeared to be paying off. I wondered how she was doing.

"Bully! Ford, can I spot 'em or what? All right, see you Monday, doll."

I couldn't stop smiling, until I got back to the office and had to tell Mr. MacKenzie that I was leaving to take another job.

"I thought you might," he said. "It's hard to keep good typists around here anymore."

"I'm sorry, Mr. MacKenzie. You've been good to me, and I'm so grateful. But my mother and my sister are depending on me. I know you only gave me that raise a month ago, but he's promised me five dollars more right away."

"I wish you'd reconsider. You're a good worker, and you've done well by us. I hate to see you go into flickers because some smooth-talking director says he can pay you a little better. No, change that. I hate to see you go into flickers, period. But I can't stop you." He made out my last check and handed it to me.

"Thank you, Mr. MacKenzie, for everything."

"I hope you're not making a mistake," he said.

"Me too, sir."

That afternoon I found a little two-piece number with a long chemise and short bloomers underneath. It was navy blue with horizontal red stripes across the bust and hem. And I also found a red scarf to wrap turban style around my head with a big bow effect and some hair fluffed out at the sides. My last investment was a pair of smart navy boxing boots. I couldn't believe Mr.

Sennett had given me an entire dollar. Neither Peg nor I had been able to buy anything new for years. Everything was hand sewn, and Peg wore my hand-me-downs.

When I got home that night, I told Mum and Peg of my good fortune and the extra five dollars a week.

"You mean I'll be able to take a day off now and then?" Mum said as I hugged her.

"At least one a week, Mum!"

"Good," Peg said, flipping through her copy of *Beauty* magazine. "I can buy lots of new frocks."

On my first day, I stepped off the streetcar and hoisted my bag with my suit, boots, and scarf over my shoulder. As I entered the lot, a fight broke out on the roof of the print shop ahead of me. There were two men—one in shirt sleeves and a navy vest, and the other one in overalls. I watched cautiously as a woman tried separating them.

"C'mon, ya bastid! Throw a punch!" The first one said.

"Gimme yer best shot, ya cake eater!" countered the second.

"Cake eater? Why I oughta..."

The smaller man threw a haymaker, but it put him off balance. The larger one swung, but although I could still hear them yelling, they moved out of my view. Suddenly, as I watched, horrified, the smaller man came tumbling over the edge and landed face down a few feet from me.

Fighting tears, I knelt down beside him, but I knew it had to be too late. No one could survive a fall like that.

"How's the stiff?" The larger man called down. Then he burst into guffaws and slapped his knee. The woman who'd been trying to break up the fight leaned over and giggled.

The absolute insensitivity of these people!

"I'm going to find a telephone and call an ambulance. And then the police!" I yelled up at them.

"I wouldn't worry too much if I were you, honey," the woman said. "Check his collar."

"What?" I said.

"Look."

Eyeing them both suspiciously, I reached for the gentleman's collar, near his hairline. A label advertised: *This mannequin belongs to the Keystone Film Company. Return and receive a generous reward.*

I touched the rubbery neck and ear, realized they'd been filming a scene, and I now looked like the world's biggest idiot. The real man in shirtsleeves then peered over the woman's shoulder with a goofy face.

I could see I'd have to toughen up if I wanted to keep this job.

"I'm not sure who the bigger dummy is here," I called up to them. "Him or *me*!"

CHAPTER THREE

MACK SENNETT STUDIOS, EDENDALE, CALIFORNIA
January 1916

"Yeah, sorry about that," Mr. Sennett said after they'd had their laugh. "Wouldn't want you to think we're completely heartless." He showed me around the lot and introduced me to the actors and crew members. I wouldn't remember all their names right away, but some were more memorable than others. Roscoe Arbuckle was a huge teddy bear of a man with high waters pants and a twinkle in his eye. Mabel Normand worked with Roscoe on many features. Her dark sad eyes belied her wicked sense of humor and impish wit.

"Hope we didn't scare you too much up there," said Chester Conklin, down from the roof for real now. He was the smaller man, only a few inches taller than me and slightly built.

I shook my head. "No. It's nice to meet you," I said, then complimented him on his impressive brush mustache. He smiled broadly then yanked it off in one deft motion. Beneath it, he was bare-faced.

"Mustaches are funnier," Mr. Sennett said by way of explanation. "You've already met Ford Sterling."

The man I'd met on both my previous visits pulled off his false goatee, round glasses, and battered stovepipe. Then he wiggled his eyebrows at me. He was quite handsome underneath. "I hope ya don't hold grudges, little lady," he said. We shook hands and had a chuckle.

The larger man from the roof, Charlie Murray, was born to be a comedian—he had the perfect face. Absolutely square, with ears the size of Idaho potatoes and Dutch chin whiskers. When I shyly stuck my hand out to shake, he shocked me with a hand buzzer.

Louise Fazenda, the lady who'd been refereeing the fight, was about my height, with light brown hair pulled up into matching braided knots on either side of her head, and a winning goofy grin. "Where ya from, kid?" she asked.

"All over," I said. "You?"

"Lafayette, Indiana. If ya wanna know 'Hoosier' best friend on the lot, that's me!" she joked, elbowing me gently in the ribs. I liked her right away.

After meeting all of them, it was off to a frame building housing the ladies' dressing room. Outside the door, Mr. Sennett nodded at the intimidating woman with dark hair who stood guard. She wore a black skirt, gray shirtwaist, and sensible black lace-up oxford shoes. She towered over me—all six feet, stern brow, and jutting chin of her.

"Marie, this is Blanche," he said. "Blanche Payson, Marie Prevost. She's going to be one of our new Bathing Beauties."

"Charmed," Blanche said in an extremely deep voice.

"Nice to meet you," I said. After we'd passed her, I lowered my voice. "Is she a bathing beauty too?"

"No. Believe it or not, Blanche used to be a policewoman. I hired her to make sure there's no hanky panky between the comics and you gals. And when I say none, I mean zilch. Zippo. Nada. She's here to make sure of it. Although I can't blame the fellas for trying." He gave a quick rap on the door, then called out. "Everybody decent? Put on some clothes. I've got a new addition!"

There was scrambling around inside amid girlish squeals until a sharp feminine voice shouted, "Ready!"

The dressing room looked like a Chinese laundry. Costumes hung on racks that stretched down one whole wall, bulging out of every spare inch of space. Vanities with large mirrors lined the other long wall. They were crammed with greasepaint sticks, wigs on stands, kohl pencils, vials of spirit gum, lipsticks, and huge tubs of powder.

"Ladies, this is Marie Prevost. I want you all to make her feel welcome," Mr. Sennett said. He presented each one in turn, rattling off their names so quickly I knew it would be hard to remember them all. "That's Mary Thurman with the black hair in red, Cecille Evans next to her in the aqua plaid, Vera Steadman with the long dark hair in green, Myrtle Lind is there in navy polka dots, and the pixie there in the black stripes holding the pink parasol is Gonda Durand."

The girls each gave me a wave and a smile when he said their names. They were all pretty, but some were more athletic-looking than others. Some of their bathing suits had ruffles or buttons or flirty little skirts. They wore slippers with ribbons criss-crossing up their calves, or boxing boots with one stocking in place, and the other rolled flirtatiously down a leg.

Some wore giant hair bows, and others wore tams or berets tilted over angled bobs or curls. Their lips were all painted in perfect Cupid's bows with deep brown lipstick, which contrasted with their overly yellow complexions.

"Get settled in," Mr. Sennett said. "There's a free dressing table down in the corner next to Vera. The girls can help you."

He retreated outside, and the girls all clustered around me.

"Lovely to meet you," said Myrtle. She had dark hair and a nasal Midwestern accent.

"Likewise, I'm sure," I said. "Where are you from?"

"St. Paul, Minnesota."

Dark-haired Cecille approached me with a grin. "I'm Cecille. We could be sisters!"

I smiled. "We do look awfully alike, don't we?"

"Welcome to Custard College," said the one called Gonda with a grin and a pat on my back.

"Custard?" I said.

"You'll see what I mean."

Mary Thurman shook my hand enthusiastically. She was also a brunette, with lovely dimples. "We're going to have so much fun!" she said. "I'm glad you're here!"

"Me too," I said.

"I'm from Richfield, Utah," she said. "What about you?"

"I spent some time in Salt Lake City and Ogden, but I've lived lots of places," I said.

"How about that! Are you a Saint?" she asked—the native's way of finding out if I was Mormon.

"No, Presbyterian," I said. "My mother's Scottish."

"Even so, it's nice to meet someone who knows something

about Utah," she said. "I'm a bit of a fish out of water here."

"Well, you seem perfectly lovely to me," I said, giving her a little wink. "Not fishy at all."

"Thanks! We'll be great friends, I know it. I've been here two weeks, and I'm having the time of my life. I can't believe they're paying us to do this."

"It's good to meet you," the one called Vera said, placing a hand on my shoulder. "How long have you been in California?"

"A little over three years. You?"

"All my life," she laughed. "I'm from Monterey originally. Mr. Sennett took one look at my legs and signed me. I'm a competitive swimmer, but I don't get to do the contest thing much anymore, what with our shooting schedule."

"I love California," I said. "It's my favorite of all the places we've lived."

"Where have you lived?"

Where hadn't *we lived?*

I told her about our constant moves. "I feel like I was born with my bag packed," I finished.

"Good Lord! Was your father a traveling salesman?"

I shook my head.

"Missionary?"

"No, we just moved a lot." How I ached to confide in someone about Frank, and about our strange nomadic life and the divorce. But I dared not for Mum's sake.

"Well, you're here now. That's what matters!" she said with a smile.

Over in another corner, Gonda petted a fawn-colored Great Dane with sad eyes and a huge studded collar.

"What an adorable dog!" I said.

"This is Teddy," she said. "He's our co-star, and he's very well trained. Watch this. Teddy, play dead."

He obediently rolled over and went limp. Then he peeked an eye open.

"Teddy, sit." He dragged himself from the floor, sat up straight, and wagged his tail politely.

"Good boy!" Gonda said. "Now shake." He held up his paw and she took it, then slipped him a treat from her pocket.

"Pepper's around here too," Cecille said. "Most likely camped out on something soft."

"Pepper?" I asked.

"Mack's cat. Another co-star. Yep, here she is." She pulled back a striped costume to reveal a deep gray cat sleeping on a furry collar of some kind. The cat let out a leisurely yawn, then rose for an extended stretch.

"How do they get a cat to do tricks?" I asked. "Aren't they very independent?"

"Pepper's your average cat," Cecille said, scratching the cat's head as Pepper preened. "She'll do anything for tuna fish."

"And cream," Gonda added, giving Teddy a hug. He drew his mouth back into a canine smile and panted in her ear.

"We'd better let you get changed," Vera said. There was a drape strung across a small alcove, and she pulled it open for me. "This is for the new girls. Those of us who've been here a while usually do it out here. It's faster."

I slipped in, put on my new suit and the boots and wound the scarf through my curls. Then I pinched my cheeks and emerged. The girls cheered.

"Cute suit," Cecille said.

"Thanks. Swelldom was having a sale."

"Now we have to make things more proper up top," Vera said.

"Wouldn't want the nips standing at attention when we get our suits wet at the beach," said Myrtle.

"Don't worry, I'll show you," Vera said. "Pull your suit straps down."

"I couldn't possibly! I..." My voice faded as my face flamed.

"Don't be silly. We're all girls here," Gonda said. She put an arm around me. "We all had to learn how to do it the first time."

"Modesty's great, but yours won't last long around here," Myrtle said. "Trust me."

"Gonda, you had the gauze last. Where is it?" Vera said.

Gonda opened her drawer, pulled out a roll of medical gauze, and tossed it to Vera. They showed me how to use the gauze to "tape up the lollies," as Mary called it, then Gonda gestured us over to the vanities.

"Now for the fun part," she said. "Bring her over here, girls!"

Mary and Vera took my hands and pulled me toward the chair at the vanity I'd claimed. I sat down.

"Try to watch in the mirror," Gonda said. "We have to do our own." She pulled open the vanity drawer. "First, grease-paint." She held up a tube-like stick of solid yellow-colored makeup and made streaks of it all over my face. Then she used her hand to blend and smooth it, covering every pore.

"Yellow?" I said. I'd wondered why the girls all had that unhealthy jaundiced pallor.

"Yeah. It's the film they use. We have to counteract the tint it gives us. Lean forward," Vera said.

I did, trying to be careful of the gauze now constricting my cleavage and diaphragm. Gonda grabbed a towel off one of the towel racks and wrapped it turban-like around my hair.

"Now, flip back up," she said.

I raised my head and smiled at all the eager faces surrounding me.

"My turn," Mary said. She took a powder puff off the vanity and dunked it in a big tub of pink-tinted powder. Then she patted it gently but firmly all over my face until the greasepaint absorbed all the powder. It covered my lips, eyelashes, and brows, making me cough.

"Now, we brush it," Cecille said. "To get all the excess off." She took a thick, soft brush and fluffed it into every facial crevice, smoothing as she did. Then, she used a kohl pencil to outline dramatic dark swaths around my eyes and a dark gray crayon to create shadows on the lids. She smudged that with her finger. Finally, she applied the same dark brown lip color the others were wearing.

"Perfect!" they squealed. "Look!"

I glanced in the mirror.

"Looks like my liver gave out last week!" I said with a laugh.

Sennett's specialty was shorts—one-reelers with simple stories, or as Mr. Sennett said, "no meat on their bones."

Mum didn't care how long they were. She was so proud of my new position. She insisted we go to the Superba to see *Better Late Than Never* as soon as it was released. And then she squealed when my walk-on as a maid happened. Other mothers might have taken a daughter off to a nunnery before they'd have let her become an actress. Especially in flickers. Not Hughie McDonald Dunn Prevost. She was tickled to tears that she could walk into Tally's or the Pantages or Clune's and see me up on the big screen.

With Peg it was a different story. She did her level best to knock my ego down, even though she was enjoying my extra income immensely.

"You're acting and all, but you'll never be famous like Mary Pickford or Edna Purviance," she observed.

"Yeah? Why not? Chaplin started with Mr. Sennett. Why not me? Besides, I'm helping Mum so we can eat and have a roof over our heads. You're sixteen now. You could start looking for a job too, you know."

That shut her up.

My walk-on parts got a little larger, and Mr. Sennett gave me more of them, until the other girls and I started getting plenty of fan mail. But since our characters had no names, the letters were addressed to "the blonde girl who fell off the pier" or "the pretty girl chewing gum on the streetcar."

When I came home from work, Mum would ask me what we'd filmed that day. She'd clap her hands and laugh uproariously as I told her about my new friends on the lot and the constant practical jokes they played on each other. There was the fellow who complained about not getting enough fan mail, so someone had signed him up for oodles of mail order patent medicine companies' mailing lists. Or the comedian Joe Jackson, who tempted you with candies in his pockets, but instead filled them with garter snakes. Once, when Mr. Sennett dressed down a group of the comedians for an uncoordinated scene, they got their revenge by rigging up a bucket of water above the door to his office. He laughed so hard he couldn't be angry, although it did take a while for his trousers to dry that day.

The Sennett publicity machine raved about my French Canadian roots, and how I'd been taught to ski as a young girl by my French father, and other tidbits of manufactured malarkey that made me sound oh-so-glamorous. Despite the invented lore, Mum loved it all. I asked Mr. Sennett if she could watch us film, and he allowed it. The merry-go-round covered with scenery was called the cyclorama. As it spun behind Charley Chase and Wayland Trask during a crazy chase scene, Mum's tinkling laugh could be heard far down Alessandro Street.

But then came the day that we filmed downtown and Mrs. Taggart happened to come out of her dentist's office on Broadway after having her new dentures fitted.

"Mary Prevost, is that you?" she demanded. "You told me you were working as a secretary. And here you are filming a flicker? How long have you been living under my roof doing this? You and your mother and your sister will collect your things and be out by the end of the week!"

Mum immediately found us another place to rent on South Hampshire.

"Hateful cow. We're better off," she said. "Naebody tells mah gu-r-r-ll what she can do for a living."

BY THE SEA
BY THE SEA
BY THE BEAUTIFUL SEA

CHAPTER FOUR

MACK SENNETT STUDIOS, EDENDALE, CALIFORNIA
February 1916

"After enough time here, every comic gets good at falling and throwing pies," Chester told me. "Falls and pies are our *Raisin Dee Etrah*. That's what the French call it. Our 'reason for being.' Mack made his name with 'em. So you gotta learn too."

It was a bright afternoon, and we sat under the lot's huge pepper tree. The longer I was there, the more I learned about flickers, about the studio, and about life, so Charlie and Chester had decided to teach me the ins and outs of comedy. And they'd set up a table with some supplies for their exhibit. I nodded eagerly and leaned forward, elbows on knees.

"There are three main types of falls. Observe," Chester said as Charlie demonstrated. "The first one is the pratfall. Watch Charlie. Somebody knocks him in the puss with a ladder. Here's what happens."

Charlie pretended to run into an invisible barrier and fell backward onto his rear until he was lying down. Then he hopped up quickly and spread his arms for a bow. I clapped.

"Next," Chester continued, "The stiff back. It's a two-pointer—falling from your feet, when somebody hits you over the head with an anvil or a plank."

Charlie pretended he'd been knocked for a loop, then fell straight onto his back. I was amazed at the control, and even more amazed that he didn't end up with a concussion. My spine ached even watching him.

"The last one's a bit more challenging," Chester said. "You go all the way up in the air, and make an all-point landing, on your back. Your entire body takes the brunt of the fall. Charlie?"

Charlie walked along, then pretended to slip on a banana peel. His feet went up in the air and as they did so, his body went horizontal and he landed on his back.

"Holy moly," I said, "He makes it look so easy."

"It's called a one-oh-eight," said Charlie, pulling himself up and massaging his hip. "Hurts like a sonofabitch when you land."

"Charlie!" Chester cautioned him. "Lady present."

"Sorry Marie," Charlie said.

"In addition to falls, Mack loves the pie in the face," Chester said. "There's nothing like it for making pompous windbags look ridiculous. We've got a couple types we use. Some of 'em, you want a lot of goo to go everywhere, but others, you want the filling to stick so people gotta peel the cream out of their eyes and off their faces."

"Exhibit #1, 'The Mess,'" Charlie said. "I'll demonstrate." He filled a pie plate with blackberries from a berry basket, then spooned whipped cream from a bowl into it. "It's an art, the perfect throw."

Chester nodded in agreement. "It's not so much tossing it as pushing it forward into somebody's face." He flexed his arm. "It's all in the follow-through. Del Lord's got the best arm on the lot."

"But nobody tops Roscoe," Charlie said. "He's one of the all-time greats. Can hit a fly from ten feet away. With either hand. Blindfolded, even."

"All right, ya got me there," Chester said. "If we're talking 'of all time,' Arbuckle is the king. It's true."

"Exhibit #2," Charlie said. "'The Goop.' For stickability, there's nothing better."

"What's it made of?" I asked.

"Paste," Charlie said.

"No custard?"

"No body to 'em. Mack doesn't like the way they film. Chester, you wanna do the honors, or shall I?"

"Oh, allow me," Chester said. He picked up 'The Mess,' pointing to his arm so I could watch it. "Observe the trajectory." His arm jutted forward, the pie exploding berries and cream all over Charlie, the table, the benches, and partially, me.

"You were off about half an inch," Charlie said, his grin breaking through the cream stuck to his face. He licked off the stuff closest to his mouth.

"Says you. That was perfect. Your turn."

Charlie picked up 'The Goop,' pointed to his arm to show me his technique, and landed it square in the center of Chester's face. It stuck to Chester's eyes, cheeks, nose and forehead. "See the consistency differences?" Chester spit out, wiping the paste from his eyes.

I nodded. "Perfectly."

Charlie grabbed a couple of moist towels that he'd set on the bench, used one, and threw the other to Chester. "It's all for the laughs. Mack wants to make people laugh. It's what he lives for. But he's got real definite ideas about how to do it," he said.

"And he won't use scenarios," Chester said. "Doesn't like 'em. Tales typed up by guys with Underwoods are too stuffy. He used to get the writers to divide up in twos and run gags by each other, with a little bit of a story to hold everything together. He'd rather see banana peels being slipped on or fellas getting knocked over with ladders like it used to be in Keystone's early days. But we've had to get more organized the last few years. More writers, more actors, more flickers. You get the point."

"He's even got a direct line to the fire department," Charlie said. "They call us when they have a big blaze so we can film it."

They related hilarious stories of shooting—beds falling through multiple floors, clotheslines pulled up to trip people, and cars skidding on sudsy streets—and Chester told me more about the man in charge. Mr. Sennett had a temper, so he'd sometimes fire even his best directors or cameramen, only to have second thoughts and hire them back the next day. Despite his mercurial moods, the folks who worked there were uninhibited, full of fun, and willing to do almost anything for a laugh. Most of Mr. Sennett's frustration lately seemed to be because of the headaches of working under the Triangle Film Company label. And there were whispers of problems in his relationship with Mabel. Mabel and Roscoe had taken a trip to the Eastern Triangle Studios in Fort Lee to get away for a while.

"Spontaneous is the name of the game here," Chester said. "Mack likes doing this so much that he'll still get in front of the camera from time to time. He likes to have fun with it."

"I have fun with what?" Who should walk up right then but Mr. Sennett.

"I was telling Marie how you still jump in once in a while. Keep the action going," Chester said.

"He's right," Mr. Sennett said. "You gotta keep it lively. I don't care how you do it. That guy from Poughkeepsie in the audience? You can't let his mind wander. The minute it does, you've lost him. Action is what flickers are all about."

"Tell her what you always say, Mack," Charlie said.

"Somebody wanna work for me, I watch the fella fall down first. Anybody can fall. And maybe get some laughs. But getting back up? That's where you see what people are made of. What comedians are made of. *Those* are the people I sign."

BEACH AT SANTA MONICA, CALIFORNIA *March 1916*

"Sun's out! Fire up the wagons!" yelled one of the crew.

When we shot our bathing beauty spots at the beach, we usually packed a couple of Model A's full of cast, crew, and equipment, and waited for the morning fog to burn off before we motored off to Santa Monica.

Eddie Cline was the architect of the Bathing Beauties, who'd first put the flea in Mr. Sennett's ear. Lee Davis was our cameraman, Phil Kersey our second cameraman, and Richard Jones, our director. His nickname was Jonesy. They rode in one car with Gonda and Mary, and the rest of us were in the other. With us was Nelson Evans, our still photographer, toting his bellows camera. The stills were as important as our film work, because they were used to promote the studio. Nelson snapped us frolicking in the waves or on the sand, or posing on top of one of the flivvers we brought with us.

Today, when we arrived, jalopies piled high, Teddy hopped out and took off after a flock of sandpipers skittering across the sand. I stood at the water's edge and let the surf lap at my toes, giggling because the receding wave tickled and left little tidal pools where tiny crabs burrowed.

"Come on, girls!" Myrtle called. "Last one in is a rotten egg!"

"Wait!" Nelson called. "Don't get your stockings wet yet! Let's get some stills first!"

Lee, Phil, and Nelson hurriedly set their cameras up on their tripods, and captured us frolicking. In the distance, the Ocean Park Bathhouse loomed like some strange Arabian palace dropped on the shore like a mirage. The flags flying above it snapped in the stiff sea breeze, which also carried the smells of clams, sardines, and abalone from the Breakers Café on the Promenade. Over the noise of the waves came the sounds of the calliope from the carousel at Looff's Hippodrome and the squeals from the Blue Streak Racer roller coaster. Boats headed up to San Francisco or Seattle passed off shore, sounding their deep foghorns.

"Here's an idea!" Jonesy called. "I brought a nice long rope from the lot. Let's have a tug-of-war!" He pulled the rope from the backseat of the flivver and tossed it toward us. Vera was the first to step forward, since her swimming had helped her to build up some nicely toned arm muscles.

"Who wants to ally themselves with the three-time Monterey Beach swimming champion?" she boasted, holding up her arm and flexing it.

"Me!" I cried, knowing she was a sure bet. Mary joined us, skipping across the sand.

"You two need a little competition," Myrtle said, planting herself at the opposite end of the rope from us.

Gonda joined her. "We can take them, no problem!" she said, winking at us.

"Three and three," Cecille said. "I'll even it up."

"Wait a minute," Jonesy said. "Let's create some rules." He grabbed a piece of driftwood and created a deep depression in the sand with the end of it. "First one to cross the line, that team loses."

We all took hold of the rope, eyeing each other across the stretch of sand. Teddy sat and watched, panting happily.

"Ready? Go!" Jonesy yelled. Lee and Phil continued cranking their Pathés as we pulled the rope from either side, and Nelson snapped away with his Graflex.

With Vera as our anchor, Mary and I tugged with all our might. Although Myrtle was small, she was mighty, yanking until I thought she'd pop a blood vessel. Gonda made some of the most hilarious noises, and between her and Cecille, they kept the rope centered over the tiny ditch for the longest time. At last, it began to move slightly in our favor.

"Come on, Myrtle! Pull hard!" Jonesy shouted. "Pretend Francis X. Bushman's the reward!"

That was it. Myrtle dissolved in giggles, and when she lost her grip (figuratively and literally), Mary, Vera, and I tumbled backward when inertia took hold.

"That was low, Jonesy," Myrtle grumbled.

"It worked, didn't it?" he said. "You got the shot, right, Phil?"

"Got it, Jonesy!" Phil said.

As I tried awkwardly to stand up, I stumbled and bumped into something solid, but distinctly male. He was tall—at least six feet. His pomaded dark hair sported a distinctive light streak, and he had sad, expressive pale blue eyes. He wore a gray suit and spats, and a straw boater with a blue band.

"I'm so sorry!" I said, still trying to find my footing.

"I shouldn't have walked quite so close," he said, helping me up. He gave us a big smile.

"Hey," I said. "I know you. You're King Baggot, aren't you? The actor!"

"I am indeed," he said. He looked pleased to be recognized, doffed his hat, and bowed gallantly to all of us. Gonda and Vera waved. Myrtle and Cecille swooned, and Mary blushed to the roots of her hair.

King Baggot had been making movies since we were girls, starring in everything from *Ivanhoe* to *Dr. Jekyll and Mr. Hyde.* But he'd left IMP after a fight with the director, Herb Brenon. Now he was back at Universal, the renamed company, but no one was sure how he'd pulled it off. Town gossip had it that Carl Laemmle really liked him and had let him back into the fold despite the drinking problem he'd developed to cope with his fall from leading man to co-star to director.

"Are you with Sennett?" Mr. Baggot asked, nodding to our cameramen.

"Yes," I said, looking fondly at the cast and crew.

"I thought I recognized you. You have a gift for comedy,

young lady. I think you could go far. Let me know if you're interested. I could put in a good word for you at Universal. What's your name?"

"Marie Prevost," I said shyly. King Baggot recognized me? This man was the greatest of the great, and I'd never been so intimidated. I didn't know what to say. Especially with the cast and crew watching. I settled on "Thank you for your offer. It's very kind."

"Certainly. I'd better let you get back to work. Ladies," he said, tipping his hat again. Then he strolled off in the direction of the pier, and the girls twittered around me like a flock of nuthatches.

"King Baggot talked to you!" Vera squealed.

"You're so lucky! He's dreamy!" Mary said.

"I should have chosen the other side!" Myrtle lamented.

As summer progressed, we developed a routine. We'd hightail it to the beach in our flivvers, work from around ten a.m. until noon or so, then the group of us would grab lunch. When we were in Venice, the Strand Café or the Iota Café; when we were in Santa Monica, the Redondo Café or Nat Goodwin's. After lunch, we'd do more shooting, then it was back to Edendale with the footage. Those of us not tasked with editing it would then catch the streetcar home.

The headlines were full of battles in Western Europe, but here in southern California, pretty girls playing in the waves was frothy fun, and for Mr. Sennett, a good financial move. We usually drew a crowd of curious onlookers, and the crew had to keep them back so we could keep filming. We played leapfrog with each other, and sometimes with the passersby who wanted to have a little fun.

On a bright June day, Mr. Sennett decided to join us for a shot at the pier. He'd had some ideas he wanted to share with Jonesy, and wanted to make sure his advice was being followed. He drew chuckles from the onlookers because he'd worn his favorite hat—an expensive Panama to which he'd taken a pocketknife and cut the crown.

"It's for ventilation! Makes the scalp healthy!" he'd exclaim. "Prevents baldness!"

We stood on the weathered planks waiting for direction, looking down at the green waves lapping against the pilings.

"For this scene," he said, "I want animated!" He snapped his fingers. "Jonesy, where's that banana you brought?"

Jonesy produced a brown paper bag and pulled the fruit from it. He peeled it and handed the peel to Mr. Sennett, snacking on the banana itself. Mr. Sennett laid the peel on the pier boards not far from the edge. Then he turned to us.

"All right. When I give the signal, run around like you're confused. Marie, you can swim. I want you to pretend to slip, and then fall off the pier."

"Where's the fun in that?" I asked.

"Because your character's a klutz. That's fun," he said.

"All right, if you say so," I said. But I was unconvinced.

"Ready Jonesy?" Mr. Sennett said, turning back to the cameraman.

"Ready, Mack," he said. But it sounded more like "Rerry Moh," his voice garbled over the last of the banana.

The slate boy clacked the halves of his board together, and Mr. Sennett took Jonesy's megaphone. "Places...and...action!"

Gonda and Mary bumped into each other, Vera pretended to fall by doing a one-oh-eight, and Cecille and Myrtle stood and watched curiously, the foils to our madcap. I approached the end of the pier where the banana peel lay.

Falling off the pier wouldn't be that funny in itself. But remembering everything Charlie, Chester, and Mr. Sennett taught me, I had an idea about what would be. I listened to my gut.

I hit the banana peel with the perfect spin to my ankle, then purposely bumped into Mr. Sennett, and dragged him with me. As we got close to the edge, we balanced there precariously for a moment, then gravity triumphed and he toppled in. Somehow I kept from following him.

I might have won the battle, but at the cost of the war. The girls' faces were pale and horror-stricken, and they whispered among themselves as Mr. Sennett let the tide pull him into the beach. Wearing an unreadable expression, he rose from the surf and made the long hike back onto the pier. We all stood quietly, waiting for an explosion, and I prepared myself for an expedition downtown to beg Mr. MacKenzie for my job back.

"You! Prevost!" he said, pointing at me, his face breaking into an expansive grin. "That was perfect! I'm upping you to twenty-five dollars a week!"

MACK SENNETT STUDIOS, EDENDALE, CALIFORNIA
July 1916

That raise gave me more confidence, so several months into my tenure at "Custard College," I decided to push my luck a little further.

"Mr. Sennett, I hate to disturb you, but I'm wondering if I

could ask you a huge favor," I said,

"Have a seat, Marie. Abdullah, take a powder, will ya?"

The masseur nodded and pulled the sheet over Mr. Sennett's back, before retreating out of the room.

I cleared my throat and began. "My sister needs a job. She looks a little like me, and she's quite funny." This was a huge risk, but I was willing to take it for Mum.

"Got a picture of her?"

"Yes, right here." I reached into my bag and pulled out the portrait that she'd had done at the Witzel Studio on Hill Street. With my money.

"You said she's funny?"

"Yes, sir. And she has good knees too." I told him about the time she rigged the bucket of snow above the kitchen doorway and caught 'our father' unawares and the time she'd made the Easter bonnet for Diablo, 'our father's' old prospecting mule.

"All right, she might have potential. Have her come talk to me next week. I'll do it as a favor to you. If she's awful, I'll cut her, but I'll give her a shot, at least."

"Thank you so much, Mr. Sennett!"

It was more than Peg deserved, the way she'd been acting lately, but I'd do anything to take more of the financial burden off Mum. That night at the dinner table, I told Peg about her new opportunity.

"What should I wear?" she said. "I'll need to buy a new dress! And my hair is a mess. I'll have to get it done. I'll need money for that."

"Mr. Sennett doesn't care about any of that. He only cares if you can make him laugh. If you can't do that, he won't care if you're dressed up like a queen."

"What should I say?"

"Hold out your hand to greet him and take a pratfall right in front of him. That'll get his attention. He likes stunts. But they have to be funny."

Later, Peg retreated to her room with the new issue of *Shadowlands* magazine and Mum and I cleared the dishes.

"Thank ye, pet. 'Twas a verra kind thing ye did. I know Peg isn't the easiest person to love, but we're family."

"I didn't do it for her, Mum. I did it for you. You're still working too hard. She's sixteen, and she can start pulling her weight around here now."

"Regardless. 'Twas sweet of ye." She caressed my cheek with her hand, and the scent of lily-of-the-valley that she wore warmed me all over. "I love you, wee girl," she said, using my childhood pet name.

"I love you too, Mum." We held each other, and I nestled my face into her shoulder. "I don't know what I'd do without you."

The next day, Peg got dolled up and had her meeting with Mr. Sennett. To my great relief, he brought her on. But it wasn't long before she began trying to weasel out of work.

"Shooting starts too early in the morning," she complained. "I want to sleep late."

"You're an adult now," I said, dragging her out of bed and pulling her toward the bathroom by her ear. "Adults work for a living."

"Not if they're smart," she said, giving me a sarcastic look.

"Oh, for God's sake," I said. Somehow I'd known that this was a lost cause. "I didn't do this for you. I did this for Mum. So take your bath and get to the studio. Now."

"No," she said.

"You'll go and you'll like it."

"You can't make me." She put her hands on her hips like an over-indulged child. And that's exactly what she was.

That did it. Years of frustration had built up to where I couldn't stand it anymore. I let fly with a backhanded slap across her face.

"You are a spoiled brat, Peg Prevost. I stuck my neck out for you. I should have known it was pointless."

She burst into tears, then ran into her room and slammed the door. As with everything else in her life, her laziness became her undoing. Mr. Sennett didn't keep her on. But she still landed on her feet.

Peg had cozied up to Henri Lehrman while she was on the lot. He was an Austrian who'd made up an elaborate lie that he'd worked for Pathé Frères in France, and had figured that'd make him a shoe-in at Sennett. It did, and people had been calling him Pathé ever since. Pathé decided to form his own studio, called L-KO Pictures, and Peg left with him. For me, it was a bonus. She had her own money, and although she was working, I didn't have to put up with her at Sennett.

A GOOD MAN IS
HARD TO FIND

CHAPTER FIVE

August 11, 1916

"**S**ee, I told you," Vera said as we strolled Main Street near Central Avenue. "I knew you'd love it. They've been advertising it for weeks."

Mr. Sennett had sent a group of us down to Newport Beach to work on *A Scoundrel's Toll*, and Vera was already registered for the ladies' diving exhibition on Sunday, so she came with us. The carnival had initially sounded like a waste of a weekend to me, but Mr. Sennett had insisted we enter the Ladies' Bath Suit Parade on Saturday.

"It's free publicity!" he said. "Of course you're signing up!"

Mr. Sennett was so testy these days with all the rigmarole about *Mickey*, and Roscoe and Mabel leaving the studio that I didn't want to argue with him.

Vera and Mary and I had eaten breakfast at Barker's Café, then watched the magnificent water pageant, with actors portraying Vasco Núñez de Balboa and his crew discovering the Pacific.

Each brightly painted booth we passed tried to outdo the other with signs for scandalous Oriental dances, Burlesque on the Bay, Willard's Famous Melodium, and Hop the Frog Boy. After enjoying the can-can girls at the Paris After Midnight Exhibit, we saw a beautiful bay named Mozart the Musical Horse paw out the beat to "The Old Gray Mare, She Ain't What She Used to Be" with his front hoof. He was rewarded with a shiny red apple. Tonight, there would be an evening street carnival with bands for dancing.

After we'd made an afternoon visit to the concessions booths, Vera gnawed her corn-on-the-cob, Mary indulged her sweet tooth with saltwater taffy, and I munched some crunchy fried clams.

As dusk descended, Stewie Stewart's Stupendous Syncopators churned out a lively version of "Sister Susie's Sewing Shirts for Soldiers."

"Dance?" A hulking blonde fellow in a sailor suit approached me, and a red-haired one asked Mary to dance. After she and I had both taken several swirls down the boulevard, we found Vera again and called it a night so we'd be ready for the regatta the next day.

Friday dawned overcast, but with a perfect breeze from the west for the regatta. It was a close finish, but the *Label* took first, outmaneuvering the *Marion* and the *Pastime* around a curve, and bringing home the loving cup. When the races were finished, the sun came out, and we decided to cool off.

After we changed into our suits, we swam out to the yachts, now anchored off the island, and played hide and seek around the hulls of the *Marion* and the *Pastime* until I started feeling the effects of the previous day's excitement and the exercise. I swam over to the *Label*, where city councilman Conwell was holding court with some older gentlemen. Most likely drinking something alcoholic, considering how much fun they were having.

"Hey!" I called up. "Mind if I hang on for a minute or two?"

A face looked over the side at me, followed by a slim muscular body in shirtsleeves, olive drab linen trousers, and a straw boater. He held out his hand.

"Get in," he said, his grin dented with dimples. His eyes were a lovely warm gray, like the driftwood on the beach, and his dark hair curled slightly around the edges of the hat.

I took his hand and he pulled me onto the *Label*. The older men gave me appreciative glances, and my entire body flushed in embarrassment. The boy encircled me with a big fluffy towel to cover me up.

"Here," he said. "Sit. Sit." He patted a cushion, and I lowered myself onto it. "Do all the mermaids around here look like you? If so, I've died and gone to heaven."

I smiled. "My friends are over there too." I pointed at Vera and Mary splashing playfully around the hull of the *Bonita*.

"What's your name, Mermaid Girl?" he said with a smile.

"Marie Prevost. What yours, Mr. Fisherman?"

"Henry Gerke," he said. "My friends call me Sonny."

"Don't throw that one back, Sonny!" one of the older men hooted. I was thankful for the towel right then, as the man's gaze crept uncomfortably from my head down to my toes.

"Not a chance," Sonny said. "I hope you won't think me too

forward, but I'd love it if you'd have dinner with me later. And we could watch the water parade."

Strange, but I'd never had a date before. Not in school, and not even at Sennett, since there was no courting between the players. It would be my first real date. Peg, on the other hand, had gone all the way already. I was sure of it.

"All right," I said, a little shyly. "I'm staying at the Balboa Hotel with some friends. Room 5."

"I'll be by to get you at five thirty then," he said.

"Little early, isn't it?"

"How can we watch the sun go down if we don't start a little earlier?" he said.

I'm not a girl who giggles easily, but I did then.

"See you at five thirty," he said as I turned back toward the water and dove in.

I found Vera and Mary, and we paddled back toward shore. I thought about the boy with the gray eyes.

"I have a date tonight," I said as the tide brought us in and we made our way up onto the beach.

"You rascal," Vera called. "With the gob who pulled you on-board the yacht?"

"Yes. We have to get back to the room," I said. "He's coming by at 5:30. It will take me forever to get ready. Look at my hair!"

Good thing I'd brought several nice frocks with me. I took a bath, then daubed on some talcum powder and carnation-scented toilet water. I dressed in my China-blue chiffon with the apron effect in the front, and I paired it with dancing slippers in the same shade.

There was a knock at 5:30 on the dot, and Sonny stood at

the door, looking very handsome in a charcoal-colored jacket and navy trousers, with a navy tie and two-toned oxfords. He doffed his hat and I showed him in to introduce him to the girls. "Mary, Vera, this is Sonny Gerke. Sonny, my friends Vera Steadman and Mary Thurman."

"Nice t'meetcha," Vera said.

"Same here," Mary said with a laugh. "You have any friends, cutie?"

"I'm afraid I'm down here with a bunch of terribly old men," he said. "Friends of my parents. All ready?" I nodded and draped my shawl over my shoulders.

After a dinner of freshly caught halibut at a café near the pavilion, we found a spot on the pier that was perfect for watching the water parade.

The boats were lit with strings of lights from bow to stern, and even up into the riggings. Reflected in the slow black swells, they twinkled like millions of tiny stars. And above us, the full moon glowed with a pale mellow light. When Sonny leaned over to kiss me the first time, it was magical. He walked me back to the hotel, then gave me another kiss, this one on the cheek.

"Will I see you tomorrow?" he asked.

"I hope so," I said.

"Be by to get you at ten?"

"I'm in the bath suit parade at eleven."

"Then all the better. Don't want anyone making a play for my girl."

I blushed to the roots of my hair.

Saturday the island awoke slowly. We girls dolled up in our favorite suits, spent extra time on our hair, and applied some kohl pencil and lip rouge before throwing on casual day frocks over the top. Then, we met Sonny in the hotel dining room, where we enjoyed a breakfast of griddle cakes and stewed apricots. Afterwards, we all strolled to the area near the beach, and Mary, Vera, and I clustered together nervously until the contest began. An assistant handed us each a number written in dark fountain pen.

"Ladies and gentlemen! Welcome to the first annual Balboa Bath Suit Parade!" the announcer called through his small megaphone. "Never in your life will you see a more breathtaking bevy of bewitching beauties than we have for you today!"

An audience formed around the pier. Young and old, male and female, they'd all gathered to see the show.

"I'll need your assistance! With such an array of pulchritudinous pleasure, it is impossible for one man to judge such a difficult contest! I'll call each contestant's name and number, and I want to hear deafening applause from you! So when your favorite steps forward, let's hear you make some noise! All right? Let's begin!"

Polite applause greeted that announcement.

"Our first contestant, in the red suit and becoming rolled stockings, number one... the enchanting Missssss... Dorothy DeVore!"

Dorothy had soft black hair and a heart-shaped face, and wore a big red bow in her hair to match her suit. The applause was respectable, but it seemed they were holding back a bit until seeing the rest of the choices.

"And now, number two, pretty Missssss Vera Steadman, appearing in Mack Sennett Studios' upcoming release *Maid Mad*!"

Vera had worn a dark-green suit and a headband trimmed

with lace. With her matching green stockings, she looked like a forest sprite. She wiggled her fingers in a flirty wave while strutting forward, then backward from her spot. The applause was louder and more enthusiastic.

"Also representing Mr. Sennett and his recent release, *His First False Step*...number three...lovely Missss... Mary Thurman!"

Mary stepped forward, did a little turn and blew kisses to the audience. She was greeted with a chorus of wolf whistles. She had chosen a plum-colored suit and a purple tam hat that she wore angled jauntily over her dark curls.

"And... appearing in Mr. Sennett's upcoming new feature *A Scoundrel's Toll*, the bewitching number four...Missss... Marie Prevost!"

I'd worn a black suit over short blue bottoms, the better to show off my pale skin. With it, to accent my eyes, I'd worn a bright blue velvet tam. The claps and whistles made me smile. I waved my arms enthusiastically, wiggling my fingers at those calling out the loudest—especially Sonny, who gave me a big wink.

A few more contestants were announced, each pretty and flirty and aiming to win a prize. Finally, the announcer got to the last girl.

"And lastly....the adorable number ten...Missssss.... Virginia Lee Corbin!"

Little Virginia was all of about five or six years old, with a perfect head of Pickford-like pale corkscrew curls, and a giant bow in them. Her mother pushed her toward us. The little girl simpered forward and dropped into an adorable curtsy.

"Isn't she special, folks? Let's give this little lady a big hand!"

At the applause, she giggled and ran to her mother's side, hiding her face in the woman's skirt.

"Let's have a big round of applause for all our contestants!" the announcer called.

After a few minutes consulting with the judges, he was back.

"All right, ladies and gentlemen, we have the results of the Balboa Bath Suit Parade!"

Vera, Mary, and I held hands. Mr. Sennett had promised us an extra five dollars each if any of us got higher than third place. Although the announcer drew things out interminably, fifth place went to a woman named Opal Doyle, fourth to Vera, third to Dorothy DeVore, and second to Mary. There was only one spot left.

"And first place goes to... Miss... Marie Preeeeeeevost! Plus, we mustn't forget a very special award to Miss.... Virginia Lee Corbin!"

Me?! I'd never won anything in my life!

A huge cheer swept through the crowd, accompanied by more wolf whistles.

I waved and smiled as the man placed a sash over my shoulder, and the local newspaper photographer snapped a photo. The other girls also got sashes, and little Virginia got a tiny tot sash that they'd cut down to size for her. We each got a small silver loving cup imprinted with our title, and I squealed as they handed me mine.

It was exciting, but at the same time, I felt a little like a piece of meat at the butcher store, being ogled like that. When Sonny gave me a congratulatory kiss and told me how beautiful I was, I shoved the thought to the back of my mind. It was only one bath suit parade. And Sennett would eventually lead to other things. I wouldn't wear this swimsuit forever.

After Vera, Mary, and I put our frocks back on, Sonny joined us to watch the water sports and the cruiser race from Balboa Bay out to the open ocean. Then he took us out for dinner—grilled sardines and vegetables steamed in butter. On Sunday, we cheered for Vera as she completed pikes, tucks, and half-gainers off the platform that had been erected in the harbor for diving stunts. She earned a red ribbon and a trophy for second place.

Vera and Mary went back to the room, and Sonny and I ordered a delicious dinner of fresh scallops at Barker's. We watched the fireworks show from a bench on the pier, where he kissed me again, then later we sat in the front seat of his Packard, nervous and unsure.

Would our three-day vacation romance last when we got back to our regular lives? Monday morning, Mary and I had to resume filming on some harbor shots, and Sonny had to return to Los Angeles. It would be at least another week until we could see each other again.

He took my hand.

"The minute you get back to town, you must let me know," he said, handing me a paper with his telephone number.

"All right," I said. So far, so good.

"I need to see you again." He nuzzled my ear.

"Promise?" I asked, as he held me close.

"Promise," he muttered against my cheek.

That night, I barely got any sleep, reliving the fireworks. The ones in the sky, and the ones in my heart.

The minute I walked in the door at home, I telephoned Sonny. After I kissed Mum hello, but before I said hi to Peg.

Over the next few months, Sonny and I spent wonderful days and nights together. One day, he took me fishing off the Looff Pier, and we both caught a couple respectable-sized croakers. We went bathing at the Venice Plunge, and made sandcastles on the beach. Sonny's family were respected wine merchants in northern California, so he had plenty of money to spend. There were numerous dinners out. One night to the Citrus Café in downtown Los Angeles, and another to the Vernon Café. One night, we even took the funicular up to the restaurant at the Mount Washington Hotel. I ate elegant foods I'd never seen before, like consommé Olga, soused salmon, and peaches in chartreuse jelly.

At the end of each night, there was the kiss, which gradually became deeper and more passionate with each outing. I wasn't sure where it would end, but I liked going steady.

CHAPTER SIX

MACK SENNETT STUDIOS, EDENDALE, CALIFORNIA
April 5, 1917

"All right, Pep," I said. "Scoot over."

When I got to the dressing room that morning, Pepper had camped out in my chair as usual, sprawled across my dressing gown. I stroked her head and she let out a yawn, then stretched a limber paw across the silk. When I nudged her, she hopped down and decided Gonda's robe was as good as mine and lighted there for the rest of her nap.

"Did ya see the paper this morning?" Vera asked, smearing Gouraud's Oriental Cream on her elbows. When she was done rubbing it in, she tossed me the front page of the *Times*.

"The Senate Adopts War Resolution by Large Majority"

it read.

"It's all anyone's talking about," said Cecille, shaking her head.

President Wilson and Congress had finally done it. They'd

taken us to war in Europe. I shivered, knowing it was bad, but not understanding the full implications of it. I didn't think any of us would for some time.

"… And here's the dressing room…" Mr. Sennett said outside. He rapped on the door. "Ladies, get decent! We have some new additions!"

We all threw something on, and then he ushered in three pretty blondes: one with a halo of honey-colored ringlets, one a taller athletic type, and the third with a capful of pale curls. It hit me immediately. I knew her!

"Phyllis O'Haver?"

"Oh, my Lord! It's Mary Prevost! As I live and breathe! What are you doing here?"

"Being a bathing beauty," I said with a smile.

"Me too! I dropped the O, though. I'm plain ole Phyllis Haver now. Mr. Sennett suggested it."

"And he said I should become Marie," I said.

"I take it you two know each other," Mr. Sennett said, chuckling.

"We went to high school together," Phyllis squealed, pumping her fist. "Manual Arts! Fight, fight, fight!"

"So this is Phyllis, as you've all heard. This is Harriett Hammond," Mr. Sennett said, gesturing to the tall girl. "And this," he said, indicating curly locks, "…is Juanita Hansen. I'll let you all get acquainted. Be on the set in twenty minutes, if you please." He retreated out the dressing room door.

"Pleased to meet ya!" Mary said, enthusiastically shaking Phyllis' hand. "I'm Mary Thurman." Then she turned to Juanita and Harriett and did the same.

The regulars clustered around, admiring the new girls,

their darling frocks, and Harriett's hat, a velvet Tudor beret in the same sky blue as her eyes.

"Here," I said to Phyllis. "Come take this vanity next to me." I patted the seat. "How are you? How have you been? I didn't get answers to my last few letters."

"Yeah, sorry about that. Georgie and I got hot and heavy about then. And after a couple months, it fizzled. When I did finally write back, you'd moved. Say," she said, looking around her conspiratorially. "There's some swell-looking fellas around the lot!"

Have I mentioned Phyllis was the biggest flirt in our class? Practically going after them with a butterfly net.

"If you know what's good for you, you'll stay away from them," I observed.

"But why?" she pouted.

"The wrath of Blanche," Mary said. She explained Mr. Sennett's no fraternization rule.

Phyllis couldn't help but look disappointed. We'd all been there. Sure, there were some old men throwing pies and chasing cars, but some of the fellas were downright yummy.

"I'm Harriett," the tall girl said a little unsurely. "Where should I put my stuff?"

"Put it down here," Myrtle said, indicating the vanity next to her. "The more the merrier." Before long, they were chatting away like they'd known each other for years.

"Where ya from, Goldilocks?" Mary said, offering Juanita a lemon drop from a small sack she'd been sharing with us.

"Des Moines. And please, call me Wah. Everybody calls me that," she said. "Except my father. He's from Denmark. He calls me 'Neeta,'" she said, imitating his stilted, Scandinavian accent. She smiled and took a lemon drop.

"I've been through there," Mary said. "I have cousins in Ames."

"Boring with a capital B," Wah said. "I guess I was expecting Hollywood to be more exciting, but it's not much different than home."

"You haven't learned where to go yet," Gonda said with a nudge and a wink. "I'll show you."

Wah giggled. "All right. I'm holding you to that."

Before long, Wah, Harriett, and Phyllis were part of the gang like they'd always been there. And Wah and Mary seemed well on their way to being best friends.

Meanwhile, my courtship with Sonny continued—walks on the beach in Santa Monica, strolls on the boardwalk, and dinners in downtown Los Angeles. Things took on a new urgency after Wilson brought us into the war, because Sonny planned on joining the navy. One June night, over chicken à la king at the Bristol Café downtown, he took my hand.

"Marie, you know what I'm gonna ask you. I'll be at sea for months. But I want a good woman to come home to. And I want you taken care of if anything happens to me. You could get my pension. I want to marry you before I ship out."

Doesn't every girl dream of hearing those glorious words? But in my case the 'before I ship out' put the kibosh on any romantic feelings I might have had. Sure, Sonny wanted a good woman, but did he want me? I supposed I should have been happy that he wanted me to have his sailor's pension, but was I only filling a role that any other woman could step into? He gazed at me with those earnest eyes, persuading, beseeching. I couldn't hurt him. I said yes.

To sweeten the deal, Sonny decided we would motor down the coast and overnight at the Oceanside Beach Hotel as mister and missus. I told Mum we were shooting there, so I'd be gone for a few days. And then I felt like the world's biggest heel for lying to her for the first time ever.

Your wedding day is supposed to be the most romantic and special day of your life. Mine wasn't much different than any other. Less special, in fact. I doubt many people want to spend a morning waiting with other impetuous fools at city hall to tie the knot in front of a justice-of-the-peace. I wore my nicest white eyelet lace dress with white stockings. I had no white shoes, so I settled for my beige kid lace-up boots. We went to a flower store and bought a nosegay of white roses, orange blossoms, and ferns, and Sonny got a white rose boutonnière for his lapel.

We nervously recited our vows, merely repeating the lines provided for us, then signed the register, like the couples before us and the ones after.

We drove straight from the marriage to the hotel, now officially Mr. and Mrs. Henry Gerke, and even though we'd done lots of billing and cooing on our dates, we'd never gone any further. In the bathroom, I changed into my ruffled white lawn nightgown and stared at myself in the bathroom mirror, thinking how my life was about to change. I was going to become a woman, and I was terrified.

My hand trembled as I opened the bathroom door. I stood there for a minute.

"I don't know what to do," I said.

"Me either," he replied.

Making love had always been this mysterious but oh-so-wonderful thing that you weren't supposed to know about until you were married. But then you were supposed to magically learn all the mechanics of it, instantly.

"If I kiss you a lot, that should make you feel less nervous," Sonny helpfully suggested.

"All right," I said.

He kissed me, lightly, then deeper, using his tongue to pry my mouth open. As he did, he lay me down on the coverlet and thrust his tongue into my mouth, bruising my lips in the process. He was getting stirred up and kneaded my breasts like he was checking avocados for ripeness at the market. He fumbled with the hem of my nightdress, and his hands moved over my nether regions.

Did all women go through this? Was there nothing romantic or wonderful about it at all? How had the population grown so large if women always had this miserable a time procreating?

Sonny figured out the engineering of it, and soon he was clumsily pounding away on top of me. It hurt worse than anything I'd ever felt before, unless I counted that time I'd accidentally stepped in the red ant nest when we were in Arizona years before.

I clutched the top rails of the brass bed, trying to cushion my head, which was repeatedly ramming the headboard. Concentrating on a crack in the ceiling and clenching my teeth so I wouldn't cry out, I concentrated on anything but what was happening to me.

Sonny was totally enjoying himself, panting and grunting and making strange faces. When he gurgled, "Oh yes, oh yes, oh yes," and collapsed on top of me, I knew something had happened, but I wasn't quite sure what until I felt the dampness on me and on the sheets.

He nuzzled my neck and caressed a breast. "Darling, that was wonderful. I think you're about the most special girl in the world."

I know it was awful of me, but all I could think was, *How soon will this be over? And when does he ship out?*

"This is the best day of my life," he said, holding me close. At least this part was nice. If all we did was hold each other and kiss a little, I was fine with that. The other part though... I'd heard people use the term round heels, but I couldn't imagine wanting to do that even once, let alone with someone different every night. We did it again over the course of the weekend. I hoped it would get better, but it never did.

When our weekend together was over, Sonny was sent to the Brooklyn Navy Yard, and I went back to my life—filming and gabbing with the girls. The only difference was that now the food vendors on the Venice pier couldn't sell more than two hot dogs to a customer. Other than that, I quarreled with Peg, and felt guilty for keeping my secret from Mum. Usually I loved keeping secrets. Since I'd been a little girl, I'd loved there being things I knew that no one else did. But this was different. I wanted to tell Phyl and Vera, but I was afraid they'd laugh at my impulsiveness. How could I ever explain making the biggest mistake of my life?

Sonny's letters continued to arrive regularly, so I dutifully wrote him back, pretending to feel something I knew I never could. Not for him, and not after our wedding night. I almost wished a well-aimed torpedo would take care of the problem for me.

The worst part was the dread of telling Mum what I'd done. That I'd lied. That I'd eloped. She'd be so disappointed in me. All mothers dream of seeing their daughters get married—the white dress, the church music, the flowers, the rice at the church door. But I'd stolen that from her. And now I had to find the perfect time to come clean.

CHAPTER SEVEN

PREVOST APARTMENT, 451 S HAMPSHIRE STREET,
LOS ANGELES, CALIFORNIA *October 1918*

"Idinna feel so weel," Mum said when she arrived home from work complaining of a headache and body aches. Clouds had moved in, and it started to rain.

"Here, come sit down," I said, helping her to the couch. I held the back of my hand to her forehead as she'd done with Peg and me when we were little, then gasped at how incredibly hot she felt.

"Mum, you're burning up. Let's get you into bed. I'll make you some chicken broth and tea."

"My sweet wee girl..." she whispered as I pulled the counterpane back and she crawled into bed. "I'll be right as rain in no time. I only need to rest..."

For the next four days, she flailed about, trying to get comfortable, kicking off the covers one minute, and cowering beneath them shivering and teeth chattering the next. She was too weak to get to the privy, so I improvised a bedpan for her and had to change the sheets at least once a day. Sometimes twice.

Peg, ungrateful as usual, protested at having to care for Mum when she wanted to be out with her friends. She had a little money from *Hello, Trouble,* and was expecting more from *Painless Love,* which was to be released in the next few weeks, but now there was talk of the theaters closing because of the influenza.

"Peg, don't you get it?" I said, grabbing her by the arms as she tried to slip out the front door. "The doctor won't come. The entire country is sick. While Mum has got this thing, we only have my paycheck coming in, and your L-KO money, which isn't much. That's it! If I get sick, you won't have a roof over your head! This influenza business is serious. Mayor Woodman is putting all sorts of restrictions on gatherings. The studio may not even be able to film for much longer. We could all be dead tomorrow. So come help me *this instant!*"

Her petulant face dissolved into tears. "Why are you always so mean to me?! It's not fair! I'm meeting Dulcie and Rosemary at the soda fountain!"

"That's what you're worried about?" I asked. "Shame on you, Peg Prevost. Mum could be dying, and all you care about is not being able to sit and gossip over an egg cream?"

"Not exactly..." she said. "I still care about Mum too... honest!"

"Then help me. I have to go to work. I showed you how to use the bedpan. I've been giving her two aspirins every four hours, and I've left a stack of rags and washcloths in the bathroom. Wet them with cold water and put them on her forehead for the fever. I didn't get a chance to change her nightdress. When she's lucid, try to do that. The tea is right next to the stove. She likes the Salada, so I mix a little whiskey with it to help her sleep. All right?"

"All right," she said with a sigh.

"I have to go. I'm running late."

That night when I got home from the lot was the worst yet. I crawled into bed with Mum, holding her as she shook with chills. I hadn't spoken to God much in my life—church had always bored me. Instead, I'd chosen to daydream or count the words in the Book of Common Worship until the service was over. But that night, I prayed as I'd never prayed before. I couldn't let her die with my ridiculous lie hanging between us. I'd planned on telling her when the time was right. But until now it had never arrived.

"Dear God," I pleaded silently. "Please don't let this turn into pneumonia like all the others. Please don't take Mum away from us. She's too young. She hasn't had a chance to be truly happy in her life yet. She deserves so much more than this. I'll do whatever you want. Please...let her live...I'll tell her. I promise."

I drifted off and awoke in the quiet darkness of early morning. A glance at the alarm clock told me it was 4 a.m. Mum was sleeping soundly for the first time in a week and a half. I touched the back of my hand to her forehead, and to my surprise, it was dry and nearly normal. The fever had broken at last.

I looked up to the ceiling and smiled at the invisible being beyond. "Thank you," I mouthed. Now to find the perfect time. I tucked the covers snugly around her and went to put the kettle on.

By the next Saturday, Mum was getting her color back. But she was still helpless as a baby bird, so I brought her soup and tea and read to her in the evenings so she could drift off.

She loved *Rob Roy* and *Lorna Doone*.

"Afternoon, Mum," I said. The tray contained Wee Mae's prized china teapot, two cups, a tiny pitcher of milk and the sugar bowl. Plus a plate of fresh shortbread.

"Ye take such good care of me," Mum said, patting the bed next to her. I set the tray down on the bedside table, poured the tea, and stirred in milk and sugar. Then I lay the plate on the blanket.

"Mum, I have something very important to tell you," I said.

"What is it, pet?" she said, taking a cookie.

"It's about Sonny."

"You must miss him terribly," she said, leaning back against the pillow and finishing her shortbread.

I stayed quiet, unsure how to answer. Mum looked at me curiously.

"This is so hard," I said. "I have to tell you, but I know you'll be angry with me."

"Angry? Whatever for? Ye saved m'life, pet. Ah couldn't be more grateful for ye." She took my hand. "What is it, wee girl?"

I sighed. "Sonny was nervous... and scared about shipping out, and..."

Her eyebrow rose.

"We're married," I blurted.

"Ye're wha'?"

"Back in June. When we went to Oceanside. I wanted so much to tell you, but I was scared. I was so stupid. It was a terrible mistake, and now I don't know how to fix it."

The shock on her face was palpable, and all I wanted was to turn the calendar back and tell Sonny no. "You're angry," I said.

"No' angry. Surprised, aye. Disappointed, perhaps. But ye're an adult now. If ye think it was a mistake, then ye dinna need me getting upset. That'll only make things worse. Ah only wish ye'd talked to me first."

"I'm so sorry, Mum. I thought I was in love," I admitted.

"I did too," she said, with a rueful smile, referring to Frank. "Like mother, like daughter. Sonny seemed like a good lad. Wouldnae say boo to a goose, that one. Did somethin' change for ye?"

"Yes, but I'm not sure exactly when." I could actually trace it back to our honeymoon, but I couldn't tell Mum that. It was too embarrassing.

"S'no' easy bein' divorced," she said. "Migh' be easier wi' no bairns, but..." She glanced at me sideways. "Mary, ye're not—"

"No, Mum, I'm not. But we did have a honeymoon down in Oceanside."

She continued to watch me for a reaction.

"It was awful," was all I said.

She nodded sagely. "Wha' will ye do? I'll help ye if ah can. You know that."

"There's not much I can do until Sonny comes home. *If* he comes home. I couldn't do that to him while he's out there defending the country."

"Then we cannae do more than pray that's soon."

The war ended a month later. I hoped Sonny and I could come to an agreement and end this farce of a marriage. But he wrote me that he wouldn't be back until the spring. I'd have to bide my time until then.

MACK SENNETT STUDIO, EDENDALE, CALIFORNIA
February 1919

"All right, ladies, time to pack up those carpetbags and see the world!" Mr. Sennett said to a group of us waiting around the jacaranda tree. He aimed a stream of tobacco toward a weed struggling through the wooden plankway near the open-air stage.

"What's going on?" Harriett said. She was sitting on the bench with Pepper on her lap.

"Harry Carr got a brainstorm—he wants a short flicker to promote *Yankee Doodle in Berlin*. Starring all of you, of course. We're sending you on a publicity junket to go with the film. Out east first, then the Deep South, a swing through the Midwest, up to the Pacific Northwest, and a twist through the desert before heading home. Whaddya say?" Mr. Sennett said.

Harry Carr was Mr. Sennett's publicity man, always dreaming of some new crazy scheme to get attention for our films. With the war over, poking fun of the Kaiser had become good entertainment. *Yankee Doodle in Berlin* did that in spades.

"Do we have to wear bathing suits the entire time?" said Gonda. She was tired of slapstick and it showed. The rest of us had hoped to become more than cabbage roses on wallpaper. Vera had tired of pie throwing and left for greener pastures at Vitagraph, and Wah had moved on to Universal. Mary missed her terribly.

"Not the whole time," Mr. Sennett said. "But you gotta show your knees, at least. That's what folks are paying for!" Seeing our frowns, he furrowed his brow. "Come on! Where's the enthusiasm? Where's the excitement? I want you all ready to leave bright and early, nine a.m. day after tomorrow."

The cast and crew met at the depot in Glendale, and we girls attracted glances from all directions—the traveling salesman here, the college student in a letter sweater there. We found our berths and hung out of them, gabbing like a flock of hens. Harriett pulled out her ukulele and strummed "They Were All Out of Step But Jim." Phyllis, always game for kicking up her heels, did an impromptu shimmy in the corridor to our applause.

Phyl and I were bunking together, top and bottom, as were Myrtle and Harriett and Gonda and Mary.

Of course, Blanche Payson had joined us as our ever-present chaperone. When I thought of her being there, I wanted to laugh. What would the girls say if they knew I'd already gone off and gotten myself hitched? I ached to confide in Phyllis, but after all this time, I was worried she might not speak to me again. For a second time.

On the leg between Chicago and Seattle, as we ate supper in the dining car, Mary updated us on Wah.

"She's been so ill. I'm worried about her," she said.

"Influenza?" I asked, since I now had experience with it myself, caring for Mum.

"Yes. It's been so horrible. All she wants to do is sleep. No energy at all." She leaned across the table and whispered, "Her eyes have crossed."

"Her what?" Myrtle asked.

"It's true. We're both terrified they'll stay that way," Mary said.

"What would cause someone's eyes to cross?" Gonda asked.

"The doctor says it's something to do with her nerves. She

sits and sits, like she's in a trance. Her mother has come to care for her, and we're both worried sick. She's not herself. When I think of how often she wrote me when they were filming *The Brass Bullet*, she was so excited. Then she moved onto *The Rough Lover* and *The Sea Flower*. She said working with Franklyn Farnum and Gayne Whitman was an absolute dream," Mary said as she stirred sugar into her tea.

"I hope she'll be okay," Gonda said. "To have this happen right as she's moved onto bigger things isn't fair. I mean, we all dream of something more. I appreciate the opportunities we've had so far, but..." she left the sentence unfinished and instead took a bite of her chicken cutlet. Her gaze drifted off, out the window to somewhere in the darkness.

"It sure would be nice, wouldn't it?" said Phyl, eating a spoonful of her creamed turnips. "Being able to move up like Wah or Gloria did...getting all that cabbage for one picture."

"B-b-b-r-r-r-i-i-i-i-n-n-n-g-g-g!!" I said, miming putting a phone receiver to my ear. "Miss Haver? Why, she's right here, operator. It's Mr. DeMille!" I whispered loudly.

Phyl laughed. "Don't I wish!" she said. "I can live in hope though."

"That goes double for me," Harriett said, savoring a piece of chocolate meringue pie. "None of my big dreams involved being background scenery for Sennett."

When we got back to our berths, Phyl rustled through her bag.

"Marie," she said. "Look at this picture I found before we left."

"Yeah?" I set down the Charlotte Perkins Gilman novel I'd brought along. She passed me a publicity shot of us playing leapfrog on the beach in Santa Monica.

"Why didn't you tell me this red plaid suit makes me look fat? I look like an elephant at a watering hole," she said.

"Because it doesn't," I said.

"Oh it does. It absolutely does," she protested.

"Phyl, it doesn't. You look beautiful," I said, handing it back.

Her hopeful face appeared at the drape opening. "You think so?"

"Of course I do. A real friend tells you the truth."

"You're a pal, Marie. Listen...I feel bad about not writing after we graduated. I want to tell you again how sorry I am."

"It's all right," I said, pounding my pillow to plump it up a bit.

"It's just...Georgie and I were spending all that time together, and he was getting jealous, and I..."

"It's all right. I understand. G'night," I said, cutting her off. I couldn't let her know how much the brush-off had hurt.

"Night," she said, retreating to her own bunk.

Seattle was the same as the other towns—a whistle-stop arrangement where we tossed leaflets off the back of the caboose. They urged folks to come to the Moore Theatre, see the show, poke fun of the Kaiser, and have a laugh. At the end of the film, we stood in the lobby, signed autographs, and posed for photos taken by newsmen and fans with Brownie cameras. After weeks and weeks of train travel, Harvey houses and being jammed together in cheap hotels, we were dead on our feet.

When we arrived back in Los Angeles, a Sennett crew picked us up at the station, then deposited each one of us on our doorsteps. The plan was to let us recuperate for a week before we had to report back to the lot. The truck gave a honk-honk, and I waved as they putted away. I'd put my key in the lock when a figure stepped out of the shadows of the oleander bush near the door.

"Hello, Marie."

CHAPTER EIGHT

PREVOST APARTMENT, 451 S HAMPSHIRE ST
LOS ANGELES, CALIFORNIA *July 1919*

I screamed, then instantly felt like a fool. The shadow stepped closer to the front porch light, and I realized it was Sonny.

"I'm sorry. I didn't mean to frighten you," he said. "I'm home. You didn't answer my last few letters."

"I've been out of town on tour. They picked me up from the depot." I gestured vaguely at the truck, still chugging off into the distance.

"I missed you," he said, stepping closer.

I am entirely too tired for this scene tonight.

"Sonny, I'm exhausted. I've been traveling for weeks, I'm rumpled, and I haven't washed since Phoenix. We need to talk, but I can't even think straight. All I want to do is sleep."

"This isn't the welcome home I imagined," he said. "Don't I even get a kiss?"

"Sure," I said. He approached, ready to leave a wet ring around my mouth. Instead, I turned my face, offering him my cheek.

Mr. Burton, our crotchety neighbor, had made it to his window, and the shutters burst open. "What's going on out there? Is everything all right?"

"Everything's fine, Mr. Burton," I said. "I'm terribly sorry."

He frowned. "You should be ashamed, Miss Prevost. Waking up the whole neighborhood that way."

"I'm sorry. He surprised me. We'll be quiet now," I said.

He continued grumbling as he pulled the shutters closed and shut the window.

"What's wrong?" Sonny asked.

"I told you. I'm tired and I don't want to talk about it right now," I said, trying to hang on to what was left of my temper.

"Then I'll be here bright and early to pick you up for breakfast. We can talk then."

"Fine," I said, opening the front door.

"Nine a.m.!" he called after me. I'd already shut the door.

He arrived to collect me precisely at nine. I'd barely had time to comb my hair, brush my teeth and wash my face. He put the car in gear and headed for the Solana Café on 5th Street, where we ordered hash and eggs.

"I thought you'd be happy to see me," Sonny said, and took a sip of his coffee.

As the waitress set down my plate, I sighed, trying to figure out how to let him down gently.

"Sonny, I wanted to make you happy before you went off to war, marrying you and all, but..."

"But what?

"It's a bad time for me to be married, that's all."

"What do you mean, bad time?"

"We've never really been married. Not like you're supposed

to do it. I went home to my mother and you went home to yours. Then you shipped out."

"That doesn't mean it didn't happen. Marriage is for life."

"You talked me into it," I said resentfully. "I'm too young to be married. It's the wrong time for me."

"Wrong time, but most importantly, wrong guy."

"Yes," I said. "I'm sorry."

What else could I say? *If your bedroom manner had knocked my socks off, I'd have tried to pretend this marriage had a chance* sounded terrible.

Sonny Gerke left me cold. And nothing he said or did made me any warmer.

"I want a divorce," I said quietly. I didn't want to make an issue out of it, but when you realize you've made a mistake this huge, you usually want to move past it as quickly as possible. Not so with Sonny.

"Got another fella waiting in the wings to take my place?" he said.

"No," I said. "I can't be married. I want to be done with all this."

"I won't do it," he said, thrusting a toothpick between his lips.

"Why not?"

"Because I love you. I still want to take you out once in a while," he said, taking my hand.

"We're not doing that again," I said, pulling it away from him.

His face fell, as I knew it would. "Can't you see I'm crazy about you?" he said.

"I'm sorry. I don't love you. I'm not sure if I ever did. I

don't even know what love feels like. I'm a child. It wasn't fair of me to marry you."

"That's it then," he said. He pulled out the toothpick and broke it in half.

"I'm afraid so," I said.

"I'm not signing anything," he said, and rose suddenly. Grabbing his hat off the counter, he dashed off, leaving me with the check and no ride home.

"Sonny!" I said, hurrying after him. "Sonny!" I only got as far as the front door before the alarmed manager stopped me and held up our outstanding tab.

ALEXANDRIA HOTEL LOBBY, LOS ANGELES, CALIFORNIA
November 1920

The Hotel Alexandria was full of expensive rugs, crystal chandeliers, potted palms, and high-placed movie men. Ones with money who liked discovering new talent. New talent like Phyl and me. It had taken me entirely too long to put in an appearance here.

Phyl and I were determined to make the move from Sennett if we could, and we'd heard about the million-dollar carpet in the lobby, where lots of deals got signed. If you wanted to move up in Hollywood, this was the place to do it.

Needing to have a little fun, we decided on a flicker, and then a visit to the Alex to socialize. We'd gone to see Wah in an episode of *The Lost City* at the Pantages. While she appeared to have recovered from her illness, there was something different about her. I noticed it right away.

"You thought so too?" Phyl said when I commented on it.

"I couldn't quite put my finger on it," I said. "She was racing around so much."

"Faster than Peggy Hopkins Joyce with a new sugar daddy. Did you see her eyes?" Phyl said.

"I was too busy paying attention to everything else. I've only seen it once before. That party at Mabel's."

"You thinking cocaine?" she asked.

"I don't know what to think."

"Remember Mary said Wah was having to work on *The Lost City* at the same time as *Rough-Riding Romance*? Plus she was still getting over that sleeping thing. Poor dear is probably a wreck."

"I'm worried about her, Phyl."

"Me too," she sighed. "She's still writing. I'll try to find out what's going on. How's Vera?"

"Happy," I said. "She's positively glowing." Vera had married in September—to Jackie Taylor, the violin player in The Ship Café's orchestra—and since she was a newlywed, we hadn't seen her as much lately. Earlier in the year, she'd started working for the Christie Company and loved it, since they'd paired her with Bobby Vernon for a series of comedies. We chatted about the wedding and made bets on how soon she'd have a new addition.

I'd just settled back into the celadon velvet settee when Phyl touched my knee. "Ooh, who's that over there? He looks important. And familiar," Phyllis said, sipping her carefully doctored orange juice. You couldn't drink legally in Hollywood, but no one went anywhere without a flask. "I'd swear that's King Baggot, the actor."

"That *is* King Baggot," I said. "I've met him."

"You what?"

"I bumped into him on the beach a few years ago when the girls and I were playing tug-of-war. He's very nice," I said.

"And so handsome," Phyl said under her breath. "I'll bet he could introduce us to anybody in the place."

"You've got a point," I said. I waved at him from across the room. He saw me, smiled, and approached us, clutching his teacup. Teacups were now the accepted method of disguising booze.

"Miss Prevost," he said. "Nice to see you again. Are you enjoying your evening out?"

"We're having a marvelous time. Mr. Baggot, this is my friend, Phyllis Haver. Phyllis, King Baggot."

"Charmed, I'm sure," Phyllis said, batting her eyelashes and offering her hand, which he leaned over and debonairly kissed.

"Are you working on anything now?" I asked him.

"We're in the process of wrapping up *The Forbidden Thing*," he said. "A comedy with Carter DeHaven and Gloria Cunard," he said with a smile. "How about you?"

"A short called *Movie Fans,*" I said. We exchanged a few war stories, then I guided the conversation around to his previous offer. "Mr. Baggot, I hate to trouble you, but you once said if I ever needed your help, you could put in a good word..."

His laugh was throaty and sounded bitter and rueful.

"I'm not sure if it's a matter of me putting in a good word for you or you putting in a good word for me," he said. He snapped his fingers at one of the waiters rushing about and hoisted his teacup as a request for another. "I'm afraid that any clout I had is fading fast," he said. "But I'll do what I can."

I gulped. He did look quite a bit older, even in only the few years since I'd met him. The waiter brought him another cup, and he downed it like a parched man who'd been stranded in the Mojave for weeks.

"See that suave-looking man over there next to Hoot Gibson, the fellow in the cowboy hat?"

Phyllis and I nodded eagerly.

"That's Irving Thalberg. They both work with me at Universal. Thalberg's a guy to watch."

Compared to the fat cats with their big cigars and fancy cufflinks, Mr. Thalberg carried himself with reserve, as if he was above all the chaos around him.

When Hoot Gibson excused himself to make time with a pretty blonde. Mr. Baggot waved at Mr. Thalberg across the expanse of rug, and Thalberg crossed it to join us.

"King. Good to see you," Thalberg said, shaking hands with our would-be benefactor.

"Irv, I see you're out for a night on the town. May I present Miss Marie Prevost and Miss Phyllis Haver."

"Delighted," he said, clasping first my hand, then Phyllis's. "I'm familiar with your work for Mr. Sennett."

I smiled and tried to think of something to say that wasn't idiotic. Thalberg wasn't overly tall, but he was taller than me. He had shiny black hair styled with pomade, smooth olive skin, and direct but friendly dark eyes. I judged him to be about my age—possibly a little younger, but not by much. His voice spoke of New York, but it wasn't the straight Brooklyn of so many of the transplants out here. He sounded cultured.

Maybe it was only an act.

"Irv, Marie and Phyllis have become disenchanted at Sennett, and they…"

"You'd like to come work at Universal," he said, shaking his glass to tinkle the ice in it.

"If you think there'd be any room for us in your organization, we'd be happy to start in the lower rungs," I said. "Bit parts even. Something to let us develop into more serious actresses. Not wearing bathing suits all the time and taking pies to the face."

He sized us up coolly, from the tops of our heads to the tips of our toes. Up, down, then back up again. We stood nervously, awaiting his verdict.

"You're both attractive ladies." He paused, then took a deep breath. "Miss Haver, I hate to disappoint, but we've only recently signed an actress named Laura LaPlante who resembles you," he said gently. Phyl's face fell.

"Miss Prevost, you have an interesting look. Women are becoming much more freedom-minded since getting the vote. Our writers have been creating some newfangled scenarios to keep up with that trend. I'd still want to see a screen test though. When does your contract end?"

"I'm not sure of the exact date, but it's due to expire soon."

He reached into his breast pocket. "Here's my card. Things are crazy right now, but why don't you schedule a visit after the holidays? Make an appointment with my secretary. We can have you take a screen test, and maybe take it further. We'll see how things go."

I nodded and we smiled at each other.

"Have a good evening, Miss Prevost, Miss Haver. See you

tomorrow, King."

King gave him a wave as he departed.

Phyl waited until he was out of earshot, then gave a low moan. "I can't believe you might leave Sennett," she said sadly. "I'll be there by myself."

"The other girls will still be there with you, Phyl. I'm sure someone at one of the other studios will be interested."

"It won't be the same," she said with a pout.

When I got home that night, Mum looked up from her copy of *Collier's*.

"Had fun, did ye?"

"Mum, Irving Thalberg was at the Alexandria! King Baggot introduced us, and he wants me to do a screen test after the holidays!"

"Ah dinna know who that is, pet."

"He's the studio manager at Universal. I might be able to go work for them!"

She looked a little sad. "Wha' of Mr. Sennett? He's been awfully good tae ye."

"I know. But I'm tired of walk-ons and swimsuit snaps. Always being window dressing. I'm a good actress. Mr. Sennett says I have a gift for comedy, and so does Mr. Baggot. This could be my next step."

She wrapped me in a hug.

"If this is what you want to do, then it's the right thing. Mr. Sennett must see that ye're spreading your wings. Her eyes danced their blue-violet jig. "Whate'er ye do, ye know yer auld mum is behind ye."

"Of course, Mum. I know."

The door slammed and Peg stood in the front hall, returned

from her date with Pathé. "What's going on?"

"Marie's excited about a meeting after the holidays with someone important."

"The president?" she quipped.

"As long as you get to do more shopping, what do you care?"

She cocked her head. "You're right. Goodnight."

CHAPTER NINE

UNIVERSAL STUDIOS, UNIVERSAL CITY, CALIFORNIA

Late February 1921

"And this is the administration building," my guide said, pausing for breath. "We're completely self-contained. That's the post office, and over there is the telegraph office. We even have our own fire and police departments. There's a greenhouse, a nursery, stables, a blacksmith shop, and a zoo. Even our own hospital." He pointed as he talked.

I was getting the tour from a fresh-faced clerk named Herman. Mr. Thalberg had someone in his office, but would see me as soon as he was done. My screen test had gone pretty well, I thought. A reading from *Romeo and Juliet* where I registered dozens of emotions. I must have done something right.

I'd thought our Keystone lot was impressive, but Universal put our setup in Edendale to shame. Universal had stood for a little over six years in its current spot, fronting Lankershim, Herman told me. But before that, it had existed several miles up the road.

The buildings were Mediterranean style, with the whitewashed stucco, red roof tiles, and sinuous lines the builders out west liked so much. The windows tilted out to absorb any stray breeze, and awnings helped to keep out the baking California sun.

"What's that?" I asked, pausing near the barnyard. In the distance were the facades of several European-style buildings covered in scaffolding, obviously a set under construction.

"That's for the new film, *Foolish Wives*. Don't tell anyone I told you, but the cost overruns have been enormous. There's been a lot of friction over it. Mr. Von Stroheim wants everything perfect, but Mr. Thalberg is trying to control the expenses. Between you, me, and this chicken coop, I don't think it will end well."

When we were done with the tour, Herman deposited me back in Mr. Thalberg's waiting room. Thalberg's secretary saw me into his office, which was decorated in subdued shades of navy and gray.

"Hold my calls, Miss Bayer," he said as she retreated. "Miss Prevost! Good to see you again. Please have a seat." He waved me in to take one of the chairs in front of his desk and held out his hand. His nails were neat and clipped.

I sat in the blue upholstered chair across from his desk, nervously clutching my handbag. "Thank you, Mr. Thalberg. As I said at the Alex, I'm hoping Universal might have more to offer. Sennett used to be fun, but it's not anymore."

"I think you definitely have potential. I hate to see you sharing what little billing you get with Teddy the Dog," he said.

"I want to be sure I'm doing the right thing. Mr. Sennett's been so good to me, and it will hurt him terribly if I leave. And all my friends..."

"Pardon me for saying so, Miss Prevost. You need to worry

about yourself first and foremost. Start with Sennett, then move on. Those other girls have the looks, like you. If they have the talent, they'll find a place somewhere. Take Gloria Swanson for instance. She had the wisdom to get out. Look at her now."

That was exactly who I'd been looking at. Gloria Swanson was now in the stratosphere of stars, making as much as a Rockefeller. And Wah had gone on to Selig Polyscope from Universal. She was becoming a serial queen like Pearl White, for goodness sake. So I could do it too. I had the looks, I had the athletic ability, and I could act.

"You have a very real talent," Mr. Thalberg continued. "I think Universal can let you shine in starring roles and allow you to grow as an actress, like you want. Have you read *This Side of Paradise* yet?"

I shook my head.

"No matter. There's a new kind of character played by the woman in it. Kind of like what Olive Thomas was doing with her baby vamp thing, but they're calling them flappers now—like her last movie. I see this as a natural progression of your work as a bathing beauty. You can still capitalize on that devil-may-care attitude, but you can keep your clothes on. Flappers drink, they smoke, they bob their hair, they pet in the backs of cars, and they dare to break the rules. There's a market that's begging to be tapped."

"What do I do first?" I said. I leaned forward in my chair, and he smiled.

"First, let Mr. Sennett know we're interested. Then, you and he can come to some sort of an agreement on your contract. Once that's done, we can get you squared away here. I have a publicity idea I want to talk to you about. Do you still have any of your bathing suits?"

"Yes, folded up in a drawer at home."

"Perfect."

LOVE'S OUTCAST SET, MACK SENNETT STUDIO, EDENDALE, CALIFORNIA *March 1921*

"Hey, Gilbert! Adjust that muslin, would ya? The sun's moving," Mal St. Clair called through his megaphone. He and John Waldron, another of the directors, stood with Mr. Sennett near the main stage.

Ben Turpin and Kalla Pasha stood by, along with Phyl, waiting for direction. Kalla was a black-haired brute of a fellow who looked like he should be standing at a sultan's palace with a scimitar at his side. In reality, he was regular old Joe Rickard from Detroit, and he was a big pussycat. The most noticeable thing about Ben was his perfect comic timing. And his incredibly crossed eyes. But he was a sweetheart, and always called me "Dawlin." He was from New Orleans.

Gilbert, one of the hands, did as he was told and tugged the rigging over another foot or two.

"Better. Places!"

The slate boy chalked up the next take on a board and clacked the halves together. "*Love's Outcast.* Scene three, take three."

"And...action!" John said. He and Mal watched as their scene progressed.

"Mr. Sennett," I said.

He looked irritated. "What is it, Marie? I'm a little busy."

"I'm sorry, but I need to talk to you. You weren't in your

office."

He sighed and stepped away from the group.

Mal supervised as Kalla moved in with his pie on the unsuspecting Ben.

I followed Mr. Sennett into his office. He closed the door behind us and tugged up his trouser legs to take a seat. Then he reached into his tin of Old Abe tobacco and wadded a mound into the crevice of his cheek. He chewed as he looked across the desk at me expectantly.

"What can I help you with, Marie?" he asked. His voice was garbled, awash in spit, and he aimed a stream of tobacco at the spittoon on the floor next to his desk.

I took a deep breath. "Mr. Sennett, I want to thank you for the last five years. They've been a wonderful learning experience for me. The friendships I've made here, the adventures we've had filming—they'll stay with me forever. But I—"

"You've been offered more money to go somewhere else, and it sounds like a swell deal," he finished for me.

I sat there speechless.

"You think I haven't seen this before?" he continued, running his hands through his hair. "You're not the first. There've been plenty before you, and I'm sure there'll be plenty after, taking what they've learned from me and using it somewhere else. I mean, why wouldn't you? I can't pay the salaries the big guys can."

"You mean you're not mad?"

"Of course I'm mad. You're one of my best girls. You've got good comic timing, you can swim, and you're easy on the eyes. Plus you fill out a bathing suit better than anybody here. I'd be an idiot not to be mad. Who'd you go with? Mutual? Famous

Players?"

"Universal," I said. "Mr. Thalberg there has some good ideas."

"Not a bad outfit," he said. "You'll do fine there." He nodded to make his point. We dealt with the details of me finishing up my contract, then he did something I didn't expect. He stood up and held out his big hand. I took it. His eyes glistened with new-forming tears. He blinked them away.

"Take care of yourself, doll," he said. "This town will chew you up and spit you out if you're not careful."

IRVING THALBERG'S OFFICE, UNIVERSAL STUDIO, UNIVERSAL CITY, CALIFORNIA *April 1921*

"Now Marie, about that changing your image," Mr. Thalberg said. We were meeting in his office, and I'd already signed on the dotted line. "Your public only sees one thing when they look at you: great legs, shocking knees, shapely ankles, and the right amount of bosom. But there's a big difference between Lady Macbeth and custard pies."

"I'm ready to change all that," I said. "But how?"

"By capturing the imagination of America. By cutting that invisible cord that's binding you to Sennett. That swimsuit of yours is ancient history, and it'll take a symbolic gesture to prove it. You're going to make a statement. At Coney Island. Fans can see you shake off your bathing beauty yoke."

"All right," I said, a little nervous and a little thrilled at the same time. "When?"

"I'd hoped for the Fourth of July," Mr. Thalberg said. "National holiday...height of summer rush... I couldn't think of anything more in keeping with the spirit of the occasion than one young woman declaring her independence from the garment that has kept her pigeonholed for so long. Unfortunately, Mr. Laemmle wants to meet with you while you're in New York, and he'll be out of town with his family for Independence Day, so we're scheduling it for May instead. You'll have two chaperones. Gordon Cash is a production head. He needs to go back east to meet with Mr. Laemmle. And Marion Graham is one of my assistants. They'll take care of all the details."

The day of our departure, Universal sent a car to retrieve me, and Mr. Cash and Marion introduced themselves while the driver secured my trunk to the rear of the Ferris sedan. Marion had lovely delicate bone structure and chestnut curls. Mr. Cash was older, brusque, and seemed irritated that he had to accompany me. While we waited at the terminal, I paid a dime for a *Variety* at the newsstand to have something to browse on the trip.

We took Southern Pacific to Chicago, then we were due to catch the Broadway Limited to New York. The accommodations were far more luxe than the day coaches I was used to traveling in with Mum and Peg. In my compartment, I leafed through the news.

Juanita Hansen Collapse, the

headline read.

Wah had been in a sanitarium for two weeks, and the snippet claimed she would not be shooting for over a month.

"Oh, Wah, no," I said. I began a letter to her that afternoon that I hoped to mail when I got a minute. I sent love and told her to stay strong.

"We've booked you a room at the Biltmore," Marion said over roast duckling with applesauce in the dining car somewhere around Nebraska. Cornfields and plains flew by in the darkness. "I hope you'll be comfortable there. It's quite a nice hotel."

I smiled. Considering the dilapidated rooms that I was used to, anything would be a palace.

"Is this your first visit to New York?" Marion asked me.

"Yes," I admitted. "You?"

She laughed. "Nope. I'm from Long Island originally. I'm getting a visit home."

"I've seen lots of the west and the southwest, but not as much of the east coast," I said.

"That's about to change," she said. "With all the premieres and personal appearances, you'll get to see plenty."

Grand Central was busier than anyplace I'd ever been—everyone wanting to be somewhere else, and rushing to get there. They stepped off their trains, engaged a porter for their luggage, and strolled through the station. Guests like us took an elevator to the hotel basement and crossed into the hotel.

The Biltmore was luxurious. My jaw dropped when I saw the interior—thick velvet benches, heavy patterned carpets, marble sculptures, and tiled bathrooms with individual water closets.

Mr. Cash and Marion got me checked in, then took me to the Palm Court for a lovely dinner. We sat right near the ornate gold clock, and I had my very first oysters Rockefeller, along with a filet mignon, and a meringue for dessert. They saw me to my room and promised to retrieve me the next day at 8 a.m. sharp to visit with Mr. Laemmle before heading to Coney Island. I went to sleep with a huge smile on my face.

After a quick breakfast of shirred eggs and stewed rhubarb in the hotel dining room, we took the hired car. New York was like nothing I'd ever seen—huge, intimidating, and humming with activity. I craned my neck out the car window and still couldn't see the tops of the buildings. Most of the places we'd lived out west didn't have electric lights or indoor plumbing. But here, there were lights, lights, and more lights!

Mr. Laemmle's office was only a few blocks away, on Broadway at 48th Street. The Studebaker Building was ten stories of red brick and terra cotta, with arched windows below a top cornice. Mr. Laemmle's secretary showed me to his office. "He's expecting you," she said.

"Thank you, Miss Wells," he said as she slipped out of the room. "Miss Prevost, iss very good to meet you!" He rounded the corner to take both my hands in a very courtly manner. "Sit, please!" He gestured toward a black leather chair in front of his desk.

He was even shorter than me—around 5'2", I judged. Balding on top, and what was left was nearly white. His suit was well cut, with a white carnation in the lapel, and his eyes were lively, even kind behind wire-framed spectacles. His teeth were like the battlements on top of a castle—all gaps and strange angles. But the most noticeable thing about him was his thick German accent.

"Enjoying your time in New York so far, I hope?" he asked.

"Oh yes," I said with a nod.

"Good, good. A little schnapps perhaps?" He crossed to the bar. I shook my head.

"Iss a weakness of mine," he said. "Am very excited for you to work with us."

"Me too, Mr. Laemmle."

"Mr. Sennett vas paying you peanuts?" he asked. He poured himself a low tumbler and went back behind his desk, where he took a seat.

"It's time to move on. That's all."

"Diss means you grow as person and as actress. Ve vill do great vork together, ja?"

I beamed. No wonder his nickname was Uncle Carl. "Ja," I said.

We chatted about my trip, how I liked my hotel, if I'd visited New York before, and if I was nervous about the big day. I was, but I was excited too. Then he spoke to me about my contract and the plans they had for me. Before long, it was time to leave.

"Now you must find Marion. I hear you haff bonfire to light." He chuckled as I left his office.

Marion met me in Mr. Laemmle's waiting room, and we took the elevator to the street, then the hired car took us all the way to the southern tip of Brooklyn.

"We've been advertising for the last week or so," Marion said. "Ads in the theatricals, flyers on the boardwalk. You're famous already." We strolled down the Riegelmann Boardwalk, past everything from astrologers' booths and tattoo artists to shooting galleries and chuck-a-luck games.

"The buzz has already started," she continued. "They've changed the name of the film from *The Butterfly* to *Moonlight Follies*, and scheduled it for release in September. We're drumming up as much publicity as possible before then."

We had to step sideways to avoid the barker outside the Wagner's World Circus Sideshow who was advertising their attractions.

"Hur-ry, Hur-ry, Hur-ry! Step right up! See Boneeeta Barlowe, the Snake Enchantress! R-r-r-right this way! And Jolly Irene! At 689 pounds of pure delight, she's the world's largest woman! Mar-r-r-r-vel at the lovely Miss Myrtle Corbin, the four-legged wonder! And don't forget Zippo and Pippo, the pinhead twins!"

The noise was a jumble of hand organs and calliopes, along with the mechanical rumbles of roller coasters and the squeals and screams of their riders. Even the pier in Santa Monica didn't compare.

We stopped at a place called Nathan's, and Marion bought us hot dogs for five cents. The man behind the counter threw in a free root beer and a pickle.

At our designated spot, Mr. Cash had set up a salamander heater, one of those oil drums used to burn trash. Black bunting and streamers were draped from the eaves behind it, and a sandwich board had been set up in front of it, with a dramatic announcement painted on it: *Today! A statement of independence! Miss Marie Prevost!*

Mr. Cash and Marion had made me dress up especially for the occasion, a navy blue dress with the dropped waist so popular for the season, and a red, white, and blue scarf around my hair. Marion had also handed me a little American flag to wave.

Mr. Cash, wearing an expensive-looking suit and a bright red bow tie with matching red carnation, stepped to a position of prominence next to the salamander. He held up a small megaphone. "Ladies and gentlemen, may I have your attention, please!" A group of strolling bystanders paused and approached.

"You may recognize Miss Marie Prevost, late of Mr. Mack Sennett's Studio in California!" he bellowed. I gave a little wave, and a round of polite applause followed. "Miss Prevost has recently signed a contract with Universal Pictures under the auspices of Mr. Irving Thalberg! She is here today to make a statement, protesting her days of hedonistic exhibition as a bathing beauty!"

More applause.

Mr. Cash handed me the megaphone, and I swallowed and took a deep breath before reciting the words I'd memorized. I felt guilty for saying them, but...

"For far too long," I said. "I have been merely a brainless bit of fluff supporting star players at Mr. Sennett's studio!" I took a deep breath. "Universal will cast me in real movie roles! Films whose success isn't dependent on me showing my legs! Today, I am declaring my independence from my bathing beauty past with this symbolic gesture!"

Marion handed me the striped number I'd worn in *She Sighed By the Seaside*. It was much worse for wear now, faded and stretched out of shape, but still recognizable.

Wrinkling it up in my fists, I tossed it into the salamander. Marion pulled out a collection of my old still photographs, and we added them to the drum. Then she handed me a box of matches, and I struck the sulfur strip on the side, watching blue flame erupt from the tip. Into the drum it went. The flames leapt up as everything was consumed.

"Let's have a big hand for Miss Marie Prevost, no longer a

slave to her bathing beauty past! Look for her soon in *Moonlight Follies*, coming to a theater near you from Universal Pictures!" Mr. Cash shouted over the din of the midway.

The crowd had swelled by this point, to several hundred, I guessed. They burst into robust applause, so I smiled and signed autographs and shook hands with the fans.

"Miss Prevost, your Sennett films are our favorite!" an older woman said, nudging her husband next to her. A little girl in pigtails offered me a seashell and a piece of saltwater taffy. A teenager in an argyle sweater vest and plus-fours asked me for my signature on a postcard, then took it gratefully before shyly asking if he might have a kiss. I gave him a kiss on the cheek, and then Mr. Cash hustled me away, wanting to avoid a riot of every red-blooded college boy on the boardwalk.

Marion and Mr. Cash took me to Delmonico's for dinner and told me to order anything on the menu. I ordered the lobster of course. When would I ever have the chance to do that again? It was delicious. And that night as I fell asleep, the applause echoed in my ears.

CHAPTER TEN

MOONLIGHT FOLLIES SET, COFFIN ESTATE, PASADENA, CALIFORNIA *June 1921*

Despite its depressing name, the Coffin Estate was a beautiful mansion on Summit Avenue, set back in a grove of trees. It was a pleasant rustic spot with a swimming pool and lovely gardens full of pastel peach roses, deep purple salvia, and bright scarlet bee balm. To the northeast, the San Gabriel mountains loomed.

William Hiatt Coffin had been a Quaker who'd settled in Pasadena and he let film crews use the grounds of his home for shooting. Rumor was that Old Man Coffin, closing in on a hundred years old, still lectured from time to time at the college. I kept glancing at the upstairs windows, feeling like he must be watching us, but I never saw anyone.

I'd been tickled to find out that Mr. Baggot was directing *Moonlight Follies*. My character, Nan Rutledge, was a flapper with a heart of gold who liked spoiled rich boys until she met a rough-and-tumble mountain man, played by Clyde Fillmore. Clyde and I got along famously, but the plot was ludicrous. He was at least twenty years older than me. Who was going to believe I'd given up the yum-yum Park Avenue pretty boys for some old miner forty-niner?

Even so, I played my scenes to the letter, the way Mr. Baggot wanted them. When I wasn't being primped and prodded by the folks in wardrobe and makeup. I sat by the pool catching up on my reading until we were ready to shoot. Right now, that was *Main Street*, by a fellow named Sinclair Lewis. My dress was a stunning white chiffon embroidered with pink butterflies and a pink underslip. But it was hard remaining dainty in the heat when I was sweating like a longshoreman. It had to be the hottest day on record. Even the cactus were looking droopy.

We'd gone to Casa Verdugo for lunch, and now some of us were regretting the heavy Mexican food we'd ordered.

"It's hot as blazes out here!" our second cameraman, Nat Ross, cried. He was dark haired, with a young, eager face, and a sense of humor that kept me in stitches much of the time. He tugged off his socks, shoes, and bow tie, stripped down to his undershirt and trousers. Holding his nose, he leapt into the glistening aquamarine pool.

"Careful, Nat, you had all those tamales," Mr. Baggot cautioned him. When Nat didn't respond, Mr. Baggot turned to the pool.

"Oh, shit," he said, kicking off his shoes. I looked in that direction and saw Nat struggling in the water.

"Cramp!" Nat gasped. Mr. Baggot dashed across the pavement and dived in, so the crew gathered at the pool's edge, expecting him to make a dramatic rescue. But he didn't surface.

Then I saw the trickle of blood in the water.

"He must have hit his head!" I said. Knowing I was probably one of the few people there who could swim, and mindless of the gorgeous frock I was wearing, I kicked off my slippers and dove in after them. I reached Mr. Baggot first and brought him back to the edge in a swimmer's carry. Bert Glennon, our cinematographer, took hold of him and placed him on the grass near the edge of the pool, so he wouldn't get burned on the sidewalk.

"Go get Doctor Aldrich!" Bert shouted. The slate boy ran off toward the house, where our set doctor had gone to relieve himself.

I swam back to where Nat was still trying to stay afloat. He struggled against me as I took hold of him in a swimmer's carry.

"Relax. I'm trying to help you," I said. I cuffed him in the head to calm him down, and he finally quit fighting me. When I got Nat back to the side of the pool, Bert pulled him out and laid him next to Mr. Baggot, whose head Dr. Aldrich was examining. Mr. Baggot came to at last.

"Wha' happened?" His fingers gingerly touched the area Doc was trying to bandage.

I held up my index and middle fingers. "How many?"

That brought a weak smile. "Two."

Someone brought us towels, so we dried off. My dress was sopping—most likely ruined, but at least Mr. Baggot and Nat were safe. We'd have to re-shoot the scenes I'd done wearing it.

"Marie pulled you fellas out!" Bert said. "You shoulda seen her!"

"You did?" Mr. Baggot looked impressed.

I smiled. "You didn't think I got to be a bathing beauty on looks alone, did you?" I gave him a little wink.

"You saved our lives, Marie!" Nat said, massaging the cramp in his side. "I don't know what we'd have done if you hadn't been here!"

"Anybody would have done the same thing," I said. "I happened to jump in the fastest."

"Anybody who could *swim*," he protested. "One thing I know. No more tamales for lunch!"

Working for Universal was like nothing I could have imagined. Especially the money. My first paycheck went to Hazel's Dress Shop, where I bought a collection of new frocks that befit a flicker star: silks, laces, brocades, velvet, crepe, and a Persian lamb coat. And as I moved into *Nobody's Fool*, I invested in a stone marten and a silver fox. Then I visited Nanette Millinery on Broadway for dozens of new hats: tams, cloches and whimsical concoctions with beads, grosgrain, and feathers.

After *Don't Get Personal* and *The Dangerous Little Demon*, I started a nest egg to buy Mum a house of her own. In the meantime, I rented her a charming little apartment on Vermont near Sunset, and helped her pick out furnishings. I was there half the time anyway, visiting. Peg got her own place too, but I had no idea how she made rent.

For myself, I splurged and bought a new car. All the movie stars were trying to outdo each other with snazzier and fancier models. I merely wanted something to get me to and from the lot. I ended up with a sporty red 1921 McFarlan. It had decent horsepower, and it made a statement wherever I went. Like to the set of my newest film, *Her Night of Nights*.

VERA AND JACKIE'S HOUSE, HOLLYWOOD, CALIFORNIA
October 1921

"They're so beautiful," I said. "So sweet. They're darling, Vera."

Vera and Jackie had two new additions—adorable twin girls who were only two weeks old. She'd had a difficult delivery, but they were all home and healthy at last, so I'd come for a visit, bearing two pink layette blankets as a gift. Vera and I had lots of catching up to do, since she'd moved to Christie Studios and I was busy at Universal.

"What are their names?" I asked.

"This one is Frances, after Jackie's grandmother, and this one is Marie. After you," she said. The babies were beginning to get real tufts of pale brown hair, and it was obvious they'd have Vera's deep brown eyes.

"Oh, Vera..." I said. I gazed into the wrinkled face of little Marie, who let out a mewl and a yawn. The lump in my throat grew as the tiny fingers closed around my thumb.

"You're my best friend," she said by way of explanation. "I had to name her after you. See, she has lots of hair like you. But Frances seems to have better lungs, which I'm sure you'll hear if you stay for any length of time."

A thump and a groan came from their bedroom. Jackie had played his usual gig at The Ship Café the previous night, and Vera glanced away, embarrassed.

"Everything all right?" I asked.

"Fine." Her face told me something different.

"What is it? Tell me," I said.

"I hate it when he gets like this," she confessed. "He comes home drunk after playing all night."

"Boys will be boys?" I asked.

"I'm afraid it's more serious than that."

"Can I help?" I said.

"Thanks, but no," she said, squeezing my hand. "This is something I have to work out on my own."

I helped her feed, burp, and diaper the babies, and I got a little extra cuddle time with my namesake before I had to leave.

"Thanks again for the blankets," she said. "They're lovely."

"My pleasure. I'll see you soon, okay?" I said. I hugged her, then chugged off toward Venice, where Phyl and I were meeting for dinner at the Strand Café.

Phyl ordered the halibut with egg sauce and I got the breaded veal cutlet and an oyster cocktail. We were comparing notes about Roscoe Arbuckle's predicament up in San Francisco when who should approach us but Mr. Sennett. With him was another tall fellow. His forehead was a massive expanse of sunburned, leather-like skin, and his eyes were intense and beady beneath a heavy swath of eyebrows.

"Marie! Phyllis!" Mr. Sennett called. "How are you?"

I mentioned I'd just come from Vera's.

"How is she?"

"She and the babies are doing well. Frances and Marie. They're both beautiful."

"Oh, where are my manners. Marie Prevost, Phyllis Haver, I'd like to introduce Al Christie. Al, Marie and Phyllis. Ladies, this man helped to found Hollywood. He's the original lessee of the Blondeau Tavern, where it all began, and the brainchild behind Nestor Films. Best thing about him? He's a Canuck like us, Marie!"

"Al Christie?" I said. "You're Vera's new boss."

"I am!" he said, pleased that I recognized his name. "It's nice to meet you both." He held out his hand and shook both of ours.

"Honestly? I don't think I've met this many Canadians outside Canada in my life," I said with a laugh. "How many of us could there possibly be here? Where are you from, Mr. Christie?"

"London, Ontario," he said. "You?"

"Sarnia," I said. "What, only fifty, sixty miles away? How about that? My mother grew up near Strathroy."

"Small world! Do you know the Hennesseys or the McRaes?"

"No, I'm afraid I don't. We moved away when I was a baby. But my grandparents were there after we left. Angus and Mary McDonald. My aunt Jessie and my uncles, Robert and William, are still there too. You should meet my mother. I know she'd love to meet you. She gets homesick, and you could chat about Ontario."

"I'd love to reminisce a little," he said. "You know, it sounds crazy, but I miss snow sometimes. And having four seasons."

"Me too," I said with a laugh.

Mr. Sennett and Mr. Christie sat with us for a little while, and before Mr. Christie left, he insisted that I call him Al. I invited him to tea the following weekend. Mum loved finding an excuse for pulling out Wee Mae's treasured shortbread recipe and her delicate china that had been painstakingly packed and moved all over the southwest. For a special guest like Mr. Christie, she might even make a cranachan.

HUGHIE'S APARTMENT, VERMONT AT SUNSET, HOLLYWOOD, CALIFORNIA *November 13, 1921*

"Mmm...so buttery! Hughie, this shortbread is perfect," Al said. He set down his plate, wiping crumbs from his lips.

Mum smiled. There weren't many who could resist Wee Mae's treats.

"When Marie told me she'd met someone from London, ah was verra surprised," Mum said. "Bu' pleasantly."

"Marie says you left long ago?"

Mum and I gave each other the "think fast, no Frank" look. I deferred to her.

"Aye, we spent some time out west, then moved to California," she said, smoothly bypassing any further discussion by asking Al questions about his own family and whether he'd been able to get back home for any visits. I was constantly amazed at Mum's gift of deflection.

When he brought the conversation back around to us again, Mum skillfully guided it to Wee Mae and grandfather Angus, and talked of her brothers and sister. Al departed with an invitation to a Hogmanay celebration at Mum's.

Now, Al often came for visits on the weekends for tea and sweets when he could squeeze it into his schedule. Once in a while, he brought his brother, Charles, and often Vera and Phyl often joined us.

Mum loved being able to play hostess—something she'd never been able to do because of our constant travels. She'd only begin making friends, then Frank would move us again. She was completely in her element.

As Mum brewed more tea, the phone rang and she answered it. She listened a moment. "Hold the line please." She handed me the phone.

"Is this Mrs. Vera Taylor's friend, Marie?" a male voice said.

"Yes, it is," I said cautiously.

"This is Doctor Thomas Alexander. I'm wondering if you could possibly come to stay with your friend today."

"Is something wrong?"

"I'm afraid there's no easy way to say it," he said. "Her daughter, Frances, died early this morning."

"Oh no..." I said, my hand going to my mouth in shock. "No...no..."

"She's quite hysterical," he continued. "With good reason."

"Where's her husband? Where's Jackie? He should be there with her!" I said.

"He's gone," the doctor said. "He came home early this morning, but he'd been drinking. He was quite abusive to Mrs. Taylor and to me. Finally, he got so angry he left the house. She says she has no idea where he went."

"Thank you for calling, doctor," I said, trying to collect my wits. "I'll be over as soon as I can." I hung up and turned to Mum and Al. Their faces were full of questions.

"One of Vera's little girls died last night, and her scourge of a husband is on the warpath. I need to go be with her."

"That bastard," Al said. "I've seen the bruises. I asked Vera if I could help, but she told me she had it under control. I'm going with you, in case he comes home. Someone needs to protect the both of you. I hate to eat and run, Hughie..."

"No, medears. This is an emergency. Please give Vera my love."

Al and I flew out the door, and I sped across town,

screeching to a stop at their apartment bungalow on Gower up the street from the Christie Studio. A hearse was parked out front, and two attendants hoisted a tiny stretcher into it. Vera stood watching them, and next to her was a man I assumed was Doctor Alexander. I came to her side, and she fell into my arms, crying inconsolably. Her eyes had huge dark circles beneath them.

"Marie!" she managed to get out between sobs. "My baby... my baby..."

With Dr. Alexander and Al following us, I led her inside to the couch, clutching her cold hand between the two of mine. Al sat on the other side with his arm around her.

"I've been treating the twins for cold and croup," Doctor Alexander said after we introduced ourselves. "Last night, their coughs got worse, and Mrs. Taylor called me in a panic. I told her to give the girls some Aspironal to break up the congestion and Glessco so they could rest."

"Jackie had the car. I didn't have any cash for the streetcar, and I was afraid to leave them alone. It was too far for me to walk," Vera said, her voice quavery and weak. She looked completely lost. "I called The Ship Café and begged him to stop at The Owl Drug and pick up the medicine, but he yelled at me. Yelled at me! 'Not now, Vera.' 'I'm working, Vera.' I was up all night with them, rocking them, singing to them, rubbing their backs..."

Al shook his head.

"Why didn't you call me?" I asked softly. "I could have helped you or gone for the drugs..."

"I didn't want to bother you..." she said, her voice fading off. "If only I'd known how serious things were... Jackie finally came home, and he yelled at me some more. It was my fault they were sick, and because of me, the guys had ended their set with no fiddle. Then he threw the sack down on the table. While I gave the girls their medicine, he started attacking Doctor Alexander, calling him a quack and a good-for-nothing sonofabitch..." Al held Vera as I paced the floor, trying to figure out what to do.

"Mr. Taylor's behavior was inexcusable," Dr. Alexander said. "He reeked of alcohol." He picked up his black bag from the floor. "Thank you for coming, Miss Prevost, Mr. Christie. I have some other patients to see. I'll be back to check on Marie and Mrs. Taylor a little later."

"Thank you, Doctor..." Vera said absently.

"I'm sorry, Vera, but I've never liked Jackie. He's no good, and this only proves it," Al said.

I escorted Dr. Alexander to the door and scribbled my address and phone number down for him. "Doctor, please let me know how much Vera owes you, all right?" I told him. "I'll take care of it."

He nodded, took the paper, and hurried out to his gunmetal Packard parked at the curb. When I turned back from the front door, Vera still sat on the couch, dabbing at her face with a lace-edged handkerchief.

"Thank you for coming," she said. Her voice was strained.

"Don't mention it," I said, looking over her head at Al. "What can we do for you? Name it."

"Yes," Al said. "Anything."

"Please stay with me for a while. There's so much to think about. I have to make the arrangements... she'll be so afraid of the dark by herself..." her voice faded away.

"Honey, you're exhausted. You need some rest." I ducked

into the tiny bathroom and rooted through the medicine cabinet until I found some Veronal. I gave it to her with some water. "Drink this. That's an order. Auntie Marie is in charge now."

She drank it down. I wrapped an arm around her shoulder and led her to their bedroom, where she hugged me, then crawled beneath the covers. I opened the door to the nursery to check on little Marie. The Glessco appeared to be working, as she was sleeping peacefully, and her color was good. In the morning half-light coming through the Venetian blinds, the other crib lay painfully empty—its occupant now at the Pierce Brothers Funeral Chapel waiting for her service and interment.

Al straightened up the place as I did the dishes, then I searched the kitchen for something to make for dinner. I found a whole chicken in the icebox, so I seasoned it and put it in a frying pan. Then I prepared some peas and carrots and boiled a quick caramel custard. I was chopping cabbage for slaw when the front door banged open.

"Vera!" It was Jackie. Of course. Right as I'd gotten her calmed down and rested, he was back. The baby began screaming.

"Hush, you fool!" I hissed. "Haven't you made enough people miserable this morning?"

"Shut up, Marie," he said. "Where's my wife?"

Al stepped in front of him and his bravado deflated somewhat.

"She's resting, you dumb ox," I said.

"Not anymore," Vera said. She stood at the doorway to the bedroom, her arms folded.

"Well?" Jackie said.

"Well, what?" her voice was ragged.

"How are they?" he said, setting his hat and violin case down on the hallway table.

"Frances is at the funeral home," Vera said. Al and I moved closer to her as a protective measure.

"She what?! She had a cold!"

"I asked you to come right home. I begged you, Jackie! Her fever was going up and I didn't know what to do! Now do you see what's happened? Do you?! How important is that set at the café now, huh? Your daughter is dead!"

He glared at all of us. "You're putting this on me? This is *not* my fault. *I'm* the one who brings in the money! I'm the god-damned breadwinner! If I leave a gig, they'll fire me! Then we'd be out on the street. Is that what you want? Is it?"

"No! But I need your help! Yelling at our doctor in a drunken rage doesn't help us! Now he'll want all his payments up front instead of letting us pay him in installments."

"He's a quack. He killed my kid!"

"Don't worry about the bill," I said. "I'm taking care of it."

"I pay my own bills," Jackie said, glaring at Al and me. "You can go now."

"Vera is our friend," I said. "She'll let us know when she wants us to leave."

A resigned look passed over Vera's face, and she glanced nervously at Jackie, then back to us. "You'd better go," she said.

"I'm not leaving," Al said, firmly clasping her hand.

"Please, Al. It will only be worse if you stay," she whispered.

"Are you sure?" he asked her.

She nodded.

"All right," he said, eyeing Jackie hostilely. "But Vera, if you need anything else—anything at all—you call me. All right?"

"And you already know I'm here for you," I said, giving her a kiss on the cheek.

She blinked back tears. "I know," she whispered. "Thank you both."

I hugged her at the door and worried about her all the way home. When Dr. Alexander sent me the bill a week later, I paid it outright, Jackie Taylor be damned. And I rarely let Vera and little Marie out of my sight.

CHAPTER ELEVEN

THEY'RE OFF! SET, UNIVERSAL LOT, HOLLYWOOD
June 1922

They're Off! was a story by Bernard Hyman about car racing, and we filmed much of it at the Beverly Hills Speedway. We even had cameo appearances from race car drivers Ralph DePalma, Tommy Milton, and Jimmy Murphy. My director, Stuart Paton, was a Scot, from Glasgow, so he and I got along famously. He'd also been by the house for a visit with Mum, and claimed her Dundee cake tasted exactly like his grandmother's.

One morning back at the lot, Prudie, my makeup girl, primped and styled me as usual, and I arrived at Feature Stage B in time to catch a snippet of conversation between Stu and my insufferable co-star, Kenneth Harlan.

"But Bill shouldn't have to be reduced to letting a woman win the race for him," Harlan said. "He's a tough guy. He should be racing even with a broken arm. Increase the suspense that way."

"Ken, that'd be great, but that's not the way the scenario was written. We're showing how much Pamela loves Bill. His arm is broken, so she steps in and wins the race for him."

"But it's not believable," Harlan said.

Harlan's hair was dark and swept back from his forehead in a casual wave. His lips were full and sensual but still handsome in that chiseled movie-star way. He was tall, masculine, and broad-shouldered, with gray eyes that tilted down at the corners, giving him that sleepy, "Darling, come to bed," look. But frankly, his attitude stank.

"What do you find so unbelievable?" I asked with my hands on my hips. "That a woman could win a car race? Or the fact that she can drive at all?"

"That's not what I meant," Harlan said, backing down a little.

"Seems pretty unmistakable to me," I said. "The hero always has to save the fair damsel. She can't ever return the favor, right?"

I'd seen Harlan in something with Connie Talmadge called *Dangerous Business*, and thought he was attractive, but his constant offhand remarks about my character, Pamela Billings, irked me. Women had now had the vote for a year, but he was stuck in a pre-suffrage era.

"Now, Marie," he said. "You have to admit it's far-fetched. A woman winning a race? Come on."

"I have to admit no such thing. Women can drive. She's as capable of winning a race as he is. *More* capable. Both her arms work."

"Fine," he said. He retreated in the direction of his bungalow.

Stu looked over at me. "Round one, Prevost!" he said with a boisterous laugh.

Later that afternoon, as we broke between takes, a shadow

covered the page of the scenario I was studying. I glanced up to see Harlan standing there. I glared at him. "What?" I said in irritation.

"Can we have a truce?"

"Are you willing to admit you're wrong?" I asked.

"About what?"

I raised an eyebrow. "No truce."

"Oh, fer cryin' out loud," he said. "You're a tough customer, you know that?"

"Yes, I know. Please move. You're in my light."

He sighed. "All right. I was wrong."

"Keep talking. What were you wrong about?" I said.

"About driving. Racing. All of it."

"And *why* are you wrong?" I gazed at him innocently.

"Because we have to work together, and I'd rather it be a pleasant experience instead of the trial that it's becoming."

"I'm a *trial* to work with?" I said, goading him now that I knew I'd had an effect. "Aren't you a peach."

"Jesus! You with the icy mitt. I didn't say that. I mean... we've been quarreling since the picture started, and I'd rather we get along. I want to make it up to you."

"How do you propose to do that?"

"Let me take you to dinner," he said. "We can talk and get to know each other as co-stars—possibly as friends—and try to make a good picture. I'm sure Stu would appreciate it. I know I would."

"You're married, aren't you?" I asked.

Indeed he was. To Flo Hart, of the Ziegfeld Follies. Rumor was that he had a wandering eye. But maybe he was serious about work.

"Separated," he said. "And I have a career that's important to me, so sometimes, dinner's dinner and nothing more."

I wasn't sure about that, but against my better judgment, I agreed. Hell, as sticking points went, I was still married too. I gave Ken my address and he picked me up around six in his shiny new Lincoln.

"Village Inn?" Ken asked.

"No. Further out," I said, wanting to avoid the Hollywood crowd and the certain-to-follow gossip.

We decided on the Valley Café in Burbank. We relaxed in a deep leather banquette in the corner, and Ken ordered orange juice for us.

"How did you end up in Hollywood?" he asked me. He reached into his jacket pocket and pulled out a flask, which he used to discreetly doctor our juice.

I explained the nomadic travels that had brought us to California, leaving out Frank. Then I told him how my job at the law firm had led me to Sennett.

"Finally, I got tired of pies and pratfalls and wanted to try something different," I finished. I took a sip of my drink. "Now I'm at Universal."

"I was excited when they told me they were pairing me up with a bathing beauty," he said. I couldn't tell if he was serious or not.

"*Ex*-bathing beauty," I clarified. "That's part of my past. I burned all that stuff at Coney Island."

"Yes, but you still save directors and cameramen who need fishing out of the water. I heard about your lifeguarding in Pasadena. That's the kind of swimming that counts!" he said.

The waiter set down Ken's T-bone and my squabs.

"I guess so," I said, laying my napkin in my lap. "But I didn't need a swimsuit for that. I jumped in with my clothes on."

Ken let out a hearty laugh and began cutting his steak. "That should rate you a few close-ups from Baggot in the future."

"I already owe him for introducing me to Mr. Thalberg and getting Universal to sign me," I said, cutting some meat off the bone. "What about you? How did you end up out here?"

"My mother mostly," he said, taking a bite of his potato.

"Your mother?"

"She's an actress too. Rita Harlan, most recently with Balboa Studios down in Long Beach. But she's been on the boards since I was a baby."

"I never got to see theater shows when I was young. We lived in some out-of-the-way places. And we didn't have a lot of money." I spooned up some buttered peas.

"It was a wonderful life for a boy. I loved waiting in the wings or out in the audience during rehearsals. One of my favorite memories was turning twelve years old and watching mother as *Camille*. We were at Steinberg's Grand Opera House in Traverse City, Michigan, and the entire cast brought me a cake from the local bakery. That was when I decided I wanted to be an actor," he said.

"And your father? Was he an actor too?" I took a bite of squab.

"He tried being one for a while, but his heart wasn't in it. He went back to Ohio, where his family was from. And mother simply kept being mother." He laughed, and took a good healthy swig of his drink.

"You mean your mother..."

"Yes, a divorcée. *Twice*. Scandalous, I know." He grinned.

Was this honestly something other women did? Suddenly I didn't feel so alone with my secret about Frank. Here Ken was laughing about it. Divorce was nothing to him.

"You have to understand my mother," he said. "She's... unconventional. My father couldn't keep up with her. But to me, as a boy—seeing her up there in all her glory—I thought she was the most beautiful, most amazing creature I'd ever seen. I suppose it's only natural that I now have an affinity for actresses. That Dr. Freud would have a ball analyzing me, I think." He took a healthy gulp of orange juice.

"You've told me lots about your mother, but what about you?" I asked. "How did *you* get started?"

"I started in a few productions with Mother, playing secondary characters—sons, neighbor boys, nephews—that type of thing. I did something called *Alma, Where Do You Live?* and then went on tour with Gertrude Hoffman, the dancer."

"You're multi-talented," I said.

"Oh, I didn't say *I* could dance," he said with a deep rumbling chuckle. "It was a lot of pantomime so I stood around posing while she did most of the dancing."

"What kind of dancing?"

"Some newfangled Oriental stuff. Honestly, it was just a paycheck. I did what I had to do to work my way up to D.W. Griffith for a couple films. That's where I met my friend Warren Kerrigan—on *A Man's Man*. And that was how the Talmadge sisters saw me and decided to take me on. I joined up during the war, so I was lucky to find something when I got back."

"It must have been hard coming back after such a long

hard break," I said.

"Yeah, a break. That's what it was," he snorted. "Like a vacation in the Meuse-Argonne."

You and your damned attitude.

I got very quiet, my face flaming. "I'm sorry," I finally said. "I shouldn't have said that. It's not what I meant. War is never something to make light of. I apologize."

"I'm sorry too. Several of my friends died in France. It's still difficult to think of them."

I was now ready for the night to be over.

"Don't look down," he said. "When you look down I can't see your eyes."

"Charmer," I said with a brittle laugh.

"I'm serious. I'm very fond of them. Not sure I've ever seen any that particular shade of blue before."

"They're from my mother. Hers are the same," I said, forking up a string bean.

"Tell me about *your* mother," he said.

"Oh, she's nothing like yours," I said, establishing any kind of distinction I could between him and me. But as I did, I realized that wasn't true. They were both 'scarlet women' to polite society, weren't they? "She's Scottish through and through. And my very best friend in the world. She's my biggest champion, but she's not had an easy life."

"How so?" he asked, taking a bite of potato.

"That's a story for another day." My eyes cautioned him not to push any further. As the challenge lay between us, he put his hand on top of mine.

"I've enjoyed our evening out," he said. "I'd love to see you again."

I pulled my hand away. "You'll see me on set tomorrow."

He looked like a boy who'd eaten all his vegetables and had been told there was no dessert.

"Ken, I know your reputation. I have no intention of becoming involved with you."

"What 'involved?' I enjoy spending time with you," he said. "Once you stop haranguing me, you can be fun."

"I don't even like you," I countered.

"Really, Marie? You wound me."

"I don't go for big brawny ladies' men like you. I like the artistic types. Pretty boys."

"I wear makeup to work every day. How much prettier can you get than that?" he said.

All right, that was funny.

I felt my face break into a grin, and forced it back. I wasn't going to let him get away with anything. Not after the fiasco with Sonny.

He paid our check and escorted me to the car. Then, he dropped me off with a chaste kiss on my forehead. I watched him drive away in his Lincoln, telling myself that it had only been dinner. All I had to do was get through one film. Then it was done.

Things have a way of working out differently than you plan.

CHAPTER TWELVE

SHIP CAFE, VENICE, CALIFORNIA
June 1922

"Say! Who's the cutie patootie toasting you from across the room?" Phyl asked. She faked a stretch, her fingers sneakily pointing off toward the corner.

Phyl and I hadn't seen each other in weeks because of our shooting schedules, so we'd agreed to meet in Venice for a drink. The Ship Café, built on a pier over the water, looked like a Spanish galleon taken from Elizabethan days and planted right here in California. The staff dressed like naval officers. Slip 'em a $20, and they could bring you whatever you wanted to drink—legal or not. Which explained why we had come. It certainly wasn't the glares Jackie was giving me over his fiddle up on the stage.

"Huh?" I looked over to where she was indicating.

In the corner, with his friends, Carmel Myers and Warren Kerrigan, sat Ken, his silvery eyes twinkling with mischief. He raised his teacup in salute, so I did the same and laughed.

"That's Ken," I said. "Kenneth Harlan."

"He's the one you told me about? The one who used to

work with Dutch Talmadge and her sister? He's positively divine. I thought you couldn't stand him."

"I couldn't at first, but he grew on me. Once I got him to drop the caveman act, he was all right," I said. "He can be pig-headed, but he makes me laugh."

"You still working on that flicker with him?"

"Yes, but they've changed the name to *The Married Flapper*. They're releasing in July."

"I'd be running in his direction right now!" Phyl said, taking a sip of her drink. "What's stopping you?"

"Phyl, I have a confession to make," I said.

"Oh yeah? What?" She gazed at me over the top of her teacup.

"It's about Sonny."

"Sonny? What are you worried about him for? You wouldn't let anyone talk about him anymore, ever ever...so why are you dwelling on him now with Mr. Perfect over there?"

"There's something I never told you," I said, lowering my voice. "We're married."

"You're what?!"

The entire population of The Ship Café turned and stared at us. Phyllis's squeak carried over the clinking of silverware, the music of the house combo, the busboys clearing away dishes, all of it.

"Shhhhhhhh!" I said. Then under my breath... "I don't want all of Hollywood to know, for God's sake."

"Too late for that," she said. Every eye in the place was fastened on us. "That's some pickle you're in."

"You're telling *me*. Promise you won't say anything, Phyl. *Promise*," I pleaded.

"Cross my heart," she whispered out of the side of her mouth. "Does anyone else know?"

"Only Mum and you. And Sonny, of course. I'd like to keep it that way."

"What are you going to do?"

"Try to find out where he's gone off to and quietly petition him for divorce," I said. "He told me no last time I asked him."

"Ladies, how are you this evening?" I looked up to see Ken standing there.

"Ken, lovely to see you. This is my friend, Phyllis Haver. Phyllis, Kenneth Harlan."

"Enchanted," he said. He kissed her hand.

"Oh, me too," she said and fluttered her eyelashes at him.

"Marie, would you care to trip the light fantastic?" The combo had struck up a lush version of "April Showers."

"Sure," I said. "Excuse me for a minute, Phyl."

"Have fun, honey," she said with a wink. "Your secret's safe with me."

"Secret?" Ken took my hand, then placed his other arm around my back.

"It's nothing," I glared at her. She smiled sweetly and waved.

Ken led me around the floor as Jackie and I looked daggers at each other.

"Kenneth Harlan, you're a perfectly fine dancer," I said.

"Gertrude at least taught me a thing or two," he said.

I laid my head on his chest, noticing from my sideways view that quite a few patrons had taken notice of us, and were smiling behind their hands.

"They're onto us," he said.

"What us? There is no us," I corrected him.

"Hey, tell me something," he said. "How soon until I can take you out again?"

"You're still married. It's too complicated."

"You might be interested to know that Flo filed for divorce back in April," he said.

"I might be, but I'm not."

"Ouch."

"I'm sorry, that was harsh of me," I said.

"Can I please convince you to have dinner with me this weekend?" He led me through a turn and into a dip, and he held me there, making a scene. "I'm going to stay like this until you say yes." His mouth curved into a sly grin.

"Ken, pull me up," I said.

"Say you'll have dinner with me."

I sighed. "Dinner. That's all it is." He let me stand up, then looked me straight in the eye.

"I wouldn't be too sure about that."

When the weekend arrived, Ken rang the bell and Mum opened the door to my place. She'd wanted to meet him to see if she approved.

"You must be Ken. S'nice to meet ye. I'm Marie's mother. Call me Hughie."

"Charmed," he said. "Hughie. That's an unusual name."

"It's Scottish. Shor' for Hughina. Please, have a seat. Marie, yer fella's arrived," I heard her say as I applied my lip rouge.

"Coming," I said.

"Marie's told me of her Scottish roots," he said. "Let's

see...'Wherever I wander, wherever I rove, the hills of the Highlands forever I love,'" he said, adopting his best Highland accent.

"Ye know yer Robbie Burns, laddie," Mum said with a chuckle.

When I entered the living room, Ken rose and swallowed hard, turning his hat in his hands. He looked so perfect—in an expensively-cut black suit and maroon silk tie. I'd worn my favorite opaline blue satin frock, embroidered in crystal bugles, and my opaline blue T-straps and blue satin bag, the better to bring out my eyes.

"You look...stunning," he said. "Absolutely beautiful."

"Thank you," I said, smoothing my skirt. I tried to look casual, even though my heart was firing on all six.

Mum stood to one side, looking prouder than I'd ever seen her. I grabbed my wrap, and Ken placed his hand on the small of my back to lead me outside.

"Have a wonderful time!" Mum called after us.

He opened the door to his Lincoln for me, and I nestled into the soft leather.

"I was thinking we might go to the Ambassador," he said.

"Absolutely not," I said firmly. "Nowhere in town."

"All right. I was only testing the waters," he said.

We ended up at the Hotel Virginia dining room in Long Beach and asked for a booth in the back. When we were comfortably tucked into it with our doctored orange juice, Ken studied me by the candlelight. I gazed back, starting to feel the effects of the booze.

"Do you live with your mother?" he asked.

"No. We're very close though. She wanted to meet you."

"See if I pass muster, huh?"

"No, because she's a fan," I corrected him.

He sighed in frustration.

"I can't explain what I've begun to feel for you, Marie," he said. "I've never met a woman who calls me on my guff before. I want to get to know you better."

"That's what this is," I said. "We're getting to know each other. But I still think you're insufferable."

"Come on. Am I that bad?"

"Sometimes."

"You don't believe in love at first sight, do you?" he said, sipping his drink.

After Sonny? Absolutely not.

"Do *you*?" I said, gesturing the waiter over for a refill. "You hardly know anything about me. We've had a few drinks, some dinner, and a dance or two. I could be a horrible person."

"Nah. I've been married to that before. Trust me. I think you're wonderful."

"How many times have you been married anyway?" I asked. "There. That's me getting to know you."

He cleared his throat nervously. "Twice," he said.

That was a surprise. "I thought it was only the once," I said.

"No, Flo's number two," he said. "Salomé was the first. We met when I was on tour with Gertrude. She was young and beautiful, but terribly naïve. I needed someone a little more worldly."

"More like your mother?" I asked, taking a piece of bread from the basket and smearing it liberally with butter.

"Something like that," he said with a smile. "But I got more than I bargained for with Flo."

"Yeah? How's that?"

"Flo was in the Follies. And the Frolic. And while she does have certain charms, she has very expensive tastes in clothes and booze. More than I felt like paying for. Let's change the subject, shall we?" he said, loosening his collar.

"Sure, if you want," I said. "But I still think love at first sight is a bunch of hooey."

"Why? I'm curious."

How could I describe what I thought I'd felt with Sonny? I'd trusted my judgment then, but I'd been wrong. So horribly wrong.

"I'd have to know someone for a while before I could consider myself 'in love' with them," I insisted. Hell, I'd known Sonny for a while, and I still hadn't been in love.

"All right, I get it," he said, waving his hands defensively. "But I'm different than that. There are times when you just know."

Pshaw, I thought.

When the waiter arrived at the table again, Ken ordered for us.

"The lady will have the rarebit...light on the cheese sauce, and I'll have the prime rib, heavy on the horseradish." We folded our menus closed and handed them to our waiter. Ken took my hand across the table. "Now where was I?"

"You were telling me about love at first sight, and I was telling you you're full of bunk," I said with a smile.

His deep laugh echoed through the dining room. "I can see I've met my match," he said.

He drove me home, although I think he would have preferred parking somewhere instead. When he down-shifted and pulled the Lincoln to a stop, he looked over at me expectantly. I leaned over, whispered 'goodnight,' and kissed him only once on the lips before retreating into the house.

"Always leave 'em wanting more," Phyllis had told me, so I followed her advice.

The next morning, I strolled down Laemmle Boulevard to my bungalow. As I approached it, there was a rustling in the huge blue elderberry planted outside.

My key suddenly halted in the lock.

Ken stepped out from behind the bush. He wore the same rumpled black suit from the previous night.

"Ken, what are you doing?" I said.

CHAPTER THIRTEEN

He nodded at the door, so I opened it and let both of us in. I reached for the light switch, but he stopped me, and we stood in the shadows. He flipped the lock.

"I've been driving around all night," he said. "You've got me turned upside down, Marie." He took hold of my forearms and held me there before leaning down and kissing me. And I don't mean some courtly little peck. I mean...a little rough, a little frightening how full of passion it was. At first I stiffened, unsure how to react, but as the kiss deepened, he pulled me closer, and I let him. I whimpered as he held me there, making me feel what *he* felt.

He slipped his fingers into my hair and held my face up to his. Gradually, I melted into the kiss, letting my self-control slip away, and inhaled deeply of his scent of rumpled clothes, Pears soap, and Bay Rum aftershave. I trembled as he kissed me—knowing where this was leading, but powerless to stop it.

He fumbled over the buttons on my dress, but finally got them all, and let the dress slide to the floor. Then I nervously lifted my arms. He removed my chemise and my step-ins, and I unhooked my stockings and pulled them off. Suddenly I realized what I was doing and panicked.

"Ken, I..."

"Shhhhh..." he whispered, putting his fingers over my lips.

"...it's been a long time, and I..."

"I'm going to make love to you," he whispered. "I'm going to erase every other man from your memory and change your life."

I unbuttoned his shirt to be closer to the furred mat of hair covering his chest, then pulled it off. My fingers fumbled over unbuckling his belt, so he helped me.

Gently, he lay me back on the daybed, his caresses soft and comforting, and his breath warm in my ear. The next hour or so passed in a beautiful blur of a daydream. Ken murmured sweet things in my ear to reassure me. But it wasn't awkward and strange and awful like it had been with Sonny. It was like being drunk, only on each other—happy, ecstatic, moving together in a tender rhythm, clasping hands. I'd never felt anything like it—the maddening friction and this pent-up need I'd never even known I had. At last, I reached the crest and went falling over the edge. I cried out, and Ken softly placed his hand over my mouth so all of Universal wouldn't know our secret.

When I was finally able to open my eyes, I wanted to lie there with him forever.

"Oh my God," I whispered, barely able to form the words. I'd never felt so happy or so right with the world. Ken was nothing like Sonny. He knew how to make love to a woman. Now I understood what poems and songs were written about. This was the mysterious, magnetic force that drew people together and made them do crazy things. This was love.

He lay on his side next to me, propped up on an elbow,

using his finger to trace a circle on my belly.

"How was that?" he asked, arching an eyebrow.

I smiled in answer. He gave my nose a little kiss and caressed a breast. I closed my eyes again and waited for my teeth to stop vibrating.

"I didn't hurt you, did I?" he asked.

"No," I said.

"Not even a little bit?"

He thinks I was still a virgin.

"Ken, I need to tell you something."

"What is it?" His brow furrowed.

I sighed. "I'm married too. It's a long story."

"Hey," he said, sitting up. "I've got all the time in the world. If some crazy husband is going to come looking for me with a gun, I'd like to be ready for him."

"I don't even know where he is," I said, "It was the war, and he asked me to marry him. It was impetuous, and he talked me into it. I realized it was a mistake right afterward. I tried to get a divorce when he got home, but he refused. Then he shipped out and disappeared. I'm trying to take care of it. But I want you to know."

"But this was your first..."

"Yes. We had a wedding night, but it was terrible. Sonny knew nothing about making love. Not like you." I kissed him again.

There was a knock at the door.

"Miss Prevost, they need you in makeup."

"Tell them I'll be right there!" I called. I began gathering up my clothes, and Ken did the same.

"This is to be continued," he said. I smiled and slipped out. There was no doubt about it now.

SET OF THE MARRIED FLAPPER, UNIVERSAL STUDIOS

June 1922

"And...cut!" Stu Paton grinned a cock-eyed grin, trying to fend off laughter. Ken and I were still kissing.

We'd been wrapped in each other's arms, the orchestra serenading the set from the corner, when the command came. But it was too hard, tearing myself away from him. We finally looked around to the amused snickers of the crew. My face flushed.

"Let's break for lunch!" Stu called. "Thirty minutes!"

As I tried to pull myself together for what now looked like the endless trek to my bungalow, Ken whispered, "Come for a drink."

I let him go first, gave him a little head start, then waited until most of the crew had filtered off the set. Then I slipped over to his bungalow, where I gave a quick quiet knock.

Ken barely opened the door, letting me slip in. He shut the door after me and after we kicked off our shoes, we boldly gazed at each other.

"This is all I've been able to think about for days," he said. Wrapping me in those big strong arms, he leaned down and kissed me. Not the tender chaste kisses we'd had to pretend with for the crew, but ones that let me know he was the boss. The kind that left my lips slightly bruised and my hair pleasantly mussed, and my thoughts a chaotic jumble of happiness, excitement, and pleasure. I kissed him back, pulled his jacket and trousers off, and smoothed my palms across his shirt, undoing the buttons. He pulled my dress off, then my slip, leaving my stockings and garters on. Every nerve ending in my body was on fire.

"How much time do we have left?" I said breathlessly.

"About twenty minutes," he muttered against my mouth.

"Plenty of time," I said.

"Not if you're good, it isn't," he said with a lopsided grin.

"Make love to me, Ken," I said, lying back on the daybed. The hungry look in his eyes sparked, and he lay next to me, caressing my face, my breasts, and then, moving lower. He took me more roughly than before, but I liked it. It felt naughty, a little wrong, a little dangerous, but oh so delicious.

I'd shuddered to think of Sonny touching me again. With Ken, I couldn't get enough. I wanted him constantly.

When I returned to the set, I carried a copy of the scenario, and I wore a completely blank expression. We'd been practicing the scene. That was all anyone had to know.

Two weeks later, I was summoned to Mr. Thalberg's office. My option was coming due, so I was expecting good things.

"Come in, Marie. Come in," he said.

I sat down and waited to hear the good news.

"There's no easy way to say this," he said. "Universal has decided not to pick up your option."

I felt my jaw drop.

"But Mr. Thalberg, I don't understand," I said. "I thought you liked my work. And Mr. Laemmle too. Aren't you happy with my pictures? They've pulled in decent money, haven't they?"

"As I said, Marie, it's purely a business decision. The studio is going in a different direction from here on out, away from the fluffy baby vamp stuff you've been doing. Perhaps in the future we may reconsider and sign you again if you broaden your repertoire a little. I'm not ruling anything out at this point."

"But for right now, I'm without a contract."

"That's correct. I'm sorry."

"Me too," I said with a sigh. I'd been so sure they'd renew me. Maybe even with a raise. Instead, I sadly took the final check he slid across the desk at me. It was a good thing I'd hoarded most of my money like a squirrel storing nuts for the winter.

CHAPTER FOURTEEN

MARIE'S PLACE, HOLLYWOOD, CALIFORNIA *July 1922*

Phyl and I had done a little shopping downtown, browsing the summer sales on frocks at Jacoby Brothers and Myer-Siegel, then enjoying some sandwiches at the Vanity Fair Tearoom. Then we returned to my place, where I shook up some orange blossoms. We were chatting about our purchases when the phone rang.

"Prevost residence," I said, picking it up.

"Marie!" It was Vera. Her voice sounded strangely nasal.

"Vera, how are you? Do you have a cold?"

"Doh! He hit be!"

"He hit you? That sonofabitch. Is he there?"

"Doh. He said he was going to fide zumwhere else to zleep."

"Good. It's better that way. We'll be right over."

I hung up and turned to Phyl.

"Jackie again?" she said. "What the hell is wrong with that guy?"

I shook my head.

"All right, let's go," she said, downing her drink for some fortitude.

When we arrived, Vera was holding a handkerchief to her nose. She pulled it away, and it was obvious that it had done a great deal of bleeding before we got there. It appeared to be tapering off at last.

"What happened?" I asked.

"He got mad that I spent some of his cash on Mellin's. He left me short this week, so I had to."

"He was angry that you bought baby food?" Phyl said incredulously.

Vera nodded. "He slugged me." She wiped her tear-stained face with the back of her hand.

I opened my arms and held her, mindless of the blood that might get on my dress. "How's the baby?" I asked.

"She's fine," she said, nestling against my shoulder. "I hadn't woken her up yet."

"I'm surprised she didn't wake up on her own," Phyl said, peeking into the nursery. Little Marie was standing up in her bed, reaching her tiny hands out to be picked up.

"Hold on, precious," Phyl said.

I pulled the handkerchief away, and Phyl and I both examined Vera's nose.

"It doesn't look broken, at least," I said.

"Thank God for that," she said. "My career would go down the toilet with a broken nose."

"Vera, you need to leave him," I said. "This is getting ridiculous. The man is a selfish bully. I'm worried he's going to truly hurt you. Worse than this, I mean."

"Believe me, I'm trying. I save every penny I can so Marie and I can make it on our own. I know he's making more money than he says he is. I've seen him stashing money all over the house, hoping I won't find it. He thinks he can spend it all on giggle water and bottle blondes and not take care of a wife and daughter."

"I'll help you any way I can," I said.

"No, Marie. You already paid the doctor bill *and* the funeral home. Besides, you're without a studio right now."

"I'll help too," said Phyl. "I don't have a lot, but I'll do my best."

Vera choked up. "I love you both. You know that?" she said, clasping Phyl's hand, then mine. "You're always here for me. For us. I so appreciate it. Thank you for coming to help me. I'll get out as soon as I can manage it."

"Hey," Phyl said. "Once a bathing beauty, always a bathing beauty, right?"

WARNER BROTHERS STUDIO, SUNSET AT BRONSON, HOLLYWOOD, CALIFORNIA *September 1922*

If you looked up cocky in the dictionary, the entry would have Jack Warner's picture next to it. I was convinced. He wore a jacket in a tiny black and white houndstooth print, and his hands were immaculate and tanned. He looked like the type to invest in manicures. He already had a receding hairline, and his eyes had a sleepy look to them, but something told me not to underestimate him. He sat behind a dark wood desk covered with scenarios, newsletters, contracts, and a half-finished sandwich.

I stood for a minute, waiting for an invitation to sit.

"Miss Prevost! Come in, come in. Make yourself

comfortable," he said, offering me the seat opposite him.

I smiled and sat down. The credenza beside me was full of photos of his wife and kids.

"I liked your screen test," he said. "Universal's loss is our gain and all that. I thought we could discuss what you and Warner Brothers could mean to each other. I'm talking multiple-picture contract."

He steepled his fingers under his chin.

"I hear you want a little grit. You want to get your hands dirty," he said.

"I like the flapper persona," I said. "I mean, it's how people think of me, and it's worked well for me so far. But I'd like to expand it a bit. Maybe work with some other talented directors."

"I'm sure the paycheck plays a part as well."

"I'd be lying if I said it didn't, Mr. Warner. A girl's gotta eat, you know."

"I gotta warn you. We're small potatoes here. We've got big ideas, but we're waiting for the right time to make our move. However, we're still rounding up the best talent to give us a star-studded roster. And I have a picture in mind for you that I think will be the perfect jumping off point for that. We've bought the rights to Fitzgerald's latest, *The Beautiful and Damned*. Helluva story, and we need the right girl for it."

"I adored that book," I said.

"How about *Brass*? Charles Norris?" he continued.

"Fantastic stuff. I finished it a month ago."

"The spurned wife part in that? I think you'd be perfect for that too," he said.

"Keep talking."

He got up from behind the desk and took a seat on the corner of it. His two-toned lace-up oxfords were spit-shined until they glowed.

"I'll even sweeten the deal. I've heard whisperings around town that you and Ken Harlan are an item now."

My smile gave me away.

"They're not rumors, I take it."

"We go out from time to time."

"Playing coy? Okay, I can take a hint. Here's my offer. You and Harlan. *Beautiful and Damned.* $1500 a week. Three-picture deal."

"For both of us?"

"Ken's gonna freelance for a while until we see what he can do."

My mouth almost fell open in shock. It was awfully generous, and Ken and I could see each other anytime we wanted. It was the best offer I'd had so far. I'd hoped for a prestige studio, but I had to get a lot more credits under my belt first.

"I'll have an option to renew for five more at $3,000," Warner continued.

"Mr. Warner, I don't know what to say."

"Say yes."

I thought about it, then after some more chit-chat, I signed on the dotted line.

Fall 1922

The Beautiful and Damned was another of Fitzgerald's tales of excess. Rich boy Anthony Patch courted and married spoiled brat Gloria Gilbert while he waited on an inheritance from his rich grandfather. I had a whale of a time playing Gloria. All I had to do was pretend to be Peg. Ken and I chewed a lot of scenery.

Louise finally got to make her break with comedy, and enjoyed the hell out of playing Muriel, Gloria's less glamorous friend. Tully Marshall played Grandpa Patch to a T. Our director, William Seiter, tried any number of new ideas, like shooting through the strings of a harp to film Anthony and Gloria's wedding scene.

Attendance broke records—a bona fide hit. But Jack Warner had been right—it wasn't up to the caliber of Universal or Paramount. The wolf was always at the door. Once in a while, we were given "coupons" instead of paychecks until the real cash showed up. And someone was always tasked with taking expensive equipment home overnight in case creditors came to the lot looking for payments.

Still, with our new celebrity from *The Beautiful and Damned*, Ken and I became Hollywood royalty. Not as big as Doug and Mary of course, but we made the rounds of the premieres. One night, *The Acquittal* with Norman Kerry at the Mission on Broadway, the next, *In the Palace of the King* at the California. And I was thrilled to see Phyl making the transition into larger roles like *The Common Law* for Selznick, working with Corinne Griffith.

Socializing was almost a full-time job in Hollywood. Rubbing shoulders with people over a gin rickey or a Buck's fizz at Ford's Castle could net you an eventual screen test or maybe even a contract. We were invited to all the best parties—to Pickfair, to Mae Murray and Bob Leonard's place, and even to

William Randolph Hearst and Marion Davies' mansion.

We couldn't dance in Hollywood—some repressed numb-skull had decided it was obscene. So for that, we had plen-ty of other places to visit: The Sunset Inn in Santa Moni-ca, Moonlite Gardens or Danceland in Culver City, or The Vernon Country Club, stuck out in the middle of some beet fields south of town.

In November, Mum and Ken and I motored out to the Mission Inn in Riverside, where Peg was getting married. The groom was Albert Berggren, a stockbroker. Mum and I had met him and thoroughly approved. We both thought Bert would treat her well. In my case, I thought he was better than she deserved.

As promised, Warners had chosen me to play Marjorie Jones in *Brass*, which began shooting right after Christmas. My co-stars were Irene Rich, whom I'd met at The Ship Café with Ken, and Monte Blue, a fellow I hadn't worked with be-fore. Monte was a tall fellow from Utah, a Mormon like Mary, and he was swell, even if he did look better in makeup than I did. We developed a warm, comfortable working relationship, and became friends off the set too. We confided in each other between takes and shared some secrets. He and his wife were unhappy, and I realized that January was turning out to be a month for a lot of people to re-evaluate marriage. Vera had finally had enough, taken little Marie, and left Jackie for good.

"I'm afraid Erma and I are done," Monte said, shaking his head. "We don't get along anymore."

I wondered about Mormon rules for divorce, and con-sidered telling Monte about Sonny, merely to let him know we were in the same boat. It seemed strange to say that at twenty-six, I was looking a divorce in the face (if I could find the guy). Just like Mum. Instead, I nodded companionably and clucked my tongue. I wanted to tell him not to give up—that he could find love again, as Ken and I both had.

Then, one Saturday morning in mid-January, I was surprised to get a call from Bert, Peg's new husband, asking if we could meet for a cup of coffee. I suggested the Topanga Diner on Vine, so we agreed on a time.

"Thanks for meeting me," he said when I sat down.

"Of course. What is it, Bert? This sounded important on the phone."

"It is. It's about Peg."

I braced myself for the worst.

"She's driving me crazy," he said.

"Crazy, how?" I asked, only too prepared for what I would hear.

He sighed. I could tell he wanted to be diplomatic, since she was my sister, but he needn't have bothered. Peg was Peg.

"Tell me straight out," I said.

He nervously turned his coffee cup in its saucer.

"I work hard every day, I come home, and she never even puts dinner on the table! Not once in two months. We have to go out, which costs money, and I can't afford to keep both of us living in high style. The minute we started dating, she quit L-KO, and she won't even look for a new studio. I love her, but I'm not sure I can go on like this for long. Can you talk to her, maybe?"

I shook my head sadly. Bert was a decent guy. I hated to see him suffering. "I'm so sorry. You're finding out what Mum and I already know."

"What's that?"

"My sister wouldn't know an honest day's work if it walked up and bit her. She's been like this her entire life. I had my misgivings when you got married, but I didn't want to say anything. You were so nice. You seemed to be good for her, and I thought... 'people can change.' But in her case, I guess they don't. I apologize for my sister, but nothing I say will make any difference."

"I don't know what to do," he confessed. "I love her, but I'm losing patience. She's bankrupting me. What would you do?"

I was quiet for a minute or two. I took a sip of my coffee and mulled things over.

"Honestly Bert, I'd get the hell out," I finally said. "My sister is lazy and she's manipulative. I'd find a good divorce lawyer and file right now. The only thing Peg understands is money or the lack of it. Without you, she might have to sink or swim on her own."

"Won't she borrow from you if I do that?"

"I'm used to it. She's been doing it her whole life. And I can afford it." I patted his hand. "I won't think any less of you for it. Believe me."

"But your mother..."

"She'll get over it," I told him. "It's hard for her to admit, but Mum knows Peg isn't ideal wife material."

"I don't want you to hate me, that's all."

"Hate you? I'd give you a medal for effort if I could," I said, and he chuckled. "Coffee's on me."

We clinked cups.

MARIE'S PLACE, LOS ANGELES, CALIFORNIA
January 1923

Although we'd become a well-known couple around Hollywood, Ken and I still couldn't commit the grievous sin of living together before marriage. But the rumblings had begun that Ken planned on popping the question. We became adept at leaving each other's places early in the morning and arriving at vastly different times to any event we attended. But for the most part, weekends were spent on the beach in Santa Monica or sleeping luxuriously late then dawdling over breakfast and the newspaper.

Within the *Times* pages this morning was a snippet about Wally Reid that made me want to cry. Then I saw Juanita's name and felt sick.

NARCOTIC AGENTS RAID REID DRUG CURE RETREAT

Film Actresses Sought Relief From Dope; Juanita Hansen Caught in Raid

Wah had been staying at a facility in Oakland owned by a Dr. John Scott Barker, who'd been helping her and others get free of dope, and she'd recommended it to Wally. He was such a nice guy, but all of Hollywood knew about his problem. Now they knew about Wah's too.

The phone rang as we were sitting down to breakfast, so I picked it up as Ken bit into a slice of bacon.

"Hello?"

"Miss Prevost, good morning. This is Herbert Howe from *Photoplay* magazine."

"Hello, Mr. Howe. What can I do for you?" I said.

"I'm wondering if you could comment on Mr. Fitzgerald's opinion."

"I can't very well comment on his opinion if I don't know what he said," I said.

"I apologize, ma'am. I'd assumed you heard."

"Heard what for goodness sakes?" I snapped.

"It's Mr. Fitzgerald, Miss Prevost. He hates *The Beautiful and Damned*. He's come out swinging against the picture. Friends have told *Photoplay* he's denigrated almost every facet of the film. Could I have a response statement from you?"

"A response? No. I have nothing to say. Goodbye, Mr. Howe."

I set the phone down and glanced at Ken.

"What is it?" he asked.

"Fitzgerald hates it," I said. I picked up my glass of orange juice and toasted him with it. "Here's to killing both of our careers."

"What does that hack know about movies?" he said. "He went to Princeton and rubs shoulders with a bunch of snobby writers exactly like him."

"We're still selling tickets, and that's what matters, I guess," I said.

"His next book will be a flop," Ken said.

"Think Warners will buy it?" I joked.

CHAPTER FIFTEEN

MARIE'S PLACE, LOS ANGELES, CALIFORNIA
August 12, 1923

"And Mr. Lubitsch wants me to play Mizzi?"

"He wants you!" Jack Warner said. The eminent German director, whom Warner Brothers had recently brought over from Europe, had seen plenty of screen tests, but he'd selected mine for his new film, to be called *The Marriage Circle*. I was going to play a flirty, frustrated Viennese wife.

The *Los Angeles Times* wanted a comment from me, so reporter Sarah Cox paid me a visit. I offered her an iced tea and some of Wee Mae's shortbread.

"These are delicious," she said, finishing her third cookie. "Very buttery."

"My grandmother's recipe," I said with a smile.

"What do you think of Mr. Lubitsch hand-picking you for this role?" she said.

"Well, naturally, I prefer dramatic roles more than comedy, because it shows serious ambition. Comedy's fun because it's refreshing rather than tiring. And as a training school for developing acting ability, there's nothing better.

Comedy's great, but drama is hard work. Having Mr. Lubitsch select me for such a role is a huge compliment."

I was expansive and hospitable, sharing my thoughts on the upcoming film, the director, and a million other things. So it was a rude awakening when I got a call mid-morning the next day. It was Miss Hampton, Jack Warner's secretary.

"Marie honey, you've got to get to the office right away," she said. "He's roaring mad. I can't hear what the matter is, but you'd better wear your suit of armor."

Uh-oh. That didn't sound good. I took the McFarlan to the studio and looked nervously at Miss Hampton as I took a seat in the anteroom.

"I'll buzz you in," she whispered. She cleared her throat then pressed the button on the machine. "Mr. Warner, Miss Prevost is here."

"Send her in," I heard.

I strode tentatively into the office, and Ken was in one of the chairs facing Jack Warner's desk. Harry Warner was in the other.

"Ken, what are you doing here?" I said.

"This concerns all four of us," Jack Warner said. His voice sounded like he'd been gargling vinegar—bitter and mean. "Anything you'd like to tell me, Marie?"

I looked around like a trapped jackrabbit surrounded by foxes.

"What's this about?"

"You know what it's about," Jack snapped. He grabbed a newspaper from his desk and held it up in front of me. When I saw the *Times* headline, it was all I could do not to revisit breakfast—all over his French rug.

Marie Prevost Secretly Wed
Sonny Gerke Starts Suit Charging Desertion

Oh, Sonny, you complete bastard.

I felt faint and slumped onto one of the chairs. While I'd been playing hostess to Sarah Cox, sharing my thoughts and dreams with her, one of her colleagues had been downtown digging up dirt on Sonny and me.

"Mr. Warner, I can explain," I said, wondering how I'd be doing that while I was painting his carpet all the colors of the rainbow.

"Explain?!" he thundered. "Explain?! Explaining would have been a good thing to do before you two started gallivanting all over town together. Instead, you've kept quiet all this time?!"

"Mr. Warner, I—"

"Who is this guy?"

I took a deep breath before beginning. While I told him the whole story, he reached into a humidor and pulled out a cigar, then cut off the tip.

"Why the hell didn't you divorce him? Or have it annulled?"

"I tried to several years ago, but he refused. Then he disappeared."

"Little bastard wants us to pony up the cash to keep this quiet," Harry Warner said.

"He can milk this bigamy story as much as he wants, and as long as the papers pay him for it, he's golden," Ken said.

He was right. I'd suddenly become much more valuable to Sonny.

The four of us looked cautiously at each other. Jack Warner puffed thoughtfully on his cigar.

"I'm so sorry," I said. "Honest I am. I didn't know how to tell you. I was waiting for the right time so I could undo the damage. I never suspected he'd do this. I wanted to take care of things quietly, but I couldn't find him."

"Did you know about this guy?" Harry yelled at Ken. Ken looked uncomfortable and swallowed hard. "Doesn't matter. You two are lucky we've got some connections downtown at city hall. I think we can make this go away."

"In the meantime, you're going to do another interview," Jack said pointing at me. "Otherwise, the papers will go after any speck they can find—accurate or not. You'll do it right away. I've got a lawyer I want you to talk to. And you will. Immediately." He handed me a business card, then nodded toward the door. We were being dismissed.

Ken and I rose and prepared to leave.

"And Marie..." We turned to hear the rest. "You ever... and I mean ever pull anything like this again, and you're through in this town. Through. The both of you."

The lawyer he had me go see was named Ray Hunt. He had an office downtown at Spring and 6th. He seemed very astute, and I needed his help. I had no idea what to do.

"Let me explain to you how California divorces work," he said. "One of you files for divorce. That's the easy part of all this. It's called an interlocutory decree. Then, there's a waiting period between the time you file your interloc and the date everything's finalized."

"How long is that?"

"They make you wait a year."

My face fell. "What? No!"

"I'm afraid so," he said. "The law is set up to preserve the holy estate as much as possible, and to discourage divorce among the general populace. In addition to that, one or both of you have to file a judgment at the end of that time. That tells the court that you've seen out the waiting period, you want to proceed, and you haven't changed your mind. Finalize it in the eyes of the law."

"That's a lot of work!" I said.

"Unfortunately, if you want to be free of Mr. Gerke, this is how you do it legally."

"Could I file in another state?" I asked. "Maybe go to Reno?"

He was already shaking his head.

"The Warners want this completely on the level. They might pay him off behind the scenes, but they don't want anything about this to look fishy. No contesting it, no asking for money, and no dashing down to Mexico."

"And this is their way of saying, "Here. This is your bed. Lie in it," I said.

He shrugged with a 'What are you gonna do?' expression on his face.

"Fine. Then let's get this paperwork filled out," I said. "What do I have to sign first?"

Three days later, I welcomed Miss Cox back to the

house. No shortbread this time. No special treatment.

"I see you're in a bit of hot water," she said.

"Yes, thanks to the *Times*," I said, freezing my face in a rictus grin.

"Tell me about this man, Gerke," she said.

"I knew he was going to sue," I lied. "But I was surprised, and yes—frightened. There isn't anything to tell. It was during the war and everybody was marrying. When the ceremony was over, we both realized what a silly thing we'd done. Mr. Gerke went to his home and I went to mine. I never truly realized I was married. We were two foolish children who ran away and married and then separated immediately. Now it's all over."

"Did you ever see Mr. Gerke again?"

"I talked to him about divorcing, but there never seemed to be much of a need until I met Ken. Then I couldn't find Mr. Gerke."

Miss Cox asked a few more in-depth questions, which I answered as well as I could. I didn't want to, but when I thought of the Warners barking across the desk at me, I followed orders.

Fortunately, I was starting *The Marriage Circle* within a week. Monte and I would be working together again. Our co-stars were Florence Vidor, who had a lovely Texan drawl, and Adolphe Menjou, a magnificently well-dressed heel who constantly raved about the threat of Bolsheviks until I wanted to rip my hair out by the roots. It was all I could do to get through my scenes with him.

Considering we played a married couple who hated each other, I think we pulled that off pretty well.

THE MARRIAGE CIRCLE SET, WARNER BROTHERS LOT, HOLLYWOOD, CALIFORNIA *September 1923*

"Was ist das hier?" were the first words I heard from Ernst Lubitsch as he examined a piece of the set design. I wasn't sure what to think about him at first. We'd only recently fought a war with these people, and I wasn't the only one wondering what it might be like to work for a Hun.

Lubitsch was short and he liked smoking cheap, stinky cigars. Next to him stood a boy, barely out of short pants, who looked eager and enthusiastic.

"Hallo," he said in German-accented English. "I am Henry Blanke, Mr. Lubitsch's assistant."

"Hi," I said. "Marie Prevost." I shook both their hands.

"Freut mich," Mr. Lubitsch said in a heavy accent.

"Mr. Lubitsch apologizes that his English is not so good. I help him with translation when he needs it," Blanke said. "He is pleased to meet you."

I'd read the scenario, and between Henry and Mr. Lubitsch, they tried to describe what Mr. Lubitsch was looking for. Lubitsch rambled on in German, then Blanke translated.

"Fun," Henry said. "Mr. Lubitsch wants for making luff to be fun. This is about matters of the bedroom. It is silly, but also sophisticated. Your character, Mizzi, is source of all kinds of trouble. She must be played as coy, flirty, and how do you Americans call it...devil-may-care."

"You are bored *mit* jour *mann*, Josef, zo flirt *mit* friend's *mann,* Franz," Mr. Lubitsch told me, looking to Henry to confirm his English.

Henry nodded.

"*Und dann,*" Lubitsch said. "Colleague of friend's husband shows her attention. *Der Freund* thinks husband is interested in third woman, so asks Mizzi to vatch him. Which is worst thing to do."

"And I'm bad news," I said with a sly little smile, understanding the name of the film now. I wiggled my hips, getting into character.

"*Ja!*" said Mr. Lubitsch, pointing at me. "*Sehr gut!*"

The shoot was frustrating, to say the least. Half the time, we had the language barrier to worry about. The other half, Mr. Lubitsch drove me crazy, wanting something I had trouble giving him. I wasn't smiling wide enough. I wasn't emoting enough. My walking needed to be smoother—not so awkward.

"Mr. Lubitsch," I said. "I've been walking since I was two years old. I think I know how to do it correctly."

"Correctly, perhaps, but not..." he fumbled for a word, snapping his finger a few times. Henry Blanke jumped into the breach.

"Stylishly," he provided.

"*Ja!*" Mr. Lubitsch said, delighted. "*Mit* style. *Mit* grace. *Und* naughty. Mizzi knows 'how to get what she wants,' *nicht war?*"

I tried again, altering my walk to something more sophisticated. A "woman of the world" gait.

Lubitsch nodded enthusiastically.

The next scene called for Mizzi to visit Franz's office.

Multiple takes later, I still hadn't gotten it right. At least, not right for Mr. Lubitsch. He had me keep repeating the same motions. Over and over, I walked a few feet, opened a door, and closed it behind myself.

"*Nein*!" he said, running his hands through his pomaded hair. "Cut!"

"Mr. Lubitsch, you've made me do this twelve times."

"*Fraulein* Prevost," he said. "Diss is nothing. Acting requires patience *und*..." snap snap snap.

"Deliberation," Blanke said.

He snapped and pointed at Blanke with a smile, as Henry got to the root of what he wanted to say.

"Again!" Lubitsch called.

I sighed.

"*Marriage Circle*, scene ten, take thirteen!" the slate boy called, clacking the halves together.

"*Und*...action!"

I ran through the same motions over and over with the door and the rest of the scene. Lubitsch was testing me. That's what this was. It was a battle of wills, and he wanted me to know that he was the boss. I quietly fought that battle through several takes.

"Cut!" Lubitsch said.

Lubitsch and Blanke gave each other a look, and Blanke cheerfully called out, "Ve take break now!"

Monte and I breathed a sigh of relief, crossing to the table laden with the coffee and fancy cakes and pastries that Lubitsch had insisted on for the cast and crew. Jack Warner vetoed them right away, but Lubitsch had called his own personal strike. "No cake, no coffee, no shoot!" he told us. Warner backed down.

Lubitsch took my hand, led me to a canvas chair that had my name stenciled on the back, and he got me a glass of water. Henry Blanke hovered nearby in case he was needed.

Mr. Lubitsch pulled another chair up close, his expression one of deep contemplation.

"Dis iss very hard," he said. "You think I am harsh man. Slave master. But iss more to acting than doing actions. Acting come from in here." He poked me in the breastbone below my shoulder blade with his index finger.

"I vatch old Sennett flickers in *Deutschland*. I haff seen you do comedy. But this..." he pointed down at the floor of Stage 2. "Iss not slapstick. Iss more mature." Snap snap snap.

"Subtle," Blanke said.

"*Ja*! You think, 'Lubitsch *ist Arschlock*,'" he said, lapsing back into German.

"An asshole," Blanke leaned over and whispered in my ear.

"*Nein*," Lubitsch continued. "Am like conductor trying for bravura performance. You are orchestra!"

I nodded, trying to understand.

"You know Mary Pickford?" he asked.

"I've met her," I said.

"We just finish *Rosita*. One scene? We do over and over and over. She not complain once. We get on *zweite klappe*. Ach...Henry...die *nummer*!"

"Twentieth take," Henry said.

Lubitsch patted my hand, then rose and went to talk to James Flood, our second cameraman, letting me stew temporarily. He knew that talk would have the desired effect, and it did. Nobody wanted to be seen as a whiner, a crybaby, or God forbid, less professional than Mary Pickford. We finally got it in the can on take twenty-two.

Then we moved into the next scene, where Mizzi attempted to seduce Dr. Braun, played by Monte.

The slate boy took his place in front of the camera.

"*Marriage Circle*, scene eleven, take one." Clack.

"Und...action!"

For our mood music, Lubitsch instructed the string quartet to play a dreamy, romantic version of "The Blue Danube Waltz." Mizzi had told Dr. Braun that she was sick to lure him over so she could seduce him. When he came to attend me, I was wearing a negligee, and I'd sprayed heady perfume and lay perfectly positioned on my fainting couch. As Monte used his stethoscope to examine me, Lubitsch softly guided us.

"*Gut, gut,*" he said. "*Und* now, you must pour de schnapps *mit...*" Snap snap snap. "...*mit* flirting, *mit...die Wimpern...* ach...Henrich!" He wiggled his fingers near his eyes.

"Bat your eyelashes," Henry said.

I did what he asked, leaning across Monte to provocatively pour from the bottle of schnapps, which was actually colored water. Monte's Dr. Braun looked suitably embarrassed and moved the little table further away.

"*Und* now, play *mit his Haare!*" Lubitsch instructed. "*Und jetzt warf dich uber seinen Korper.*"

"Drape yourself over him!" Henry called. I did.

"*Sehr gut.* Cut!"

Lubitsch only made us repeat this scene ten times, so I

knew I was improving.

Over another Strauss waltz, we filmed the dance after the dinner scene. I tried to remember what I'd seen from Theda Bara and Nita Naldi, combining looks and moves from them, but adding a bit of my own, inner baby vamp. Monte did his best to look bored and uncomfortable with Mizzi's antics.

"*Ausgezeichnet!*" Mr. Lubitsch called, clapping his hands. Henry assured us that meant we'd done a very good job. By the end of the shoot, I was down to two takes per scene. It seemed I was a real actress at last.

CHAPTER SIXTEEN

THE MARRIAGE CIRCLE PREMIERE, GRAUMAN'S RIALTO,
DOWNTOWN LOS ANGELES *January 16, 1924*

The line of limousines wended its way down Broadway to the intersection at 8th. I wore my Bordeaux silk with dropped waist and matching silk flower at the hip, wine-colored silk pumps, and a burgundy-patterned silk scarf draped artfully over a shoulder. I'd painted my lips a matching shade, but Ken complained when I kissed him, so I took a handkerchief and rubbed at the lip print his cheek. He looked perfectly cool and collected in his tux, but my knees wouldn't stop knocking. I watched out the window as our car approached the marquee. Spotlights moved in pale discs through the dark skies.

The crowd buzzed in anticipation, kept back by cordon ropes. The KHJ announcer stepped to the microphone and winced as it let out an ear-splitting whine. He backed away, then began again, keeping up a running commentary as directors, stars, and spouses strode the red carpet into the theater.

"Good evening, ladies and gentlemen! We're so pleased to be speaking to you tonight from the Rialto Theatre in downtown Los Angeles for the premiere of Warner Brothers' fine feature film *The Marriage Circle*! The stars are beginning to arrive and excitement is building in the crowd! Oh, look, it's Florence Vidor, wearing a becoming pink silk frock edged in diamonds and spangles!"

What he didn't point out was the glaring absence of Flo's husband, King Vidor, who'd been shacking up with Eleanor Boardman of late. She said a few words, but the announcer let her pass without much fanfare, as the bigger fish were arriving. The limousine in front of us pulled to a stop, and Monte got out, accompanied by Tova Jansen, whom he had started squiring around town after his divorce from Erma.

"Here's Monte Blue, another of the stars of the picture! Monte, do you have any comments to make about the film?"

"We're all very proud of it," he said. "Thank you for coming to see it." Tova stood by his side, pretty as you please, then they strolled in.

"And next here's Monte's co-star, Marie Prevost, who plays the mischievous Mizzi! She's accompanied by actor Kenneth Harlan, a star in his own right. Marie, you look lovely this evening, and Ken, you're a lucky man. Anything you'd like to say to the fans?"

I swallowed hard to calm the butterflies that suddenly felt like bats in my gut.

"Thank you so much to the Warner Brothers, and to Mr. Lubitsch, for helping us make such a wonderful film. And thank you to our fans."

"Any truth to the rumor that you and Ken will be tying the knot soon, Marie?"

"Not as far as I know," I said with a nervous laugh—trying

to pawn off our lack of nuptials as a whim of Ken's rather than a legal matter. Ken and I stepped away from the microphone, attempting to fend off any more questions that could lead to Sonny being brought up.

The announcer moved on to my next co-star, now approaching down the red carpet.

"Here comes Adolphe Menjou, who plays Dr. Stock!"

Menjou sauntered to the microphone like he was a king sizing up his subjects. He droned on about the film, his work on it, and his working relationship with Mr. Lubitsch. He'd been arrogant, dismissive, and he'd made fun of Mr. Lubitsch's accent. All I could think as he stood there was what a colossal, blue-nosed pill he was.

As we milled around the elaborate lobby, Mr. Lubitsch saw me and crossed the room within seconds. "Marie!" he said. I smiled as he took my hand. "Dis iss quite de event, *ja*? More festiff than in Berlin."

"It certainly is. I don't think you've met my fiancé. Ernst Lubitsch, this is Kenneth Harlan. Ken, this is Mr. Lubitsch."

"Pleasure," Ken said, shaking his hand.

"Your schweetheart is genius!" Mr. Lubitsch said, pumping Ken's hand enthusiastically. "I wish all my actresses were as wonderful as Marie."

"You're too kind," I said.

"Pah! Is well-deserved praise. You are Mizzi. I want efferyone to know of this gift you have for bringing her to life."

I leaned over and gave him a kiss on the cheek, and he beamed. The house lights blinked, alerting us to the start of the film.

"Shall we?" I said.

He nodded. The ushers took us to places of honor, along with Mr. Menjou, Florence Vidor, and across the aisle, the Warners.

The lights dimmed, the introductory titles began, and the audience quieted for the show. From time to time, I snuck a peek around me in the dark. Faces were lit up at the titles and our performances. The titters and laughs echoed throughout the theater. Mizzi was a hit.

When it was over, the applause was thundering. Menjou rose first, then the rest of us. Florence Vidor fluttered her fingers at the crowd. Monte smiled and waved. Mr. Lubitsch grinned in glee then took my hand and clutched it excitedly. A chorus of whispers and comments swept through the crowd toward us.

"Wasn't she wonderful?" I heard. "Such a bratty coquette!"

"Blue was stupendous, but Miss Prevost was still my favorite."

"Lubitsch is a genius!"

"It's like watching champagne flow—so much fun and so bubbly!"

We stood in the lobby afterwards, and the audience members heaped on the praise. I was the toast of Hollywood, and it was thrilling. I won't lie. We were all invited to a party at Harry Warner's place, where we could greet the sun.

"You were glorious, darling. Positively glorious," Ken said, placing a hand on my knee as he leaned into the deep leather of the limo's backseat. We headed west on 8th Street.

"Mr. Lubitsch made me work harder than any of my other directors. I think he's rubbed off on me." We smiled at each other, and despite the recent mess with Sonny, I was happy.

The limo eventually pulled up at a red brick Georgian in Hancock Park.

"Marie! Ken!" squealed Phyl when she saw us walk in the door. I hadn't seen her at the premiere. "You look simply divine." Phyl had chosen a baby blue frock in silk charmeuse, with matching shoes and bag, her blonde curls now cut into a smart bob.

"You look beautiful too," I said, "Thanks for being here to cheer me on."

"Don't mention it," she said with a shrug. The whole time, her eyes wandered the room until they found what they were looking for. "Excuse me, honey. I gotta go see a man about a dog."

And off she went like that. Same old Phyllis. I rolled my eyes and turned back to Ken. When I looked back a few minutes later, Phyl had cornered Darryl Zanuck near the French doors overlooking the patio, and was feeding him olives from the hors d'oeuvres tray.

Over in another corner, Monte stood with our other co-star, Creighton Hale, deep in conversation. The bartender was mixing sea breezes and orange blossoms right and left. At the sound of a spoon being pinged against a glass, we turned to see Harry Warner ready to make an announcement.

"I'm glad to see each and every one of you here tonight," he said. "We owe a great debt of the success of this picture to our director. I'd like to present to you: Mr. Ernst Lubitsch!"

A smiling Mr. Lubitsch stepped forward to applause from those present, and Henry Blanke stood close to him, in case he needed prompting for a word.

"Can we get a few words, Ernst?" Mr. Warner said.

"*Ja, ja*! I vant to thank you all for support and attention you give dis film," he said to light applause. "Everyone did marffelous job on picture. But I would like to make comment, iff I may."

Warner looked confused, and Ken and I looked at each other. Drinks paused midway to mouths, and cigarettes stayed poised in mid-air for a moment longer than necessary.

"Miss Marie Prevost vas *ausgezeichnet* as Mizzi. Iss unforgivable that she iss not given top billing. She is one of few actresses in Hollywood who knows *unter*playing de comedy. She stole effery scene!"

Oh shit.

Menjou glared at me as if he were trying to set me on fire with his eyes. And Florence Vidor? The syrupy sweet was gone, to be replaced by the most hate-filled glance I'd ever seen. Mr. Warner? I was too terrified to glance in his direction.

Before anyone could react, Menjou flourished his silver-topped walking stick and stalked toward the door, slamming it once he was outside.

Florence Vidor, nursing a spritzer for the last twenty minutes, moved closer to Mr. Lubitsch and tossed it in his face.

He stood there staring at her, then bowed elegantly before turning back to Ken and me.

"*Danke schoen*, Mrs. Vidor. That was quite refreshing," he said. He pulled out a handkerchief to absorb some of the mess. Calling her Mrs. was a nice barb. It was all over town that she and King were in the process of a divorce. Florence too headed for the door, looking near tears before her exit.

The party resumed, but far more subdued, and eyes rested on me far too often. After her *tête-à-tête* with Mr. Zanuck,

Phyllis worked her way back to my side with what I estimated had to be at least her fifth seabreeze.

"Jesus, it's like Siberia in here."

"Tell me about it," I muttered. "For someone appearing in such a successful movie, I feel about as successful as dog shit right now. You wanna get out of here? Come over to my place and we can have a little fun."

I started to take a sip, then changed my mind and gulped down the rest of my drink.

"Sorry to disappoint you, honey, but I may need to hang around a little while, if you know what I mean."

She waved across the room to Mr. Zanuck. Even as I watched, she moved a foot or two away from me so it wouldn't look like we were together. If she'd slapped my face I didn't think it would have hurt quite as much.

"I guess I'll see you later then," I said. Our evening was over. All because Mr. Lubitsch couldn't keep his opinions to himself, flattering as they were.

From *The Marriage Circle*, Warners moved me into *Three Women*, once again with Mr. Lubitsch. Which was good because I still enjoyed working with him, but bad because I'd developed a real love of his favorite cream-filled Napoleon pastries.

Starring with me were May McAvoy and Pauline Frederick. Warners made a big deal of the huge society carnival they'd had constructed. Lew Cody played a cad who romanced both May and Pauline, as mother and daughter.

And I played Harriett, the third woman in his romance plot.

And even though I was less popular on the lot, they still negotiated a five-year contract with me in March.

My assembly line of upcoming films included *How to Educate a Wife* and *Being Respectable*, both with Monte. Then a loan-out to B.F. Zeidman to work with a new girl named Clara Bow, in a picture called *Daughters of Pleasure*. Clara was a marvelous actress. But as I closed in on thirty, the doubts started settling in. She was also competition.

CHAPTER SEVENTEEN

KEN'S PLACE, HOLLYWOOD, CALIFORNIA *August 1924*

"Oh my darling Kenny! I'm so happy to see you! And this must be Marie. Charmed, my dear. Utterly charmed." She took my hand.

"It's wonderful to meet you, Mrs. Harlan," I said.

"You simply must call me Rita. Mrs. Harlan is my ex-mother-in-law."

Rita Harlan swept into the room, clad in teal sateen, with a dark sable collar and a turquoise turban sporting a peacock feather, which tickled my nose as she strolled by. She embraced her son, kissing the air on either side of his face.

"How was New York, Mother?"

"Ugh. Dreadful." She flung her wrap onto the couch and made herself at home. "You can't get a decent cocktail anywhere anymore. You have to go to these seedy-weedy places pretending to be a bookstore in Greenwich Village or a barber shop in Harlem or some-such. Rector's has closed, more's the pity. I'm not sure I'll ever have such scrumptious Lobster Bordelaise again. But Flo and I had a lovely chat. I ran into her at Café des Beaux Arts."

"Let's not bring up Flo, if you please," Ken said, trying to change the subject.

"I can't help it if I'm still friends with your ex-wife," Rita said. "Fix mummy a drink, would you, darling? There's a good boy."

At last she came up for air and looked at me intently. She leaned back against the couch cushion as Ken shook up drinks at the bar.

"She's lovely, Ken," she said, like I wasn't sitting there right in front of her. "Preeee-vost. That's a very unusual name, dear. Is it French?"

"It's Swiss," I said.

"Swiss! How delightful!"

It wasn't that delightful. She'd never met Frank. I took a seat on the couch instead of pointing that out.

"And what of the rest of your family origins?" she asked.

"All Scottish," I said.

"Aaahhhh...the land of Rob Roy, Robbie Burns, heather and lochs, golfing and bagpipes...." She thought a second, then wrinkled her nose. "Well maybe not the bagpipes. But I'm enthrrrrralled by all things Scottish. I was supposed to play Mary, Queen of Scots years ago for the Frohmans, but then Charles went down on the *Lusitania*, and I'm afraid that was that."

"Here you are, mother," Ken said, handing her a drink, then presented me with mine.

She took a sip. "Perfect. You will have to give mummy the name of your bootlegger. What are you working on now, darling? Whatever it is, I shall be first in line at the cinema." She held her glass aloft with her pinkie elegantly raised.

"Something called *The Man Without a Heart*. And Marie

is in *Lover of Camille* at Warner Brothers."

"Aah yes....*la Dame aux Camellias*..." she said dreamily. "I played *Camille* back in '03 in a run through the Midwest."

"Ken told me about watching you in it. I loved working with him," I said, looking up at him affectionately.

"Me too," she said.

"Mother knows what she's talking about. She was my first leading lady," Ken said.

"He was divine too. As a youngster of seventeen, Kenny played my brother in *A Man's Game*."

"Then I moved on to being her sweetheart and her husband, if you can believe that," Ken said with a chuckle.

"But he drew the line at playing my grandfather!" Rita laughed heartily as she opened a platinum cigarette case, drew out a smoke, and inserted it into an ivory cigarette holder. "He ripped off his white beard and stomped out like a spoiled six-year old. Ugh. Do you know who I saw at the depot in Glendale? That awful Von Stroheim fellow." She shuddered.

"Think of having to work with him for months on end," Ken said, sitting down in one of the armchairs.

"He was at Universal while I was there," I said. "Honestly, he was a perfect gentleman whenever I encountered him."

Rita cringed. "I could never take direction from a Hun. Kenny, remember that little stage hand we had when we were in Milwaukee with *At the Cross Roads*? Gunther? Was that his name? What a peevish little person. And he ate that disgusting sauerkraut and bratwurst backstage for his lunch. It took me a week to air out my costume so it didn't reek of pickled cabbage."

All I could think was how much I'd loved working with Mr.

Lubitsch after we'd finally come to an understanding about working styles. Hun or not, he was a hell of a director. Kind and well-meaning, even if he might have angered the Warners and the cast of *The Marriage Circle*.

"When were you in Milwaukee?" I asked them.

Rita furrowed her brow as she thought. "Must have been...1906, I think. Ken was about ten or eleven. Weren't you, darling?"

"How nice that you had Ken with you while you toured," I said. "I would have thought it might have been easier to leave him at home."

"At home with whom? His bastard of a father left me. I was mother *and* father to my children," Rita said, bringing me up short.

"You have brothers and sisters?" I asked Ken. "Where are they?"

"Two sisters. Gladys and Dorothy. They're here in California."

"And three more babies I barely had a chance to love," Rita said sadly. "They all died very young."

"I'm sorry about that," I said. "And about Ken's father."

"Don't be. I'm not," he said.

"Kenny's father tried acting for a time, but the man is a milksop," Rita said. "Always has been, and always will be. In my younger years, I thought that perhaps he'd be a calming influence on my dramatic ways, but the truth was, he was a clerk. That was all he ever aspired to being. And he wanted me to be... conventional." She shuddered again.

"Something you definitely aren't," Ken said, leaning over and clasping her arm affectionately.

"*Sapho* was the nail in the coffin for him," she said with the throaty laugh of a woman of the world.

I almost spit Buck's fizz out of my nose, so Ken patted me gently on the back as I regained my composure.

"You did *Sapho*?" I asked.

"Of course!" she tossed off with a flick of her wrist.

Now that explains a lot.

The most scandalous play of the early twentieth century had meant an obscenity charge for Olga Nethersole, the English actress who'd originated the role on Broadway. Now I could see how Ken's opinion of women had developed. With his mother as Sapho, all other women looked like prudes by comparison—even a bathing beauty like me.

"Shall we head out to dinner, ladies?" Ken said.

"Capital idea, my darling. Where shall we go?"

"Marie and I are quite fond of the Grenadine of Beef at the Ambassador," he said.

"Oh no no. The Chicken Fricassee at the Palais Royal is far superior."

"Then what are we waiting for?" Ken said.

When we were seated at the Palais Royal and had ordered teacups of the house special, Ken and Rita reminisced about their traveling theater days. I barely got a word in edgewise, but I was fascinated with her divorce.

"What happened to your father?" I asked Ken, taking a bite of my chicken.

"Most likely boring the population of bustling Zanesville, Ohio with stories of his ex-wife, the harlot actress, I expect," Rita answered for him, puffing on her cigarette in its holder. "Or alternately, his incredibly handsome son." She patted his hand on the table.

"Or talking about Uncle Otis," Ken said.

"Oh, yes. Uncle Otis," Rita said dismissively.

"Father's brother Otis is also an actor," Ken said.

"How did everyone in your family end up in the theater?" I said with a laugh.

"Hardly everyone," Rita said, quick to correct me. "Although I urged them to revel in their artistic sense, Ken's sisters have embraced mediocrity by becoming housewives. I even got them bit parts in some of my productions—Dorothy in *Friends* and Gladys in *Hazel Kirke* when I had my own stock company. But alas, the theater bug didn't gnaw at them like it did with my Kenny." She gazed at him with adoration and squeezed his arm in its brown tweed jacket. "Have you kids thought about the wedding or the honeymoon at all?"

"We have to wait until our divorces come through before we can do much," Ken said.

"That will happen soon enough," Rita said. "And then you'll wish you'd planned for it."

"She's right, Ken," I said, trying to curry a little favor.

"Well, we've talked about seeing the Hawaiian Islands..." he began.

"They're utterly splendid!" she said. "Exotic...foreign... tropical. Do you know that they roast an entire pig in a hole in the ground there? It's quite grand when they pull it out. They have a big dinner party they call a luau, with dancers who do something called the hula. It's marvelous. I highly recommend it."

"I guess that settles it," Ken said. "Hawaii it is."

YOU'D BE SURPRISED

CHAPTER EIGHTEEN

MARIE'S PLACE, LOS ANGELES, CALIFORNIA
October 7, 1924

"I never knew I could feel so relieved," I said. "Thank you for calling." I hung up the phone with a yelp of triumph. Barring any unforeseen complications, the divorce would be final on Tuesday, the fourteenth. After all the years of sneaking around and keeping secrets, I felt lighter than air. Ken and I held each other, finally able to do it legally without looking over our shoulders.

"I already talked to Reverend Eby at Wilshire Presbyterian," I said. "But I should have asked you. We've never discussed religion in any depth. What are you anyway?"

"If you want to get absolutely technical, I'm Jewish."

"You're what? No, you're not." I looked at him seriously to see if he was pulling my leg.

"Not observant of course, but Judaism is passed through the maternal line. Don't tell Mother I told you."

"Rita's Jewish?"

"She swore me to secrecy. Her family, the Wolffs, were merchants. They settled in the West Indies in the 1700s. Her father moved the family to New York, and that's how she ended up there, going into the theater. Her real first name is Sarah."

I'm sure I had a strange look on my face.

"Don't worry. I won't make you convert," he said with a laugh. "Look at Mother, for goodness sakes. She's the least observant person I know."

I spoke to Reverend Eby again, and we called all our friends to alert them of the date, October fourteenth, right after the official divorce was signed. Our abbreviated guest list included Mum, Peg, and Phyllis, as well as Rita, Vera, Mr. Sennett, Irene Rich, and Monte Blue. I wore a cream on cream floral imprint chiffon with a handkerchief hemline and a simple cream-colored cloche covered in embroidered appliqués of the same color. We stopped by Wilshire Flowers and bought a bouquet of baby's breath and mums in fall colors and a matching mum boutonnière for Ken. When we retreated down the aisle as man and wife into the bright sunshine and blue skies, the day couldn't have been more perfect.

Our much anticipated trip to Hawaii wasn't in the cards any longer, since we each had shooting schedules to adhere to, and Warner's would not be kept waiting. Instead, we decided to postpone the tropics and make a quick trip to New York instead. The cast and crew generously stayed up most of the night finishing my scenes in *Recompense* so Ken and I could have our precious time together. A luxurious seven days—five on The Golden State Limited and the Pennsy, and two together at the Astor in New York—before Ken had to begin shooting *The Crowded Hour* there with Bebe Daniels. Then, he had to stay behind while I returned to California.

The fold-out bunks in our private compartment weren't the most practical or comfortable, but we got inventive. In the dining car, we fed each other decadent desserts and reveled in each other's company without having to worry about Sonny, or the Warners, or anything else.

When we arrived on the platform at Penn Station, a gaggle of reporters followed us, even as we collected our trunks.

"Mr. Harlan, how does it feel to be a married man again?" One of them called.

"It feels perfect," Ken said. "I'm married to the most beautiful woman in the world."

I beamed at him.

"Miss Prevost, you certainly didn't waste any time remarrying after your divorce," one of them baited me.

"Well, I wasn't happy with Mr. Gerke. That's not the case with Mr. Harlan," I tossed off as we sauntered away.

"The Astor," Ken told the hired car driver.

Ken lay his hand protectively over mine as I leaned my head on his shoulder.

"We're going to be so happy," he whispered, leaning down to kiss me.

When the chauffeur deposited us in front of the Astor, Ken peeled off a bill from the stack in his pocket and slipped it to him. "Get the luggage for us, would you?"

The man nodded and unstrapped the trunks from the rack as Ken and I checked in and floated up to our room. He insisted on carrying me over the threshold, and I squealed as he hoisted me up.

"Happy, Mrs. Harlan?" Ken asked as we embraced.

"Exhausted but happy," I said. "Let me freshen up."

I enjoyed a luxurious soak in the tub, then we made love in the big hotel bed, multiple times, like newlyweds are supposed to do. As we lay there blissfully afterward, the phone rang. Pulling on his robe, Ken padded to it and answered.

"Harlan," he said. There was a pause. "What? You're kidding. Yeah, I know but..."

"What is it?" I whispered.

"I'm on my honeymoon, for Christ's sake," he said, running his hand through his hair in frustration. This didn't sound good at all. "Yeah, yeah. All right." He turned to me with a defeated look on his face as he hung up. "They need me at the studio tomorrow."

"What? No! They can't do that! We were going to go sightseeing!"

"I'm sorry, darling. I truly am. They moved up production."

I sighed. "We're slaves to our shooting schedules."

We had a subdued dinner at the St. Regis that night, and when we made love later, it was the same. We said a tearful goodbye at the depot the next day.

"I love you," Ken said. He placed an affectionate kiss on my nose. "Try to stay busy while I'm gone. We need to find a new place now that we're hitched. Why don't you look at some houses? Maybe talk to an architect?"

"But I don't know what you like," I said.

"I'm not picky," he said, kissing my forehead and then my lips. "As long as you're there and we're together, I'll be happy."

"Anything you want especially?" I asked.

"Plenty of windows. A big garage for all the cars we're going to buy. A swimming pool. And you."

I smiled and kissed him. When I got back, I rented us a

two-story white clapboard with charming yellow and green awnings, where we could live until we could build a place of our own.

Then, I purchased a lot on a developing street called Camden Drive in Beverly Hills, an up-and-coming subdivision that was filling with fellow movie folk. I discussed plans with an architect, planning to capitalize on our new status as a glamorous Hollywood couple. When Mr. Neff showed me renderings of how he visualized our house, I fell in love with the two-story terra cotta, red roof tiles, wrought iron, and big stone fireplace.

"As you can see..." he said, showing me his colored pencil drawings of how the rooms would look. "...it's quite spacious. Lovely light throughout. The kitchen will have all the modern conveniences." He pointed out the Westinghouse icebox and stove, plenty of cabinets, and a beautiful built-in wooden china cabinet in the dining room, which would come in handy for entertaining. So would the large bank of French doors out to the swimming pool.

We exchanged thoughts, and I asked him to incorporate my changes for the five enormous bedrooms and more terraces. I also pictured a charming garden full of roses, topiaries, and citrus trees. So while he perfected the final designs, I hired movers to pack all our things and move them into our temporary rental.

When he returned from New York, Ken and I found the most beautiful antiques we could, imagining how the house would look when it was finished. I'd need help to keep it tidy, so I advertised in the *Herald* for a maid. I interviewed several women who didn't seem right. Then

Delilah Washington showed up.

She was older— maybe late 40s—with a shuffling walk, a moon face with shiny white teeth, and an infectious laugh. She wore her hair up in a kerchief and listened intently to everything I said. I couldn't imagine not having her around.

"And you've been a maid before?" I asked.

"Yes'm, Miz Prevost. I worked for Mr. Wallace Reid and Miz Dorothy until he died."

"That was very sad about Wally," I said. We lowered our heads in observation of Wally's tragic decline and death, and I worried once again about Wah, wondering how she was doing since the raid at the hospital in Oakland the previous year. "You'd certainly be welcome here."

"Mist' Wally always said my waffles wuz one of his favorite things in the world," she said with a chuckle.

"Ken, what do you think?"

"I think I need to try one of those waffles for myself, to be sure," he said with a wink. He retreated to let us chat.

"I got the job?" she asked.

"Of course," I said. "Will we see you tomorrow morning, then?"

"I'll be here wid' a smile on!"

Along with bringing on Delilah, I splurged on clothes I'd always dreamed of, and Ken indulged his passion for automobiles. I picked out a Stutz, and Ken started looking for something that befit our new status.

I was relaxing by the pool in the afternoon sun when a steady honking began out front. And it wasn't stopping. I moved to the garden gate and opened it to see Ken sitting at the wheel of a shiny silver Packard convertible.

When he saw me, he gave me a broad grin and spread his arms. "Ta-da! Isn't she a peacherino?"

"Spiffy," I said, gazing at it appreciatively.

"Here's the best part, look!" He hopped out and pulled me toward the front grille. There, in the frame of the hood ornament, was one of my promotional photos from *The Marriage Circle*.

I laughed and clapped my hands. "I love it!"

"Then hop in!" he said. He revved the engine like a boy with a new toy. "This thing's faster than a cheetah with a firecracker up its ass. Let's take her for a spin!"

I dashed into the house for a scarf and my motoring goggles. When I returned, Ken put it in gear. We motored up the coast to Ventura, then had a dinner of fresh perch at a beachside hut called The Catamaran.

And a few weeks after that, Ken returned home with the ultimate luxury—a Rolls Royce. I gasped when I saw him at the wheel. It was the most beautiful car I'd ever seen.

To drive it, we hired an out-of-work extra named Eugene Melton as a chauffeur. We gave him the bedroom above the garage so he could be available when we needed him. There was nothing quite like it for making others green with envy, and Ken quite liked that. He also bought up lots of real estate in town. He'd heard it was a good investment, so we purchased three more houses and rented them out.

TERRACE, MARIE AND KEN'S PLACE, HOLLYWOOD, CALIFORNIA *February 10, 1925*

"You know what I've always wanted and I've never been able to have?" Ken said in a faraway voice as we watched the sun sink low in its peach and lilac glory.

"Me?" I said with a giggle.

"Of course," he said. "But besides that? A dog. Actually, more than one. I want a whole houseful. I could never have one when mother was traveling hither and yon."

"Me too," I said, marveling that he was echoing my long ago dream. "We could never have a dog because of all the moves."

"What type of mutts shall we get? Wolfhounds?" he asked.

"No, wolfhounds are so common now. Mum used to tell me stories of the little terriers Wee Mae had back in Scotland. Cairns, they call them. There's an old photo of Mum as a little girl holding one they had in Strathroy years ago. He had such an expressive little face. His name was MacDuff, from the character in *Macbeth*."

"Then let's ask around. We'll see if we can find a breeder. Maybe the library might have some information?"

"I love you," I said snuggling up close. "I'll check tomorrow."

Mrs. Perkins, the librarian, referred me to the American Kennel Club, which in turn referred me to Bannockburn Breeders near Riverside. Ken and I negotiated with them, and our new arrivals, two girls and a boy, arrived right after Valentine's Day. We named two of them Pooch O'Sheila, and Jinx Ballantrae. The third I had to think about a bit more. He was one of Pooch's puppies from her last litter, and he was a chubby rascal who loved to play. But his name eluded us.

They were a handful, but I'd never been so happy. Ken and I were married at last, I had a career I loved, and I had three adorable dogs who thought I was the most wonderful human who'd ever lived. Oh, they liked Ken well enough, but they followed me around the house, panting happily when they weren't growling and wrestling each other on the living room rug. There was nothing I loved more than lying on the soft, plush green grass in the backyard and letting them tumble over me, licking, nipping and snuggling. And they loved taking flying leaps into the pool and paddling over to me. I'd put them back on the concrete edge and they'd do it again. It was their favorite game.

They captivated Delilah, as they'd captivated me. She could always be counted on for soup bones or chunks of roast when they fixed those pleading eyes on her. But they could be naughty too. I had to fight not to laugh when I saw Delilah trying to grab the mop away from Jinx, who'd mistaken the head for a long-haired vermin species, and was intent on fighting it to the death.

"Oh, no you don't," she muttered. "You done let go dat mop, Jinx. You's a bad dog. Very bad."

Mum was entranced by the pups, and visited as often as she could to play with them, reliving her girlhood.

"Wha' do ye call this one, pet?" she said, playing with our as yet unnamed addition.

"We're still trying to find the perfect name," I said.

"He looks like my wee MacDuff, with his gaucy belly. Oh, ye're a scamp, aren't ye, dug? Who's a good boy? Who's a good boy?" He lay on his back, and she rubbed his tummy.

"What's that mean, Mum? Gaucy?"

"He's fat and jolly. That's what he is."

"That's it! Gaucy Bairn O'Sheila he is."

She laughed. "Ye should show them in dug shows," she said. "Especially this one. Bonny lass she is." She ruffled the fur on Jinx, then offered her a piece of ham from the tea sandwiches Delilah had made us. Jinx gobbled it up eagerly.

"Like in competitions?" I said, tossing Pooch and Gaucy some ham of their own.

"Aye! She's a natural! Look a' her!"

Jinxie gazed up at us and cocked her head, quivering in anticipation of another luscious morsel.

"She'll get a big head," I said, ruffling her ears. "Won't you? You'll be insufferable."

"Ah've never been so happy or so proud of you, pet. Ye finally have everything ye've worked for. Sennett...Universal...'twas leading to this. Ye've fans who adore ye, a husband who loves ye, and this bonny home. Be verra grateful every day fer this."

"I couldn't imagine a better life," I said.

Delilah returned from the kitchen. "Mo' tea, Miss Hughie?" she asked, offering the pitcher.

Mum held a chair out for her. "Delilah, ye're werkin' entirely too hard. Si' down and relax wi' us."

"Oh, no, Miss Hughie. That wouldn't be right."

"Ye must be exhausted from changin' the beds. Please have a sit with us."

Delilah looked to me as the mistress of the house. I patted the seat of the wrought iron chair.

"That's mighty neighborly of you, Miss Hughie, Miss Marie," Delilah said, lowering herself into the chair with a little sigh of relief.

"S'too much pretense everrrywhere between the stars an'

'the help,'" Mum said. "Ah used to be 'the help.' Ah've done nothing differen' to be sittin' here on me daughter's bonny terrace. We're all alike in God's eyes."

"That's a true fact." Delilah looked at my mother with such love right then, I realized what an incredible person Mum was. Such a gentle spirit. Such concern for every single person.

Mum drew Delilah out, asking about her family back in Georgia, her husband Archie, and her children. Delilah spoke lovingly of them, and about her home off Central Avenue, and how lucky she was to be working for Ken and me.

Too soon, the shadows began shifting across the terrace, and we headed inside. The dogs traipsed in behind us.

That month, Ken started a new contract at Warner's. We were able to see each other between takes and would often grab lunch together at the commissary. I didn't think I could ask for more, and then we were cast in *Bobbed Hair* together. Filming in San Diego, and staying at the luxurious Hotel Del? Who needed Hawaii?

HOTEL DEL CORONADO, CORONADO ISLAND, CALIFORNIA
April 25, 1925

"The ads aren't exaggerating," I said. "Look at that place!"

The hotel was a fanciful Beaux Arts building of white wood and red shingles, with multiple wings and dramatically sloping roof lines. To the west, white sands stretched to water of a beautiful jewel blue, like an illustrated postcard.

After driving off the *Morena* ferry at the northern tip of

the island, Ken steered us south, avoiding a rabbit that scurried past. Eugene had asked for some time off, so we'd left the Rolls at home and took the Packard out on the road to see what it could do.

As we pulled into the circular drive out front, a bellhop hurried to unhook the trunks. Then we strolled into the rotunda, which was paneled and beamed in imposing dark wood. A gallery ran around the perimeter on the second floor.

"It's an honor, Mr. Harlan, Miss Prevost," the clerk at the desk said. "We're quite excited about the filming. Will the rest of the cast be joining you this evening?"

"Yes," Ken answered, signing the guest book. "They'll be down on the AT & SF later tonight."

"Could you please let me know when Louise Fazenda checks in?" I asked.

"Certainly, Miss Prevost."

The bellhop guided us to our room, lugging an overburdened cart that held our trunks.

"Bridal suite, here we are," he said, unlocking it. He handed the key to Ken.

I smirked at Ken as we followed the man into the room. Through the windows, the panorama stretched for miles—nothing but beautiful coastline and waves. The rich fabrics, thick carpeting, and overstuffed pillows welcomed us. I had no desire to budge from this spot.

Bobbed Hair had originally been a story serialized in *Collier's* magazine, with each excerpt from a different author. Sensing a hit, Warner's had snapped up the rights. I was to play charming, willful Connemara Moore, whose wealthy spinster aunt wanted to ensure that Connemara didn't end up unmarried and lonely like she had. Wealthy Aunt Celimena had put a clause in her will that if Connemara hadn't married by her twenty-first birthday, she wouldn't inherit. Connemara was forced to choose between two suitors: Saltonstall (Salt) Adams and Bingham (Bing) Carrington. One liked bobbed hair, and the other didn't. Thus, the name.

Eventually, Connie ran away with a third fellow, David Lacy, and craziness ensued when they tangled with rum-runners and revenue men. Ken played David, Reed Howes would be Bing, John Roche would play Salt, and Emily Fitzroy had signed on as Aunt Celimena. I'd been thrilled when Louise accepted the role of Sweetie, the rum-runners' tomboy accomplice. Alan Crosland was directing.

Planning ahead for all the nautical action, an advance crew had secured various boats for us to use—a small schooner, which would stand in for David's yacht, the *Bloody Nuisance*; five or six yawls, a tug, a couple of fishing boats, and a dinghy or two with outboards for shuttling us around between takes. In addition, they'd commissioned the *Benecia* ferry for a scene or two.

Ken and I got checked in and enjoyed a dinner of fresh scallops and sand dabs at the hotel dining room, and after a dessert of lime tart, we returned to our room to relax. Being newlyweds, we did what came naturally to pass the time.

It must have been around three in the morning when a knock at the door woke us from a sound sleep. Ken went to answer, while I flicked on the bedside lamp and tugged up the covers.

"Mr. Harlan, I'm sorry to disturb you. We've just received a message that the cast and crew of your film have been in an accident. Their train derailed on the Sorrento grade north of town."

CHAPTER NINETEEN

"Is anyone—"

"They don't know yet. They're starting to get the news in bits and pieces," the clerk said. "It happened hours ago. Someone stopped to call from La Jolla. They were hurrying to the hospital behind the ambulance."

"Oh my God, Louise..." I said. "Emily..."

"Thank you for letting us know," Ken said.

The clerk hurried back down the corridor, and Ken shut the door. I jumped out of bed and pulled on one of my more utilitarian frocks- a deep violet blue silk. Then I slid on stockings and wrapped a turban around my hair—this was no time to worry about my coiffure.

"What are you doing?" Ken said.

"I couldn't possibly go back to sleep. Our friends are on that train. I'm going down to the lobby. Whatever news comes in, they'll get it first. Since we don't know which hospital they'll be taken to, it seems like the most logical place to wait. Coming?" I said, lacing up my boots.

"Yeah, okay," he said. He pulled on an undershirt, gray trousers, and a white shirt. When he ran a hand over his unshaven face, my heart leapt a little. So handsome.

We camped out in a corner of the rotunda, surrounded by potted palms. The hotel staff kindly opened the kitchen and brought us hot cups of coffee, some sandwiches, and toast and jam as we waited, although neither of us felt much like eating. It had started raining overnight, and now there were looming thunderheads.

At this point, I was so full of coffee and nervous energy that I paced the length of the lobby. At nearly six, a man covered in mud dashed in. Despite his strange blackface, I recognized him. It was Leonard Peltzer, one of the hands.

"Leonard!" I cried. "How are you? Are you hurt?"

"Marie! Ken!" he said, pulling out a handkerchief and wiping his face. "I'm fine, don't worry. I'm glad I didn't have to wake you."

"Are you kidding?" Ken said. "We've been awake for hours. What news is there?"

"The engineer was killed. Our prop boy, Bobbie Webb, found him and pulled him out," he said. "But all of ours are fine," he began. "I saw Louise and Emily right afterwards. They seemed to be all right. A couple of cuts and bruises like me. Since I was in the best shape of the bunch, I rode with the ambulance driver down here so I could relay the news."

"Oh, thank God!" I said, breathing a momentous sigh of relief.

"The rain's been making it hard to find and help people," Leonard continued. "They had to make some improvised torches to see in the dark, but the rain kept putting them out. They'll be able to do more now that there's a little daylight. I made that driver go like a bat out of hell. Kind of scary on the wet roads, but...I knew you'd be worried."

"Thank you," I said, clasping his hands. "Louise, Emily... where are they?"

"They got a relief train right after midnight, but it took forever to get it loaded and switched to a new track. They took a few of the most injured to La Jolla Hospital because it was closer. The rest are at the new hospital. Mercy, I think it's called. To get their injuries checked out and wait for news of the others."

"Thank you again, Leonard." Seeing his mud-covered face, trousers, and jacket, I said, "Please, use our room. Get washed up and have a rest. You've earned it. The front desk can get those clothes laundered for you. Come on, Ken."

I got directions to Mercy Hospital, then we ran to the Packard, and waited in the downpour for the ferry. Ken carefully maneuvered onto Harbor, to 1st Avenue, to Broadway, then hung a left onto Fifth Avenue and headed north, skirting the edge of Balboa Park. Screeching to a stop outside Mercy, we hurried inside, getting soaked in the process.

Out of breath, I asked the nurse at the registration desk, "Where are the passengers from the derailed train?"

"Second floor," she said, pointing to the elevator.

We took it up to find Louise and Emily in the waiting room, signing autographs. Louise had a small bandage on her forehead and her non-signing wrist was wrapped. Emily stood up to embrace Ken and me the minute she saw us. Her arm was in a sling, and she had a bandage stretching from her collar around her neck. Louise looked up, eyes full of exhaustion, then introduced her fan.

"Otto Steinmetz," he said eagerly. "I can't quite believe my luck—a healthy baby boy and autographs on the same day!" He gave Ken and me that look—the "I'd like an autograph but I'm unsure how to ask" look. We both obliged him.

"Thank goodness you're okay," I said, turning to Louise. "Was it as awful as I've been imagining?"

"Oh, Marie," she said. "We were all merry as can be in the observation car, and the musicians were playing jolly tunes. It must have been getting close to ten...maybe a quarter to, and suddenly there was a terrific impact. I was thrown against the seat in front of me. Larry, the second cameraman, said, 'Hold on, Louise! Keep low and brace!' So I did. There were two more dreadful crashes. It must have been as the train broke apart."

Emily shook her head. "Harold, the cello player, flew through the air to my left. His cello broke into splinters, and there was a terrible jumble of people and bags and chairs. Vincent, the violinist, got his hand caught between two seats. It was awful."

Otto Steinmetz looked properly ashamed that he had come looking for autographs in the middle of all this. He thanked us profusely, then retreated in the direction of the nurses' station.

"Your head..." I said, reaching toward Louise's bandage.

"Oh, this is nothing," she said. "It's a little cut. They can cover it with makeup."

"And my shoulder is only sprained," Emily said. "Doctor says I'll have a lovely bruise though."

"We were lucky," Louise said. "Ours was the only car that stayed upright. One of the others was carrying our film stock and it caught fire. It was one of the few sources of light we had for hours. All the props were destroyed. Harry Warner's going to blow his top."

"We should wire them. We'll need replacements for everything. But I'm so relieved you're both okay," I told them.

"Can someone check on Pal? He was with Alan in the car ahead of ours," Emily said. Pal was the collie who was playing Bugle, the story's dog.

"I will," I said. "Any news of Alan?"

"Last I saw of him, he was arguing with an ambulance driver that he didn't need medical attention. He was going to stay there until the others were loaded in ambulances, then he was going to catch a ride on the last one to see how we were all doing."

Turned out, Alan still had Pal with him. He'd paid a teenager a buck fifty to stand outside under the portico with the dog so he could come in and check on everyone. We took Louise, Emily, and Pal back to the hotel with us so Alan could stay at the hospital until they were all treated.

"I know one thing," Louise said as we took the *Morena* back over to the island. "If it's all right, I'm grabbing a ride home with you!"

GLORIETTA BAY, CORONADO, CALIFORNIA *April 30, 1925*

After several days for our co-stars to recuperate from their injuries, and for replacement props, film stock, and costumes to be sent down with new crew members, filming began. Since we were doing night shots, the cast and crew met at the San

Diego Yacht Club, based at the boathouse, which faced into Glorietta Bay.

The old tub had gotten a sprucing up, including a white-wash job. The new name, *Bloody Nuisance*, was splashed across her side.

Alan was deep in discussion with our head of lighting onboard the *Rumrunner*, Swede the gangster's yacht. They'd secured flood lighting to some of the smaller boats, which could float alongside if the seas were calm. Although the night was clear and balmy, the tides were rough. Alan had considered filming off the Point Loma lighthouse, but decided that Glorietta, standing in for the Long Island Sound of the original story, would be much calmer.

When my character, Connemara, left Aunt Celimena's celebration of her mystery engagement, she did it disguised as a nun, so no one could see that she'd turned yellow and only had one side of her hair bobbed. The voluminous robe and habit were hot, and the wimple made my head itch. Still, I made the best of it.

While hitchhiking, Connemara got a lift from chivalrous David Lacy. And, as passengers on the ferry, they were taken for fellow Prohibition scofflaws by the hulking but not very bright gangster, Mr. Pooch, who crawled into the back of their car. After being separated from David by an accident, Connie was dragged on-board a boat by Pooch. Coincidentally, the boat was the *Bloody Nuisance*, piloted by Mr. McTish, a Scotsman, played by Otto Hoffman.

Eventually, they were joined by more gangsters, Walter Long playing Doc, and Sweetie, played by Louise. Meanwhile, Aunt Celly, accompanied by her lawyer, Mr. Brewster, and

Connemara's suitors, Bing and Salt, were searching for her on a boat called the *Filomena*, which they'd borrowed from a neighboring boathouse to give chase. Then it was discovered McTish was in league with another of the gangsters, Swede, played by Pat Hartigan.

"Ahoy, Admiral!" Ken called up to Alan.

Alan waved and strolled down the gangplank to meet us. "Ahoy!" he called back cheerfully. "David? Sister Connemara? Ready to get started?"

"Am I!" Ken said, cracking his knuckles. Then he looked more closely at our craft. "Say…Is this thing seaworthy?"

"I've been assured by the fellas in the know that she's perfectly ship-shape," Alan said, slapping her side affectionately. "Okay, here's how I see this. We've got two *Bloody Nuisances*, two *Rumrunners*, and one *Filomena*. Plus, Jack Warner kindly got us some old tubs that were going to the scrapyard, so we can do some practice shots before we try to capture this on nitrate. Study this diagram very closely before we get started."

We moved closer to the illustration he'd drawn of the arrangement of the boats. I felt like Red Grange in the huddle with coach laying out the next play. Alan gestured at some even less seaworthy looking vessels moored to the dock.

"David, Connie, Sweetie, Pooch, Doc, and McTish—that one's yours this first go-round." He pointed to one called the *Sad Sack*. "Pat, you and your buddies are over there in the *Bathtub Gin*. First, let's make sure you all have your sea legs, then we can try to create the crash. Ken, can you aim for the middle of the bay? Then come about and give her a north heading. Pat, start from a western heading, and ram them amidships. I can guide you from there. I'll call cut and we'll bring in the lifeboats to pick you up if she sinks. Ready, rescue boats?" he yelled through the megaphone to the fellows already standing by. They nodded and yelled back.

"Aye-aye, skipper," Ken joked.

We scrambled toward our various craft. Those of us on the *Sad Sack* climbed the gangplank, and Ken started her up. As he did so, a huge cloud of blue-black smoke wafted up from somewhere in the bowels of the boat.

"Let's see if she makes it that far," Ken chuckled. He put the *Sad Sack* in gear, and we chugged protestingly to the center of the bay.

"That's good, Ken!" Alan yelled through the megaphone. When we reached a good spot, we assumed our positions as agreed upon.

"All right, Pat!" Alan's voice drifted across the water, as did the loud clack of the slate boy. "Let 'er rip! And...action!"

The *Bathtub Gin* sounded like a bullfrog with hiccups. Pat looked to be giving it full throttle, and it limped along gamely, but didn't have enough power to do much damage to the *Sad Sack*. It bounced off the hull, leaving only a dent. Pat's bow was crushed, but we were merely taking on a little water.

"Cut!" Alan yelled.

A rescue boat came by and picked up Swede and his goons, depositing them on the next disposable boat, another version of the *Rumrunner*.

When they were in place, the noise of the slate boy could barely be heard over the wind that had sprung up. Alan yelled again. "Places...and...action!"

Because it was also hard to hear Alan's commands, Ken hadn't yet gotten back to his spot at the wheel. He and Louise had joined me at the rail, so we were unprepared for the impact when the next boat hit us. I grabbed the rail and held on for dear life. Ken and Louise were caught unawares and tossed unceremoniously into the drink. Louise squealed and Ken let out a hearty "Shit!" right before they went under.

Ken struggled to the surface in time to hear Alan call, "Cut! That was great!"

"Great?!" Ken yelled. "I think I broke my god-damned rib!"

CHAPTER TWENTY

"What?!" Alan called back. He ran a hand through his hair in frustration.

With difficulty, Ken dog-paddled over to the rescue boat. They retrieved Louise, and after four attempts to lift Ken out of the water, and his bellowing in response, they finally dragged him in.

Alan got his boat to pull closer, and they conferred for a minute, but I couldn't hear what was being said.

"Ken's going to be a trouper and help us finish this shot!" Alan called. The rescue boat putted toward shore, where the on-set studio doctor treated Ken and the wardrobe staff saw to it that he was dried off and changed, and his makeup reapplied. Alan sent a boat over to let me know that the doctor said it was broken.

Louise had survived her dunking unscathed. She was toweled off, donned another set of trousers and newsboy cap, and after having her makeup reapplied, she climbed the rope ladder on the *Bloody Nuisance*.

"Any updates on Ken?" she asked me, and I gave her the bad news.

"Oh, no. What does one do for a broken rib?"

"Not much. Ice and aspirin. When we get done, Ken's going to have to take it easy until it knits on its own."

When Ken was brought back out in one of the motorboats, he climbed with difficulty onto the deck of the *Bloody Nuisance*, and lifted his shirt to show me the huge roll of gauze wrapped around his middle.

"Are you okay?" I asked him. I gave him a gentle kiss.

"I'll be all right," he said. "Unless I get a cold or something. Coughing's a bitch right now."

I kissed him again. "When we're finished with the shoot, you'll have a week to recuperate. You won't move from our bed unless it's to laze on the beach. I'm waiting on you hand and foot. That's an order."

"Aye-aye, Cap'n," he said, his smile becoming a wince, as he moved too much in the wrong direction.

"All right, we're going to try this for real," Alan called. "Very carefully!"

Once again, we reached our appointed boats. Most of us aboard the *Bloody Nuisance*; then Emily, Reed, John, and Tom Ricketts playing Brewster, the lawyer, in the *Filomena*. Finally, Swede and his group of thugs, in the newest *Rumrunner*. Alan was now on the *Nuisance* with us, so the lighting needed adjusting again.

"Charley! Aim that flood over here! Little lower!" Alan called. "Perfect!"

Bad guys Pooch and Doc were tied up and lay on the deck, as they'd been taken prisoner by David and McTish. Louise took a seat on Francis' back, since Sweetie was taunting Pooch and considering turning on her bootlegging pals. Francis looked up at her with a grin.

"I ain't crushin' ya, am I, Francis?" Louise asked.

"It'd take a lot more of you than that," he joked.

"Good," she said, bouncing up and down teasingly.

"David, if you please," Alan said, helping Ken into place. "You're still annoyed at Doc for trying to signal the other bad guys. Get your foot right up against him like you're thinking about punting him. Good. Now, Marie, right up against the rail...perfect."

Alan turned to confer with our cinematographer, Byron Haskin, and gestured to the slate boy to do his thing. "Places..." he called through the megaphone.

"*Bobbed Hair*, scene 12, take two!" said the slate boy. Clack. "And...action!"

At the rail, I turned out toward the bay.

"Connie, you hear an approaching boat! It sounds bigger! Look a little more confused, Marie. That's it. David, Sweetie, you hear it too. Who could it be?" He turned to Pat's boat and called across the water. "Swede! Bring that boat into frame! Good...steady as she goes..."

The *Rumrunner* plowed through the waters toward us.

"Little closer..." Alan called. "Okay now...camera #2... gimme a close-up of Pat. Pat, show 'em you mean business!"

"Stand by or we'll shoot!" Pat yelled, wielded his gun. The craft began to circle us.

"Camera #1, get the circling, please. Camera #2, aim for a close-up of Ken. David, you're thinking! How can you get rid of the bad guys? Think hard...little harder...they're made of wood...you've got a steel nose on that tub...that's it!"

Ken clutched the wheel and got a determined look in his eye.

"That's it, Ken! Aim right for dead center amidships! Keep

'er right about that speed. Steady as she goes!"

The *Bloody Nuisance* scored a direct hit in the side of Swede's boat. Then, wincing from the pain of the impact, Ken jammed the boat into reverse and backed out of the injured craft.

"Looks good... looks good..." Alan said. "Stand by with the lifeboats. Okay! Cut! That's a wrap for tonight!"

Thank God. Ken was in a lot of pain, and I wanted him to get back to the room so he could rest.

The next night, we worked on the scenes on the *Filomena* with Aunt Celly and the suitors, and the ones with McTish, Pooch, and me. Eventually, we crammed all the shots in. Ken worked through them all without complaint.

When we finished shooting, he and I stayed on at the Hotel Del for a few days, and as promised, I waited on him hand and foot. We opened the windows to the sea air, ordered room service, and luxuriated on the beach for hours every day.

"I could get used to this," he said.

"What a coincidence," I said, kissing him. "There's more where that came from."

MARIE AND KEN'S PLACE, *May 1925*

The phone woke me far into the night.

"Hello?" I pulled up my eyeshade and flicked on the bedside lamp to see that it was a few minutes after one a.m.

My recent shooting schedule had been brutal. I'd finished up *Kiss Me Again* with Mr. Lubitsch, and all that entailed. We'd developed a comfortable working relationship, but he was still the same exacting director, calling for obscene numbers of takes. If not from me, then from Monte or Clara Bow, once again worrying me in a role that had the potential to upstage me.

Now, I'd started *Wanted by the Police* with Clive Brook. Ken had stayed late at the lot working on *The Marriage Whirl* with Corinne Griffith, and I'd fallen into an exhausted sleep after a quick dinner. I'd been out for hours when the phone jarred me out of a dream of Ken and I on a beach in Hawaii.

"Hello, darling! It's me!"

"Ken? What is it? What's wrong?" I was instantly awake.

"Nothing. I'm still at the studio. I wanted to let you know so you wouldn't worry."

"I wasn't worrying. I was asleep," I mumbled.

"Sorry about that," he said.

"It's midnight. You're working too hard," I said sleepily. "Be careful of your rib."

"Shooting ran late. Alf wanted to get this scene perfect."

"All right. Is there anything else?"

"No...no...I'll be home soon. Goodnight, darling."

"Night," I said. I hung up the phone and pounded on my pillow to get it to its perfect shape, then lay back down, turning out the light.

I drifted off again, to a far different dream. Mum and Peg and I were on a train threading its way through the Rockies, and Frank was the engineer driving it. When we pulled into the next depot, Mum and Peg and I got out and he drove away. Every few hours, he'd come through town, pick us up, then drop us somewhere new. Relieved that he was gone, Mum pulled out a plate of shortbread and offered it to Peg and me.

"We won't have time," Peg observed. "The next train is coming. Hear it?"

The bell was insistent, and wouldn't stop ringing. So much that it yanked me out of my subconscious and back to reality. It was the phone again.

"Hello…"

"It's me, darling!" was the exuberant reply.

"Ken? What's wrong?"

"Nothing! I didn't want you worrying in case you'd woken up again. Several of us decided to go get a drink."

"Ken, the only thing that's waking me up is you. Where are you now?"

"The Red Rooster," he replied.

Great. A speak downtown.

"Fine. Don't get arrested, it'll make the papers. I have to go. I need my sleep, goodnight."

I was seething. I'd been telling Ken for weeks how nervous I was about my new role. The director, Lewis Milestone, was a gruff Russian, with an accent as thick as borscht.

I wasn't sure how I was supposed to take direction from the guy when I couldn't even understand him. I wanted to give him my best right off the bat, but I had no idea what he expected. Unfortunately, Mr. Milestone turned out to be nothing like Mr. Lubitsch. Where Mr. Lubitsch was courtly and polite, Milestone was curt and impatient. He didn't demand as many retakes, but he was harder to read.

"*Bozhe moy*," Milestone said when he saw me. "You look terrible. Vhat happened to you? You look like someone dropped a piano on you."

"I'm very sorry, Mr. Milestone," I said. "My husband was

late getting home last night. Very late. And kept calling to let me know he was going to be late."

"Zounds like Mizter Harlan need to be more zympathetic to his hardworking wife," he said.

"You're telling me."

Despite his manner, Milestone turned out to be a big softie. His gruffness was only put on to intimidate people. He was as easy to work with as Mr. Lubitsch had been difficult. At least for me. And that was good because Ken's late night phone calls were becoming regular enough to affect my health. I was tired all the time.

Sure enough, my worries over my performances were well-founded. None of my latest had done stunning box office. *Wanted By the Police* was released as *Seven Sinners*, and no one was sure if it was a mystery with funny parts, or a comedy with mysterious parts.

When Ken started *For Another Woman* with Mary for Rayart and had to travel to New York, I was thrilled because I'd finally get some sleep. But the minute he got back, the calls started again.

CHAPTER TWENTY~ONE

After we wrapped *Seven Sinners*, Mr. Milestone and I were both available, so we were rushed into *The Caveman*, a lightweight comedy about a socialite who began seeing a coal porter. She introduced him to her Park Avenue friends, but hilarious complications ensued, like his horse following him around town while the porter wore his monkey suit.

I nabbed every wink of sleep I could, even dozing in my chair between scenes. At home, I could usually expect at least one call in the wee hours, no matter how many times I told Ken to stop. In my latest dream, the phone rang and rang and rang, and when I picked it up, it kept ringing. I stared at it dumbly, unable to comprehend what was happening.

My consciousness finally jarred me awake. I fumbled for the telephone and the bedside lamp so I could see what time it was on the little clock next to the bed. Midnight this time.

"Hello?" My voice was hoarse and sluggish.

"Marie? It's me! I'm still at the studio, darling!"

Jesus. Not again.

I put the phone down without replying.

Knowing it would be hard to get back to sleep, I jammed my feet into my white marabou mules and stomped to the kitchen, where I gnashed my teeth and heated up a small saucepan of milk.

The dogs, asleep on their pillows in a corner of the kitchen, peeked eyes open to see what was going on.

"Relax, babies. Everything's fine. Mommy's up late, that's all."

When the milk was heated through, I poured it into a lowball glass then flicked the light off. The whiskey Ken had ordered from our bootlegger sat reassuringly on the bar, a balm for any ill. I poured in two fingers and gave it a stir with my finger, licking it for good measure. Then I took my cocktail into the bedroom and Jinx decided to join me by jumping up on the bed.

"All right, but only this once," I said. Ken hated it when the dogs got on the bed, but I spoiled them when he wasn't around. Jinx grunted as I petted her belly. Not wanting to be ignored, Pooch and Gaucy joined her. With the other hand I finished my drink, then picked up my copy of *So Big* and propped myself up with pillows. I must have drowsed off with the light on. The next thing I remember was the jingling of the phone again. A glance at the alarm clock said it was now one a.m. Right on schedule.

"What?" my voice sounded raspy.

"We must have had a bad connection before!" Ken shouted over the noise of traffic. "I'm at a phone booth outside the Red Rooster! I didn't want you worrying!"

"I wasn't worrying, Ken. I was asleep! And we didn't have a bad connection. I hung up on you!"

"Well, that's a fine how-do-you-do! Why you so sore?"

"Ken, I love you. You know that. But you keep telling me

you're coming home, and then you don't! You can't keep calling me to give me updates. I have to be on the set at seven!"

"I'm sorry, darling. I only came in for a little belt! Then I ran into Warren and Irene. They asked about you!"

"Terrific," I said, trying to keep the sarcasm out of my voice. "Are you coming home now?"

"I'm not sure. The band's revving up, and I'm a little ossified."

As if I couldn't tell that.

"Do me a favor, please. Come home. And use your key to open the door quietly. I have to get some sleep."

"All right. I love you. You know that?"

"Yes, I know," I said. "But don't call again unless you're at the hospital." When I hung up, I flicked off the light and buried myself under the covers with Pooch, Gaucy, and Jinx tucked against my leg. I didn't know anything else until I'd been asleep for hours and felt an arm slide around me in the dark, then boozy breath in my ear and an insistent erection against my back.

"Ken, no," I said, swatting away his hand.

"Come on, honey. I missed you."

"No. Bank's closed."

"Marie..." he pleaded.

"I'm sleeping!" I spat out, even though it was obvious that I wasn't anymore.

"You used to love early morning nooky," he said, pouting. He made a test grab for a breast and I smacked it away.

"I asked you to come in quietly since you already woke me up twice last night. I'm exhausted. So mitts off until I'm better rested!" I yelled. I took a pillow and the blanket draped over the foot of the bed and stomped off to sleep on the couch. Jinx joined me, squeezing in by my side, with Pooch and Gaucy on the floor nudging my hand for pets. I stewed until I finally dropped off again.

"Miss Marie, it's five a.m.," said a voice. I reluctantly opened my eyes to the tangerine-tinted eastern sky visible through the living room drapes. Delilah stood over me, doing her best to be gentle.

I came to slowly, stretching my arms and legs, which had cramped up being in the same position for two hours.

"I'm runnin' the shower for you," she said. She glanced at me with a confused expression, no doubt wondering why I was out here while Ken was in our room. "Breakfast be ready in a jiffy."

"Thank you, Delilah," I said, pulling off the blanket. "Only coffee and a hard-boiled egg for me, please. I need to get to the studio."

"Yes, ma'am. Any breakfast for Mist' Ken?"

"I have no idea. I have a feeling he'll be sleeping until noon or so."

I peeked into the bedroom, and sure enough, he was down to his boxer shorts, his head thrown back, snoring as loud as a V8 Auburn Brougham.

After my shower, Delilah served me my egg and coffee and I headed to the studio. It was a relief when Ken traveled to Oregon a week later to work on *The Ice Storm*. Once again, I'd be able to sleep through the night.

JACK WARNER'S OFFICE, WARNER BROTHERS STUDIO
November 1925

"Thanks for coming up, Marie," Jack Warner said, gesturing to a chair.

"I couldn't imagine what this was about," I said, unsure why I was there. His face was unreadable.

He sighed. "You know the receipts for *Seven Sinners* haven't been that great."

"Yes, I know, but Mr. Milestone and I work very well together. And *The Caveman* has a lot of potential. Now that Phyllis is working here too..."

"...And as much as we spent on *Bobbed Hair*—with the salaries, the train wreck, the boat crashes—it didn't earn that much back," he continued.

"The wreck was an unfortunate accident. We both know that. You're not blaming the performance of the film on that, are you?"

"It happened, and it cut into profits. That's all I'm saying," he replied. "There was also the downtime because of it and because of Ken's rib."

"That fall could have killed him," I said angrily. "We're lucky it was only a broken rib. And my films with Mr. Lubitsch have *all* made you money."

"That's true, but Mr. Lubitsch's schedule is already filling up for the new year, and you're not assigned to any of those films."

"Yet. I'm not assigned any of those films *yet*," I corrected him.

"Before your work with Mr. Lubitsch, the returns for

Recompense were also disappointing. Even *The Beautiful and Damned*..."

"*The Beautiful and Damned* broke records, Mr. Warner. In San Francisco, people were lined up down Market Street to Turk. Four deep!"

"The author hated it."

"And that's my fault?"

"Not singlehandedly."

"I'm proud of my contribution," I said. "Ken is too."

"But that brings me to the reason for our conversation."

Then it dawned on me.

"You're firing me?" I said, incredulous. "You can't do that! I have a signed contract. You can't end it any time you want."

"I'm not firing you," he said. "Not in so many words. I'd like to see if we could come to some kind of arrangement about your contract."

"What kind of arrangement?" I said, raising an eyebrow.

"The wolf is at the door, Marie. I told you. Small potatoes. You can't tell me you haven't seen Henry Blanke taking equipment home at night to keep the creditors from seizing it. Half your checks have been coupons because we didn't have enough to pay you until we got the cash from ticket sales."

I stayed quiet.

"We have to do that to keep the doors open. If our films don't make money, we don't stay in business. Unfortunately, your flapper pictures aren't doing that well for us. We're going for more realistic drama than what you're known for. I'm offering you a convenient out."

"Or what?" I said, crossing my arms.

"Or I tell the world you've become undependable, and we

were forced to fire you."

"You're kidding," I said, beginning to panic.

"I never kid about money," he said.

"How is this different than firing me?"

"It's a much different announcement. We both came to the realization that you weren't happy working here, and we weren't happy with the performance of your pictures. We're agreeing to end the contract amicably, giving you a small pay-out, and keeping both of our options open. That way, if we do happen to run across a part that's perfect for you later, we can always invite you back."

"And if I hire a lawyer to fight this?"

"We have lawyers too," he said. "And they can make mince-meat out of that contract. Plus, the publicity would give you such a black eye, it would kill your career for good. Your choice."

I sat there glaring at him. He calmly looked back.

"Sam's working on something huge for us, and I need to get rid of the dead weight around here," he said.

"Dead weight?! How dare you."

"I won't apologize to you for doing something that could save this studio," he said. "That's my best offer." He sat back in his black leather chair and watched me.

"So take the offer, get a little coin and a nice referral. Don't take it, or get a lawyer to fight it, and I get…"

"*Bupkis*. Or worse than *bupkis*. You'll be out all that mon-ey for lawyers' fees, and we'll blackball you in this town. No studio head worth his salt will hire you. Even as an extra."

"Are my movies that bad?" I asked, suddenly near tears.

"No," he said. "But they're bad for us. That's the difference.

It's business. That's all this is."

The room got very quiet as I considered. Hire a lawyer to fight for this job? Stay at a studio where I was no longer wanted? I could only imagine the lousy choice of parts I'd be getting that way. Or go quietly with my parting gift and smile like it was a fancy bouquet instead of the silver-plated turd it was in reality.

I went with option #2.

"All right, fine. What do I sign?"

He passed it to me, and I signed. Then threw the pen across the desk at him and stalked out.

A week later, the trades announced that Warner Brothers and I had parted by mutual agreement.

CHAPTER TWENTY-TWO

December 1925

Dear Marie, the letter read.

So good to hear from you. Mary and I are in New York. I'm doing better these days, but Mary isn't, unfortunately. Poor dear got a case of malaria, if you can believe that. While she was working on Down Upon the Swanee River *in Florida. I thought people only got malaria in the Belgian Congo or tootling down the Amazon on a riverboat. The doctor is dosing her with oodles of quinine, but she's fighting off chills like she's at the North Pole with no igloo.*

Thankfully she's in the big city now so she can get better treatment than those Podunk doctors gave her. I've wired her mother to meet us here. Throw the poor girl a prayer if you think about it. I feel rotten for her.

Love and kisses,
Wah

I hoped Mary's Mormon savior would recognize my humble Presbyterian prayers. Ken was still at the studio, filming *The Fighting Edge* with Patsy Ruth Miller. So I sat down and scribbled a quick letter back to Wah before bed and the inevitable early morning phone calls. I had a big meeting with a friend of Al Christie's in the morning. He said the guy was interested in signing me, so I needed my beauty sleep.

The next day, Al's secretary, Irma, buzzed me into his office, where both men were already smoking cigars and having a chat.

"Miss Prevost," the stranger said, holding out his hand. "It's an honor to meet you. I love your work. I'm William Sistrom."

Sistrom was a handsome fellow, with dark hair combed to the side, dark eyes, big ears, and a British accent. I smiled at him, but also looked to Al for a little guidance.

"Bill is the general manager at Metropolitan Pictures," Al said.

"And DeMille Pictures," Sistrom added. "Since Al's company and mine are both being distributed by PDC, he suggested I talk to you. We at Metropolitan are very impressed with your previous work, especially your roles for Mr. Lubitsch. So impressed that we're prepared to offer you a contract. No screen test."

"They're Hodkinson's old outfit with a new name," Al said by way of explanation.

DeMille? I thought. *What woman in her right mind wouldn't jump at this opportunity?*

But it wouldn't do to look too eager. We chatted a little, then I got down to brass tacks.

"What type of salary are we talking about here, Mr. Sistrom?"

He pulled out their standard contract, filled in a few of the blanks, and passed it over to me. I read the high points—like the $2500 a week, $1000 more than Warner's—and skimmed the others.

Mr. Sistrom and Al watched me expectantly. I deliberated, then signed in my loose scrawl and passed it back. Sistrom signed and we shook. Al looked proud that it was all done under his watchful eye, and we opted for lunch at Musso & Frank to seal the deal. Over rarebit, jellied consommé and shrimp sauce poulette, we chatted about properties in progress and the possibilities he was imagining for me. Sistrom even picked up the check.

That night, while Ken was again shooting late, I invited Vera and Mum over to celebrate. Delilah prepared a crown roast, jacket potatoes, and Wee Mae's Dundee cake, which Mum had showed her how to make.

"Marie, what's the blue ribbon for?" Vera asked, seeing the new display on the wall when she arrived.

"That," I said proudly. "Is Jinx's latest Best in Breed ribbon from the Pasadena Dog Show. And we're entered at the one in San Diego on the fourth."

"Ah told you she was a champion," Mum said, looking over proudly. "Aren't ye, dug?"

Jinx sat delicately, waiting for a pat on the head, then let out a mighty belch, which sent us into peals of laughter.

Over dinner, we chatted about plans for the new year. My plans were contingent on the roles that Mr. Sistrom planned for me.

"I'm going to Miami to race my boat in the Biscayne Bay Boat Races," Vera said proudly. "End of March."

"Vera, ah'd love to see ye race yer boat!" Mum said. "What's i' called again?"

"The *Baby Mine*," Vera said with a chuckle. "I need to get away for a while. Since the divorce, I've been a wreck. Mother's going to watch little Marie for me."

"Ye could say hello to Peg fer us," Mum mused.

After her divorce from Bert, and being fired from her job dancing at the Café Lafayette downtown, my sister had worked her connections and somehow nabbed a job with Ziegfeld at his new show, *Palm Beach Nights*, in Florida. She'd written us about it every chance she got, but she'd been spending all her spare time in rehearsals since they were opening in January. I was amazed she hadn't blown this opportunity yet.

"You know what, Hughie? You could come too!" Vera said. "Let's make a trip. You and me together. We could both visit Peg. You'd love Florida."

Mum clapped her hands. "What an adventure we can have! Tha's six or seven whole states away! Ah've traveled before, but ah've never been to Florida. You should come too, pet," she said, placing her hand over mine on the table.

"Oh, Mum, I can't. I wish I could. I won't be able to get away that long." Bastard that he was, Jack Warner was holding my last check until I did some follow-up work on *The Caveman*, and there was no telling what Sistrom would schedule.

"Should I book us on the Chief?" Vera said with a smile.

"We could drive," Mum said.

"Drive? But it's so far!" I said.

"Aye, it's far, bu' think of everythin' we'll be able to see along the way! The Grand Canyon, the Alamo, New Orleans, a state capitol or two. We'll hae plenty of time," Mum said. "Wi' all the moving we've done out west, there's still so much I've wanted to see and never had the chance!"

She and Vera giggled like two schoolgirls as they began planning their expedition. Several days later, Mum called me with even more good news.

"Vera spoke to Al Christie. He's coming with us as far as El Paso and meeting his brother there. Charles has been scouting locations in Texas. Won't that be nice?"

"This is shaping up to be quite a trip, Mum," I said.

"I've already started me packing," she announced. "But ah've no idea wha' to take! Wha' does one wear to a regatta?"

"A sailor suit," I teased her.

She let out a hearty laugh. "Ah should take some gifts to Peg. If ye think of anythin' yer sister needs, let me know."

What she always needs. Money.

As the date of their departure grew closer, I called Peg. I had to judge the best time since she worked the late shift and slept mornings.

"Operator, long distance, please. Florida. Palm Beach 9-1026."

"I'll ring you back when your call connects," she said.

Soon, the phone jingled.

"Hello?" Peg answered in a husky whisper. I pictured her in her silk pajamas, pulling up her eyeshade as she reached for the phone.

"Long-distance call from Los Angeleez..." the operator said.

"Peg, it's me, Marie. How are rehearsals going?"

"Fine. The tickets are going for $200, if you can believe that."

"Two-hundred? Do you get a Duesenberg with the ticket?"

"There's a gambling joint here—Bradley's. Fellas walk outta there plumb with cash. So Ziegfeld's trying to give 'em something to see. Top-notch talent, glamour, the works. Are you coming with Mum and Vera?"

"Sorry, but I can't get away," I said.

"That's too bad," she said. But her voice told a different story.

"Mum wants me to ask if you need anything," I said.

The line went quiet as she thought. "I can always use extra stockings. And you know what I'd love? Those little chocolate cream thingies from The Owl Drugstore. We don't have them here."

"We'll see how they make the trip. Don't blame Mum if they're completely melted."

"Oh, and Marie..." she began.

"Yes, Peg." I knew what was coming.

"I'm a little short this month," she said.

Of course you are.

"I'll give her a check for you," I said.

"Thanks, sis. You're swell."

CHAPTER TWENTY~THREE

KEN AND MARIE'S PLACE

December 22, 1925

"Ken wrote and told me he had his first encounter with a rattlesnake," Rita said.

"Sounds like a couple of studio heads I know," I said.

Mum's laugh trilled across the dining room, and Rita stood at the bar, having poured herself three fingers of some Bushmills Ken had gotten hold of.

"Well, thank goodness my darling boy is all right," Rita said indignantly.

Although I was tired and not feeling my best, I was hosting early Christmas dinner at our house, even though Ken himself was in Arizona working on *The Golden Strain*. My side had been aching for a day or two, but I wanted friends and family to have somewhere nice to go. Vera and little Marie were there, and Rita was in town from New York, so I didn't want her spending Christmas alone. Although she kept goading me with tales of visits with Flo, Ken's ex. I kept a smile glued to my face and tried to make the evening festive.

Ken had telegraphed me often, letting me know of his first

glimpse of roadrunners and kangaroo rats. He'd reassured me the snake hadn't been that close, and that one of the hands had taken care of it with a well-aimed shotgun.

"Delilah, that's the handsomest bird ah'v ever seen!" Mum declared, as Delilah presented the turkey and set the platter down on the dining table. It was trussed, burnished, and glistening gold. Delilah beamed at Mum then bustled back and forth with side dishes. Mum had shown her how to make Wee Mae's cock-a-leekie soup, and also how to make neeps and tatties and dressing with chestnuts the way I liked them.

Vera cut everything on little Marie's plate into tiny pieces, and as we were ready to dip our spoons into the soup, the doorbell rang. Delilah waddled to the door and answered it as we took our first sips.

"Miss Marie, telegram," she said. "Western Union here."

I wiped my lips and rushed to the door, expecting to have a message from Ken. Hopefully, he was still avoiding snakes. The messenger boy stood on the front porch clad in his military style uniform, jodhpurs tucked into black boots, bag across his shoulder.

"Telegram for Marie Prevost," he said. "It's an honor, ma'am." He lifted his little pillbox hat and smiled through buck teeth. "Sign here, please."

I smiled back and signed, then he handed me the message and rushed down the front walk to his motorcycle parked at the curb. After he putted away, I read it and gasped.

WESTERN UNION TELEGRAM

MARIE STOP MALARIA GOT WORSE THEN TURNED TO

PNEUM STOP MARY DEAD STOP HER MOTHER SHIP-
PING BODY TO UTAH STOP FUNERAL PLANNED FOR
29th STOP LOVE AND SADNESS STOP WAH

"Oh, no. It can't be true. It can't," I said, slumping against the wall with my hand over my mouth.

"What is it?" Mum said. She got up from the table and came to my side.

"It's Mary. She's dead," I said, holding out the wire.

Vera moaned. "Mary? Oh, no...no..."

"What's wrong, Mommy?" Little Marie said, looking up from her soup with alarm.

"It's Auntie Mary," Vera said with tears in her eyes. "She's gone to heaven."

"Like Frances?" Little Marie said.

"Yes, like Frances."

Mum mouthed a short prayer. "Mary Thurman," she explained to Rita. "Delightful lass. Used to work at Sennett with Marie and Vera."

Rita clucked her tongue and shook her head. "Poor dear," she said.

It seemed impossible that the beam of sunlight we'd all known and loved had ceased to shine. Mary had been so much fun–so vibrant and full of life.

"I don't feel well," I said, and slumped to the floor.

"Marie..." Mum said. Her voice faded in and out. "Delilah, call the hospital! We must have an ambulance!"

I remembered Mum's worried face, and the attendants lifting me into the back of the vehicle, but nothing after that. When I came to, everything was white—my pale hand against an even whiter sheet, white walls, and white ceiling with an incredibly bright disc of light from the fixture above me. I glanced to the side. Mum dozed in the chair. I tried to pull myself to a sitting position to look around, but it was impossible. A stitched-up wound in my middle pulled painfully when I tried.

"Ow," I murmured.

Mum woke then, and looked at me with relief.

"Oh, pet. I was so worried."

"What happened?" I asked, still woozy from the ether.

"A wee cyst on your ovary, the doctor said. But it wasnae as small as they thought. They had tae remove it and the tube."

I may never have children.

I frowned, still trying to find a comfortable position somewhere between lying down and sitting up. Most importantly, I tried not to cry. "What day is it?" I said.

"The fourth," Mum said.

I shook my head, trying to wrap my head around the number. "The fourth? Of January?"

"Aye." She pulled the chair closer to the bed and took my hand. And then it all came rushing back. Christmas dinner. The telegram. Mary. The dog show I was supposed to be attending today.

"Mary's funeral. I missed it, didn't I? Oh, God, what a terrible friend I am," I said, succumbing to tears.

"Pet, ye've been in and out of consciousness for two weeks. They had to knock you out so you wouldnae bust yer stitches. You kept tryin' to leave the hospital. Vera went to the service for both of ye. Mary knew ye loved her."

"Has anyone heard more from Wah?"

"Vera wired an' said she's in a state, the poor dear. But tha's to be expected."

"I'm not sure I can ever forgive myself," I said.

"Stop it. This wasnae yer fault. It wasn't." Mum said. "Guilt is a useless emotion. Only Catholics can do it properly."

"Is Ken back yet?"

"Aye, I called him to come home after ye collapsed. He was here for a few hours before me. He went home to get some rest before shooting. He starts *The Sap* tomorrow."

"Oh, yes. Now I remember. And when do you and Vera and Al leave for Florida?"

"No' till the end of the month. But I'm no' goin' anywhere until ye're up and able to do for yerself, my lass. Trip or no trip, someone must care for you until then."

"Delilah takes good care of me," I said.

"Ah cared for you long before she did, and ah plan on continuing that, if ye don't mind," she said with a sarcastic smile. She reached behind me to plump up the pillow.

I winced as I finally found an angle to sit that wouldn't tug at my stitches.

"Are ye in a lot of pain, pet? Shall ah call the nurse?" she asked as she sat back down.

"No. You're here. That's all that matters," I said.

"Here's somethin' ye might like to see," she said, handing me a magazine folded open to the middle. "Vera brought this by last night during her visit. The new *Film Daily* announcing your deal with Metropolitan. Even though they know ye're stuck here for a while longer, they're publicizing it. Good to see."

"Are you getting excited about your trip?" I asked, leaning

back into the plumped pillows.

"Aye! Vera's even hired a chauffeur. Yer ole mum will be living in the lap of luxury with a posh driver, sitting in the back, eating caviar, and drinking champagne."

"Mum you hate champagne," I said with a laugh, wincing when I realized how painful it was.

"That's fer show," she said. "No self-respecting Scotswoman would drink champagne when there's a bottle of brown plaid nearby. But ah do like the way it tickles me nose."

"I wish I could go with you," I said. I didn't want to see Peg, but spending a trip laughing with Mum, Vera, and Al would have been a kick.

"Ah know, wee girl. Ah'll be back in no time. Don't ye worry," she said. She leaned over and kissed my forehead. And for the next few weeks, she proceeded to spoil me rotten. I was still weak from the surgery, but I'd bounced back more every day.

The night before Mum was to leave, I went and spent the night at her place so I could help her pack. On the first, Vera and Al arrived in Vera's Lincoln Phaeton, driven by a chauffeur Vera introduced as Mr. Todd. Mum approached the car with a wave.

"All right, Hughie," Al said, leaning out the front passenger window. "I have whatever you need right here. Cards, dime novels, and even a pillow for sacking out in those monotonous desert states. I can wake you up for the good parts."

"Ah couldn't ask for a better travel mate than that," Mum said. She laughed merrily as Mr. Todd attached her trunk to the rear rack, then she turned to me. "Goodbye, wee girl. I'll see you when I get back." She folded me in a big hug. "Mind yer tummy, and don't strain yerself. Get Delilah to do things for ye. Mum's orders."

"Bye, Mum."

She crawled in the backseat with Vera, and we quickly clasped hands through the open window before Mr. Todd pulled out of the driveway.

"Have a wonderful time!" I called. I waved until they were out of sight.

KEN AND MARIE'S HOUSE
February 5, 1926

Four days later, I'd gone to bed earlier than usual, after making myself a toddy and reading *Manhattan Transfer*. Ken had started *The Ice Flood* with Viola Dana for Universal, so the house was quiet, and the dogs had tucked themselves around me. Ever since I'd come home from the hospital, they'd been glued to my side. It must have been after midnight when the phone rang.

I felt for the receiver and picked it up, my head still muddled from sleep. I figured it was Ken with one of his drunken updates, momentarily forgetting he was away. I didn't even bother turning on the light for these anymore.

"Long distance from Lordsburg, New Mexico..." the operator said. The phone clicked several times.

"Marie, it's Vera."

"Vera!" I said, pulling myself to a sitting position. I tugged up my eyeshade and flicked on the light. "How are you? I figured you'd be in El Paso by now."

There was a long silence, and then a sigh. "Marie, something awful's happened."

CHAPTER TWENTY~FOUR

I sat straight up. Pooch opened a cautious eye and Jinx and Gaucy stirred next to me.

"What is it? Are you all right?" A note of fear crept into my voice.

She paused, and her voice cracked as she spoke. "There was an accident with the car," she said. And then her voice broke over the worst of the news. "It's Hughie, Marie. She's dead."

Vera kept talking, but it was only a buzz in my ears.

"No..." I moaned. "Oh no....no, no, no....please no..." My head swam, and I realized that keening noise was my own voice.

"We were driving through the desert, having a marvelous time," Vera continued. "One minute, we were singing songs and having a laugh, and the next, we were careening across the road. A rear wheel came off, and we flipped. Al and I were trapped underneath the car until someone happened by, and the passerby and Mr. Todd were able to lift it off us. We're both cut all to hell, but we'll be all right. We had to flag down a car on its way to Lordsburg since we were twenty miles outside town. Hughie got the worst of it. Her back was broken. We tried to keep her alive until an ambulance could get there, but it took so unbearably long. I'm sorry, Marie. I'm so sorry." She dissolved in tears.

If I opened my eyes, maybe I could make this distorted nightmare end. But my eyes were already open. This was real. There was no waking from it.

"Is Ken there with you?" Vera asked, pulling herself together.

"Still up in Oregon," I whispered.

"Try to get him home as soon as you can. He needs to be with you. Can you call him?" she said.

"Huh?" I was in a daze. I couldn't seem to put thoughts or words together.

"Do you want me to call him for you?" she said. When I didn't answer, she repeated herself. "Marie? Do you want me to call Ken?"

"Ken? No...I'll call him..."

"I'll call Peg, all right? She was already expecting a call from me anyway."

"Okay." My mouth was having problems forming words, let alone saying them.

"Marie, don't you worry about anything. Al's already contacted Mr. Sistrom at Metropolitan. They know not to expect you in. We'll get Hughie home to you on the train. I know Mr. Fitch at Fitch and Company. I'll call him and let him know what's happened. We'll be back there as soon as we can. You were so good to me when Frances died. I won't let you go through this alone. Can someone come and stay with you until I get there? Maybe Phyl or Irene?"

"Sure..." I whispered. I was so tired. So very tired. "I have to go, Vera..." I put the phone back on the switchhook and sat down in a daze. Jinx, always a little bolder than the others, gave my nose a tentative lick as if to say, "Chin up. It's not as bad as all that."

That sweet gesture caused everything to burst forth, overwhelming me. I lay down with my legs tucked up to my chest and cried. Scenes from our life together passed through my head—innumerable train rides curled up on a seat with my head in Mum's lap, the softness of her arms, the delicate scent of lily-of-the-valley that she loved, and her always making the best of a bad situation, laughing despite it all. Now I'd never feel her embrace again. All I could do was sob. The dogs whimpered against me, not understanding my sorrow or the awful noises I was making. They looked at me with their deep soulful eyes, like they were hurting too. They never seemed to know what to do with themselves when someone else was in pain. Every so often, one of them would give my nose another lick. Eventually, I drifted off to an exhausted but fitful sleep.

I came to right before dawn. The house was silent. I lay there for an hour or so, trying to find the will to get up or even to move. I was completely immobile. My stomach groaned, but the thought of food made me sick. Over and over in my head, I saw the Phaeton skidding, then flipping across that sandy desert road. Why hadn't I gone with them? What were Mum's final thoughts? Was she thinking of Peg and me? Of my father? Or was she too frightened to even understand what was happening? How much pain had she been in? I was afraid to imagine that.

I should have told Jack Warner to stuff it. It all seemed so pointless. Peg or no Peg, I should have been in that car. I should have been there to comfort her in her last moments. I wasn't sure I could ever forgive myself for choosing work over being with her before she left this earth. She'd told me guilt was a useless emotion, but I couldn't help feeling bushels of it.

I closed my eyes, trying to see her face as I always had before—laughing, singing, and joking, even after all she'd been through in her life. Now it was twisted in pain and fear, and spattered with blood.

I sobbed into my pillow even more than I had the night before until my throat and chest hurt. My sinuses ached and drained like I was drowning. At last, I dropped off again out of exhaustion.

"Miss Marie?" Delilah said. She peeked in, her dark face curious. "D'you need to be at the studio today?"

I slowly came to, a little at a time. My face had that dried out, exhausted feeling that crying gave it—the skin stretched uncomfortably over the bone. I must have looked a fright because she recoiled when she saw me.

"No studio..." I mumbled. I was cold, so cold, and Mum was gone. I had to call Peg. Or had Vera said she would do that? Yes. That was it. It was Ken I needed to call. I couldn't do this all alone. I had to think. "Delilah, could you bring me some tea?" I whispered.

She nodded and retreated to the kitchen with a worried look on her face. I clutched the phone.

"Operator, long distance, please. Klamath Falls, Oregon. The Earley Hotel."

"Yes, ma'am. I'll ring you back when your call connects."

It took a few minutes, but the connection was finally made.

"Earley Hotel."

"Hello, I'm calling long distance for Mr. Barney Google," I said, asking for the alias Ken used when he traveled. Could I leave a message please?"

"Of course, madam. What is the message?" the clerk asked.

"Please tell him to call home as soon as possible. Mark it urgent. This is his wife."

"Certainly. We'll give it to him as quickly as we can."

"Thank you," I said, hanging up.

"Miss Marie?" Delilah stood in the doorway. "I brought your tea."

I pulled myself to a sitting position, trying to dry the tears that had started pooling again. "Thank you," I said hoarsely.

I made room on the nightstand for the cup and saucer, and she set it down and stood there, waiting for me to tell her what was wrong. I didn't even recognize the croak that came out.

"Delilah, Vera called last night. They were in a car accident in New Mexico." I said. "My mother is dead." The words felt foreign and wrong, like poison in my mouth.

She sat down next to me on the mattress, her face a mask of sadness. "Oh Miss Marie, no. Not Miss Hughie." She cupped her hand over her mouth, and tears sprang to her eyes too. That was when the dam burst again. I collapsed against her shoulder and didn't come up for air for I don't know how long. I couldn't catch my breath. Delilah cried with me, rubbing my back and hugging me. When the tears ebbed a little, she reached for the tea. She held the cup up for me and I sipped it gratefully. We shared a glance full of shared pain.

"Miss Marie, Miss Hughie surely was a special person. One of the nicest ladies I ever met. Always askin' how I was and carin' 'bout what I said. She never saw nobody's color. Only that they was human beins. I never met no one like Miss Hughie. Is they anything I can do to help?"

"Even your being here helps," I said, and patted her knee. "Thank you. I'd hate to be alone right now."

"I ain't goin' nowhere. I'ma tuck you in. You lie back and rest now, y'hear?"

She brought me more tea and aspirins throughout the day, ministering to the pounding headache that wouldn't relent. By late evening, I still hadn't heard from Ken.

"Delilah, could you please try Ken's hotel in Klamath Falls for me again?" I said. "He's at the Earley Hotel, under his usual name."

"I surely will, Miss Marie."

She used the phone in the upstairs hall, and the operator called back and connected her.

"Could you please leave anoth' message for Mist' Barney Google? We done had a death in the fambly, and he need to call home right away, please. Thank you."

The phone hook clicked again and Delilah lowered her voice.

"Miss Phyllis, this's Delilah, Miss Marie's maid. I don't mean to disturb you, ma'am, but Miss Marie ain't well a' t'all." She paused. "Her mama done died. Yes'm, Miss Hughie. If you could possibly come over, I'm sure she'd be most grateful. Thank you, ma'am."

She hung up the phone, then it rang again. The muffled conversation was hard to hear. Then Delilah's heavy waddle arrived back at the bedroom door.

"Miss Marie," she said. "I done left another message for

Mist' Ken, and I called Miss Phyllis. She say she be over short-
ly. Miss Vera called too. She say to let you know she and Mist'
Al are taking the first train they can get back to California.
And she called Miss Peg."

"Thank you, Delilah."

"You try and get some rest now. I'll bring Miss Phyllis up
when she get here."

I lay there in a daze until Phyl arrived. As usual, she tried
to help me remember the good times instead of dwelling on
the sadness that swallowed my soul right then.

"Here," she said, handing me a Whitman's sampler box full
of chocolates. "I thought this might cheer you up a little." She
tucked her leg beneath her and sat down on the bed next to
me.

I smiled and lifted the lid. A cashew cluster called to me,
so I popped it in my mouth, instantly feeling a little better as
the chocolate sweetness dissolved on my tongue. Phyl got me
chatting about Mum and our life together.

"Remember the time that you and Hughie went as Fat-
ty and Mabel to the Keystone costume party? And she wore
the bowler and the pillow under her shirt and the high waters
pants?" she said.

"And Roscoe said, 'Hughie, you can be my understudy!'" I
said with a wistful smile.

"Or..." she continued. "...that time she was so excited to try
that new cake recipe for your birthday and..."

"...mixed up the sugar and the salt..." I finished with a
chuckle.

"Or that time that Louise tried to show her the perfect
pie-throwing technique, and she hit Mack square in the face?"

"I'd forgotten about that," I said with a sad chuckle. "I'm so lost without her, Phyl. There's so much she'll never get to see...I can't even think of it. It breaks my heart. She was so full of love...to have lived through all she did..." I almost said, "with Frank," but stopped myself. "...and to end up like this... so young..."

"She's still here with you," Phyllis said, placing her arm around my shoulder. "In fact," she said, looking up at the ceiling. "She's got the best seat in the house."

I smiled through my tears thinking of Mum in a heavenly cheering section. When I imagined her and Mary having a marvelous time in the afterlife, it lightened my mood. I took another chocolate—a coconut one this time. And then a molasses chew. Phyllis helped with one or two. Soon they were all gone. I looked down at the box regretfully, then let loose with the full-blown waterworks again.

"Oh, honey, I'm so sorry," she said. "I'm so incredibly sorry." She held me as I cried. When I'd gotten more of the frenzy out of my system, she rose, went to the bathroom, and poured me a tumbler of water. Then she was back.

"Here," she said, reaching into her purse. She pulled out a pill bottle and emptied a few tablets into her palm. "Take this."

"What is it?"

"Phenobarbital. Doc gave me these when I wasn't sleeping a few months ago. I started feeling better, so I didn't finish them. You need them more than I do right now." She handed me the water and watched as I took the pills. "Now, please try to rest, sweetie."

"Ken's supposed to be calling me back. We left messages."

"Don't worry. I'll let him know what happened," she said.

"You need some sleep."

"If Vera or Al or Peg call..."

"I'll take care of everything, I promise." She continued to murmur comforting words and rubbed my back.

"Thanks, Phyl." We chatted for a few minutes until the drugs gave everything a fuzzy look, and my eyes wanted to close. I lay down and she pulled the covers over me.

"Come here, babies," she said, patting the counterpane. The terriers hopped up on the bed, tails wagging, and nestled in close to me. Phyl stroked my hair, and I petted the dogs as I drifted off.

"Delilah, will you help me keep an eye on her? I'm phoning her damned husband again and telling him to get home or at least call her. What the hell is wrong with him?"

That was the last thing I heard.

It took Phyl dispatching hotel staff to personally fetch Mr. Google to the phone and giving him a piece of her mind to get him back to California. But the damage was done. After barely communicating for two weeks, Ken finally arrived home on the Shasta route, almost three weeks after Mum's death.

"I'm sorry, honey," he said. "I am. But you can get a little hysterical about things, and I thought..."

"Hysterical?! My mother *died*, Ken! She was the best friend I had in the entire world. *I* called you, *our maid* called you, and *my best friend* called you. Repeatedly. Didn't you wonder if maybe this might be serious? I realize you have responsibilities, and couldn't leave the shoot, but do you think you might have been able to call and reassure me a little?"

He sighed. "I'm sorry. All right?"

I didn't answer. Instead, I reached over to the bar and

poured myself a whiskey. It gave everything the blurriness I needed to keep going so I could pretend all this wasn't real. And it gave me the strength to deal with my horrible guilt. I was such an unhinged mess that Metropolitan had to bring in Patsy Ruth Miller to take over for me in *When Girls Go Back Home*. Not the most auspicious start to my time there.

I arranged Mum's funeral service for February eleventh at Forest Lawn. Rita, Vera, Phyl, Monte, Mr. Sennett, Irene, and Al all sent flowers. Wah was still in mourning for Mary too, but sent a bouquet of purple orchids. And I bought Mum the most beautiful funeral wreath I could find, all in lily-of-the valley with pretty, deep blue ribbons and swatches of her familial Gunn and McDonald tartans. A quartet at the grave site played "Abide with Me," and I hired a singer who sang a heartbreaking Cockburn version of "Flowers of the Forest." There wasn't a dry eye. Ken couldn't be there with me because he'd had to go back to Oregon.

Peg came back from Florida for the burial but couldn't stay long. I gave her the check I'd originally sent with Mum, which had still been in her purse.

"Sorry, Marie. Flo doesn't offer bereavement leave, and I need the coin," she said as I handed it to her. "By the way, I called dad. He's been living at a rooming house in San Berdoo, spending his money."

"What money?" I asked. That $42,000 he'd lost still stung.

"That's the funny part. One of the mines actually paid off after Mum divorced him," she said.

"Swell."

When we were told the house on Camden was complete and ready to move in, I walked through the rooms and hallways, but they were empty and quiet. The planning that had given me such delight now brought me no joy. I wasn't sure if Ken and I could be happy there, and Mum was still gone.

CHAPTER TWENTY~FIVE

BROWN'S, HOLLYWOOD, CALIFORNIA
March 1926

"Help you, miss?" the soda jerk asked. He wore the usual white paper cap and red bow tie.

I deliberated. One wouldn't hurt.

I'd almost passed the ice cream parlor and its reassuring, overly sweet smell of cream and cold and chocolate. But then I stopped short and gazed in the window at the people inside— mothers and children having a cone, a couple cooing at each other over a banana split, and one or two stars trying to en- joy a non-alcoholic vice in a little peace—happy people. Phyl's chocolates had made me feel instantly better, and I needed that cheerful spark again. It would be a little treat, I told my- self. I'd been feeling so low since the funeral. Especially today.

Mum had died without a will, but thanks to a lifetime of her Scottish thrift and tidy record keeping, I could find no debts. And with very little to her name other than what I had shared with her, her estate would not be complicated. But it had taken a month for me to find the strength to go clean up the little apartment I'd rented for her. Vera helped me, and so did little Marie. We took a bunch of boxes for collecting everything.

I let Vera take care of the sentimental items I knew I couldn't bear to look at—family heirlooms, baby books, and photograph albums. I handled the practical items like dishes, linens, clothes, and the items from her dressing table, making a pile to keep and a pile to take to charity. I held it together until I got to the small glass bottle of eau de toilette that she'd loved. Then I fell apart again.

"I'm sorry," I said, when Vera came to check on me. "I thought I was better now."

She sat down on the floor next to me, and little Marie joined us. "You have nothing to apologize for," Vera said. "We all miss her. We do. You have a good cry if you need it." She held me as the tears came, and little Marie held my hand.

Now as I stood deliberating, all I wanted was to be happy like the people here.

"One hot fudge sundae, please," I said, taking a seat on one of the stools at the soda fountain.

"Hot fudge sundae, comin' right up!" the soda jerk said. He flipped his scoop into the air and caught it in a master piece of showmanship. A minute later, he presented me with a footed metal dish piled high with ice cream, fudge sauce, whipped cream, and a cherry. Alongside was a small glass pitcher of more fudge. "That'll be fifteen cents, miss."

I slid my coins across the counter and reached for the spoon. Then I took a bite and let it roll around in my mouth, savoring the sweetness as it swept over my tongue. Bite after bite, I lost myself in the lusciousness, and when I looked up, the dish was empty. All I could think of was how I'd be paying for it later. The buttons on my dresses would be harder to do up, or the wardrobe mistress might have to resort to a girdle to hold all of me in. I hurried out of Brown's and headed home to the house on Camden.

Ken was out when I arrived, but the dogs greeted me at the door. Plenty of nose licks and I wasn't in half as sad a place as I'd been before. But there was still something that needed doing.

"That you, Miss Marie?" Delilah called from the kitchen. "Have dinner ready in a jiffy."

"Thank you, Delilah!" I called.

I slipped into our elegant black and white tile bathroom, closed and locked the door, and stuck my finger down my throat. It produced the needed results. The sundae was only a memory in my gut, and I wouldn't need that girdle.

I flushed and rinsed my mouth, then turned as the phone rang. Delilah picked up the extension downstairs.

"Miss Marie, it's Mist' Al on the line!"

"Thanks! I'll take it up here!" I called. I picked up the candlestick phone next to the bed. "Al, hello. How are you?"

"I should be asking you that," he said. "I've been thinking of you all month, wondering how you are."

"Oh, you know. Coping." That was a lie. I wasn't doing well at all.

"I have a proposition for you," he said.

"What type of proposition?" I asked.

"A loan-out to me, thanks to Bill Sistrom."

"What do you have in mind?"

"Come see me at the studio tomorrow and I can show you the scenario. You need to get out a little."

I could continue to dwell in the horrific sadness, or I could go back to work and try to stop wallowing in it constantly. Mr. Sennett's words came back to me:

"Anybody can fall. But getting back up? That's where you see what people are made of."

"All right," I said. "When?"

"I'll see you in my office at 8 a.m."

When I got there, he welcomed me in, made sure I was comfortable, then let me know I was perfect for *Up in Mabel's Room*.

"I know you've been low since Hughie's death and the end of the Warner's contract," he said. "Since they had to replace you in *When Girls Go Back Home*, I figured you might be at loose ends. We added Phyllis to the cast too, so that should sweeten the deal."

Even the mention of Mum brought the familiar prickling of tears in my eyes again. I blinked them back. "Thanks for this, Al. I appreciate you trying to keep me distracted."

"It's the least I can do for you. I feel responsible. There was something horribly wrong with that car, and I didn't know. You have no idea how awful I feel."

"It's no one's fault," I said. "I've been torturing myself, feeling angry and sad and guilty at the same time, but I can't anymore. Let's talk about this scenario. Please."

He showed it to me, explaining some of the details, and we made it official.

Up in Mabel's Room had been a stage hit by Wilson Collison and Otto Harbach about a ditzy girl named Mabel, played by me, who met Garry, played by Harrison Ford, in Paris. After a whirlwind courtship, they got hitched in a hurry, and Mabel got miffed because she saw him buying lingerie and assumed it was for someone else. When she finally glimpsed the delicates, she saw they'd been embroidered 'To Mabel from Garry,' and determined to get him back after the divorce. Complications ensued, with Phyl playing the new interest in Garry's life.

Our director was E. Mason Hopper, and it was a fine shoot—despite the fact that I had to keep a full bar in my bungalow for before, during, and after shooting. With my trusty friend whiskey, curtain calls didn't seem to be so brutally early, and quitting time wasn't so awfully far away. Though I was sleepwalking through real life, I still managed to be animated on camera.

"How are you doing? You look tired." Al saw me coming out of my dressing room one day and asked with genuine concern.

"I don't sleep much," I said. "It's something I've learned to deal with."

"Is Ken any help to you?" he asked.

I let out a bitter chortle.

He definitely isn't that.

Al could see right away that the answer was no.

I was four times as tired, thanks to Ken and his ridiculous early morning phone calls.

"Can I help?" Al said.

"You've already done plenty," I reassured him. "Mabel's keeping the bills paid a little longer. Thank you, Al."

"If there's anything you ever need, please ask," he said.

"I'll be all right," I said. "Thank you for the offer. If there's anything I can't stand, it's pity. I'll be on top again soon. Bootstraps, you know?"

"I have no doubt," he said.

Mum's death did give me some perspective, even if it was a gloomy one. After *Up in Mabel's Room* wrapped, I decided to leave town for a while. Metropolitan was still trying to get casting done on *For Wives Only*, and I needed to get away from Ken before I killed him. Since he'd returned from Oregon, our bickering was out of control.

When I stopped by Christie's and mentioned the trip to Al in passing, he hooted like a barn owl. "Perfect!" he crowed happily. He slammed his palms on the desk in approval, making the framed photos on his desk jump.

"What is?" I said.

"We're premiering *Mabel* at the Strand in New York on June 27th. You can make a personal appearance while you're there! You wouldn't mind, would you?"

"Of course not," I said, hoping I could hold it together that long. "I'll buy a gorgeous new frock for the occasion. Who wouldn't love that?"

"Good girl," he said. "I'll let Charles know. He can meet you there and you can work out the details."

Delilah helped me put my trunks together and accompanied me. She was excited, never having seen New York before. We departed on the Gold Coast Limited bound for Chicago, but it rained for three days through the Midwest. Rivers had crested all over, but the Mississippi was the worst. I prayed none of the bridges were out. We reached Chicago safely, then took the Golden Arrow to New York, and arrived May 30. I had a cab take us to a suite at the Astor.

Four days after we arrived, Delilah and I were on our way to catch a cab to Bergdorf Goodman. As we passed the front desk, the desk clerk called out to us.

"Oh, Miss Prevost! Message for you."

We approached and he handed it to me. It was from Mr. Sistrom:

Cast locked in earlier than expected. Shooting date on For Wives Only *moved up. Need you back on coast as soon as possible. Sorry for any inconvenience. Sistrom*

Well, it was nice while it lasted. I'd had a few days of shopping and nice restaurants. Now it was back to work. And Ken. But I'd actually missed the big lug. Delilah and I arrived back at Los Angeles Central Station on June 10, to a crowd of reporters on the platform.

"Miss Prevost! Harold Beckham, *Orange County Reporter*. You were originally going to appear at the *Up in Mabel's Room* premiere in New York. What changed?"

"Production dates got moved up back here," I said. "It happens all the time."

"Were you eager to get back to Mr. Harlan?" another reporter called.

"Of course."

Ken approached right then with a mixed bouquet of lilies, carnations, and snapdragons, and gave me an affectionate kiss on the cheek for their benefit. Then he plucked a carnation out and jokingly handed it to Delilah. She let out her trademark chuckle. I nearly started crying again. This time, tears of happiness, as flashbulbs crackled from the photographers gathered there.

"All right, boys," Ken said. "I've missed my wife. That's all the questions for now." He pulled me close and laid a tender kiss on the top of my head. I inhaled the scent I'd missed so much—bay rum, hair tonic, and Kiwi shoe polish. I'd never seen him without a glossy spit shine on his black brogues.

"I missed you, darling," he said, smiling down at me.

"I missed you too," I said. "What'd you do while I was gone?"

"Started *Twinkletoes*," he said. "With Colleen Moore, the queen of close-ups. She's a giant pain in *my* ass."

We strolled out of the depot and into the bright sunshine. Eugene waited outside in the Rolls. He doffed his hat at me and smiled, then he and Ken got the trunks loaded, and we all piled in. We chatted on the way back to the house, and when we pulled up to the garage, Eugene went to take care of the trunks, and Delilah went to the kitchen to start supper.

As soon as we walked in the bedroom, Ken took me in a rough embrace.

"I missed you so much," he said again, mussing my hair and cupping a breast through the fabric of my dress. He kissed me hard. "It's been so long, Marie." He tasted of bootleg bourbon and peppermint drops.

"Make love to me, Ken."

He removed my silver fox coat and lay it across the expensive brocade coverlet. Then, he pulled off my pale pink picador crepe frock. Beneath it, I was wearing some pretty delicates I'd bought in New York along with the long string of pearls he'd bought me for our first anniversary.

"This is new," he said with a smile as he admired the silk chemise. Then he peeled it and my step-ins off and rolled down my stockings. I left the pearls on and lay back on the soft fur, shivering as I undid his belt and untucked his shirt.

He kissed me deeply and we lost ourselves as we hadn't in months. In those precious moments, we were in love again, we were close, and the rest of the world was far, far away.

When we lay together afterward, I lay my head on his chest and played with a dark coil of hair.

"We haven't had it easy lately, have we?" I said.

"No, we sure haven't," he said. He put one arm behind his head and pulled me close with the other.

"Between Mary and Mum going, and me losing my Warner's contract, I'm afraid I haven't been the best company," I admitted, nestling closer.

"We've both been distracted," he said.

"We need to care for each other and be newlyweds again," I said.

"I know a good place to start," he said, leaning over to kiss me again.

IF YOU DON'T
WANT MY PEACHES
(YOU BETTER STOP
SHAKIN MY TREE)

CHAPTER TWENTY~SIX

The pale discs of Klieg lights arced through the velvety blackness of the perfect Hollywood evening. In front of the theater, a line of limousines dropped off glamorous stars to walk the red carpet. First, Mary and Doug, Gloria Swanson and her marquis, Elinor Glyn in an outlandish wine-colored satin getup, then the guests of honor, Count and Countess Tolstoy. Gloria wore a long red Chanel dress with her hair in a twist styled low on her neck, and she was the one all the reporters wanted to see. The popping and hissing of the cameras were relentless.

Rod La Rocque arrived with his wife, Vilma Banky, who was wearing elegant cream silk enhanced with seed pearls. *Resurrection* was the latest big hit for Rod. It was taken from Tolstoy's story of a Russian peasant girl bedded and then deserted by a roué prince. Starring with Rod was a new actress who'd been getting more attention since she'd starred in *What Price Glory?* with

Edmund Lowe, Victor McLaglen, and Phyl. Her name was Dolores Del Rio, and she was a stunning Mexican woman with dark hair and deep, flashing eyes. I coveted her gown—a black velvet number with burnout designs of deep maroon flowers on the underskirt and a black lace mantilla.

Ken had worn his tux, and I'd chosen a cloth-of-gold frock, embroidered with jade thread, with tiny diamonds sewn into the hem. If only it had been as gorgeous on me as it had on the hanger. I felt like a lump of dough dressed up in cinnamon sugar. Still plump.

The hot fudge sundaes at Brown's and custard pie at the Brown Derby had made me feel better at the time, but I regretted them now. I wanted to be back to normal, but it was a balancing act that I was losing. The drinking and the rich foods I'd been eating had not been kind to me on screen. I had a hard time putting the brakes on and going back to salads. I'd also neglected my regular swimming regimen while working through my sadness. I felt like the world's biggest fraud.

I'd sleepwalked through *For Wives Only*, and by the time I plowed through *Almost a Lady* and moved onto *Getting Gertie's Garter*, my face was wider, my eyes were tired, and I was developing a paunch and double chin. But I couldn't seem to stop. My grief faded a little as time passed, but my thirst for booze had replaced it. By the time I got to *Night Bride*, I was sauced pretty much twenty-four hours a day. I gargled Listerine, eau de cologne, and whatever else might disguise my breath. But I was also self-conscious enough to begin buying lots of Doublemint gum.

After the casual nature of working with Al and his company, Metropolitan's methods were hard to get used to. Plus,

I was forced to do far more publicity appearances. It kept me away from home enough that Ken and I continued bickering. We alternated between tenderly making love and threatening each other with hurled insults or household objects. He flirted with other women right in front of me, and his late-night calls continued unrelenting. I loathed the sound of the phone ringing.

To anyone from the newspapers or the trades, we had the perfect marriage. Our friends never saw us quarrel in public. But at home, Delilah heard the yelling, the slammed doors, and the nasty barbs thrown back and forth. The dogs cowered or escaped to another room when we went at it. Delilah also had to clean up the aftermath of broken dishes and carpet stains. It was only a matter of time before we hit a tipping point.

Ken and I found our seats for the film, and he sipped from the flask he'd brought with him. I was in tears by the heartbreaking conclusion. First because of the story, but also because my flask was already empty.

When *Resurrection* was over and the audience stood in the lobby, newspapermen interviewed stars, and photographers took shots of the gathered celebrities. Ken and I posed for them, as we always did, but he was being louder and more obnoxious than usual. I put up a good front for the public, but the minute we got back in the Rolls, the gloves came off.

"Jesus. You smell like a distillery," I said as he moved in for a boozy kiss.

"I smell like one? It never bothered you before. And you're one to talk, honey," he said.

"Well, you weren't embarrassing me in front of all of

Hollywood before, *darling*."

He lit a Fatima. "I embarrassed you?" he slurred and laughed.

"You asked Tolstoy if he knew any places to get good vodka these days," I countered.

"I'll bet he does, though. That bohunk bastard has the biggest gin blossom I've ever seen."

"He had a cold, Ken. Didn't you see him pull out his handkerchief? He sneezed three times during the film!"

He shrugged. "Well, since we're pointing out foibles, it's my turn. The Listerine isn't working, Marie. Mother noticed it too last time she was here."

"How kind of your mother to constantly point out my faults. I'm still grieving my own mother, thanks." I said with a glare.

"Jesus, it's been a year since Hughie died. If I can smell it, and mother can smell it, so can producers, directors, and co-stars. Cut back on the cougar juice yourself or double up on the mouthwash."

When we pulled up in front of the house, Eugene opened the car door for us. Instead of waiting for Ken as I usually did, I got out first and stalked off toward the house. The minute I got inside I crossed to the bar and poured myself a drink.

"Give me one of those," he said. "Since it's your solution for everything these days. Hey, we're being out in the open about it, right?"

"At least I'm still working," I said. "How many movies of yours have they released this year? What's that, little bird? Oh yes. None."

"I'm working some deals," he said. "And I'm in better shape

than you."

"Better shape?" I spit out my next words. "I'm hanging on by my fingernails right now, Ken! But I still have to go to work and smile and laugh like everything is fine. I get no sleep thanks to you, and I honestly don't think you care. You're a free agent with no shooting schedule, so you insist on calling me multiple times a night and waking me up, even though I have to fight for every wink I get. Are you punishing me? I'm not sure what for. Frankly, I'm finding it very hard to be in love with you right now."

"Mother says I should have stayed with Flo," he said.

"Does she." It had been completely obvious since I met her that Rita Harlan didn't think I was good enough for her son. My bathing beauty past made that impossible. Never mind that Florence Hart had taken her clothes off for rich men at the Ziegfeld Follies. For some reason, her position carried more caché than mine.

"I'm tired and I'm going to bed. Are you coming?" he said.

"No," I said, pouring myself another.

"Suit yourself."

I fell asleep on the couch after a few more belts. The next morning, Delilah woke me. As I rose to shower, I saw a piece of paper on the coffee table. It was a page of the scenario from *Getting Gertie's Garter*.

GONE TO SANTA BARBARA. KEN

Gone to Santa Barbara for how long? Forever?

After a few days, he came back, looking sheepish. When he showed up, I was sitting near the pool, tossing a ball for the dogs. Pooch brought it back, coated in slimy dog spit, and set it in my hand. I recoiled a little, tossing it again, and Pooch growled as the back gate opened. Then all three terriers let out yips of delight when they saw it was Ken. He wore my favorite warm gray tweed suit—the one that brought out his eyes—and he stood by the sago palm holding his hat.

"She's getting pretty good at that," he observed.

"How was Santa Barbara?" I asked, not caring.

"Not bad. Pretty boring. You weren't there."

I gave him the most cynical look I could summon. "Did you come here to beat your gums or what?" I said.

"I'm sorry for the other night. I shouldn't have drunk so much."

"Me either, evidently. But I accept your apology. Thank you."

"That's it? Thank you?" he said, looking offended.

"What do you want me to say? You were the one who struck out for parts northwest. I honestly wasn't sure if I'd see you again."

"I'm here, aren't I?" he protested.

"Yes, but for how long?"

"For good, I hope. I want us to work. I want us to be happy."

"Well, it is part of the whole marriage contract. You know... 'til death us do part."

He sat down on the poolside recliner next to me, and the dogs gathered around. I continued to look down at the cement as he took my hand.

"I love you. You know I do. I don't understand why marriage has to be so hard."

"It doesn't. Marriage is a give and take situation, Ken. I

need a little more consideration from you right now. I wish I could make you understand. My mother and one of my good friends died within two months of each other. I'm not as young and pretty as I used to be. Even if I hadn't burned my bathing suits, I wouldn't be able to *fit* into them anymore. I'm *scared*, Ken."

He held my hand to his chest. "I get stupid when I drink, but I'm trying to do better. Can I come home please?"

"I don't know," I said, pulling it free. I was not going to make this easy for him. "Can you promise you won't call me late at night anymore? I mean it. I've told you to stop, and you haven't. I need my sleep. I need to know that you're behind me on this. And tell Rita to butt out. There are two people in this relationship—you and me. If you want to go back to Flo because Rita likes her better, the gate's right there. Use it."

"I don't want to use it. I want to stay."

"But *why* do you want to stay?"

"Because I love you," he said simply. "I don't want another divorce. I don't. I want us together and happy. I'm sure we can be. Let me show you."

I thought long and hard before I answered.

"This is serious, Ken. Don't blow it."

He leaned over and kissed me, and I dared to hope. For the first time in a long time, Ken was a changed man—sweet and considerate, leaving me nice notes in the morning before he left to drum up interest at the studios. He hadn't worked since he'd made *Easy Pickings* at First National back in January. He played golf with friends who had studio connections, and he brought me flowers at night. We enjoyed romantic dinners out again and made love regularly.

I tried to pare off the extra pounds, but it was hard when liquor and sweets were two of my weaknesses. I couldn't get over the feeling that Ken was judging me when he saw me naked. I told myself I was imagining it. He was my husband, he was home, and he was trying. I couldn't blame him for my own self-doubt.

Instead of eating, I swam laps in the pool, trying to remember what it felt like to be young and beautiful.

CAMDEN DRIVE HOUSE, BEVERLY HILLS, CALIFORNIA
May 19, 1927

This time, it was music that jarred me from a sound sleep. The tinny sounds of *Yes, We Have No Bananas* traveled up the stairs. I sat straight up, tugged off my eyeshade, and flicked on the bedside lamp. When I glanced over at the alarm clock, it was 2:37 a.m. The Grafonola had been fired up, and raucous shouts and cheers traveled up through the floor. I was exhausted from filming *The Azure Shore* at DeMille's Studio.

It sounded like Ken had brought his entire retinue from the Red Rooster with him, forgetting everything we'd talked about.

Groggily, I tugged the sheets aside, threw on a dressing gown, and trudged down the stairs, following the light coming from the parlor, where the merriment was underway.

Ken sat on one of the couches with a blonde on either side of him. Both wore bathing suits. Richard Dix sat on the facing couch, and a girl with dark hair and bee-stung lips sat in his lap. Hoot Gibson and another girl did the Charleston with wild abandon. I worried they'd kick over my Ming vase.

"Darling! You're up! Come have a drink with us!" Ken's voice was slurred. "This is Maisie, Helen, Geneva, and Dorothy."

"Hi, Marie!" Richard called, cuddling the brunette. She laughed, and so did her friends, like there was a hilarious joke I wasn't in on.

"Ken, it's two god-damned thirty in the morning. I have to be in Culver City in four hours!" I turned the volume knob on the Grafonola all the way down, then flicked it off.

"You said you wanted me home, honey," Ken said.

"Not if you're going to be this loud, I don't," I replied.

"We're having some fun, that's all!" He didn't realize it, but he'd started shouting.

"We've talked about this. I have a contract and I need my sleep," I said.

"What are you shooting this week, Marie? *The Flapper*? *The Flirt*? *Homewrecker's Blues*?" he teased.

I put my hand on my hip and glared at him.

"Do you get to do any swimming in this picture? Or do you just lay around in your bathing suit? Ladies and gentlemen, let me present my wife, the smick-smack girl! Hey Marie, remember when you used to look this good?"

He leaned over to nuzzle the prettiest blonde and listed so much he almost fell over a side table.

I blinked back hot tears, willing myself not to cry in front of the others and rushed from the room. The only reassuring thing I could think of was the flask I'd stashed in my sable hanging in the foyer closet. I slipped back upstairs with it, slamming the bedroom door as the Grafonola fired up again.

I crawled back in bed, gulped my prize, and did a lot of thinking. Eventually, the noise of the crowd and the phonograph faded. The next thing I knew, the sun was streaming in the window. My eyes felt glued shut, but I padded to the bathroom, took a bath, and brushed my teeth. And when I was done, I'd come to a decision.

Delilah fixed me a quick breakfast, then helped me pack. She hurried back and forth between the closets and my upright wardrobe trunks, gathering frocks and hats and underthings.

"Don't worry, Delilah," I said. "Ken simply needs to learn that he can't treat me like he did last night. He can't act any old way he wants to."

"Who can't act what way?" Ken said, appearing bleary-eyed at the door to my dressing room.

"Where are your friends?" I asked. "Asleep on the couches?"

"They left hours ago."

"Too bad. They could have kept you company."

Delilah handed me an armful of my furs—the ermine, sable, stone marten, and silver fox. I gently laid them on the bed to begin hanging them inside a trunk. She quietly stepped into the closet, giving us space to argue.

"Where are you going?" he asked.

"I'm leaving you," I said, fitting the stacked hat boxes into the niches in a trunk.

"Why, because of last night?"

"Yes, because of last night, and because of your trip to Santa Barbara, and because you were an insensitive ass when Mum died, and because of all the times you've woken me up multiple times a night to tell me you were coming home when you weren't."

"But that was—"

"I've told you I can't be up all night babysitting you or being the fifth wheel for your little parties downstairs. Last night, you were insulting and awful to me. In front of Richard and Hoot. Friends of ours!"

"We were zozzled, that's all. I didn't mean anything."

"Fine. Have all the parties you want without me. I need my sleep," I said.

"You can't leave. That's desertion," he said.

"Oh, that's right. You're an expert at this divorce thing now, aren't you? You can't claim desertion if I claim mental cruelty and alienation of affection first."

"With whom?"

"What do you suppose Maisie, Helen, Geneva or Dorothy would tell me about your other late nights out?"

He at least had the decency to look ashamed. Kind of like Gaucy, when he'd pooped on the silk Isfahan rug in the parlor that I'd paid $2,000 for. "They're only friends," he said.

"Banana oil," I replied.

Delilah returned from the closet. "That's all, Miss Marie."

"Thank you, Delilah."

She hovered, waiting for instructions.

"Delilah, I can still keep you as my personal maid, if you'd like to continue on, working downtown with me," I said.

"That's an easy choice, Miss Marie," she said. "I wouldn't leave you now."

"Good," I said with a smile. "Then I'll give you a chance to collect anything of yours you need to take with you."

She retreated to do that and I turned back to Ken.

"Don't leave," he said.

"I have to get my head together."

"Then get your head together. But do it here. You know what will happen if the papers pick this up."

"Yes. You might have to think about how you treat other people for a change," I said, flipping the locks on one of the steamer trunks. "I'm contacting the papers myself. The story should be out by tomorrow morning, if I have anything to say about it. I'll be at the Biltmore."

He stood there watching me, then turned on his heel and walked out. I got Eugene to help me with the trunks.

Never had such a fancy hotel room seemed so damned lonely. But after another day and a lot of deliberation, I decided to take the big step. Vera had recommended her attorney, Kimpton Ellis, of Ellis and Vickers, but their calendar was too full, they told me. They recommended Ralph W. Smith, a colleague of theirs. His office was also downtown, so that was my next stop.

CHAPTER TWENTY-SEVEN

OFFICE OF CHANDLER & SMITH, A.G. BARTLETT BUILDING, DOWNTOWN LOS ANGELES

July 15, 1927

If Ralph W. Smith hadn't been a lawyer, he could have been an actor. On the one hand, he was staid and well-spoken, with graying patrician hair. On the other, he appeared to have studied drama and knew how to use that spark to his advantage, which would be very useful in the courtroom.

"What you're saying then, is that I have no right to the house," Ken said.

"I chose the design," I said. "I commissioned it, I met with the architect, and I picked the furnishings and the colors. It's mine."

"You left," he said. He'd initially chosen not to dispute the divorce, but now he'd changed his tune.

"I couldn't look at you anymore. And I knew you wouldn't leave. Voluntarily anyway," I answered.

"All right, fine. Let her have the house," Ken said. We'd already given him two of the properties we owned, and I took the other.

"Duly noted," Ralph said. He scratched that onto the property agreement he was drafting.

"I'll get something nicer," Ken tossed off. "Besides, the bathing beauty needs a swimming pool."

"Let's move onto the cars, shall we?" Ralph said, attempting to change the subject. After some negotiation, I got the McFarlan and the Stutz, and Ken got the Lincoln, the Rolls, and the Packard.

"Of course, I'll have to change the photo in the hood ornament," he observed.

Ralph said nothing, but continued down his list. Delilah would stay working for me, and Ken retained Eugene as his chauffeur.

"Now for the antiques. The first thing on my list is the Ming vase, then the dining room breakfront," Ralph said.

"Give those to her. What do I need them for?" Ken said.

"Good. I plan on doing plenty of entertaining, so I'll need the breakfront for my dishes," I said.

"Then...the dishes? Ken? Any objections?" Ralph said.

"What do I care about dishes? I eat out all the time anyway."

"We know," I said, thinking of Maisie, Helen, Geneva and Dorothy. He glared at me. I smiled sweetly back.

"Next...the living room rug," Ralph said, trying to keep us on track.

"That's mine," Ken said. "I want it."

"But it's Aubusson," I argued. "We spent hundreds for it!"

"Exactly why I'm entitled to it. You're getting two houses, two cars, a Ming vase, an antique dining room piece, and the dishes in it," Ken said.

"Fine," I replied, wondering whether I'd ever find anything

with the same beautiful colors again. "Then I get the Isfahan in the parlor."

Ken shrugged. Ralph wrote it down.

"One pair of Battersea enamel candlesticks. Approximate value... a thousand dollars?" Ralph said. He looked shocked at the amount.

"They were pretty," I said. "...and they matched the rug."

"Then I'll take the candlesticks," Ken said. "They match the rug."

I seethed a little.

"What about the dogs?" Ralph said.

"I love the dogs," I said.

"So do I," Ken protested. "Since you show her, the obvious solution is for you to take Jinx and me to take Pooch. But that still leaves Gaucy."

"The only thing that's missing here is King Solomon," I said. It broke my heart, but I knew it was for the best. "You should take him so he can stay with his mother."

"Fine," he said.

We gradually got through everything, from the Hepplewhite tea table to the George III secretary bookcase, from the silver tea set to the Louis XIV bed and matching loveseat to my Duncan Phyfe dining room set. The gilt and ebony console tables went to me, and the Chippendale wingback chairs to Ken. Finally, we got up to leave. Ken followed Ralph and I out.

"You need anything else from me for a while?" Ken said, as we boarded the elevator down to the lobby.

"I don't think so. Why?"

"I'm finally going to Hawaii," he said. "Going to do all the stuff we said we were going to do."

"Must be nice. Some of us still have to work for a living," I said.

He made a noise somewhere between a chuckle and a snort. "I'll get a new contract soon. I figured I'd go while I have some leisure time."

The elevator doors opened. Ralph and I began walking away.

"Aloha," I said.

MALIBU, CALIFORNIA *Late July 1927*

The Hollywood crowd had all been flocking to Malibu, so I decided to join them. I leased a lot and had a weekend cottage built. It would help me escape my memories of Ken, and all the swimming and walking Jinx along the shore would keep me fit and far away from Brown's and temptation. I was over the moon, since DeMille had picked me for his latest, *Girl in the Pullman*, to be directed by Erle Kenton.

The house was finally finished in mid-July, so I took a free weekend, retrieved the key, and drove up to see it. It sat right on the beach among a little stand of other celebrity houses in the colony, to the north end. It was a gorgeous two-story stone cottage with pretty flower boxes on the windows overlooking the beach, and a small palm just outside the door. There was a rough-hewn fireplace on the north wall.

The floors were natural Mexican tile, and the walls were painted a color somewhere between cream and vanilla that fairly shimmered in the afternoon light reflecting off the

Pacific. It was especially beautiful at sunset, when the pinks and purples of dusk glowed through the windows facing the water.

For the kitchen, I'd chosen the latest in Westinghouse appliances, and picked cheerful sunshine yellow and bright royal blue for my dishes, canisters, and tea towels. Yellow because Ken hated it.

There were two bedrooms—one a larger master for me, a smaller one for guests, then a tidy little bathroom in black and white tile. I had lots of wall space with room for bookshelves and art.

As I investigated the amount of closet space I'd have and considered which pictures to hang in my bedroom, a cheery "Yoohoo!" came from the open door leading to the beach.

I peeked around the corner. There was Louise Fazenda waving to me from outside.

"Marie!" she squealed in delight.

"Louise! What are you doing here?" I asked. "Do you have a place in Malibu?"

"Hal and I are up for the weekend. The brown clapboard with the dark picket fence is mine. I've been waiting to see when someone would move into this place!"

"How is Hal these days?" I asked.

Louise's squeeze, Hal Wallis, worked in the publicity department at Warner's. Nice guy. A real go getter. I loved the fact that two of my good friends had fallen in love. Rumors had been flying over when they'd tie the knot.

"He's good. He's been running himself ragged working and driving back and forth to Burbank to keep an eye on things at First National since the merger. Warner's has something huge in the works that will really put them on the map.

If you thought *Don Juan* was wonderful, their new offering is coming out in the fall. It's going to be a real humdinger! I'm so glad you're here. This end of the beach will be so much livelier now."

"I decided to buy myself a divorce present," I said.

She frowned. "I'm sorry about you and Ken. You seemed so happy. But I suppose the rest of us only knew half the story, hmmm?"

I nodded.

"Now that you're here, I must throw a party to welcome you," she said. "I can introduce you around! Clara Bow, Wesley Ruggles, Buddy DeSylva, Allan Dwan, Jack Gilbert..."

"Clara and I worked together on *Daughters of Pleasure* and *Kiss Me Again*," I said, not voicing my uncertainty at Clara's staying power and my struggle to stay relevant. "A party sounds marvelous."

"I have to get going, since we're headed back into town," Louise said. "But I'm nosy. I simply had to come and spy on the new neighbors. I'll let you know when the party is but stop by anytime. You can borrow a cup of sugar. Or gin. Bye now!" She gave me a quick wink, then scampered to the parking pad out back where a sleek navy Packard sat parked next to my McFarlan. With Hal at the wheel, they waved as he pulled out and headed toward Coast Boulevard.

A few weeks later, Louise invited me over to meet my neighbors. She'd hired a caterer who'd supplied oysters Rockefeller, salmon mousse, stuffed mushroom caps, tiny meatballs on toothpicks, deviled eggs, spiced nuts, olives, table water crackers, and little tea sandwiches with the crusts elegantly trimmed off. They'd found some French champagne, claret, and Bordeaux. And a colored bartender shook up rickeys, champagne cocktails, Bronx cocktails, and orange blossoms. Louise had even hired the Swinging Syncopators to play.

Jack Gilbert was there. Leatrice Joy had divorced him two years earlier, but he wasn't wanting for female companionship. A pretty blonde I didn't recognize was draped all over him like a raccoon coat.

Louise introduced me around—to Buddy DeSylva, the songwriter; director Wesley Ruggles; Clarence Brown's cinematographer Oliver Marsh, and actress Virginia Valli. We chatted amiably, and at the sound of a knife pinging on glass, we turned to see Hal trying to get our attention. We turned to face him.

"Hello and thank you for coming. Louise and I are delighted to see you all having such a good time. And to our guest of honor...Marie, we're so excited you've joined the colony, and we're hoping for many enjoyable memories here with you in Malibu." He raised his glass to me, and I did the same, smiling at my new friends.

"Now I know you've heard about the merger, and the rumors of my little project, and you're dying to know about it, but all I can tell you is to be patient a while longer, and the suspense will soon be over. It will change the industry, my friends! To Warner Brothers First National!"

The guests held up their glasses in a toast to Warner Brothers. Except me. I downed mine and handed it to the bartender, snatching up another and doing the same with it as a chorus of voices echoed:

"To change!"

SAINT VINCENT'S HOSPITAL, LOS ANGELES CALIFORNIA
October 9, 1927

"Could somebody get me some bicarbonate?" was the last thing I recalled saying before collapsing on the *On to Reno* set. My director, James Cruze, summoned an ambulance.

I remembered them readying me for surgery, but after that, things got pretty fuzzy. When I came to, I once again had no idea how long I'd been laid up. All I knew was that my gut was no longer on fire.

Someone had been in the room recently. There was a *Los Angeles Times* laying on the bedside table. With some difficulty, I picked it up. The date was the sixth. I scanned the front page to see what was new.

The headline jumped out at me:

Jazz Singer Premiere in New York
Warner Brothers Talking Picture a Hit!

So that was what Hal had been up to. Talking pictures. I kept reading to learn that Al Jolson had been a huge success, singing and dancing. The lines were out the door and around the corner, and critics were seeing a revolutionary new direction for films. It figured that Warner's had gotten rid of me before they became a big player. No one would have to take cameras home to hide them from creditors now.

With something approaching panic, I wondered if all the other studios would follow suit. They'd need new equipment and new technology to do these pictures. And what about the voices? Some of the stars would be fine. But what about the foreigners? What about the accents from Alabama or the Bronx? When I imagined Norma Talmadge talking in a movie, I laughed out loud.

I looked up at a rap on the door and lay the newspaper down on my lap. I could barely see Phyl behind the beautiful bouquet she carried. It was full of roses and gladioli and irises, made lovelier by the smile behind it.

"Oh, Phyl, you shouldn't have!" I cried, delighted.

"Whaddya mean? Of course I shoulda!" She set the flowers down on the chest across from my bed, then crossed the room to give me a sideways hug.

"What was it this time?" I said. "That put me in here."

"Ulcer, the doctor said. And I probably shouldn't be doing this, but…" she said, reaching into the pocket of her coat. "Happy birthday!" She pulled out a flask.

"Phyllis Haver, you know very well that my birthday isn't until next month," I said with a giggle.

"Then we'll celebrate early!"

She peeked behind her to ensure there were no nurses and poured a little into the water glass beside the bed for me. Then she hoisted her flask.

"Bottoms up," she said as we clinked. "This is medicinal, you know."

"I know," I said, taking deep thirsty gulps.

Dear God that's good.

"Hey, slow down. Don't want the doc sore at me for getting you tight."

"Sorry," I said, realizing how it must have looked. "I just heard about the next big thing." I gestured to the front page. "Figures Warner's waited until they dumped me to go big-time."

"But on the bright side, we're at the same lot again, so we'll see each other more often." She paused. "This is where you're supposed to say 'Gee thanks, Phyl. I hadn't considered that. You're right!'"

I gave her a forlorn smile. "You're right. I am glad about that."

"You don't know how crazy things have been out there the last few days!" she said. "Half the studio heads are mad that they didn't think of sound first, and the others are trying to figure out how long it will take them to catch up. I've heard some of the dirt at parties. No one knows how they'll sound, and they're scared to death."

"That's reassuring," I said, grimacing.

"It'll take the studios a while," she said, pulling out a package of Chesterfields. "To get converted, I mean. We shouldn't have to worry yet." She lit one and inhaled, using the empty aluminum bedpan as an ashtray.

We chatted about the sound conversion, about who was seeing whom at the latest parties, and about me taking it easy. Then she stood.

"Sorry, honey, it's getting late. I better run," she said. "Shooting bright and early tomorrow for *Chicago*. I'm playin' a murderess! This could be my big break. My phone hasn't stopped ringing since *What Price Glory*!"

She departed, wiggling her fingers in a final goodbye. I glanced at the headline again, and like everyone else in Hollywood, I worried about the arrival of sound.

CHAPTER TWENTY~EIGHT

SUPERIOR COURT, CIVIL DIVISION, LOS ANGELES, CALIFORNIA

November 16, 1927

R alph sauntered in front of the witness box, casually resting his hand on the polished wood and asking me guided questions about the marriage. Eventually, I revealed Ken's repeated calls in the wee hours. And then the last big party.

"You say they were sitting around in bathing suits?" Ralph asked.

"Yes. Wet ones too. On my thousand-dollar loveseat. They'd been in the pool," I replied, coolly looking across the benches at Ken.

"Did their being in the pool wake you up?" Ralph said.

"No, the phonograph did."

"The phonograph?" he said.

"They were playing 'Yes, We Have No Bananas' very loudly and dancing."

"That seems terribly rude," Ralph said.

"Objection. Speculation," Ken's attorney said.

"I'll rephrase. What did you do when you were awoken this way?"

"I confronted them all—Ken in particular—and told them that I needed to sleep," I said. "Then I switched off the phonograph."

"Mr. Smith," Judge Bowron said, looking through the papers in front of him. "I don't see any mentions of this early morning drunkenness in the original complaint."

"No, Your Honor. We believed that the constant early morning phone calls were sufficient to prove cruelty, since Mrs. Harlan's sleep was continually interrupted, and it affected her work at the studio."

"As I look this paperwork over, I'm not sure about the thoroughness of your examples." Judge Bowron pushed his spectacles further up the bridge of his nose. "I think if you file an amended complaint that includes this incident, your case will hold more water."

"Of course, Your Honor. I can see to that right away."

"Fine. Do that and I can make my judgment. Court is adjourned for the day," he said, banging his gavel.

Not quite a week later, we were back with Ralph's amended complaint. Vera served as my witness. We'd both been at Al's studio while I worked on *Up in Mabel's Room*, and she was able to testify about the death of my mother, its impact on me, and how Ken's phone calls and the lack of sleep were affecting my health. As the person who'd phoned me with the original news of Mum's death, she'd been in a unique position to know how I was doing. Her testimony was incredibly powerful.

As we left the courtroom, a sudden jolt of pain shot

through my gut. I clutched my side.

"Marie, are you okay?" Vera asked.

"I'm fine."

"No, you're not. Look at you. You can hardly walk. I'm taking you to the doctor," she said, getting under my arm and helping me down the corridor.

"Vera, honestly, I'm all right."

"Hush," she said, steering me toward the car, and then driving me to St. Vincent's and Dr. Baldwin's office.

"I don't like that you're still having pain," he said. "There may be adhesions."

He had me admitted, and I was quickly prepared for another surgery. When I came to hours later, Vera sat next to the bed, and one lone bouquet in a vase stood on the bedside table.

"You're awake," she said. "Good. I was wondering when you'd come to."

"How long was I out?"

"About four hours," she said. "Can I get you anything? Do you need a nurse?"

"Maybe a glass of water," I said, with a mouth that felt like a herd of Cossacks had ridden through it.

Vera took the pitcher next to the bed and poured one for me. I gulped it down.

"More?"

I nodded, and she obliged. We both looked up when Dr. Baldwin approached.

"How's my favorite patient?"

"Fine," I said. "My middle doesn't hurt as much."

"That's good. There *were* adhesions, and we'll need some follow-ups."

"Doctor," I told him. "I don't have the time to deal with all these appointments. I'm starting *Blonde for a Night* next week. I can't blow this. I can't!"

"Tell you what," he said. "I don't do this for all my patients, but I'll do it for you, since you're also my favorite actress. If the studio will agree, I can come there to attend to you, perhaps on your lunch breaks. How does that sound?"

"I'm so grateful, doctor. I'm shooting at the DeMille lot in Culver City. I hope it's not too much trouble for you."

"We'll figure out some way to make it work," he said.

In *Blonde for a Night*, Mr. DeMille had insisted that I go platinum blonde, even though I argued with him.

"A wig would work too," I said.

"It's not realistic enough," he said. "If you're supposed to be blonde, I want you blonde."

So that was that. The man knew what he wanted. I spent what seemed like weeks in the salon getting progressively lightened. At least Mr. DeMille worked with me to squeeze in root touch-ups and doctor visits, where Dr. Baldwin poked and prodded my middle to ensure that I was healing properly.

"Hey, don't knock it!" Phyllis said when she saw my new look. "You know what Anita Loos says!"

Let Phyllis appeal to those who liked blondes. As soon as we were done shooting, I dyed it right back. I didn't feel like myself. It wasn't for me.

Imagine how excited I was when January rolled around, and DeMille wanted me blonde again for my next role, in something called *The Godless Girl*. We met in his office, and he gave me the latest copy of the scenario, while we discussed the film.

"Jeanie's finishing up the last of the edits right now," said Mr. DeMille. Jeanie MacPherson was Mr. DeMille's screenwriter and assistant. A more supremely capable woman I'd never met.

"What's it about?" I asked.

"At its most basic, it's going to be a treatise on atheism."

"Atheism and reform school?" I asked.

There's something you don't hear every day.

He smiled broadly. "I've had a couple spies working for me. I got a boy to infiltrate the Preston School of Industry, and I snuck a girl into the California School for Girls in Ventura. You wouldn't believe some of the reports they sent back. It'd make your hair catch fire."

As if the constant blonde treatments weren't bad enough.

"Tell me more," I said.

"Lina Basquette is signed as my starring actress, and I think I've locked in Tom Keene as the male lead. He's a religious boy, and she's an atheist girl. They're on a school campus, and she and her friends hand out leaflets for an atheist meeting. He and his friends decide to break it up, and when they do, there's a brawl. One of the atheist girls gets shoved against a rail on the landing about four or five floors up, and it breaks. She dies from the fall."

"Then what happens?" I asked.

"They're all sent to reform school together. You'll be Mame, one of the harder girls who's been in for a while. You show Lina the ropes. That's why I need you blonde. More of a contrast with her."

"Sounds good so far, but...atheism? I mean...how will it play in Peoria? It could be risky," I said.

"Wait til you see what I do with it," he said, and gave a deep chuckle. "Let's suffice to say that all are redeemed in the end. Even the bad guy."

"Who's the bad guy? The atheist?" I asked.

"Actually, no. Remember the spies I told you about?"

"Then the guards are part of the problem."

"Bingo."

Jeanie poked her head in the door. "Mr. DeMille, the monkey is here. The one I told you about."

"Marie, do you mind?" he said. "I found a fellow with a trained monkey, and I've been needing to see how he does. Come with me. You can meet him too."

"Monkey?" I raised an eyebrow.

"It's a novelty. For a little comic relief," he said. "On the whole, it's a rather dark picture until the redemption at the end."

"But why a monkey?"

"He's a gimmick. The atheists use him to attract students to their meetings."

When we reached the outer office with Jeanie, there stood a dark, swarthy man wearing a workman's shirt and pants, and a gray tweed newsboy cap. A Capuchin monkey wearing a matching red pillbox hat and vest sat on his shoulder.

"Giovanni Petrelli, this is Mr. DeMille. Mr. DeMille, Signor Petrelli," Jeanie said.

"Pleased to meet you, Signor Petrelli," Mr. DeMille said, taking his hand.

"Please, call me Joe," the man said in a strong Italian accent. "And this is Rocco."

The monkey held out his tiny paw, and Mr. DeMille

obligingly took it between his thumb and forefinger and wiggled it.

"Joe, this is Marie Prevost," Mr. DeMille said. "She'll be one of the stars of the picture."

"*Piacere*," Joe said, lifting his cap.

My time being introduced as *the* star was long past. As it was, I was merely pleased to be working. The sound conversion was hitting Hollywood hard. I'd already warned Lina that although her name came above mine in the credits, I'd be trying to steal every scene we were in together.

"Deal," she said with a wink.

Poor Lina. She had married Sam Warner when she was only eighteen and he was thirty-eight. They were deeply in love and had a daughter, Lita. But the night before *The Jazz Singer* put Warner's on the map, Sam had died of a brain hemorrhage. His family, who'd always considered her a gold digger, got custody of her little girl, and wouldn't allow Lina to see her. We were both coming out of hard times, and we were determined to make the picture a hit. Moreover, both of us hated the Warners. But I wondered long and hard about Mr. DeMille's decision to film *The Godless Girl* as a silent.

"Jeanie tells me you're an organ grinder by trade?" Mr. DeMille said to Petrelli.

"*Si*. And Rocco is my star. So many tricks he is doing! Very smart is Rocco."

"Would you mind showing us a little of his repertoire?" Mr. DeMille said.

"*Que cosa?*"

"All the things that Rocco can do," Jeanie clarified.

"Of course!" Joe cried. "Rocco, *tifa!*"

Rocco sat up and raised his arms as if he was cheering. Joe fed him a chunk of banana as a reward.

"*Bene, bene.* Rocco, *abbassati!*"

Rocco huddled over and clutched his paws above his head, as if bombs were being dropped from above. Jeanie and Mr. DeMille watched, their smiles growing even wider. Joe gave Rocco more banana, and the tiny, greedy paw took it.

"*Bene.* Rocco, *balla!*"

The monkey did a little jig on the desk, then let out a short screech.

"Marvelous," Mr. DeMille said, clapping. "Do you think you could train him to hand out pieces of paper to the actors?"

"*Cosa vuoi dire?*" Joe said, looking confused.

"Like this," Jeanie said, taking a piece of paper off the desk and handing it to Mr. DeMille.

"Aah...*la carta. Si. Si.* Rocco, *distribuisci.*" He handed the monkey a stack of papers from the desk, and Rocco handed them to me, to Jeanie, and to Mr. DeMille.

"I do on street...paper invitation to street fair," he explained.

"Perfect," Jeanie said.

"One last thing," DeMille said. "Is he housebroken?"

"Aah! *Il gabinetto. Si.* I take outside."

"Then Jeanie will stay here and sign you and Rocco to a contract," Mr. DeMille said. "Miss Prevost and I have some business to do. Thank you very much, Joe. Jeanie, can you take care of that?"

"Of course, Mr. DeMille," she said, guiding Joe and Rocco to a chair in front of her desk.

Joe doffed his hat at us as we retreated to Mr. DeMille's office.

"I don't know about you, but I think Rocco's going to

upstage all of us," I said.

Because of Mr. DeMille's vision, *The Godless Girl* was actually far more artistic than I'd originally imagined it might be. The brutality of the reform school began to soften the atheist and harden the devout boy. Wallace Beery was deliciously evil as the guard who finally got his comeuppance. DeMille's artistic touches abounded—from the atheist girl's fall during the brawl as seen from above, to Lina's character's stigmata, received from clutching an electric fence.

Mitchell Leisen was Mr. DeMille's art director. His light brown hair, twinkling eyes and natural grin were attractive, but there was something different about him. Although he was married, it was also whispered that he was a homosexual. All I knew was that he was a genius. A sadistic genius.

Mitch had great ideas for the film, but between him and DeMille, things got pretty hellish for the rest of us on the set. We filmed either on "Forty Acres," the back lot at DeMille's studio, or at Las Tunas Ranch in the valley, where it was always a million degrees hotter.

For the giant reform school fire at the end, DeMille wanted to torch the old sets on the lot that dated from when Thomas Ince had owned the studio. It would be difficult, if not impossible, to do retakes, and it had to be done safely. Mitch had a special keyboard that he used to control the fire effects, and he "fireproofed" us as much as possible. Our costumes were washed in an asbestos solution, then more of it was painted onto them. Afterward, the salon staff sprayed more of it into our hair before they styled it. The stuff smelled awful, and at the end of the fourteen-hour day, all I wanted was to lose myself in a hot bath and a bottle of Bushmills. It took at least a week for my sinuses to get back to normal from all the smoke. Lina was less lucky. Her eyebrows were singed off, and months later, she was still having to pencil them in.

Mr. DeMille was a titan. I was pleased I'd had the chance to work with him. But if I'd expected him to see me as another Swanson...giving me an affectionate nickname like "Young Fella," or putting his arm around me, taking me for a stroll around the studio grounds and saying, "Stick with me, kid, you'll go places!" I was mistaken. We never even had the chance to develop a greater working relationship. With DeMille Pictures and PDC limping along financially, and with Mr. DeMille spending way over-budget for *King of Kings*, something bad was bound to happen eventually.

LET'S KISS
AND MAKE UP

CHAPTER TWENTY~NINE

"The reason I called you, Marie, is to let you know that Mr. DeMille has left the company." Mr. Sistrom said, looking uncomfortable. He loosened his tie.

My jaw dropped. "What? But it's his company. It has his name on it," I protested.

"We've been bought out. Mr. DeMille's expenditures were considered too costly for the business, I'm afraid. *The Godless Girl* was a complete flop. Worse than a flop. And now we have a new financier who's come in to help us recover financially."

"A financier. Would this be a huge bank trying to cut their losses?"

"Not that you'd know, but his name is Joseph Kennedy. He's from Boston, and he's making lots of changes, all in the name of profitability."

"Thanks for telling me. Is that everything?"

He swallowed hard. "Unfortunately, Mr. Kennedy has also decided to terminate a number of contracts, to bring us back to solvency."

"I'm one of those players," I whispered. The writing was on the wall again.

"I'm afraid so."

"This cannot be happening."

I was now an old pro at being fired. I cleaned out my De-Mille bungalow, then went home, poured myself a stiff belt, and took stock.

Back in January, Phyl and I had made one last visit to the old Sennett lot. It was being taken over by eminent domain, and Mr. Sennett had built a new lot out in Studio City. But a part of history would be gone forever. Maybe my life might have been different if I'd never left the Fun Factory and my friends there. Phyl and I sat with our legs dangling off the sides of the empty pool and had a good cry.

Putting the word out that I was once again a free agent, I waited for new offers to come rolling in. Every day, I read the *Times* over my egg and coffee, convinced that my next great part was out there. But the silence was deafening. One morning, I got an extra gut punch from the front page.

She Has Jolt For Film Star

I read on to discover that Ken hadn't even waited until we were officially divorced to take up with someone new. He'd done it to Flo with me, and I'd bet if I checked with Salomé that he'd done the same to her with Flo.

Ken had taken up with Gertie Henry, the wife of a wealthy manufacturer from Detroit. They'd trysted in Ken's bungalow at Universal, but had the bad luck to be seen by a studio caretaker named Paula Schultz. Now, Gertie's geezer husband was suing her for divorce in California, calling Ken as co-respondent. Ken had already been called to the stand, denying that he and Gertie had taken a moonlight cruise to Catalina. I hadn't realized I was making a face.

"Bad news?" Delilah asked, refilling my coffee cup.

"He didn't even wait until the divorce was final," I said, gesturing to the headline.

She shook her head sadly.

"I shouldn't be upset. I was the one who filed to end this thing, after all. But I still love the big lug."

It was true. From the top of his brilliantined head to the tips of his shoe-shined brogues, he drove me crazy with his late-night phone calls. But it still hurt to think of him with someone else—whether she was a permanent new arm decoration or merely some floozy he'd taken up with.

Delilah laid a comforting hand on my shoulder, then diplomatically let me stew. She could read my moods so well, knowing when I was better left alone and knowing when to be sociable. There wasn't much of that these days.

In quick succession, I finally nabbed two parts. Both independents, but at this point, I wouldn't sneeze at them. Their money was as green as everybody else's. As long as the checks didn't bounce, I was up for the part.

One morning in May, the phone rang. I held up the damp cloth on my forehead, knowing Delilah would let me know if it was anything important.

Her heavy footfalls labored up the stairs and she hovered at the door to the bedroom for me to acknowledge her.

"Who is it, Delilah?"

"Miss Marie, terrible sorry to interrupt yo nap. It's Mist'

Ken on the phone." She shrugged helplessly in a plea for guidance.

"Ken? What could he want?" I said to no one in particular. She tried to hide a smile as she retreated.

I rolled over and picked up the bedroom extension.

"Yes?"

"Marie, it's me," he said.

"I know. What is it?"

"I've been thinking of you. I wanted to call and...and...see how you were doing. How you are."

"How I am? I'm nearly divorced. How was Hawaii?"

"Hawaii was wonderful. I stayed right near the beach. I saw volcanoes and ate all sorts of strange new foods. And I got a helluva suntan."

"How's Gertrude? Take any trips to Catalina lately?" I hated the cattiness in my voice.

"I deserve that," he said with a sigh.

"You don't waste any time, do you?"

"Well, the divorce was proceeding, and I was lonely, and I thought... well, I don't know what I thought. Gertie only made everything more complicated."

"You do seem to have a thing for married women, don't you?" I said.

"Like I said, it's complicated," he said.

"Yeah? Why's that?"

He sighed. "Because I still love you, Marie. I've been such a stupid clod. I'm calling to see if we can still save this thing. I realize what an idiot I've been. Could we meet for dinner? Talk things over, maybe?"

"What do we have to talk about? We'll only end up fighting

again," I said.

"We don't have to let Bowron finalize the divorce. Let's get back together. I miss you. I miss what we have."

"Had, Ken. What we had," I corrected him.

"It's still here. Open your eyes and you'll see it. Please, Marie. It's one dinner."

I sighed. "All right. But I'm meeting you out. Wherever it is."

"The Cocoanut Grove?"

"Jesus, no. Everybody in Hollywood will see us. Someplace small and dark. I'll meet you at King's Tropical Inn in Culver City. Last booth in the back near the kitchen. The light's burned out. I'll reserve it. We'll come in separately."

"When?"

"Tonight. Seven o'clock." I hung up before he could say whether the time worked for him or not.

At quarter to seven, I pulled the McFarlan into the lot outside King's. It was a dull, reddish, adobe building with mullioned, Tudor-style windows. The front beds were full of short palms. The inside was dimly lit, and the dark, lacquered bamboo-covered booths had tall, wraparound sides and backs—the better to keep every busybody in town from knowing your business. The palm fronds of the fake trees inside provided extra camouflage from prying eyes.

Ken entered a few minutes after me, looking around like a spy.

"For God's sake, get in here and sit down," I said. "You couldn't look more suspicious if you tried."

He took a seat and grinned. He wore my favorite gray-green tie—the one that made his eyes glow—and the devilish expression he wore made my heart flutter a little, despite everything.

When the waiter returned, we ordered teacups of the house special.

"Give us a minute for food," Ken told him. The man nodded and hurried away. I leaned back to size Ken up.

"I love this place," he said. "Reminds me of Hawaii. I ate poi and kalua pork and laulau..." He told me more about his trip—catamaran rides and visits to Kilauea.

"You're looking good, Ken. I think single life agrees with you," I said.

"No, it doesn't," he said. "I'm miserable without you."

"You don't *look* miserable." I crossed my arms and looked more closely.

"This suit is hanging on me. I've lost ten pounds!"

He did look a little thinner, come to think of it.

"See these gunny sacks under my eyes?" he said, pulling at the skin underneath them. "I'm not sleeping well."

"I'll bet," I observed.

He frowned. "You know what I mean."

"I don't know what to say, Ken. I love you, but I don't think you know how to be in love. It requires two people not always thinking of their *own* needs and considering the other person. Waking me and the neighbors at three a.m. is rude. Calling me multiple times a night is worse."

"But I—"

"Don't tell me you were zozzled or souped up or splifficated. It doesn't matter. I drink too. I admit it. I drink too much. But I'm a solitary drunk. You're not. You're loud and obnoxious, and you can be downright mean," I said. It was harsh, but there it was.

"I'm sorry. I don't know how many times I can say it before you believe me." He cast his eyes down, looking suitably ashamed.

"A few more would be nice. But it doesn't do any good if you don't want to change," I said.

"I'll change if it will get you back," he said quietly.

"Excuse me for being skeptical."

"Waiter!" Ken called. Our waiter reappeared. "We've changed our minds on the drinks. Could you bring us two nice cold glasses of milk instead?"

The man looked at us with a confused expression, and I burst into giggles. The waiter returned to the kitchen shaking his head.

Ken looked at me with a big enthusiastic grin.

"Marie, we can be good together. We don't have to get tight. Both of us will stop drinking. Then we won't have to worry about any of that other stuff."

I must have looked cynical.

"Doesn't it mean anything if I tell you I truly want to try?"

"Of course it does, but..." I shrugged helplessly.

"But what?"

"After Santa Barbara, you said you'd straightened up. It was only for a little while. I don't want this to be the same way."

"It won't be. I promise. We'll love each other again. Really care for each other."

"Like before we were married?" I said. "Getting married was when things started going wrong for us. And Vera said the same thing about Jackie. It only got worse when she had the girls."

"I'm not Jackie," he said. "And I swear to you I'm a changed man." He took my hand and gazed at me adoringly.

"Slow down, Ace," I said, pulling it free. "You've got some more convincing to do."

"Of course! I don't want to pressure you. But I want you to see that things will be different. I've talked to mother and told her butt out."

"It's a start," I said. "But we're going very slow. Glacial even."

"All right. I can do that. Glacial. We'll talk. Like normal people. On a date. What are you working on right now?"

I told him about no longer being with Metropolitan, and about the two independent films I'd signed up for. One was produced by the people of Utah, so I'd be traveling there as soon as I got the wire that shooting was starting. I took a quick glance at the menu and decided on the Chicken Tropico.

The waiter reappeared with our glasses of milk. "Have we decided?"

"Yes!" Ken cried joyfully. "She's taking me back!"

When it came time to go, I insisted on leaving separately. I wasn't ready to give the papers any dirt yet. We sat there in the booth staring at each other. Neither of us were in a hurry for the evening to end.

"I want more, but I don't want to scare you," he said.

"I have shooting in the morning. And I need to be sure of you first. Sure of a lot of things."

"Can I call you tomorrow?" He looked so hopeful.

"Call me Thursday," I said. That was five days away. I'd let him stew a little. But we could maybe make plans for the weekend.

We decided on the White House Café in Laguna Beach. Nice and remote. I stupidly let him come pick me up instead of meeting him there. When he took me home, he leaned over to kiss me, and the combination of his nearness and his familiar smell was enough to break through my resolve. He nuzzled my ear, and when my head fell back, hard, he took my head in his hands. We lost ourselves in that kiss.

"I want you so much..." he said hoarsely.

The headlamps of an approaching car played over the Packard, and suddenly distracted me from the trance I'd been in.

"I have to go," I said, rushing from the car and from him.

"Marie, wait!" he called after me.

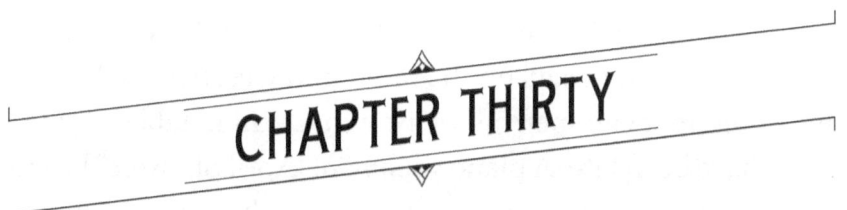

CHAPTER THIRTY

BEVERLY HILLS HOTEL, BEVERLY HILLS, CALIFORNIA
June 1928

K en knew I was skittish, and to his credit, he tried to put me at ease. He let me pick where we went—always to out-of-the-way spots in the valley, or Glendale, up to Ventura or out to Pasadena like we'd done in the early days. All it would take was one wagging tongue, the papers would have a field day, and I'd be left with egg on my face. I was testing the waters—that's all this was. Right now, there was still heavy undertow with no lifeguard on duty.

But a month after Ken's initial phone call, we went for a drive along the finished portion of the Roosevelt Highway, then came back to the Beverly Hills Hotel. Ken checked in, and I brought the car around on Crescent Drive to keep our ruse going. Our favorite bungalow was #4, with a jaunty palm out front and pots of dahlias and poinsettias on the porch. We kicked off our shoes and opened the bottle of contraband champagne for which he'd slipped the concierge an extra forty bucks. He poured both of us a drink, and we clinked glasses before downing it.

The room was bathed in a warm glow from the candles we lit, and suddenly, his lips were forceful on mine. I couldn't resist anymore. I had to break the kiss so my brain could work. It was all jumbled. I pulled away from him and tried to catch my breath, then flicked on the radio in the corner. KQFZ was finishing up a commercial for Bromo-Quinine tablets, but it must have been fate. A piano version of "April Showers" began to play, and Ken opened his arms to me. I lay my head on his chest and he pulled me close as we moved together. Like my heart, his was hammering a mile a minute. This time, when he kissed me, the song ended, and we stood there stupidly, neither wanting to be the first to break the spell.

He lowered the volume, then took my hand and led me to the bedroom. I unbuttoned his shirt so that he stood in front of me, the most magnificent example of manhood I'd ever seen.

"I missed you," he whispered, nuzzling my ear. "Let me..." His hands gently cupped my breasts through my silk frock. My hand drifted to the V of his trousers, and I unbuttoned them. He stepped out of them, then lifted my dress over my head, breaking the kiss only long enough to do so.

Whipping off his shirt, he pushed me down on the bed. Then he began the exquisite process of adoring each breast. I closed my eyes, drinking in the sensation, every nerve wide awake. He moved lower, kissing my belly, then traveled even lower than that.

"What are you doing?"

He showed me, wringing cries out of me the likes of which I'd never made before. Then it was happening, and as we moved together, Ken bellowed triumphantly. The tears rolled down my face—tears of joy, tears of sadness? I wasn't quite sure which. We clung to each other desperately, murmuring "I love you, I love you," until we were spent.

When the hunger got too much, I rose, threw on a dressing gown, then picked up the phone to order some food. "I'll have two orders of the broiled squab on toast with cress please. More champagne, and two chocolate meringues. Bungalow four, please."

"Right away, madam."

Ken approached, nuzzling me from behind and laying his chin on my shoulder.

"That was the most amazing night of my life," he said, kissing my neck.

"You weren't so bad yourself," I said.

"Does that mean what I think it means?"

"It probably means what you think it means," I said. "What do you think it means?"

"Don't tease me, darling. You know what I'm asking."

"I'm willing to try this one last time, Ken," I said. "Last night was perfect. But we've had our problems. And I'm scared they're still here. Sex has never been a problem for us. We both know that. Our problems are everything else."

"We can do this," he said.

The food arrived, and we ate the squab with our fingers, having a picnic on the floor beside the fireplace. We clinked glasses and kissed, then he nuzzled my ear and caressed a breast. We stumbled back into the bedroom again.

The next night, we were quiet on the drive back to the house, each of us lost in our own thoughts. When Ken pulled to a stop at the curb, he looked over at me, his face a massive question mark.

"I want to move home—" he said.

"—I want you to move home," I said at the same time.

"You do?"

"Yes. But not yet," I clarified. "I like the way things are right now. The romance, the passion... things haven't been like this for a while. Let's enjoy it while we can. Besides—I'll be leaving for Utah in another month or so. The distance will help us. We do better when we're apart."

"All right," he said.

"You mean it?" I asked.

"Whatever you want, I'm willing to do it."

THE RACKET SET, GOLDWYN STUDIOS, CULVER CITY, CALIFORNIA *June 1928*

One of my new independent films was with a small outfit owned by a Texas millionaire.

"Howard Hughes," he said, introducing himself with a broad drawl, so that his first name came out 'Ha-ard.' But I got the feeling I was expected to know that anyway.

He missed nothing when he looked at you, and his eyes scared me a little—they were so direct you had to look away—otherwise it'd be an undeclared competition. That gaze was bold, unrelenting, and solid. His hair was as dark as his eyes, and he had a small pencil-thin mustache. He peered out from under a gray fedora and constantly drummed his fingers on the arm of his canvas chair. He was a little too cocky for his own good. But at the same time, he was strange. Fidgety. Not bad looking, mind you, but he acted like a butcher, with me being the prize porterhouse.

He took me around and introduced me to everyone. My co-stars, Louis Wolheim and Thomas Meighan, were both seasoned pros like me, and Lewis Milestone was directing again. With two pictures under our belt already, we worked well together.

It was a crime picture, set in Chicago, and I'd be playing Helen Hayes, a gangster's moll. The bad guy was named Scarsi.

"He named the bad guy SCAR-si?" I said with a laugh when I read the scenario. I couldn't imagine a more pointed barb aimed at Al Capone. "Is he suicidal or stupid? Or both?"

Hughes, for all his intensity, had a constant look of exhaustion about him. Tom gave me the skinny.

"He's also shooting another film up at Caddo Field near Van Nuys. Some big aerial thing. Says it's going to be bigger than *Wings*. They've been filming wherever the weather's cooperating—Chatsworth, Santa Cruz, Oakland...the travel alone is grueling."

"What are they calling this aeroplane epic?" I asked.

"*Hell's Angels*, he's named it. I overheard him talking with one of his money man friends. The guy must be dead on his feet. He goes from before dawn to after dusk every day. And he's partially deaf. Mumble. It drives him crazy."

While *The Racket* earned rave reviews from critics who were able to view it in larger cities, Mr. Hughes had stepped on some toes. Not only did Al Capone get his feathers ruffled by Scarsi's name and disfigurement, the Chicago police demanded that it be sliced up like a Thanksgiving turkey for the corruption angle. Will Hays, the Hollywood censor general, was only too happy to oblige. Even after they were done, we were told *The Racket* would never play Chicago. But at least it was a success, even without Chicago's dollars.

On the personal front, Ken now came by the house and picked me up for dates. He tried to be gentle and kind—the way he hadn't been for years. He brought me flowers, and a beautiful topaz necklace, my birthstone. I cleaned out the bar and gave the good stuff to friends of ours. Instead, I filled the house with fruit juice, Coca-Cola, and ginger ale. And of course, at night, things were better than they'd ever been. Sometimes Ken stayed over, but always pulled into the garage so his car wouldn't be recognized.

We finally got brave enough to go to Judge Bowron and ask him to stop the divorce proceedings. He frowned as he re-read the paperwork from my filing.

"Mrs. Harlan, you claimed your marriage was a 'hellish existence.' What's changed?" he asked.

"*We* have, Your Honor. We're trying again. Isn't that what the interlocutory decree is for?" I asked. "To get people to change their minds?"

Bowron harrumphed and banged the gavel, and it was done. Ken and I were still married. The papers churned out story after story on the reconciliation.

We even began discussing a second honeymoon, since our first had been so disappointing. As always, it depended on when and where we'd be filming. Hawaii was out for me now. Maybe I'd make it there someday, but it was ruined, thinking of Ken there by himself with any number of nubile young native girls. I'd settle for Florida, but New York was always a good option.

THE OUTRIGGER CAFE, SANTA MONICA BOARDWALK
July 1928

"Did you hear about Wah?" Phyl asked, taking a bite of her Crab Louis.

"No. How is she?" I said. I was almost afraid to ask. Wah had gotten clean of the heroin that had nearly destroyed her life, but we all still worried about her. I looked longingly at the bread basket, then moved it closer to Phyl and ordered a large green salad and steamed vegetables.

"She was staying at the Hotel Lincoln in New York, and mistook the hot water tap for the cold. She got scalded pretty bad."

"Oh God. That's all she needs after everything else," I said. I took a sip of my water with lemon.

"It's been one step up, two steps back for her since Mary's death," Phyl said.

"Let's hope she's strong enough to make it through this without backsliding," I said, thinking of me with the booze nearly as much as Wah with the junk.

I was leaving in a week for Salt Lake City. Dozens of names for the film had been tossed around, but nothing had been decided yet. As the good citizens of Utah had financed it, we all called it "The Mormon Picture" in the meantime.

"How's Stephen?" I asked. Phyl had been seeing Stephen Goosson, a set designer. From everything she'd told me, she was crazy about him and expected him to pop the question any day. He'd worked on *Blonde for a Night*, and he'd seemed like her type, so I'd introduced them.

"He's fine," she said. "I told him I wanted a romantic vacation, so we're escaping to Catalina for a few days. He kept telling me he had to work, but I finally got him to say yes. I had to butter him up like a yeast roll!" She let out a little giggle. "Congratulations, by the way. I mean—it's all over the papers about you and Ken."

I smiled. "Thanks. I took him back. We're even planning a second honeymoon, since our last one was a bust."

"That's wonderful," she said.

"Phyl, have you ever loved someone so much it hurt? That you think you might die if they were to leave?"

"Yeah, sure. Isn't all love like that?"

"But have your feelings ever changed so drastically that five minutes later you'd gladly hit him over the head with a sash weight like that Ruth Snyder woman?"

Phyl paused, fork halfway to her mouth. "No, I can't say I have," she said.

"I love him so damned much, but there are times when I wonder if it can last. We make love, and two hours later, we're at each other's throats like wild animals in the Serengeti." I angrily stabbed at a tomato.

She covered my free hand with hers. "He told you he's changed," she said. "Why not give him the benefit of the doubt?"

"He's been insensitive before, and I'm worried he will be again. About my weight, about my drinking, about Mum... Mum was my very best friend in the entire world, Phyl. I miss her so much. The only time it doesn't hurt is when I drink.

I can forget then. When I have Bushmills in warm milk at night. Or only Bushmills. We're both on the wagon now, and it's so hard. I have to deal with the pain again."

"There's something important that we need to talk about then."

"What's that? My drinking?" I said, not in the mood for a lecture.

"No, silly! Your supplier! I wanna know where you're getting Bushmills!"

I had to give her credit. She was trying to make me laugh. But this time, her cheerful way of making light of everything only came off as a lack of concern. I think I would have preferred the nagging.

I'LL NEVER BE
THE SAME

CHAPTER THIRTY~ONE

October 1928

"Miss Prevost!" Miss Prevost! Dan Snyder of the *Salt Lake Review*! Would you care to make a comment on the reconciliation with Mr. Harlan for our readers?"

"We're ecstatically happy," I said, as Ken and I strolled to the ticket desk.

"Mr. Harlan! Buck Johnson of the *Ogden Standard*! Do you have any remarks?"

"She took me back and we worked out our troubles," Ken said. "We're happier than we've ever been!"

It's amazing how a fresh start seems to grant everything around you a rosy glow. Especially when you're wearing your favorite navy duvetyn suit with caracul collar. Ken arrived in Salt Lake City, and we spent a romantic night together before we were due to depart on the Royal Gorge Route. A gaggle of reporters followed us into the depot, eager for the big scoop of our second honeymoon. The snapping and hissing of the cameras hounded us the entire way.

I'd been in Utah for not quite three months. The cast had stayed at the Hotel Utah off Temple Square, and the days were hard, sweaty work. But during my time there, I'd taken several days off to travel to Richfield, visit Mary's mother, and pay a visit to her grave. I stood in front of the stone, letting the tears fall. Mary's mother took my hand.

"She loved you girls so much," she said.

"We loved her too. Rest in peace, dear girl," I said, laying the bouquet of lilies on the grave. Mary's mother hugged me.

"Thank you for coming," she whispered.

I cried on the train back to Salt Lake, not caring who saw me. Maybe as much for lost youth and innocence as for my friend.

It was a relief to see Ken after that. On the train, we found our sleeping compartment and relaxed together on the pull-out bunk. Ken traced a finger down my cheek and kissed me. He'd deepened the kiss and led my hand to his crotch when the conductor unceremoniously burst in.

"Tickets, please," he said, holding his hand out. Then, "Terrible sorry. Didn't mean to interrupt."

Ken and I tried not to look like two guilty teenagers up to no good in a rumble seat. Ken handed the man our tickets from his jacket pocket.

"All th' way to Denver. Thank you, suh. Good day, ma'am." He touched the brim of his hat.

"You too," I said, as he backed out of the compartment.

The minute he was gone, we dissolved into laughter.

"Now, where were we?" Ken said, leaning over toward me again.

"You were about to punch my ticket," I said with a wink.

It was as if we'd never been apart. The miles passed in a blur. By the time we hit Denver and had to change to the Burlington route to Chicago, we'd gotten some of the frenzy out of our systems. Something about the rhythm of the train, I think.

We settled down to a relaxed dinner on our third night out. Ken had the breast of veal and I had the baked haddock with sharp sauce. After dinner, we strolled to the lounge car and played dominoes until my recent shooting schedule caught up to me.

"I'm going to retire, darling," I said, yawning behind my hand.

"I think I'll stay up and find a poker game to join," he said.

"Don't lose too much," I said. I leaned down and gave him a peck on the cheek, then filed down the corridor to our compartment. It must have been after midnight when a loud bang and a curse came from the corridor. I sat up on the pull-out bed, suddenly wide awake. The door rattled and finally opened. Ken gave me a shaky grin, then fell face first across the bunk. I caught a whiff of Habanita perfume and bootleg hooch, and there was lipstick on his collar. Not my shade.

"You sonofabitch," I muttered.

"I'm not that drunk," he slurred.

"God damn you, Ken Harlan!"

I wasn't sure who I was angrier at—him or myself for believing we still had a chance. I'd look like a laughing stock in front of the entire world for taking him back, then filing for divorce a second time. What a prize idiot I was. I couldn't remember how many chances Mum had given Frank. Like I couldn't remember how many I'd given Ken. All I knew was that it was too many. And here I was. Like mother, like daughter.

I pulled on my dressing gown and went to find the conductor.

He touched the brim of his cap when he saw me. "Evenin' ma'am."

"Good evening," I said. "Could you tell me if the train is full? Are there any vacant compartments I could move into?"

He glanced at the door to our compartment, then furrowed his brow, obviously confused by my request. "But ma'am, that compartment has been paid for. Double occupancy."

I sighed. "Mr. Harlan and I have had a disagreement, and I can't stay in ours. I can pay for a separate cabin when we get to our next stop. I can pay *you* if you like. I need to change compartments right away. Please." My voice broke as the tears took over.

"Oh no...no ma'am. Please don't cry. We'll figure this out, I promise."

He looked around to see if anyone had viewed our exchange. There was no one. Tugging a ring of keys from his pocket, he moved a few compartments down from ours and unlocked the door.

"We're lucky this trip. The car's not full," he said.

"I need to rebook my ticket too. Where would be the best place? And when?"

"We get into Chicago tomorrow evenin'," he suggested.

"Then that's what I'll do. Could I possibly take my meals here instead of the dining car?" I asked. "I don't want to run into him. Do you understand? I could pay you extra to bring it here to me."

"Yes, ma'am. I'll make sure to come by for breakfast in the mo'nin. At eight, maybe? And lunchtime around noon?"

"Yes, perfect. What's your name?"

"Woodrow, ma'am."

"I can't thank you enough, Woodrow. I'm going to go get my things from the other compartment."

When I returned, Ken had passed out face down on the bunk. Working quickly around him, I got my clothes and accessories moved into the new compartment. I scribbled out a quick note—enough for him to know not to come looking for me.

Ken—
You blew it. I don't wear Habanita and that's not my shade on your collar. I've had enough of your 18-carat lies.

PS The divorce is back on.
Marie

For a day, I did nothing but stew and read *The Canary Murder Case*. Truth be told, I didn't do much actual reading. What terrified me the most was that Ken's non-drinking policy had kept us both sober. Now that *he* was off the wagon, my own craving was starting again. I needed something to make my head a little hazy. Something to make the pain less acute. Wee Mae had called it, 'wrapped in warm flannel.'

As I watched the cornfields of Iowa fly by the window,

I worried what I would do when I returned to Los Angeles. Twice divorced, alcoholic (but trying not to be), and now the changeover was coming. I had no idea how my voice would sound on the big screen. Terror didn't even begin to describe what I felt. Somehow, I avoided Ken when I got off the train in Chicago, and got a porter to retrieve my trunk from the cargo area. I even booked a hotel near the station for an extra day so I wouldn't have to run into him.

On top of everything, when I got home, I came down with a nasty flu. And that became a horrible cough. Thank God for Delilah. Especially on the morning that I collapsed on the bathroom floor while readying my morning shower.

"Miss Marie! Miss Marie!" Delilah was frantic when she found me. She slipped a pillow under my head and used the bedroom extension to call an ambulance.

"You gave us quite a scare," The doctor said when I finally came to. His name tag read 'Dr. Mullen.' "You've been delirious for days. I thought we might lose you. Your influenza turned into pneumonia."

There were three Dr. Mullens standing there. I focused on the one in the middle, hoping he was the correct one.

"How am I not dead?" I croaked.

"It was touch and go for a while," he admitted. "We used serum therapy, and it appears to have worked. But you're going to be very weak for a while. You need rest and lots of it."

"But I have to work, doctor. I have a screen test for *College Coquette* at Columbia. What day is this?" I hacked out.

"Miss Prevost, I must insist that you delay your screen test and everything else. This is serious. I enjoy your films, but I'd like to see you around to complete more of them."

I sat and listened, thinking of the bills piling up while I wasn't working. Unfortunately, Columbia would have to wait. I'd blown it by getting sick.

Dr. Mullen checked my vital signs and, satisfied that I was on the road to recovery, he retreated to continue his rounds. Several pretty flower arrangements covered the table next to my bed. The card on the closest one, a bouquet of stargazer lilies, was from Louise.

Get better soon, honey! Love, Louise.

The minute I was able to sit up in bed, and I was only coughing every tenth word instead of every fourth, the time had come to officially announce that Ken and I were done. I scheduled a press conference at the house, and Delilah helped me change into my nicest pair of periwinkle silk lounging pajamas. When I was ready, she ushered the press men into the living room.

"Miss Prevost, Tom O'Halloran, *Culver City News*. You've separated from Mr. Harlan before. How do you know this is forever? Wasn't that what you said when you initially filed for divorce?"

"Yes, it was. But we all make mistakes, Mr. O'Halloran. I thought Ken and I could patch things up, but I was wrong."

"Miss Prevost, Michael Nash, *Glendale Sun*. So, you've spoken to the judge already?"

"No, Mr. Nash. As you know, I've been quite ill. But as soon as I'm well enough, I'm heading downtown to advance our divorce through the courts. For good this time."

"Miss Prevost, Tony Kirk of the *Petaluma Register*. It seems an awful shame. Your fans have always thought of you as a perfect Hollywood couple. Do you have a statement for them?"

"I hate to disappoint our fans, Mr. Kirk, but they didn't have to live with Mr. Harlan, and I did."

"Would you care to comment on the cause of the divorce?"

"No, I would not."

My next phone call was to Ralph, my lawyer. He was surprised, but he met me downtown, where we told Judge Bowron to activate the case again.

"I'm disappointed to see you back here after your last change of heart, Mrs. Harlan," Judge Bowron said.

"Not half as disappointed as me, Your Honor," I said.

That night, I broke my number one rule about drinking. I'd never let myself lose control before, but by nine p.m., I was blotto, and practically howling at the moon—ranting about Ken and Hollywood and life in general. There was no one to listen but Delilah. Jinx cowered outside my room, afraid of the new Marie who'd arrived.

The next morning, as the sun blared through the blinds, Jinx woke me with a wet nose to the face. I moaned and pushed her away, then yanked the pillow over my head.

"Miss Marie," Delilah said from the doorway. "I tried to wake you earlier, but I couldn't. Mist' Feld called. He sounded real mad. Said he talked to you 'bout comin in today t'add some dialogue fo' *The Godless Girl*?"

"Oh, no!" I said. The conversation had barely registered. He'd called while I was home recuperating, and I'd agreed to come in to get him off the phone. I leapt out of bed and flew to the shower, trying to scrub off the stink of my late night. After throwing on a loose frock and giving my teeth a quick brush, I sped to the studio and screeched to a stop in a parking place near the new sound stage.

Fritz Feld had been tasked with getting the dialogue bits tacked onto the very end of the film. He was a Kraut who'd come over back in the early '20s for a Max Reinhardt play. All eyebrows and attitude. A nice guy, I suppose, but boy was he in a thankless job.

I had a nip from my flask in the car to steel my courage and gargled some Coca-Cola to disguise it. Then I hurried inside.

"Marie!" Feld thundered. "Where the hell have you been? Your maid said you were fast asleep when I called. We talked about this!"

"I'm very sorry," I said. "I'm still recovering from my pneumonia, and..."

He got a little closer and sniffed. "It's not working."

"What isn't?"

"Whatever you drank to cover up the booze. Be careful, Marie. You're going to earn yourself a reputation. And I don't mean for your acting."

"I'm sorry, Mr. Feld."

"Don't apologize to me. Apologize to Lina and Tom Keene if you see them again. Now, let's get your vocals down."

Feld and the sound engineer worked with me for the rest of the afternoon to get my part done. *The Godless Girl* had not done well as a silent. But the studio's hope was that adding noise effects throughout—bells, alarms, a hose, fire crackling, and then Judy, Bob, and Mame having a conversation after church at the end of the movie, they'd be able to attract those audiences who were only interested in sound films.

It took several takes, but I finally synced my voice up with my original silent mouth movement of the immortal line, "Ooh! My puppies are barking!" while rubbing my aching feet, and another, "Cool your motor, baby, or I'm gonna sock you in the nose."

Now that my work at DeMille and PDC was officially done, I drove home, more depressed than ever.

CHAPTER THIRTY~TWO

THE MONTMARTRE, HOLLYWOOD, CALIFORNIA
Late December 1928

"It can't possibly be that bad," Phyl said. The cheery Christmas music being played by the house orchestra only contrasted with my sour mood.

"Worse," I said.

"What can we do?" Vera asked.

"Come on, tell Auntie Phyl about it," Phyl said. She was in an exceptionally good mood, since she was readying for a trip to New York. After playing Roxie Hart in *Chicago*, she could write her own ticket anywhere. I'd have done anything to be in her shoes right then. Even her breakup with Stephen hadn't seemed to faze her much.

"Well, let's see. My divorce from Ken should be final next month, I can still barely breathe from my pneumonia, and I'm not sure what I'm going to do for work now that I'm between studios again. Everything's peachy," I said. I gestured at the waiter for a refill on my grapefruit juice so I could doctor it from the flask in my garter.

Phyl lit a Chesterfield. "No need to be testy," she said. "Vera and I are trying to help."

I sighed. "I know. I'm sorry."

"For work, we can put our heads together. Has your agent run out of ideas?" Vera asked.

"I don't have an agent," I said.

"You don't have an agent? Well, that's your first problem. There, I solved it for you," said Phyl.

"What do I need an agent for?" I asked, munching on a piece of celery as I glanced enviously at her Spaghetti Tetrazzini.

"They've got connections, they've got pull, and they can do the wheeling and dealing to get you jobs when you're too busy to look. You work on your craft, and you have more time to run errands or rehearse or do what you do best. They get you auditions and screen tests and you do the rest."

"I don't understand why I have to pay someone to get me jobs."

Phyl shrugged. "That's how things work now." She reached into her bag. "Here. Shelly helped me get *Chicago*. I'd be nowhere without him."

The card was thick and vanilla-colored with embossed navy copperplate font.

SHELDON KIRSCHNER

KIRSCHNER AGENCY

9000 WILSHIRE

HOLLYWOOD, CALIFORNIA

MADISON 62-400

"Can I keep this?" I asked.

"Sure. He's in my address book already. I'll call and give him the heads up for you."

"Thanks, Phyl."

After her call, Mr. Kirschner ("Call me Shelly!") invited me to his office on the far western reaches of town.

He was swarthy, with a slim pointy, nose, and surprisingly kind brown eyes, which compensated for the overly strong hair pomade he wore and the Turkish cigarette hanging out of his mouth. His manner was bold and brusque, but if it got jobs coming in, I wouldn't complain.

"Phyllis tells me you need some help," he said, pulling his chair up to the desk after offering me the seat opposite him. "You'd be amazed at how much a star's career can flourish during a round at Hillcrest."

"I don't like golf," I said.

"Think of it this way," Shelly said with a wink. "I play golf so you don't have to."

I sat down and clutched my purse nervously.

"Let's take a look at your history," he said, looking over the list of roles and studios he'd asked me for. "Hmm...started with Sennett. Made a very anti-bathing beauty statement on the board-walk at Coney Island. That took some *chutzpah*! Sennett's old hat these days anyway. He has that new lot in the valley, but I don't think he's doing much better than you are, to tell the truth."

I waited quietly as he worked his way through my list.

"Universal...flapper parts for a year or so. Contract not renewed. Burn any bridges there?"

"I don't think so," I said.

"You worked under Thalberg, right? Before he moved to Metro?"

"Yes."

"Good. Onto Warner Brothers. How was that? Three-year

contract. Ended by mutual consent. What happened?"

I cleared my throat. "Last couple of pictures were stinkers. They told the papers we ended the contract by mutual agreement, but the truth is that they forced me out."

Shelly looked at me and stubbed out his cigarette in the ashtray, then continued sorting through my list.

"I think I embarrassed them," I continued. "My marriage to Husband #1 came out while I was being courted by Husband #2 during shooting for *The Beautiful and Damned*. Before I was officially divorced. I'm now divorcing #2."

"Oh, yeah." He nodded. "I remember seeing that in the papers. I can see them being a little *baroygis*." Realizing he hadn't been truly hospitable, he offered me the little bowl on his desk. "Peanut?"

"No, thank you," I said.

He flicked one into his mouth and continued reading while he crunched. "Recently you've done some work for PDC—Metropolitan, Christie, and DeMille. Contract terminated from their end."

"Financial problems. Mr. Kennedy came in and cleaned house to save money," I said.

He nodded. "No work for Roach? Smaller outfits?"

I told him about Howard Hughes and the Mormon picture. "And *The Sideshow* for Columbia. It came out last month. The director, Erle Kenton, got me the job."

"Receipts?"

"Average sales for Columbia," I said. "And *The Racket* did all right, but the other…"

He let out a rumbling chuckle. "Flop. You don't have to tell me. I might be able to make a golf course deal for you though. It's all about finessing things."

I leaned forward to hear this part.

"I got contacts all over this town. Secretaries, prop hands, grips, set decorators, publicity men... I play poker with Hal Wallis at Warner's, and I know Teet Carle at Paramount. Few more guys on Poverty Row..."

"I'm friends with Hal," I said.

"That's good. Could come in handy. Those connections feed me information. Louis B. Mayer's looking for a tough guy? I can do that. Ingénue at Columbia? I got that too. Bonus points for the round-heeled ones, 'cause Harry Cohn likes those best. Now, we both know your ingénue/bathing beauty days are past, but what I'm seeing for you are the wise-cracking, gum-chewing best friend parts. There's plenty of those out there, believe you me. Your problem is that you haven't had the Shelly Kirschner grapevine working for you up til now."

I let it all sink in. I'd been saying I needed an in for a while. It had been hard not knowing what was going on at the studios at any given time. Maybe Shelly could help me.

He paused and gave me a good hard look. So hard that I grew uncomfortable.

"If I were you?" he said. "I'd lay off the banana cream pie. I got a great diet here."

He rummaged through a desk drawer. Finally he pulled out a typewritten page. SHELLY`S REDUCING DIET was typed in all capital letters at the top. The diet consisted of grapefruit, more grapefruit, tomato salad, lots of water and black coffee, and a few hard-boiled eggs. I took it. I should have been insulted, but my self-respect was already in the toilet. This was all about getting work. If it was effective, I could swallow my pride.

"That's a gin blossom you're getting," he said matter-of-factly.

I swallowed hard and felt my face flush. "How do you know that?" I asked, my voice raspy and unrecognizable.

"You think I ain't seen it before? Talkies have been hard for everybody," he said. "If I'm gonna represent you, you'll have to nip that in the bud."

"I'm trying very hard..." I said. "Ever since my mother died nearly three years ago, I've been trying to bounce back. But with my divorce and..."

"Don't wanna hear excuses. I wanna see you drinking Coca-Cola and eating salads and grapefruit. My clients are either on their way up or on their way down. You may not be making the cover of *Photoplay* anymore, but you're not a washed-up lush either. Understood?"

"Understood," I said. "How much of all this do you take?"

"Ten percent off the top," he said, reaching into his top drawer for the standard contract. When I winced, he got his back up. "That's standard!"

He lay the contract in front of me, and I looked it over. The party of the first part, blah-blah-blah. In short, his duties would be to use all reasonable efforts to assist me in procuring employment in the motion picture industry.

"I understand," I said. "I need all the help I can get, Shelly. Grapevine or whatever else you've got."

"Glad you realize that," he said. "Sign on this line right here."

When I got home from his office, I got the mail since Delilah was out. The final divorce decree had arrived, which made it official. Ken and I were done forever. I poured a drink and gazed at the paper, imagining getting back on top with Shelly's help. I'd run into Ken at some premiere—me in some slinky black silk number once I'd whittled my waist back down—and there he'd be, in last year's tuxedo, squiring some Hollywood matron around, scavenging crumbs down in Gower Gulch because all he was qualified for were two-bit westerns. Raising my glass in a toast to no one and nothing in particular, I chugged it back and felt about a hundred times better. The pale wooziness slipped over me, and I poured another for good measure.

Because I was lost in thought, I finally realized that Jinx hadn't greeted me at the door like she usually did. I found her in my bedroom. She lay on her side, panting hard, obviously in some kind of distress.

"What is it, girl?" I asked, kneeling down next to her. Her stomach was hard when I touched it, and I knew something was terribly wrong. I scooped her up and sped to one of the few veterinarians in town, Dr. Taylor, who had an apartment above his office on Alvarado. When he was able to see her, she was drooling and panting even harder.

"Doctor, please help her," I begged.

"I'm sorry, Miss Prevost. I'm not sure what's wrong with her. Could she have eaten something poisonous?"

"Nothing. Only her regular food."

"Perhaps it's a cancerous situation. Her stomach is quite firm and distended. I could try to use a poultice, but it doesn't look good. Hydrogen peroxide might make her vomit if she ingested something bad for her, but it could make things worse."

"What should I do?" I asked.

"I'm afraid this is a wait and see situation."

Jinx whined, her little face clenched in agony. I took her front paw gently as my eyes blurred with tears. "Tell me what to do, girl. I hate seeing you like this," I whispered. She nuzzled my hand.

"I can keep her here overnight for observation," Dr. Taylor said.

"I'll stay too," I said. I sat down in the chair next to the exam table and caressed her soft fur.

About four in the morning, Doctor Taylor woke me, since I'd nodded off.

"Miss Prevost, Jinx is dead. I'm very sorry."

I pulled myself awake and looked over to see her eyes frozen open. "No no no…" I said, trying to understand. "She was fine, only yesterday…"

"I'm afraid the canine part of veterinary science is not that developed. A few years ago, we all treated horses. We're only beginning to learn about dogs, and we don't know as much as we should. I'm so sorry."

When I returned home, I crossed to the bar and poured myself a whiskey. The house was eerily quiet. No clicking toenails on the linoleum, no happy panting, no joyful yapping. Exhausted and heartsick, I cried myself to sleep.

CHAPTER THIRTY~THREE

CAMDEN DRIVE HOUSE, BEVERLY HILLS, CALIFORNIA
February 1929

"I'll connect you now," said the operator. "Long distance from New York."

"Marie!" came the voice at the other end. "It's Phyl! How are you, dearie?"

Trying to get over the disaster of my whopping four-year marriage now that things are officially over. Still panicking that I have no contract. Missing Mum desperately. Sad that Jinx is dead and I couldn't do a thing to help her. Lonely as hell. Why do you ask?

"Oh, you know," I said. "Getting by. You?" I shook the ice in my rocks glass and downed the rest of the whiskey.

"I have wonderful news! I met someone. And we're getting married!" she crowed.

"You only broke up with Stephen two months ago, didn't you?"

"Yes, but I'm over him," she said. "Billy is such a darling. Stephen didn't compare."

"How did you meet?"

"A party at Mayor Walker's house. Billy's good friends with him. We started chatting, and it was pure magic!"

I wasn't sure how many of Phyl's meet-cutes I'd heard described as magic until the magic wore off and she was on to the next.

"His name is Billy Seeman. He's owns a wholesale grocery chain, and he has buckets of money. I can finally be a lady of leisure!"

"I thought you always wanted to be an actress," I said.

"I did, but I'm tired of it. Now I want to be rich and in love. I told DeMille I was invoking the 'Act of God' clause. 'What Act of God clause?' he says. I said, 'Well, if marrying a millionaire isn't an act of God, I don't know what is!'" She gave a great hooting laugh and I joined her.

"Please tell me you'll be my maid of honor!" she said.

"I'd love to be your best girl, Phyl. But it depends when and where. If I'm working, it'll be hard to get away during a shoot. You know that."

"It'll be in April. Billy's cousin is Rube Goldberg, the cartoonist. He lives out on Long Island, and we're having it at his house. Mayor Walker's going to marry us. Please say you'll come."

"I'll try, Phyl. Honest I will."

"Good. I'll send you a picture of the attendants' dresses I've chosen, a bolt of the fabric, and the pattern."

I found a reasonably priced seamstress and had the frock made. For their wedding gift, I bought a set of twelve footed crystal sherbet dishes, which I planned on personally taking them on the train. Phyl loved sherbet.

Despite Pathé being under Joe Kennedy's thumb, Shelly

had persuaded them to cast me in *The Flying Fool*, and it had been taking up all my spare time. They'd made me read the nursery rhyme about Old King Cole for my sound test, and I miraculously got the thumbs up.

It was my first real sound film, but it was an extra challenge. They also wanted me to sing, since I played a night-club singer named Pat Riley.

"Sing?" I said, horrified. "I can't carry a tune. Even in the world's biggest bucket."

"Don't worry," said Tay Garnett, our director. "We'll get you a voice coach."

"I don't think you know what you're asking," I said. "But I'll do my best."

I spent every minute practicing scales and arpeggios, but it was no use. I wouldn't be ready to sing in my scenes, so Tay got someone to dub my voice. *Photoplay* knew no different, and crowed that I'd be crooning along fabulously by my next film. Liars.

To my horror, as the wedding date approached, production fell further and further behind.

"I'm sorry, Marie," Tay said when I asked him about getting my scenes done before I left. "We still have multiple scenes to shoot. We're running way behind if we want to get this thing out on schedule. There's no way they'll say yes—wedding or no wedding."

"She's my best friend," I moaned.

"You know how it is," he said. "Production schedules."

I dreaded making the phone call to Phyl. She'd be hurt, but how could I explain how badly I needed the coin from this film? If she'd only stayed in California where she had belonged instead of hitching her wagon to some east coaster, we'd all have been happy. It had been so long since my pre-Sennett days at the law firm—those lean years when Mum and Peg and I had nothing. I'd had to return to that mindset—saving every penny, wearing last year's frocks, and mending my underwear when it began to fray instead of buying the fancy silk stuff from France to replace it.

"Here goes nothing," I muttered. "Operator, long distance, please. Manhattan, New York GRamercy 4-3000."

"Of course, madam. I'll ring you back when your call connects." She did.

"Haver residence," said Phyl's maid, Hortense.

"Hortense, it's Miss Prevost. Is Phyllis there?"

"Hello, Miss Marie. Hold the phone."

"Marie!" Phyl squealed. "How are you?"

"I'm fine," I said, reluctant to be a killjoy first thing.

"There's still so much to do!" she said. "The flowers, the photographer... I found a baker in Manhattan who's making this incredible five-tier thing with spun sugar angels and it's going to be so beautiful! Is your dress all ready?"

"Phyl, I'm afraid I have some bad news," I said. "I can't get away for the wedding."

"What? But you promised!" she cried.

"I said I'd try. And I did. Honest I did. But our shoot has fallen behind. I can't get away. Ralph's bills are pouring in for the divorce, and now I have the hospital bills from my pneumonia in November too. I *have* to work now. I don't have a choice."

She sighed dramatically. "I'm not sure who else I can find on such short notice," she said. "I'd always assumed it would be you standing next to me." Amazing. I could actually hear her pouting over the phone.

"I'm not sure how I can make it up to you, but I will," I said. "I'm still sending your gift. I think you'll like it."

"Thanks for letting me know," she said. "I have to go."

"Phyl, I..."

Click.

I stood holding the phone after she hung up. My heart physically hurt.

COCOANUT GROVE, AMBASSADOR HOTEL, LOS ANGELES, CALIFORNIA
Mid-May 1929

"Marie!" the man exclaimed, raising a hand in greeting. He threaded his way through the room with a younger fellow in tow. It took me a minute to realize it was Buster Collier, who'd worked with me at Sennett. "It's wonderful to see you again! It's been ages. Absolutely ages!" He gave me a hug and a kiss on the cheek.

It had been ages. I hadn't been out on the town for a few months. But Shelly had come through with a film called *Divorce Made Easy*, so I'd decided to have a little fun.

I'd always liked Buster. He was a fatherly type who had worked with me in *Better Late Than Never* when I'd first started in flickers. It seemed strange to say it about the manic, go-go-go eccentrics at the Sennett lot, but Buster had always been a court-ly fellow. His salt and pepper hair and sensitive eyes seemed more respectable than the other clowns on the lot who'd do any-thing for a laugh. We caught up for a few minutes—he'd moved on from Sennett, doing some work at Selznick and Fox—and I told him about my work too, meanwhile sneaking glimpses of the younger man. This had to be his stepson, Buster, Jr. Talk about drop-dead gorgeous. His dark hair was brushed back in a natural wave from a high forehead, and his eyes were friendly and open. I'd seen him in the *The Bugle Call* years ago as a child actor. But he was all grown up now and sporting a five o'clock shadow to die for.

"How are all your pals?" he asked. "You girls were like the three musketeers—you and Phyllis and Vera."

"I suppose you heard about Phyl's marriage," I said. "Unfortunately, I couldn't make it." I couldn't tell him how hurt I'd been by Phyl's brush-off. "And Vera was supposed to be getting remarried last year, to a fellow named Russell Dougherty, but it fell through. She's never told me what happened. It must have been pretty serious, whatever it was."

"That's too bad," he said.

"You heard about Mary?"

"Tragic news. She was such a lovely girl. So sweet. I've been worried about Juanita too," he said.

"Yes, that awful shower episode," I said. "And everything else she's been dealing with." We shook our heads.

"I was sorry to hear about you and Ken," he offered.

"Thanks," I said. "There are some people who care about each other very much, but they can't live together. That's me and Ken."

The younger Buster's eyebrows perked up in interest.

"I'm sad all the same," he said. "You always looked so happy together."

"We had some good times," I agreed. "We also had some

crummy ones."

"Oh, where are my manners? Marie, this is my stepson, also Buster." He chuckled. "Buster, Marie Prevost."

"Nice to meet you, Marie," he said.

"Me too," I said. Then felt like an idiot. *Me too, what?*

So this was the fellow who made the gossip columns every week with a new girl. Connie Talmadge had been the last.

The combo broke into the first few bars of "That's My Weakness Now" and Buster got a gleam in his eye.

"Would you care to dance?" he asked me.

"Sure," I said, giving him a sideways smile. He led me to the polished, parquet dance floor, where we shimmied, laughing and chatting the whole time.

"My dad talks about working at Sennett all the time. He loved it there," he said as the orchestra lapsed into "Always," a slower song. He led me around the floor with polished style.

"We all did. He used to tell us about you when you were younger. He was so proud of you. Hard to believe that was nearly fifteen years ago."

"Not that hard," he said. "You were beautiful as a bathing beauty, and you still are." Fifteen years might have been a blink to you."

If this guy thought I was going to fall for his smooth, ladies' man routine, I had news for him.

"Why, Mister Collier. You've had that tongue of yours silver-plated," I said.

"That's what they tell me," he said with a grin. He whipped me around in a turn. "What say I lose the old man and we go have some real fun?"

"Real fun?"

"Yeah. I know of some great speaks downtown."

Ugh. The Red Rooster? No thanks.

"No. Absolutely not," I said. *That's all I need. A looker like this and all the booze I can drink. Trouble with a capital T.*

"How come?"

"Two reasons. Number one, I'm trying to cut down my drinking. Number two—I know about your reputation."

"What reputation is that? That I'm an actor capable of stunning depth and breadth?" He looked down at me and smiled.

"No, your way of breaking hearts from here to La Jolla, documented by Miss Grace Kingsley of the *Los Angeles Times.*"

"I'm no lothario, I assure you. I'm completely honest with all the ladies I see. I tell them upfront I'm too young to wed. I'm irresistible, that's all."

"And humble too, evidently," I said.

"Everyone knows about you and Ken Harlan. Surely you don't want to dive right back in the marriage pool, do you?"

He had a point.

"Then how about it?" he said as we came out of a final turn.

"More dancing is a good start."

And that was how it began—my affair with a younger man.

It was not quite a full six-year age difference, but Buster was like a breath of fresh air. He sired me around town to the Cocoanut Grove, the Brown Derby, and George Olsen's Supper Club. I ate sensibly and watched the booze, I swam a lot, and we did plenty of dancing. But I always met him at the door, we left immediately, and he dropped me off afterward with a chaste kiss.

But finally, the night arrived where he pulled up in front of the house in his sporty Cord Cabriolet and looked over at me for his customary kiss goodnight. At last, I felt ready to say goodbye to the past.

"Come in for a nightcap?"

He raised an eyebrow. "I'd love one, thanks."

He made himself comfortable on the living room sofa while I shook up some Bronx cocktails at the bar.

"Nice house," he said looking around.

"Thanks," I said, thinking of all the maintenance it needed that I couldn't afford. "We can go in the parlor if you like. It overlooks the pool, and it's a little less stuffy."

He didn't say a word, merely took both our drinks. Then, with a Cheshire grin, he moved down the dark corridor toward the parlor. I flicked on the light, and the backyard sprang to life from the darkness.

"We could go swimming," he said.

"I might still have one of Ken's old suits in the cabana," I replied.

"Who needs suits?" He winked.

Although I was self-conscious, he persuaded me to join him. The warm water caressed our limbs and the booze made me a little heedless, but I was still nervous. Sonny and Ken were the only men I'd ever been with.

"It's been so long," I whispered.

"Then relax," he said. "Let me make you feel good." He nuzzled my ear, then kissed my neck. His lips traced a trail down to my shoulder, and his thumb worked a maddening rhythm on my nipple. My body came alive as he whispered sweet nothings in my ear that before, might have made me blush. Then he cornered me against the wall of the pool and took me roughly until I cried out in pleasure. He put a gentle hand over my mouth to keep the neighbors from hearing. When we were done, we dried off, then went inside and kept it up until the wee hours. He tried positions Sonny and Ken didn't know a thing about.

Buster treated me like a princess. Like I was still beautiful and desirable. When we made love, it was the way it had been with Ken in the early days—sensual, exciting, and satisfying. And because he was younger, there was never a question of him being ready. He was always ready.

It was all the best parts of a new love—the dancing, the sweet words, the flirting, the romantic dinners out, but none of the hassle of a marriage—no stealing the covers, no onion breath in the mornings, no drinking the last of the orange juice without telling me, no late night phone calls waking me up. Buster only wanted to have fun. When he'd said, 'Let me make you feel good,' he knew what he was talking about.

CHAPTER THIRTY~FOUR

November 1, 1929

"**L**ong distance from New York," Delilah said. "Mist' Thatcher."

"Marie, it's me, Ernie," Ernie Thatcher said when I picked up.

Ernie was the stockbroker that Ken and I had hired when we'd decided to get serious about saving and investing. The last time I'd heard from him was when we'd divvied up the assets.

"Ernie, how the heck are you? I hear Wall Street is in an uproar."

"I've been waiting to call you until I knew for sure, but I've got very bad news," he said.

"How bad?" I said, feeling a little queasy.

"The worst," he said with a sigh. "It's gone down the toilet. Along with the rest of America. We've all lost fortunes the last few days."

"Can I re-invest?" I asked.

"There's nothing to re-invest, Marie. It's gone. Every cent."

"Twenty-thousand dollars? Gone?" I gasped. Suddenly, those headlines yelling doom and gloom the last week made horrible sense. "I don't understand how this happened. This can't be real."

"I'm afraid it is. If I were you, I'd start selling what you can. Cars, houses, anything. Do it while there's still time. This is going to get worse. You're going to need some liquid capital. I don't want to scare you, but every day here, the newspapers are full of fellas who've either jumped out skyscraper windows or blown their brains out with antique pearl-handled derringers."

I tried not to scream into his ear.

"I want you to understand how serious this is, and I want to protect you," he continued. "As I said, I would start selling the houses and the cars right away. Keep only what you absolutely need. I know Hollywood's a boomtown right now with the talkies taking off, but this crash is so bad, it's going to affect all of us. Hollywood can't make any money if no one can afford to go to the pictures."

"Dear God," I said, collapsing onto the Louis XIV loveseat. Jesus, how much had we paid for this thing? Suddenly, every expensive bauble I'd ever bought came back to haunt me. Mum would be tsk-tsking at me right now.

"I'm sorry to give you such awful news, Marie. I need to go. I have more clients to call. I can't apologize enough. I really can't."

We said our goodbyes, and I put the receiver back in the cradle, my hand shaking. My body quaked like I had palsy.

I started making plans.

I sold the McFarlan to a junior screenwriter at RKO. That left me with the Stutz. Slightly used, but still glamorous enough to be seen in around Hollywood.

I called a realtor friend named Ned Davidson and told him I wanted to put the Camden Drive house up for sale, in addition to the other property Ken and I had split up in the divorce. The Malibu house would be fine for me and occasionally for Buster. I didn't need all that wasted space anyway. Ned came and visited me that weekend. I served tea and cookies and he asked me about my decision.

"Are you sure about this?" he asked, taking a bite of Wee Mae's shortbread.

"I don't have a choice, Ned."

"Are you sure you wouldn't rather unload the Malibu place? It seems like this one would be closer to the studios. For work." He hadn't had to add the last bit. But we both knew what he meant. The studios. Plural. Those of us with no contract could never tell where our next job might come from.

"This place has too many memories. Happy ones, sad ones, broken dreams of my life with Ken. The Malibu house is a new start for me. I'd rather stay there. It's symbolic, I think. A fresh beginning." I gave him a little smile.

"They don't even have phones up there yet, do they?"

"There are some college boys who make extra scratch running errands for us. They've got a nice little racket going, and they bring me my phone messages. Helps me stay in touch with my agent."

"I understand. But I want to make sure your decision is

well thought out before I place my sign out front."

"I know," I said.

I walked him to the door and stood at the window, watching him pound the For Sale sign into the lawn. It had been impossible for Delilah not to hear everything going on between Ned and me, and I knew it was time to give her the bad news. I slipped into the kitchen as she wrung out the mop in the kitchen sink.

"Mist' Davidson gone? I was gonna bring out some mo' iced tea."

"He's putting the For Sale sign out front, then he's going to go list it," I said.

"Tha's too bad," she said. "Lots of nice mem'ries in this house."

"Some not-so-nice ones too, but all houses are like that."

"You's here to tell me you got ta let me go," she said sadly.

"Yes, I'm afraid I am," I said. "I'm so sorry, Delilah. You've been a wonderful maid and an even better friend. I don't know what I'll do without you." I put an arm around her broad shoulders.

"I've known it was coming for a while," she admitted.

"You did? I've only just now figured it out myself."

"'Course," she said. "I wash yo clothes, Miss Marie. I do the mendin' on 'em. Used to be, you bought all them fancy French silks and whatnot, and you ain't done that for a long time." She stopped rinsing and turned toward me.

"I kept hoping things would turn around," I said. "A new contract or a rich husband like Phyl got. But the big man upstairs has decided to throw me some curveballs. With talkies and this economic issue hitting at the same time,

I've never been so afraid. I'm trying to put on a brave face, but it's hard."

"You been a good boss to me. You ain't mean and snooty like some. I'll miss you, Miss Marie."

"I'll miss you too. After I lost Mum, I'd have been lost without you," I said, my voice breaking. "But I'll write you a sterling reference for your next job."

"I 'preciate that. Shore won't be the same though."

"If you could see out the rest of the week, I can pay you then."

"'Course," she said. "I'll do anythin' tuh help."

"Maybe someday I'll be able to bring you on again," I said, with more optimism than I felt.

"I'd like that."

Several weeks later, the house was sold, to a young, aspiring actress named Frances Langford and her family. A truck filled with my possessions followed me up to Malibu. My possessions minus a few pieces I sold to tide me over.

After a quick telegram announcing her arrival, Phyl came west for a visit, so we made a weekend out of it, unpacking and organizing things, and then we drove to Sam's, a place on the beach closer to town that sold the freshest seafood that you could buy. We sat on the patio, dressing our flounder with lemon and watching the seagulls frolic over the dunes. Marriage appeared to agree with Phyllis. She was tanned, and her summer togs looked expensive. The rock on her third finger left hand dwarfed any stone I'd ever seen before. She still hadn't apologized, but at least we were talking again.

"Billy will be back in two weeks," she said. "We hate

being away from each other. Why didn't you tell me this was what marriage was like? I would have done it a long time ago!" She speared a bite of fish.

"Marriage *can* be like that," I said, sipping my ginger ale. "Sometimes it's not."

"I'm sorry, honey," she said, patting my hand.

"Yeah, me too." I took a bite of carrot, but coveted her baked potato, all smothered in butter and sour cream.

"You know what I wish more than anything?" she said.

"What's that?"

"That even once, we could be in the same place at the same time."

"I may be imagining this, but we are here together on this patio, aren't we?" I said, confused.

"You know what I mean. Your career takes off, I'm still busting my hump for Sennett. You're going to glamorous premieres and rubbing shoulders with bluenoses, and I'm still buying off the rack at Nordlinger's. Your career goes into a lull, and I make *Chicago* and have directors beating a path to my door. You marry Ken, I'm still testing the waters. You guys get divorced, and I meet the man of my dreams."

My God, she's right.

"I wish we could congratulate each other on our mutual good fortune instead of one of us always having to console the other—whether it's a movie contract or a marriage."

"It could be worse. We could be in Wah's shoes," I said.

"Actually, she's doing better," Phyl said. "Did you hear? She got over $150,000 from that hotel where she got scalded. She came to the wedding, but she had to use a lot of pancake makeup to hide the scars."

"How'd she look other than that?" I asked.

"Remarkably well, considering everything she's been through the last few years. Heard from Vera lately?"

"She's been busy," I said. "Little Marie's in ballet. And she has piano lessons, and Brownies, and..."

"She's seven."

"Vera thinks she has potential," I said. "Oh, and I got a Christmas card from Gonda. She and Bob are doing fine. I need to send her a change of address." Gonda had married Bob Kortman, a cowboy actor, back in 1922.

"I got one from Myrtle," Phyl said. "Only her signature. Not much to say."

We chatted more as the shadows began angling across the flagstones of Sam's, then Phyl said the words I most loved hearing from others these days. "I'll get the check."

When it came time for her to catch the train back to New York, I drove her to the depot and waited as she confirmed her ticket on the California Limited.

"We'll talk soon, honey. It was so good catching up with you again." She hugged me, then snapped her fingers to get the attention of a porter.

"I'm on the 2:10 to Chicago," she said. "Can you get me set up?"

He touched the brim of his cap and hefted her trunks onto his luggage cart.

"Take care of yourself," she said. "Let me know if you need anything."

Pretty words, but if the last few months were any indication, Billy would be all she thought about for months until I got a Christmas card filled out by her personal secretary. If

I was lucky, I might get a fruitcake to go with it. Til she was ninety-seven years old, Phyllis would be flighty and expect everyone to buzz around her like bees around a fat pink peony.

BUSTER'S HOUSE, HOLLYWOOD, CALIFORNIA
February 1930

The jangling tore through the layers of bourbon and pills and sleep. I almost thought it was one of Ken's late-night phone calls until I remembered. Buster and I had been out late at the Cocoanut Grove. I had no desire to emerge from under the covers.

"Marie," Buster said. "Phone. It's Shelly."

I took it and rasped hello.

"It's past noon, toots. Time to get up. You sound like shit."

"I'm catching up on my beauty sleep," I lied.

"Yeah? Well, I hope you're well-rested. Take a Smith Brothers. I need you bright-eyed and bushy-tailed. I nabbed you a screen test."

Buster nuzzled me and I swatted his hand away, all ears for Shelly.

"Screen test? Oh…" I snuck a glimpse in the mirror across from the bed and could only think one thing: disaster. Pasty complexion, puffy face, multiple chins, hair that hadn't seen a comb since yesterday, and purple bags under my eyes—so big I could have used them for a trip to the tropics. "Who? When?" I was so choked up I couldn't speak.

"I had lunch the other day with Harry Cohn over at Columbia. They've got some new vehicle they're working on for a dancer in their stable—Barbara Stanwyck."

"I've met Barbara. Up in Malibu," I said, still trying to wake up.

"He's worried. She's had two flops in a row, but they've given her to this up-and-coming director of theirs named Frank Capra. It could be another complete mess, but at least it'll keep the bills paid for a month or so. When Cohn asked me how you're doing, I fibbed and told him you're in fighting trim. Don't make me look like an asshole here, okay? You been following the diet?"

"Yes," I lied. "Shelly, that audition for *Madam Satan*... did you hear back from MGM yet?"

"Bad news. They chose Kay Johnson."

I sighed. That one stung. DeMille had moved over to MGM, and I'd been so hopeful. Deep down, I guess I'd known it. But I hadn't wanted to admit it to myself.

"Sorry, kid. He said you're too heavy. He didn't think anyone would buy you as Angela Brooks. Now, remember. Two weeks from today. Monday the eighteenth, 8 a.m. sharp. Afterward, go to Harry Cohn's office. He's expecting you. Mention my name at the gate. You'll be fine."

"Eight a.m.," I repeated.

"Sharp."

"Got it, Shelly. I can't thank you enough."

"Call me Monday night," he said. "Let me know how it went."

"I will," I promised.

CHAPTER THIRTY~FIVE

OFFICE OF HARRY COHN, COLUMBIA STUDIOS, HOLLYWOOD, CALIFORNIA
February 1930

You know you've sunk pretty far in the looks department when Harry Cohn doesn't make a pass at you. The man's casting couch was already legendary. I wasn't sure if I needed to be insulted or relieved. The sad thing was, I was so desperate for a part that I would have done nearly anything he asked. I hadn't had to deal with him before since Erle Kenton had helped me get *The Sideshow*, but this time, it was inevitable.

Cohn peered at me with those strange pale blue eyes of his under looming brows. His plaid jacket was louder than the Los Angeles Philharmonic. And that god-awful cologne he wore. One of Peg's old boyfriends had worn the same stuff. "Carnival in Venice," he called it. Combined with the cigar smoke from his Larrañaga, it was enough to give a girl the heaves right there in his office.

"Shelly tells me you're free to do this picture," he said. "I still wanna see your screen test footage, but *The Sideshow* did okay for us. I'm willing to give you another try."

"Thank you, Mr. Cohn."

"I got this new gal from the Follies. Barbara Stanwyck. I ain't been that impressed with her so far, but this director, Capra, he liked what he seen, and he's insisting on her bein' in the picture. I like the guy, I'm figuring what the hell. She oughta do better if she's got a pro like you showing her the ropes."

"That sounds great," I said. Playing the ass end of a horse costume sounded great right then as long as it paid the bills. But I couldn't tell *him* that.

"Think you're up for it? Shelly says you're hurtin' for work. But don't dare tell nobody you had an in. I didn't get where I am by bein' nice. You got that?"

"Sure. Not a word from me."

Anybody else would have asked what the film was about or who the co-stars were. Not me. That's how bad things were. *Ladies of Leisure* was going to save my bacon, flop or not.

Barbara was a hoot. A tough Brooklyn broad with a wicked sense of humor. She wasn't a typical beauty, but she knew how to work with what she had. Auburn hair, hazel eyes, and a nose a little too long to be considered conventionally pretty. She gave her all on the first take, so the rest of us had to rehearse like crazy beforehand, so we'd be polished when she was ready to go.

Ladies of Leisure was the story of Kay Arnold, a party girl on the make who was hired by a guy named Jerry Strong to be an artist's model. I played Dot, the wise-cracking, gold-digging best friend. Only Dot's jokes were usually at her own weight, and she was often shown eating to drive the humor home. God, it hurt saying those lines. Marie Prevost, the smick-smack bathing beauty, now reduced to a bad punch-line. When I saw the rushes of me stuffing my face on camera, I had to go be sick. It didn't help my ulcer any.

And it didn't bode well when we were a week into shooting and I doubled over in pain again. No. Not now. Please God. It felt like I was trying to pass a watermelon through my gut. Not eaten and chewed. Whole. That week, I'd tried Fletcher's Castoria, ginger ale, and milk of magnesia, and nothing seemed to work.

"You okay, honey?" Barbara asked.

"I'm fine," I said, pooh-poohing her as I lowered myself into a canvas chair near the set. But the pain wasn't going away.

"We need to get you to a doctor, Marie. You're positively green."

"Green?" I grabbed a prop mirror from the small table next to me and looked for myself. She was right. I was chartreuse.

"You want us to shoot around you today, Marie? You don't look so good," Mr. Capra said as he approached.

"Jesus," I said, pulling myself up out of my chair. "What's with everybody? I'm all right. Perfectly fi—" The real pain hit then—I hadn't realized it could get that much worse—and I collapsed to the ground with a moan, curling up in the fetal position.

"Frank, call an ambulance!" Barbara said, kneeling beside me.

Capra dashed off to find a phone, and Barbara stayed with me, holding my hand. Ralph Graves, our other co-star, gathered a couple pillows from the set and tucked them under my head, then lay a blanket over me. When the ambulance arrived, the attendants hustled me into the back and sped off to St. Vincent's, my new second home. Then I was promptly wheeled into surgery.

When I came to, it felt like someone had wrapped me in layers of gauze. For a minute, with the bright lights over my bed, I thought I was on set, and had blacked out for a minute. But then my sense of smell kicked in, and I recognized the antiseptic odor from so many other stays.

"How are we feeling?" A nurse stood beside my bed, looking down inquisitively. She had a clipboard in her hand and noted something with the stub of a pencil. I recognized her from my last stay.

"Like I've been punched by Gene Tunney, the bastard," I said, pulling myself up.

"You've been in bad shape," she said, hanging the clipboard from a hook at the foot of the bed.

"The ulcer?"

"Yep," she said.

A tally of new medical bills rolled through my head, making me even sicker. "When can I get out of here?" I asked.

"You're out of harm's way now. The doctor might even let you go home this week. But he'll give you the prognosis when he's ready. Have to get back to shooting, do you?" she said. She arranged the pillows behind me.

"As a matter of fact..."

"I love your films," she said. "If you need anything, you let me know. I'm Ruth."

"Thank you," I said. After her footsteps echoed off into the hallway, I crawled out of bed and looked at the cards and flowers. Vera had sent pink carnations. "Feel better soon, sweetie!" said her card. Barbara Stanwyck had sent a pretty mixed arrangement with a card she'd had the cast sign. There were also some gladiolus blossoms from Mr. Lubitsch, some irises from Louise, and a beautiful bouquet of twelve red roses from Buster.

In a few days, I felt well enough for shooting. Barbara and I ran through our lines, but I had to sit down a lot more between scenes. Often during them.

"Don't worry about it, honey," Barbara said. "You're still not a hundred percent yet."

When *Ladies of Leisure* was released, Barbara became a star overnight, and Mr. Capra was suddenly a director to watch. The trades loved me as Dot, and it looked like I could carve out a new gum-chewing best friend niche for myself. The flapper could turn over a new leaf, evidently. Still, Harry Cohn didn't have me sign a contract. After I got the heave-ho from Columbia, Al offered me a small film called *Sweethearts on Parade* with Alice White until Shelly could find me something else.

Shelly called two days after we wrapped. "I got good news!" he crowed. "Screen test at MGM, bright and early Wednesday. Give em my name at the gate. It's a Great War picture with Anita Page and Robert Montgomery called *War Nurse*. I worked my *tuchus* off to get you this one. That L.B. Mayer is a tough nut to crack. I had to keep extending the one-mulligan rule. So make it count."

"I'll be there," I said. "Thank you, Shelly."

You know what? He was right. I did fine. Louis B. Mayer wanted to see me in his office afterward. And fortunately,

Shelly had let me know to dress up. Mayer liked things formal.

I'd filmed at MGM before, back when it was still the Gold-wyn lot, for *Red Lights*, a loan-out when I was still at War-ner's. I entered at the colonnade, found a spot to park not far past the main gate, and followed Shelly's directions. Mayer's office was on the first floor of the Administration building. When I entered, three women sat at desks outside. The oldest one had steel gray hair styled in unflattering curls, an unre-lenting stare behind wire-framed glasses, and a double strand of pearls. Her nameplate said Ida Koverman. Shelly had been right about her too.

"Now when you get there," he'd told me. "The old lady in the office is in charge. She may look harmless, like your *bubbe*, but she's got fangs for days. Mount Ida. To you, she's 'Yes, Miss Koverman,' and 'Anything you say, Miss Koverman.' Got that?"

"Got it."

"Have a seat, please," Mount Ida said when I introduced myself. "I'll see if he's available."

I sat down in a chair in the reception area, with my purse and gloves in my lap, trying not to fidget.

Mount Ida pressed the button on the intercom. "Mr. May-er, Miss Prevost is here."

"Send her in," the intercom buzzed. I rose and entered the sanctum sanctorum.

"Miss Prevost!" he said. "Come in! Please have a seat."

I did as I was told. The man at the desk was imposing, as I'm sure he meant to be. On anyone else, his long sloped nose would have simply looked big. But it gave his face char-acter. Like his secretary, he wore wire-framed spectacles, and observed you without a word until he was good and ready to speak. The office was all white—the desk too—and it was up on a raised dais. The carpet, phone, and grand piano were all white too.

"I was quite impressed with your screen test," he told me. "I figured that with the way Shelly kept going on and on, he was full of it, but I figured...a man that ready to lose at golf must be doing a damned good job for his clients. So I thought... what the hell. I'm prepared to offer you a choice role in *War Nurse*. If things go well, we could look at a longer contract."

I wanted to do a jig around his office.

"But," he continued. "This is all contingent on you staying your current weight or up to five to ten pounds below it. I saw *Party Girl* and I can tell you. There will be none of that weight gain here. Got it?"

"Yes sir," I said.

Shooting started at the beginning of August. My character, Rosalie, was one of the nurses who signed up, thinking the duties would be easy, only to quickly change her mind. Anita Page had the choice part of Joy, and Robert Montgomery played heroic soldier Wally. Also in the cast were Hedda Hopper and ZaSu Pitts, who'd made such a splash in *Greed* years before.

The shoot went well, I got along with the cast and crew, and I was the soul of professionalism. Not one drink anywhere near the set, no losing control, nothing. MGM were so impressed, they offered me a contract. A real live contract. I starved myself silly living on lettuce leaves and grapefruit, and I vibrated everywhere I went from all the time I spent on the reducing machine. I rubbed on fistfuls of Melto Reducing Cream, and I religiously wore my Davis Chin Strap. I even invested in a pair or Madame Willmarte's Electrolastic Ankle Reducers. Shelly was overjoyed.

At my next checkup, my regular physician, Dr. Baldwin, frowned as he unwound the blood pressure cuff from my arm.

"Marie, you know I want you to be thinner, but I also want you to be healthy," he said. "Overweight isn't good for anyone, but I'm worried about your methods."

"I'm fine, Doc, honestly," I pooh-poohed him.

"What are you eating to make you drop so quickly?"

"My agent gave me a plan to follow. Lots of grapefruit, water, tomatoes, coffee..." I said.

He shook his head. "That's extreme. All that acid from the grapefruit and tomatoes isn't good for your ulcer either. I'd lay off those for a while. I'd like to see some grilled chicken or fish, green leafy vegetables, some cottage cheese, more fruit other than grapefruit, and some grains..."

"No bread," I said. "Bread makes me fat."

"Piffle. Bread does not make you fat. The *amount* of bread you eat makes you fat."

I wrapped my paper gown a little tighter around my middle. "Doc, you don't understand. I'm fighting for my life here. I'm an actress. When I saw myself in *Party Girl*, I wanted to throw up. *Ladies of Leisure* too. Half the dialogue is me and the other characters making jokes about my weight. Do you have any idea how humiliating that is? When I'm not thin, I don't work. I'm over thirty now, and there are lots of younger, prettier girls coming in. Girls who don't have to hear producers telling them, 'You used to be a bathing beauty for Chrissakes. What happened?'"

He looked at me with sympathy. Or maybe it was pity. I

wasn't sure.

"I had some bad luck," I said. "With my mother passing away and the divorce and everything, but I'm fighting my way back. Once I'm back where I was, then I'll stop."

"You'll continue to eat sensibly after this?"

"Of course," I said. Sensibly except for the sundaes at Brown's, or the potato pancakes at the Brown Derby or the Boston cream pie at The Redondo Diner, or the deliveries from Blackie O'Toole, my bootlegger. When he looked a little cynical, I smiled. "Honest."

"How's the drinking?" he asked. I'd confessed I had a problem, but I couldn't tell him exactly how many deliveries Blackie was still making. At least he wasn't a dry, so I didn't need to worry about him informing on me.

"Better," I said. "I've cut way back." It was the truth. *This* week.

"All right. Everything else looks good. Put your dress back on and I'll have Nurse Anderson bring you some of the ointment I mentioned for your dry skin."

When I left my checkup, I strolled down Fourth Street, window shopping at The Broadway, and ignoring the siren song of the orange cake at Pico Café.

Not getting *Madam Satan* had hurt like hell. I was determined not to lose out again, simply because I was too fat to even be considered. When I heard about another smart ass best friend role up for grabs, I knocked off ten pounds in five days to get it.

CHAPTER THIRTY~SIX

SOUND STAGE, WITHIN THE LAW, LOT ONE, MGM STUDIOS
CULVER CITY, CALIFORNIA *May 16, 1930*

I got the part. The first day of shooting, I felt like a new woman. I'd been eating one meal a day, one cup of black coffee, and avoiding starches, sweets, and meat. The constant dizziness and headaches were harder to avoid. I hadn't cut back on the booze as much as I should have, but I was trying.

The *Herald* featured a story of Ken's remarriage to a woman named Doris Booth. I couldn't let anyone know how much it hurt. It hadn't even been two years since we'd split the final time. I wondered what she was like. If she was prettier than me, or smarter, or better in the sack, or...

"Say, you're Marie Prevost, aren't you? It's great to meet you at last."

"Yes, I am. And you're Joan. It's nice to meet you." I closed the newspaper and held out my hand.

Joan Crawford had made a splash the previous year in *Our Dancing Daughters*. Not bad in the acting department, and the gal could dance. I'd already met her husband, Doug

Fairbanks, Jr., the previous year, when we'd both been in *Party Girl*.

I enjoyed working at MGM. The people were friendly, the matzo ball soup at the commissary was delicious and cheap, and the guard at the colonnade gate, old Floyd, told me *Bobbed Hair* had been one of his favorites. He always gave me a cheerful "Good morning, Miss Prevost!" and a friendly wave. At last, I could relax a little. I was able to pay off a few bills, have work done on the Stutz, buy some new frocks for summer, replace my threadbare undies, and even stash some cash for a rainy day. I hadn't met my co-star yet, until now. But here she was. Joan Crawford. Her aqua-blue eyes were alive with excitement.

"I love your films," she said, pulling up a chair. "*Three Women* was marvelous. And I must have seen *The Marriage Circle* at least four times."

"That's very kind," I said. "If you get a chance to work with Mr. Lubitsch, I would definitely take it. He's a tough taskmaster, but a hell of a director."

"You were perfect in that part. As Mizzi I mean."

"Unfortunately, I can't be considered perfect at all these days. Ten extra pounds, and no one in Hollywood wants to know you."

"You look fine to me. Some grapefruit and salads and you'll be back on top in no time."

Joan was now considered Hollywood royalty, although some of it was reflected glory. Being married to Doug Jr meant she was princess to the King and Queen of Hollywood. It had to be a charmed life she was living. I'd been there once too.

"You know Harry Beaumont?" she said.

I nodded. I'd worked with Harry on *The Lover of Camille* and *Recompense*.

"Harry directed me in *Our Dancing Daughters*," she said. He told me the camera adds ten pounds. Eat less and you'll be fine."

If only it were that simple. I didn't tell her about my other problem. It was too embarrassing.

"What's it like being a daughter-in-law to Doug and Mary?" I asked. Nobody used their last names. No one needed to.

She rolled her eyes. "Why, they're just as wonderful as they can be. I hate going to Pickfair," she said. "Doug's father ignores him, and he and Mary pretend I'm not there. I think I'm a major inconvenience, reminding them of their ages. She wants to stay a girl to the public forever, and he refuses to grow up. I respect them for what they've accomplished, but they're not the nicest people in the world. They're royalty, and I'm plain old Lucille LeSueur from Kansas City. You're from Canada, right? That's what the fan magazines say. And we both know how reliable those are." She gave me a wink.

I laughed along and told her of Sarnia and the moves all over out west.

"How'd you end up out here?" she asked, leaning forward, elbows on knees.

"My mother moved us here after...my father died. And you? Are you from Kansas City originally?"

"No, Texas. Then Oklahoma. But my stepfather got into some trouble, so we ended up in KC."

"Trouble?" My ears perked up. "I know it's none of my business. I'm sorry."

She shrugged. "He was friends with an embezzler, and I

found the loot down in the cellar. My mother divorced him," she said matter-of-factly. I couldn't believe how casual she was about it all.

Suddenly all the years of keeping everything bottled up came rushing out.

"*My* stepfather lost $42,000 walking from a hotel to a bathhouse," I admitted. "At least that's what he told us. I personally think he got rolled by a woman of easy virtue."

"Mine managed a theater," she said. "What about yours?"

"Miner."

"And they divorced?"

"Yes," I said. There it was. Mum was gone. There was no need to keep up the pretense any longer.

She laughed. "Well, what do you know? The only way we could be more alike is if you have an ungrateful brother always begging you for money."

"Sister," I said. "Actually, half-sister."

Joan had been there. She understood. I had finally found someone I could talk to about all of it—Frank, the divorce, his dragging us all over the southwest in search of precious metals, his carelessly losing all that money.

"We should chat more," she said, hooting with laughter. "You must come to El Cielito Lindo this weekend for luncheon."

"El wha?"

"It's the name we gave our house, Doug and me. Please tell me you'll come!"

"I'd love to."

When I arrived, she welcomed me into their home. It was a stunning mix of antiques, upholstered with rose and green chintz. Her dining room had a huge Phyfe dining table that had to be at least nine feet long, with a set of eight matched chairs. The entire place was spotless. Not even a throw pillow out of place. She was wearing a flowing pantsuit, of the type that Marlene Dietrich had popularized recently. Her hair was elegantly marceled, and her makeup was flawless, red lips painted on in a perfect parabola.

Joan's cook, Hattie, made us precious little tea sandwiches and macaroni salad, iced tea in glasses garnished with fresh mint, and a delicious fruit salad with sweet liqueur added. After a time, these visits became the only special thing in my life. She knew how hard I was trying to claw my way back.

This Depression had changed a lot of Hollywood friendships. Phyllis had married, Vera was busy with little Marie's activities, Juanita was dealing with the courts after her settlement with the hotel had been overturned, and Louise was working on a slew of films, mostly for Warner's and First National, thanks to Hal's influence. Buster and Joan were two of the friends I could count on these days.

Coming as it did so soon after the arrival of sound, the Depression had sorted the talent in Hollywood into a couple of groups: those who made the conversion with flying colors like Joan or Ruth Chatterton, those who hadn't (and hadn't saved for a rainy day) like Alla Nazimova, or those who hadn't made it but were too rich to care, like the Talmadge sisters. I think the ones who'd made it were terrified of associating with those of us who hadn't. Almost as if it was catching—the looks not matching the voice, the delicate features emitting pure Jersey or Brooklynese. The ones who'd fared the best seemed to be from the Midwest or the stage. Theater actors had perfect diction and knew how to project their voices to be picked up by the small microphones planted in a vase of flowers on a table, on a ficus tree, or the lace fichu of a co-star's blouse.

Then there were those like me, who fell through the cracks. I had the voice for sound, but I also had a fluctuating waistline and a gin blossom. I was in a class by myself. I'd made the transition, so I wasn't deserving of real pity like Karl Dane, but I still didn't have a penny to my name. Honestly, I wasn't too proud. I could have used some pity, but I got lost in the shuffle. Not a success, not a complete failure, but not enough of either to be able to survive. Fortunately, Joan had a big heart.

I had moved onto *It's a Wise Child* with Marion Davies, but I was now the less-than-svelte family maid, Annie. Buster reassured me—telling me he still thought I was the most beautiful woman in the world. But the problem with younger men is that when you get clingy and possessive, they still want to sow wild oats. They say they love you, but still won't commit to anything more serious than the next date. Bless the guy though. When he was with me, he didn't touch a drop so that I wouldn't either. He kept me going.

Joan and Doug would have us over for a delicious dinner, and then Joan, who enjoyed backgammon, would throw together a match afterward. She'd wind up the Victrola with some Paul Whiteman records, and after two or three Dubonnets on the rocks, winning wasn't quite as important.

Joan was generous to a fault—always insisting that I take home leftovers or giving me small presents. I explained to her that it worked the other way—I brought her gifts since she was the hostess. She smiled that huge painted smile and pushed the gift into my hands. To Joan, I wasn't the broken down co-star. I was a little down on my luck, and she wanted to help get me going again.

She always seemed to know when I was hurting and when I was tired of tuna fish sandwiches and other gourmet delights only to be found in the cheap aisles at the market. I'd been eating a lot of rice and beans, since they seemed to go a little farther.

I'd virtually stopped hearing from Phyl. Her card this past Christmas had contained her signature and nothing more. Perhaps feeling guilty for the previous annual notes detailing their exotic travel and extravagant lifestyle, she'd decided to scale back. Either way, it still hurt. My best friend had done what she'd always done—thrown me over for some guy. Only this time it seemed to be for good.

Peg was now up in San Francisco. She sent me Christmas cards, but now the shoe was on the other foot. She had to send *me* money from time to time. That was a bitter pill to swallow.

CHAPTER THIRTY~SEVEN

"Fire! Fire!"

One of the most terrifying words there is, and people were suddenly yelling it outside my bedroom window.

I whipped off the sheets. "Buster! Buster! Wake up!"

"Wha? What is it?" he said sleepily.

"There's a fire! Get up! Get dressed!"

He tugged on his undershirt, boxer shorts and trousers, and I threw on a ratty old pair of sailor pants and a sweater I'd spent the day in.

"I'm going to go see if I can help," I said. "Grab the photo albums and my memorabilia box. And my purse!" I yelled as I rushed to the door, determined to help however I could. One of our problems in Malibu was our reliance on volunteer fire-fighters from the surrounding areas, and the closeness of the properties to each other.

I looked up the beach. Bright orange flames were consuming David Butler's garage and Buddy DeSylva's house, and slowly, menacingly, they advanced on Oliver Marsh's cottage.

My first thought was for Louise so I ran to her place. All the lights were off except for her bedroom.

"Louise! Hal! Wake up! Louise! There's a fire! Oh, please wake up!" Bang bang bang.

She came to the door, her hair in curlers, and a pink silk robe wrapped around her in a hurry.

"Marie? I heard the shouting. Where is it? How close?"

"Buddy's house is on fire! Get dressed and grab whatever you can!"

Louise caught up with me, then she went one way and I went the other. I continued sprinting up and down the beach, knocking on doors and yelling "Fire!" along with calling the names of the people I knew personally to wake them. Wesley Ruggles' had house guests—they'd been out playing tennis and beach baseball that afternoon. Seeing the living room light on, I banged on the window. The group was in the middle of a game of bridge.

"Marie! You look like hell! What are you doing out there?!" Wesley said.

"The colony's on fire! Get out and protect yourselves! Save what you can! Hurry!"

Oliver's house was now engulfed, and the flames had Mal Taylor's cottage squarely in their sights. I dashed back down the beach to find that Buster had set my photo albums and my handbag near my sad palm tree and gone back to work, God bless him. He'd organized a bucket brigade in the interim until the fire companies arrived.

I hurried back in for my jewelry box and some of the mementos from Ken I couldn't bear to part with, plus a few of the more expensive gewgaws—hunks of jade, an amber caché box he'd bought me for our second anniversary, and a solid gold parrot he'd bought during his trip to Hawaii that he'd given me as a make-up gift. I rushed in and out as long as I could, for the car's registration papers, Jinx's awards, and the Hurrell portrait of me that hung above the fireplace. I also took my memories of Mum—the baby book she'd lovingly and painstakingly created for me, her sepia portrait, and old family photos of Wee Mae and Grandfather McDonald. Then I gathered up whatever antiques I could. They were the only currency I still had. Several fire brigade vehicles now came screaming into the colony as Allan Dwan's house was consumed. Allan stood outside mourning his loss, flanked by Buddy and Mal.

Louise was doing the same as me—running to and fro from her place, trying to save clothing, keepsakes, jewelry, and expensive antiques. She and Hal had moved their Louis XV tables and her small Cézanne painting out of harm's way.

Despite the hoses spraying full force, Allan's house was a lost cause, and the fire was closing the gap between there and Louise's. Sparks were already spraying across the roof toward it, and we both watched in horror as they ignited the shake shingles. It was engulfed in mere minutes. We could only stand and watch helplessly. There simply weren't enough fire companies from the surrounding areas for the help that we needed.

I helped Louise move everything she'd saved further away from the flames. By the time we'd finished that and I turned around, the flames were licking at my roof. Buster had already directed the bucket brigade in our direction, but we couldn't reach where the fire was taking hold. "No...no..." I moaned.

"Please no..."

The fire teams finally hooked up their rotary pump machine, and using water from George O'Brien's swimming pool, they sprayed my roof. But it was too late.

I was astounded at the incredible suddenness of it all. This couldn't be happening. Not after Mum, and the divorce, and the canceled contracts, and my health problems, and the stock market, and...

"Come on, honey," Louise said, dragging me back to reality. "Let's move your stuff." She was right. The palm tree offered no protection. Everything was now in danger from the stray sparks and the deluge from the firehoses.

After three hours of battling the blaze, the firefighters finally got things under control, and we could assess the damage of what had been the Malibu colony. Sixteen houses destroyed or nearly in ruins, along with priceless furniture and baubles, and Buddy DeSylva's library of first editions, his pride and joy.

I sank to the sand in a sobbing lump. Now, on top of all I was dealing with, I'd lost my home too. I had exactly one pair of pants and a sweater to wear. I wasn't sure how many "fresh starts" I had left in me. I was exhausted. Louise and I held each other and cried.

Within the Law, now rechristened *Paid*, was released a little over two weeks after the fire. And although the reviews were good, I was still morose as I moved into my next film.

During shooting for *Gentleman's Fate*, Jack Gilbert and I were both nursing our wounds from watching our lives in Malibu go up in smoke. My character, Mabel, was always munching on something—an extra insult since I was doing my best at staying trim. I liked our director, Mervyn LeRoy. He didn't mind me sometimes needing to argue on the phone with insurance adjusters.

During one of our breaks, I flipped through my paperwork looking for my claim number when I felt a presence next to my chair.

"Marie. Good to see you again."

I looked up to see Irving Thalberg standing beside me.

"Mr. Thalberg. It's been a long time."

"Ten years," he said.

He didn't say it, but I knew what he was thinking. *The years haven't been kind to you. What the hell did you do to yourself?* At least that's what I heard in my head.

"What do you have there?"

"Insurance. You may have heard about the colony…"

"Oh, yes. The fire. Terrible business. Have they pinpointed a cause yet?"

"They think it started in David Butler's garage. Doesn't matter anyway. I'm still homeless. I'm lucky that Buster is so generous."

"I'm very sorry," he said. The discomfort led him to change the subject as soon as possible. "I'm looking for Merv. Have you seen him?"

"He was heading toward the commissary with Mel Gerstad. I can tell him you're looking for him."

"Would you please? It's a budget issue. Thanks."

I didn't think greetings could get much more perfunctory. I thought it couldn't get worse than scripts and critics ridiculing my weight, but I hadn't realized how far I still had left to fall.

SPORTING BLOOD SET, MGM STUDIO *April 1931*

I still remember the day I met Clark Gable. What woman wouldn't? Your knees get weak like that only a couple times in your life. I saw him across the set, my throat went dry, and I found it tough to speak. I had to wait to introduce myself until I'd sipped some water.

MGM had cast me in a role with their new find, who'd recently given Norma Shearer's rich brat character in *A Free Soul* quite the talking to. The public loved him for it.

Gable was a tall fellow, with dark hair greased with pomade. He filled the doorway, nonchalantly lighting a Camel like he owned the place. I had a good feeling about the guy. Saw big things for him. He moved with practiced grace and barely contained power—like one of the racehorses who were our co-stars.

Sporting Blood was the story of an abused racehorse named Tommy Boy. Gable was starring with Madge Evans. I played the haughty wife of one of Tommy Boy's owners. Charles Brabin, Theda Bara's husband, was directing.

Clark and I developed a great working relationship. Joan let me know lots about him since they had an on-again-off-again thing. And even though he propositioned me (Joan said he couldn't help himself), I refused out of respect for my friendship with her and my love for Buster. Call me a one-man woman. It's out of fashion in Hollywood, but there it is.

I was lucky enough to work with Gable again in *Hell*

Divers, where we filmed on-board the USS *Saratoga*, anchored down in San Pedro. Wallace Beery, a hard-drinking sonofabitch who'd also worked with me in *The Godless Girl*, co-starred with us. It was just as frustrating this time, because he'd never learn his lines. But he was always ready with a putdown of some kind, and now I remembered why I'd wished that Mitch's fireproofing had been less effective for him.

His insults should have been my first clue that I'd let down my guard. The dinners out with Buster, bridge nights at Joan's, and occasional visits to Brown's caused the pounds to creep back up.

The Sin of Madelon Claudet began life as *Lullaby*. It was a tearjerker of a French woman who has an affair with an American who deserts her and leaves her pregnant and alone. She becomes the mistress to a rich man and leaves her son to the care of her friends, Rosalie and Victor. I played Rosalie in a small part, and it didn't matter that I looked matronly, because I needed to be.

Unfortunately, it was to be my last for MGM.

L.B. MAYER'S OFFICE, METRO-GOLDWYN-MAYER, CULVER CITY, CALIFORNIA *November 1931*

"Come in, Marie. Come in," Mayer said.

I'd received the note the previous day that he wanted to see me, and I'd been dreading this meeting ever since. Stiffly, I lowered myself into the white chair before the white desk and waited for the axe to fall, as I was sure it would. I'd been this route too many times not to know what was going on.

"There's no easy way to say this," he began. "I'm going to come straight out with it. We signed you as a regular free-lancer contingent on you keeping yourself trim. That potato clause is there for a reason."

"This is it?" I asked, seeing that my dread had been justified.

"I'm afraid so," he said. "You've become too hefty, and we're having trouble finding parts for you at your current size."

He passed a final check across the battleship of a desk. I took it hesitantly, then got up, turned, and headed for the door without a word.

"You're not going to say anything?" he asked.

"What can I say?" I shrugged. "You're right. I've put on the pounds. I've been distracted. You don't need to hear excuses, and I don't have any."

"We're not the only studio in town, you know."

"I know."

"If you lose more, we might be able to bring you on again," he said, in a conciliatory manner.

I thanked him and took hold of the doorknob.

"Good luck, Marie," he said, not unkindly.

"Thanks," I murmured.

"Have a good afternoon, Miss Prevost!" one of Mount Ida's assistants called out cheerily as I rushed out. I finally let my-self collapse behind a stall in the ladies' toilet down the hall. I cried until I didn't think there was a drop of moisture left in me. God only knows who heard the commotion. Several peo-ple came and went while I was in there.

After twenty minutes, I emerged, with nearly all my

makeup gone. I dampened a handkerchief at the sink and cleaned up the rest, then somehow got myself home. When I felt like I could do it without falling apart, I called Shelly the next day from a pay phone on Broadway, where I'd gone to pick up a few cheap frocks on sale.

"Marie!" he said when he picked up. "How's everything going? I saw *The Sin of Madelon Claudet* last weekend. Tearjerking! Emotionally wrought! I'm talking powerful! The missus and I were impressed."

"Thanks," I said. "Unfortunately, you won't be impressed by what I tell you next."

"I don't like the sound of that," he said, now more subdued. "What happened?"

"Mayer sacked me," I said.

"The weight," he said. "God damn it. I knew you looked heavier."

"I'm sorry, Shelly. I did so well for so long, but I got careless, and..."

"You quit following the diet, didn't you?" he thundered.

"I had to. The doctor told me that all the tomatoes and grapefruit were bad for my ulcer, and..."

"And?! Who you gonna listen to here? Some doctor? Or your agent who works his *tuchus* off to keep you employed? Take a milk of magnesia. You know how hard I work? Mayer will play completely hardball next time I want anything!"

"I'm so sorry. You have no idea."

He sighed. "Lemme try Harry Cohn again. He's a real bastard, but once in a while, he shows a little humanity. And he owes me a favor."

"Thanks, Shelly."

"This may be the last time I can help you. I wouldn't hold your breath."

Click.

Since I had to buy all new clothes, the fire convinced me for good that Malibu hadn't been worth it. Filling up the Stutz for the back and forth had also become an expense I couldn't afford. I deeded my lot back to Malibu Ranch and returned to the city.

THREE WISE GIRLS SET, COLUMBIA PICTURES, HOLLYWOOD, CALIFORNIA *January 1932*

"Oh my goodness. Who is that?" I asked Mae Clarke. In 1931, Mae had co-starred in *Frankenstein* and *Public Enemy*, and both had been runaway successes. I was hoping a little of her previous year's caché would rub off on me.

"Our newest co-star," Mae said. "Have you met Jean Harlow? She worked with me in *Public Enemy*. Lovely girl."

"Is she wearing any underwear?" I whispered.

"I don't think she owns any," she whispered back.

So this was the new find who'd made such a splash in *Hell's Angels* and then in *Public Enemy*. I could see now why Howard Hughes hadn't paid as much attention to *The Racket*. Jean was wearing a slinky crocheted dress and sporting the whitest blonde hair I'd ever seen. Every man on the sound-stage seemed to be struck dumb at her presence. Plus, I think the rest of us were too.

True to his word, Shelly had managed to get me some

work at Columbia. He never said what he had to offer Harry Cohn to give me the job. Thankfully, Mae and I had already worked together in *Reckless Living* and *The Runaround*. We got along great.

I was intimidated by Jean, but despite the tough-talking character she played on screen, she was a sweetheart in real life. My character, again named Dot, was another comic foil, and Jean and Mae were remarkably easy to work with. I wasn't sure, but evidently, the name Dot had come to be equated with a fat smart ass.

One January afternoon, I started feeling woozy during shooting. I'd had an egg and coffee for breakfast and a tomato and one lettuce leaf for lunch (along with a nip in my dressing room).

"Marie, you okay, sweetie?" Jean said. She reached for me as I started to wobble.

"Grab her!" said Bill Beaudine as I felt myself fall.

Four co-stars caught me as I tumbled over and promptly passed out.

"Oh Jesus, no," I said when I woke up to the familiar white sheets and too bright lights of St. Vincent's again. I recoiled at the smell of Lysol.

This time, there were three lone flower arrangements. One was from Buster, one from Mae, and one from Joan. Dr. Baldwin hovered over my bed, consulting his clipboard.

I blinked a couple times before trying to speak. My throat was so dry.

"You're conscious," he said. "I'm glad to see it. We were worried about you."

"I'm fine," I said.

"You are *not* fine," he said sternly. "You're malnourished, and you passed out because of it. You told me you were going to begin eating healthfully when you got the part you were after, Marie."

"Parts," I corrected him. "Unfortunately, it wasn't only one. This is an ongoing struggle. I'd hoped that I could score a couple plum roles and then I could relax. But I can't, Doc. I honestly can't."

"This isn't healthy. Your body is showing obvious signs of distress. Your fainting was one. You're also jaundiced, which means you've been drinking more than you indicated to me. You cannot live on lettuce leaves and booze. You simply can't."

"Please don't be angry at me, doctor."

"I'm not angry. I'm frightened for you. Your body—especially your heart— cannot survive the abuse. You can't keep this up. It will kill you."

I started to cry, and he handed me his handkerchief.

"I don't know what to do," I moaned. "I have to work. The only thing keeping me working is dieting."

"There are sensible ways to diet," he said quietly. "A piece of roast chicken without the skin, a piece of fish dressed with lemon, an egg, an apple for a snack. You need more fruits and vegetables for the vitamins your body requires. You can't drink your calories."

I gazed up at him though eyes blurry with tears.

"Promise me you'll try to eat better," he said. "The next time your body goes into distress like this, it may be the last. Do you understand?"

I nodded somberly.

"Please take my advice," he said.

I nodded again for his benefit, but I knew it was impossible.

NOBODY KNOWS YOU WHEN YOU'RE DOWN AND OUT

CHAPTER THIRTY~EIGHT

WILSHIRE BROWN DERBY, HOLLYWOOD, CALIFORNIA
March 30, 1933

T he Derby was more packed than usual, with celebrities jammed in as far as the eye could see. I waved at Mae, who was seated under the wall of caricatures opposite us. People were feeling more light-hearted since Roosevelt had taken over for Hoover. There had been a mandatory bank holiday a few weeks ago on the day he took office, but I'd been living on cash from selling everything valuable that I still owned. The stock market had already cleaned me out.

Buster flagged down a waiter and ordered sauerbraten with potato pancakes for himself and a piece of roast chicken and a scoop of cottage cheese for me. Dr. Baldwin would have been proud.

"Very good, sir," the waiter said, and returned later with our plates.

"What did you want to talk about?" I asked.

"Hmmm?" he said, cutting his sauerbraten.

"You mentioned earlier that we could talk over dinner. We're here," I said with a smile.

"Oh yeah. That. I wanted to wait until we were done. Let's enjoy our dinner first."

"All right," I said with a shrug. I took a bite of cottage cheese and grimaced. I hated the stuff.

We shot the breeze during dinner, about Buster's latest role in *Behind Jury Doors*, and about Shelly, and if he'd gotten any more nibbles for me. Since the fire, moving in with Buster had allowed me to save a little until the next role came along. Buster ordered a slice of lemon meringue pie for himself, and I watched him eat it enviously.

"This is probably a good time to bring up what I wanted to talk to you about," he said, covering my hand with his. "We've been through a lot together—your health issues, and the fire, and—"

"—and I couldn't have gotten through all of this without you," I said. This sounded like question-popping material. With Buster, even with the age difference, I could definitely consider marriage again.

"...and what I want to say," he continued when I was done. "...is that even though I love you and care for you a great deal, I need my freedom, Marie."

"You what?!" I exclaimed in the middle of the Brown Derby. The clanks of silverware on plates stopped cold, along with every conversation in the place.

"Ssshhhh..." he said, patting my hand to calm me down, as other diners turned in our direction.

"You did it here so I couldn't make a scene, didn't you?" I hissed under my breath.

"I told you what I was like when we got together. I'm not ready to settle down. I did for a while, because I do care for you. But this isn't me, this playing house thing. I don't want to be tied down, and lately we've been more like roommates anyway."

"Because I'm self-conscious about my body and I'm nervous about you seeing me naked, you want to break up?"

"No. I told you. I need freedom. I can't be a one-woman man. I'm sorry."

My face burned so badly I knew it had to be bright red and the lump in my throat prevented me from saying much, other than, "When?"

"When what?"

"When do I have to be out?"

"Marie, I'm not a monster. I know it'll take you a while to find another place. You don't have to rush, I only wanted you to know."

"Know that this has all been a big inconvenience and you want me to scram."

"Please don't make this any harder than it has to be. I still care for you. I'll even give you a little scratch to get by so you can get back on your feet until Shelly coughs up the next gig."

"Thanks," I said quietly. I sat there fighting tears, feeling like a boat with no rudder—drifting, with nothing to anchor me anywhere—no Mum, no home, no job, no pets, and now no love. It was as if a cyclone had torn a path clean through my life, leaving nothing but wreckage.

"Come on. I'll take you home," Buster said.

"What home?" I muttered.

He took care of the check, then escorted me outside to the Cord. When we got back to his place on Laurel Canyon, he put the key in the lock, and we entered the darkened living room. As I turned toward the guest bedroom instead of the one we'd shared, he took my hand.

"Marie, I'm so sorry. Please forgive me."

I stood there before him, tears streaming down my face, completely stripped emotionally. I had nothing left. Nothing. He pulled me close and held me, but I was dead inside.

"Night, Buster," I rasped before escaping. I couldn't look at him. It hurt too much.

Even with no roles taking my time, I still got up early the next day. Unable to stare across a breakfast table at Buster, I left the house before he woke, and ordered a cup of coffee, eggs and bacon at the Good Day Diner downtown. Lately, I'd been reading the *Times* at the newsstand, then sliding it back in the stack, but today I splurged for a copy to circle ads for places and cross off the duds.

I got lucky at the Potrero Arms, on Hawthorn off La Brea. The landlady, Mrs. Polansky, welcomed me in when I gave her a cash deposit in full. I began moving my stuff in the next day. It was only a bare room with a bed and a chest of drawers, but it would do until I found something better.

I sent Peg my address, but it still came as a surprise when she wrote me at the beginning of October.

Hi Marie –
Writing to let you know that Frank died Sept 28th in San Berdoo. The lawyer called me, and I went to their office yesterday to hear the will. I'm enclosing your portion of his estate.
Peg

Inside was a crisp new one-dollar bill. All I could do was

laugh hysterically. That was Frank. Rubbing my nose in my former wealth. He hadn't changed a bit.

Unfortunately, it didn't take the bill collectors long to find my new address. They'd begun sniffing around in Malibu before I left, but the watchmen at the colony gate had kept them out. They'd lost me at Buster's, but they hovered around Potrero constantly. I'd sworn that if I got the money, I'd pay back every cent. But it looked like a pipedream. I took to wearing a red-headed wig and prop glasses to get back into the apartment. One of them even approached me outside and asked me if I knew Marie Prevost.

"Never heard of her," I said. pushing the glasses further up my nose.

JOE'S NEWSSTAND ON LA BREA, LOS ANGELES, CALIFORNIA *December 5, 1933*

PROHIBITION REPEALED read the headline.

I'd never been so happy to see a newspaper story in my life. Blackie had been charging me a fortune that I no longer had. A bottle of Old Crow would do the job too, and for far less. The craving was already gnawing at me.

"You gonna buy that?" said the news vendor.

"Sorry," I said, placing the *Times* back on the pile. He scowled at me. Now that the pinch of this economy was affecting us all, drinking was the only thing helping many of us to cope. God bless Franklin Roosevelt for doing what he could.

Instead of a paper, I bought some real legal whiskey. I'd been surprised to find it so soon, but a couple mom and pop shops had prepared for the announcement and stocked up early. It had been a long thirteen years. But now there was no need to pretend anymore. Might as well make it official. I was an alcoholic.

HANDS ACROSS THE TABLE SET, PARAMOUNT PICTURES HOLLYWOOD, CALIFORNIA *Mid 1935*

Have you ever been eternally grateful to someone you barely know? Someone you found out did something you'd never be able to repay? I discovered how close I had come to Mitchell Leisen sacking me when I talked to my co-star, Carole Lombard.

I adored Carole the minute we met. Not only was she stunning, with silken blonde hair and dramatic cheekbones, but she had a mouth like a Marine and said exactly what she thought. Right before shooting started, my guts had decided, like clockwork, to act up again, requiring another hospitalization I could ill afford. But darling that Carole was, she'd fought for me. Because of her, I'd be working for another month.

"Don't worry about it, honey," she said when I thanked her. "I couldn't let the fucker treat you like that. We ex-Bathing Beauties gotta stick together."

"Once a bathing beauty, always a bathing beauty," I whispered.

She grinned.

Then I did what any desperate, grateful, paunchy, middle-aged, alcoholic actress would do. I burst into tears.

"Oh, no! No! Don't cry!" she said. She put her arm around me and walked me to a nearby canvas chair with her name on it. I didn't have one anymore. Anywhere. At this point, I was lucky to even see my name on the screen at all.

"Thank you so much," I said. "I barely know you, but you went to all that trouble for me."

"It wasn't that much trouble. I merely threatened to walk. 'Have you ever had a run of bad luck?' I asked Mitch. 'Don't be a complete bastard,' I told him. I smeared on the guilt like frosting on a cake. I wouldn't let him fire you. You were an inspiration to me when I was younger. Howd'ya think I became a bathing beauty in the first place?"

She gave me her dazzling smile, and I couldn't help but smile back through my tears.

"I'll find a way to thank you, I swear it," I said.

"I was happy to help," she said, taking my hand. Then she hopped up and strolled toward the stage door. "See you after makeup!"

SIDEWALK ON HAWTHORN STREET, LOS ANGELES, CALIFORNIA *September 1936*

This year had been harder than the last four combined. I'd sold anything of value that had made it through the fire. My clothes, my jewels, my furs, my Hurrell portrait, the savings I'd amassed while staying at Buster's...there was nothing left.

I'd had three tiny roles all year. For the last, in Mitch Leisen's *Thirteen Hours By Air*, with Fred MacMurray and Joan Bennett, my credit was the lowly "waitress in Omaha."

I rarely found myself seeing more than the bottom of a bottle these days, so I was on the outs with Shelly. He said that I owed the job to Clark Gable and Buster Senior, who'd put in a good word for me with Jack Warner. That nobody was listening when he sang my praises anymore.

Cain and Mabel was the story of a prize fighter and a dancer who both wanted to boost their careers by inventing a sham romance for the reporters. Clark was the boxer, and Marion Davies was the dancer. I was the secretary for Jake Sherman, played by Walter Catlett. And there was a whole stable of we washed-up silent folk backing them up. I appreciated the way they'd kept us employed. Marion was known for her generous nature.

I was only on screen for a few minutes, but even so, I was exhausted. I wasn't sure if it was my age, the booze, a combination of the two, or mere hopelessness that made me tired all the time.

I'd had to sell the Stutz. Now it was the streetcar or my feet everywhere. I was on my way back from the streetcar stop when I noticed a small brown shape under a bush near the sidewalk. Thinking it was a squirrel, I ignored it at first, but then the full sausage-y shape of a small dachshund waddled out and wagged his tail at me.

"Well, hello!" I said.

His tail wagged a little harder.

I leaned down to pet him. His fur was short, but as soft as velvet.

"I bet you're hungry, aren't you, fella?"

The tail kept going, so I reached into my bag for some leftover crackers from my lunch. I offered him some, and he gobbled them up, looking up expectantly for more. He was so thin, poor thing. He actually looked more desperate then me. And after missing Jinx, Pooch, and Gaucy for so long, I found myself gazing into his soft brown eyes, and knew that he needed my help.

"All right, buddy. You can come home with me. I'll give you a nice respectable name. Nothing silly and German like Schatzi or Strudel. A real name. How about Max?"

He wagged his tail in agreement and let me pick him up. I snuck Max into the apartment, telling him it was important that he not bark. He did pretty well with that, and we did okay for a few months, until he saw Mr. Hexum across the street walking his poodle, Trixie. He kicked up a fuss, and Mrs. Polansky promptly evicted us. She gave me three days to find a new place.

CHAPTER THIRTY~NINE

It wasn't a dive, but I guess anything looks that way when you're falling from where I was. It had been no's from most of the places in the neighborhood, including the Amesbury across the street. When Mum and Peg and I had been struggling, one of these apartments would have looked like a palace. An old Scottish proverb says, "Get what you can, and keep what you have," and I've been pretty lousy at the second part. It doesn't matter how you end up poor. The result is the same.

I strolled up the walk, pulled open the main door, and knocked at another on the first floor marked **#3 Building Manager**.

A gray-haired woman opened the door and eyed me suspiciously. She had the voice of a lifelong smoker.

"Yes?"

"I was inquiring about the vacancy you advertised—the studio?"

She softened a little.

"Oh yes. It's furnished, forty dollars a month, plus utilities. We've got a houseboy that comes once a week to clean up, and he lets me know about maintenance problems. My husband takes care of that type of thing. I'm Mrs. Jenks, the landlady."

"Do you take pets?" I offered hesitantly. I couldn't try to risk moving in and not telling her about Max. Not after Mrs. Polansky's reaction. He was too much of a barker for her not to notice.

"What kind of pet?" she asked.

"A dog. A little dachshund. He's very well-behaved."

She was shaking her head before I even finished.

"I'm sorry. Cats I'm okay with. They're quiet, they lay around, and they sleep all day. Dogs rip the place up."

The exhaustion hit me all at once. Twenty places I'd looked at over the past two days. Twenty. And all of them with something wrong. Too small, too expensive, too far from the street-car line to walk...I couldn't bear to give up Max. He was all I had left. I started bawling. I could tell she was horrified, but at this point I couldn't stop.

"I'm sorry. It's not just this," I said between sobs. "It's everything."

She peered at me curiously over the tops of her glasses, probably wondering if I had a screw loose. I'd had too much self-respect for too long to admit how far I'd fallen to any-one. But I decided to see if Hollywood could grant me one last request.

"Mrs. Jenks, do you like moving pictures?"

"Of course. Especially now—we gotta forget this awful economy somehow, don't we?"

"I'm in them." That felt like a lie, considering my resume lately, so I qualified it. "I used to be pretty well-known, actual-ly. I'm Marie Prevost."

"The bathing beauty, right? And you were in *The Marriage*

Circle! I recognize you now!" Then her face twisted into confusion and disbelief that the sad specimen in front of her was the same person from the movies. "But what—"

"It's a long story," I said. "I've had a run of bad luck. But I'm working again. I'm trying to get back on my feet. I could sure use some help. I've looked at twenty places and none of them were quite right. This place is perfect." Perfect for someone with a nearly empty pocketbook who liked that there was a liquor store not far away.

She softened right then, as I thought she might.

"This Depression's hit everybody hard," she said in understanding.

"It sure has," I agreed. It looked like I might be reaching her.

"My husband's out of work too," she said.

I nodded sympathetically.

"This dog you got. Does he bark?"

"Sometimes," I admitted. "Mostly when people knock at the door. But I don't have many visitors!"

"I want a twenty-five dollar deposit upfront for any damage," she said. "And you keep that dog quiet."

"I will," I said, breathing a sigh of relief. I pulled the latest check from Joan out of my purse and showed it to her. She was so impressed I knew Joan Crawford that she let me sign it over. It wouldn't last forever, but it could get me moved in.

"Make sure the rent's on time. And remember what I said about that dog," she said, taking the check and putting it in the pocket of her housedress. "It's apartment ten."

It didn't take me too long to move my stuff across town. Only Jinx's ribbons, some photo albums, and a couple kitchen things. Everything else was gone. Gone in the fire or sold to keep me going. Maxie waddled behind me on his leash, exploring all the smells in his new neighborhood, and then the ones in the building.

When we reached the Aftonian, a colored boy was walking out the front door. Seeing the box in my arms and the dog in tow, he held it open for me and gave me a big smile.

"Cute little fella," he said, bending down to pet Max's soft head.

"This is Max," I said.

"Good to meet ya, Max, my name's Bill Bogle." He took Maxie's paw for a pretend shake. "I'm the houseboy here."

"Aah, Mrs. Jenks mentioned you. I'm Marie Prevost."

He did a double-take, his eyes a question.

"Yes, that Marie Prevost," I said. I was used to it now.

"Welcome to the building. I'll take good care of ya."

"I'm glad someone will," I said. Movie stars got rich and stayed rich. Not like me. But there was no sense dwelling on the unfairness of it all, how life had frayed down to this bit of nothing. "It's nice to meet you, Bill. Come on, Maxie."

Max waddled behind me, up the stairs to the apartment.

After unlocking the door and trying not to gag from the musty odor of a room closed up for too long, I opened a window to get a little fresh air circulating. I reached for the box I'd set on the bed and gulped from the reassuring, nearly full bottle of Old Crow inside. Then I scribbled a note on a piece of scrap paper floating around in the box.

Please do not knock on this door more than once. It makes my dog bark. If I am in, I will hear you, as I am not deaf.

Since I had no tape, I wedged the note in between the door frame and the apartment number frame a few inches away and shut the door again. Pushing the box aside, I collapsed on the bed. Maxie whined, demanding to be picked up, so I set him next to me on the bare mattress.

I leaned over and let him snuffle my nose. It always made me smile.

"Young man, we're home," I said, holding up the bottle in an artificial toast before I guzzled some. The amber liquid seeped into my bones, spreading warmth and consolation.

Setting the bottle on the side table, I lay with my head on the striped ticking pillow as tears rolled down my face and into my ears. Maxie curled up in the curve of my arm, his head on my stomach. When I woke up, it was morning.

JOAN CRAWFORD'S HOUSE, 426 ROXBURY DRIVE
BRENTWOOD, CALIFORNIA *November 1936*

We sat on the back terrace beside the pool. Joan's bougainvillea was in full festive bloom, and the other plants were all thriving. The opposite of me. But out here, it was easy to pretend that things were still the same. Except my dress was from some cheap little shop on Broadway and my underwear was two years old and had been mended multiple times. My shoes needed new heels too. My one concession to modernity were my stockings, which were still in good shape, having been picked up on sale on Tuesday.

Joan and I caught up, chatting about her latest film, *Love on the Run*, with Franchot Tone, her new husband, whom she'd married the previous year. Also about Irving's death. Joan was one of the few who wasn't mourning. Norma, Irving's wife, might actually have to work for a living now, rather than automatically getting every part Joan wanted, simply because of nepotism.

Picking at the remains of her honeydew melon, she looked at me across the table. I'd put on makeup of course, but no matter how much I put on, I couldn't hide the bags. I wasn't sleeping. When I did sleep, it was because I'd had one too many belts. And then I always woke up boozy and out-of-sorts.

"Marie, be honest with me, please. How bad is it? Tell me the truth," she said, setting down her fork.

Tears pricked at my eyes, and all the emotion I'd been holding back bubbled up.

"Bad," I said, trying not to cry.

We sat there quietly with the sun playing over our faces.

I had about $100 left in the account, and still had bills to pay. That was it. After twenty-something years of work—with millions of dollars having passed through my fingers, I didn't have a damned thing to show for it. One broken marriage, one that didn't even count, and some lovely memories. There were friends too, I knew that, but relationships changed when one of you had money and another didn't.

"Let me help," Joan said.

"Joan, no," I said. "You've been so kind to me so many times. I can never make it up to you. I could save for twenty years and never come close."

"Please. I'm happy to do it. Franchot and I have so much, and I hate to see you dealing with all this. How much do you need? Be honest now."

"A hundred?" I asked. "I'm behind at a couple places, and I bounced a check at the grocer's."

"You're sure you don't need more?"

"No." I shook my head stubbornly.

"Write an IOU and hold onto it," she said.

"That's not how it works," I said. "I'm supposed to give it to you."

She reached into her pocket and slid a $100 bill across the table to me. I took it with tears in my eyes.

"Look," she said. "I've been where you are—desperate and not knowing where your next meal is coming from. The way I see it is—those of us who have made it have a responsibility to the rest. We all developed this art together. And now some people want to move on and pretend that the silents never happened, and neither did the stars. That's not right. So you work hard, do your best, and if you can pay me back, you will. All right? Let's talk about something more pleasant than money."

As I left, she also slipped a check into the pocket of my dress and gave me a kiss on the cheek. I left feeling lighter than I had in weeks.

AFTONIAN APARTMENTS,
HOLLYWOOD, CALIFORNIA *January 20, 1937*

"All right, Max," I said, slipping on my shoes. "Let's go, pal." I had to run down to Weiss's Deli on Vine to deal with a bounced check. It'd be a chance to take Max for a walk and stretch my legs. I had to keep the Weisses happy because it was the closest grocery for picking up essentials.

Maxie shoved his wet muzzle into my hand and gave me that look I loved—like I was the only one in the world who mattered...the only one who cared. The truth was, this goofy little boy, with his sweet dark eyes and his funny floppy ears was probably the one thing keeping me from offing myself. Sad to say, but there it was. Maxie and the huge streak of Scottish stubbornness I'd inherited kept me going. I was determined not to quit—if only because it meant that all of Hollywood would say that chubby ole Marie Prevost couldn't hack it.

I flicked on the little gas heater in the corner so it would be warmer when we got back, then took a swig of the bottle of Old Crow from the bedside table. Breakfast went down smooth, warming my gut with its fiery reliability. After a few more sips, the world took on the fuzzy cast that made it bearable again. I set the bottle in the sink with the others.

As we passed the door to #12, I could hear Mr. Hudson's radio on with the volume up. President Roosevelt was being inaugurated for his second term. He talked about America coming far from stagnation and despair, preserving vitality, and restoring courage and confidence. He obviously hadn't been sitting where I'd been sitting. I'd never felt less vital, courageous, or confident in my life.

Max and I strolled along until we got to Weiss's Deli. I tied his leash around the leg of the bench outside, our usual routine, then pushed the door open. The bell gave a cheerful jingle as I entered and approached the counter.

"I'm so sorry, Nathan," I said, handing him the cash from

my pocketbook, plus a little extra for the trouble. "I was down in Laguna Beach shooting, and I couldn't get back up here very well."

"I know," he said. "And I understand about the rubber check. Times are hard all around right now. Thing is—I know you're good for it, see. Some *schmucks* I've had to take to court to get dough outta." He took the cash with a grateful smile. "Not you, though. You're a *mensch*, Marie."

If he only knew how many bill collectors I'd stiffed. You couldn't get blood from a stone though. Truer words were never spoken.

"Say, Marie," Bernie said. Bernie was Nathan's son—all of eighteen years old, and quite a looker. When he lost a bit more of his teenage awkwardness, the boy was going to break hearts from here to Canarsie. "Did you hear anything back on that screen test you did?"

"Nothing yet," I lied. It had been a rejection. I took a pack of Parliaments from the display on the counter. I'd never been much of a smoker, but they'd come in handy when the hunger pangs hit later this evening.

"I'll keep my fingers crossed for you," he said.

"Every little bit helps. Thanks, Bernie."

"See you later, Marie." He gave me a little wave.

"Bye, now." I said, pulling the door open. When Maxie saw me, his tail wagged furiously. "Missed me, huh? I was only gone five minutes."

He whined a little and wagged harder. I worked the knot loose and giving the leash a tug. We strolled back to Afton Place, avoiding the massive crack in the sidewalk where the alley met the street. Max gave a dandelion an extra sniff, then lifted his leg on it to mark it as his.

I wasn't sure I'd ever consider the Aftonian "home," but right now it had to do. We climbed the stairs and I unlocked the door, considering heating up a can of soup. I decided against it, and feeling lazy, kicked off my shoes.

Then I stretched out on the bed for a nice long nap.

EPILOGUE

MOTION PICTURE COUNTRY HOUSE, WOODLAND HILLS, CALIFORNIA *September 27, 1942*

The announcer stepped to the podium and cleared his throat. "Hello, ladies and gentlemen. I'd like to welcome you all to the official dedication of the Motion Picture Country Home, a project of the Motion Picture Relief Fund. Please let's give a warm Hollywood welcome for Governor Culvert Olson, who has a few words."

There was a round of polite applause.

An older white-haired man stepped onto the constructed platform. Governor Olson spoke, droning on about the Woodland Hills area, the home itself, and the care that had gone into the selecting of the site, which would be an honorable project that the state would be proud to claim.

"And now, ladies and gentlemen, let me introduce the man whose brainchild this was. A man for whom honor and charity are two very strong principles. A man who deeply cares about his fellow motion picture alumni. A respected actor, and the president of the Motion Picture Relief Fund, Mr. Jean Hersholt."

Enthusiastic applause followed.

Hersholt stepped to the podium, his gray hair closely cropped, and his kind blue eyes twinkling as he nodded at members of the audience. He wore a small gray mustache and tugged on a pair of wire-rimmed glasses before reading from the paper he pulled out of his jacket pocket. His Danish accent was much fainter now, but still charming.

"Good afternoon, ladies and gentlemen. Welcome to Hollywood's newest showplace. This, however, is not just another mansion in Hollywood. It is a work of art with heart. From now on, the Hollywood community can care for those individuals who have given so much of their talent that others may find happiness and enjoyment in their work.

"The home will be available to anyone in the motion picture business who finds himself or herself without work, without resources, or without a home. Those with money will pay for their stays. Those without that ability will pay nothing. This home will provide future security for so many who have contributed to our art. It has been a project with which I am proud to be associated. Both as a planner and a financier. There are plenty of others who have stepped forward with either monetary resources or other forms of support. I'd like to introduce one of those to you now. I present the lovely....Miss Joan Bennett."

Miss Bennett was elegantly clad in mulberry silk. She delicately made her way up the stair onto the platform and spoke about the need to care for their own. Her last words echoed passionately among the group: "And I myself pledge to maintain this place as a permanent home for those who are no longer able to provide the necessities of life for themselves. We should all do that, to ensure that the home will always have our support. I urge you to give to the fund, so we can keep the home running at optimal levels for some time. Your generosity is appreciated. Please speak to one of the representatives about making a donation or setting up a recurring payment. Thank you!"

More applause thundered across the wide lawns and neatly kept beds of bright impatiens, vinca, and pelargoniums. As soon as the speeches were over, most of the crowd headed for the tables set with glasses of punch and tiny tea sandwiches. Rationing had begun, but the variety was still good, and Hollywood had always followed its own rules.

In the audience were two ladies sitting side by side. One was a stately blonde in her mid-forties, fashionably dressed in a forest green bengaline suit, with an expensive Cartier watch and emerald earrings dangling from her ears. The other was a brunette, her hair shot through with gray, less well dressed, and without the jewels. The most noticeable thing about her was the elaborate back brace she wore. They sat quietly, in no hurry for food or drink. If anyone had examined them carefully, they might have recognized the two as relics from another time. But no one looked too closely. They were busy oohing and aahing over the features of the home, admiring the architecture of William Pereira, and socializing with the modern-day cadre of movie stars present.

"I heard about the accident, Vera," Phyllis said. "I'm so sorry. Are you in a lot of pain?"

"Usually," Vera said. She moved with difficulty. The previous year, she had been hit by a car, tossed into the air, then hit again as she landed. She'd only recently been discharged from the hospital, after many surgeries. The road back had been hard and painful. But this was one event she'd sworn not to miss. She was wracked with guilt for the death of a friend over five years before. "And you? How are you, Phyl?"

"Fine." Phyl was now dwelling on the impending breakup of her marriage to Billy Seeman. She had plenty of complaints, but none of them compared to the fact that their friend was dead. And the guilt was overwhelming. She lived with it every day.

"We should have been there for her, Phyl," Vera said on a long sigh. "Either one of us could have helped her, but we didn't. She was so close-lipped. She'd never complain out loud. I never knew how bad things had gotten. I could have let her move into our spare bedroom. I could have given her a place to live. You could have helped her back east—maybe tried to help her get some roles on Broadway with all your connections. But we didn't. I didn't realize how badly she was floundering. I didn't check in with her often enough toward the end. I didn't think about her as often as I should have. And now I think of her every day. And how we weren't there for her. And how I wish more than anything that we had been."

"I know. All the money in the world, and I didn't help my best friend." Phyl shook her head and began to cry.

"I was so worried about little Marie," Vera whispered. "After Frances died, I got so overprotective. I was afraid to let her out of my sight. I was so concerned about my daughter, but I failed my best friend. We both did." Tears pooled in her eyes too.

"I made a donation to the fund for the home," Phyl said.

"Me too," Vera said. "It wasn't much, but I had to do it."

"Do you think she knows? Do you think she can watch everything from up there and see how sorry I am?"

"I hope so," Vera said. "I hope she can forgive me. Forgive us. And remember us as we were, all those years ago."

"Once a bathing beauty, always a bathing beauty..." Phyl whispered.

THE END

AUTHOR'S NOTES

- The Motion Picture Relief Fund (incorporated in 1921) built the Motion Picture Country House in 1940. Many people pointed to Marie's death as the impetus that spurred them into action.

- Technically, the Bathing Beauties didn't really get started until 1917. I hope Sennett aficionados will forgive me for their nudge into 1916 for plot and simplification purposes.

- Marie's story of how she and Sonny met was featured in the February 1929 issue of *Motion Picture* magazine. She said she was in Balboa on location, Vera was with her, and one day there was a regatta. I later found a newspaper photo of Marie at the Balboa Water Carnival and was able to find ads for that same carnival with attractions and other information.

- Ken was a cardboard cutout until I discovered his mother had also been an actress, and so had his uncle Otis (who voiced Happy the Dwarf in Disney's animated *Snow White* in 1939). Cross-referencing between newspapers.com and familysearch.org was eye-opening for lots more data about the family, which you're now reading here.

- The story in the *Film Daily* announcing Marie's deal with Metropolitan didn't appear until January 24, 1926.

I adjusted this date slightly backward.

- Marie and Ken's chauffeur was named Frank Melton, changed to Eugene here to avoid confusion with her stepfather.

- Although Charles Foster's *Stardust and Shadows* is often cited as a source for "facts" on Marie, nothing in the book is sourced. I found no independent sources to back up most of what was included (such as Warner Brothers wanting Marie and Ken to marry on the set of *The Beautiful and Damned*, Marie's supposed affair with Howard Hughes, etc. I chose not to use it.

- Newspapers of the day were full of stories about Ken and Marie's breakup, divorce filing, reconciliation, and eventual final divorce. Evidently, Marie wasn't Ken's only wife who couldn't deal with his issues. The man was married a staggering *nine* times. He passed away in 1967.

- Phyllis committed suicide in 1960. I'd like to think that part of the reason was her guilt over deserting Marie when her financial help could have helped the most.

- Vera married twice more after her disastrous marriage to Jackie Taylor. Facts of she and Jackie's marriage and Frances' death were contained in Los Angeles County divorce record #D19253. She was hit by a car as I mention here, and eventually became a dedicated volunteer with the Salvation Army. She passed away in 1966.

- *Paid* was shot a little later than I set it here, which was necessary for continuity purposes.

- Bernard Weiss, the boy at the deli, was mentioned in one of the stories about Marie's death. This tip led me to search the 1936 Los Angeles directory for delicatessens. This, in turn, led me to a deli owned by Nathan Weiss (most likely Bernard's father) at 1334 Vine Street, which is around the corner from The Aftonian apartments.

- Officers Sanderson and Filkas were the actual police who responded to the call at The Aftonian. The Jenks couple were really her landlords, and Bill Bogle did find her body.

- I wanted to include Marie's intended trip to Scotland in 1935 (for an inheritance, it was announced), but nothing ever appeared after the one clipping I found. It appears the result was not what she had hoped for.

- Although I searched and searched for Hughie and Frank's divorce, I couldn't find it. I checked Los Angeles County, the collection at the Huntington Library, and the State of Nevada without success. It might have occurred far earlier than their arrival in California, or perhaps it never occurred and they simply lived apart for the rest of their lives. Yes, Frank gave Marie $1 in his will. Cheap bastard.

- With only one copy of *Bobbed Hair* known to exist in a foreign archive, I was not able to view the actual film. But I was fortunate enough to find the story serialized in multiple newspapers in 1925 and 1926, so I was able to suss out the basic plot of the movie. Ken's broken rib was only mentioned in one paper that I could find.

- Apologies to the animal lovers reading. Jinx, Pooch, and Gaucy were really Marie and Ken's dogs. Because of their relatively young ages, and because Marie ended up with only Max at the end of her life, certain drastic measures were needed here. Bloat had not yet been diagnosed, and it's serious and sudden. Please look it up and watch your dogs for it. Get them to a vet immediately if they exhibit symptoms.

THANKS

- None of this story could have been created without the painstaking research of Stacia Kissick Jones on her blog, *She Blogged By Night*. She disspelled many of the rumors about Marie and provided cold, hard facts.
- My Patreon patrons Shawnna and Elizabeth for your enthusiasm and monthly financial support!
- Michael G. Ankerich - Thanks to his very thorough notes in *Dangerous Curves Stop Hollywood Heels*, I was able to take his research and follow it. Digging up more sources in old newspaper archives, I was able to understand Frank Prevost and his constant travels through the mining communities of the west and southwest. If I'd been Hughie, I'd have gotten tired of the moving too. Diamond stickpin or not!
- Martin Turnbull - As usual, my friend, for support, camaraderie, and the best damned tough-love beta read known to man! From strolls on Venice Beach to drinks at the Miramar, you are a gal's best friend!
- Franchesca Todd, whose heartwarming stories of her grandma, Wee Mae, lit a little spark in my brain. Much love!
- Heidi and Mary for beta reads full of good feedback!

- The helpful employees at the Los Angeles County Supreme Court Archives, who work a thankless job and don't get half the credit they should. Thank you!
- Michael and Even, my Air B & B hosts, for their lovely lodgings in the heart of Silverlake, which allowed me to fully explore Sennett country. It was impossible to visualize until I saw it up close!
- Superfan and now good friend Lauren Semar for all the cheerleading and that fantastic Polo Lounge lunch!
- The wonderful folks at Book Soup for their support and enthusiasm for this newbie!
- Kim Cooper and Richard Schave at Esotouric Tours for their always fascinating glimpses into Los Angeles history.
- Joe Ditler for his knowledge of Coronado and environs (especially early ferries).
- Dana Thorne and Pat McEvoy at the Lambton County Archives for the data about Marie's family in Ontario.

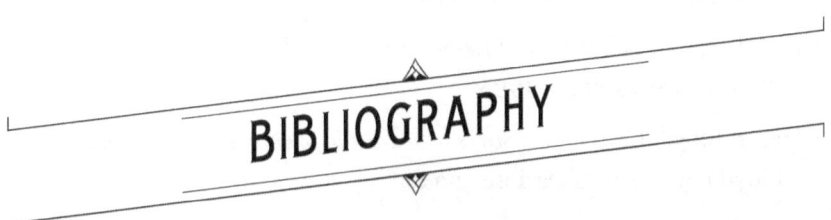

BIBLIOGRAPHY

BOOKS

Alexander, Carolyn Elayne, presented by the Venice Historical Society. *Images of America: Venice, California.* Charleston, SC: Arcadia Publishing, 1999.

Ankerich, Michael G. *Dangerous Curves Atop Hollywood Heels: The Lives, Careers, and Misfortunes of 14 Hard-Luck Girls of the Silent Screen.* Duncan, Oklahoma: Bear Manor Media, 2011.

Ankerich, Michael G. *Hairpins and Dead Ends: The Perilous Journeys of 25 Actresses Through Early Hollywood.* Duncan, Oklahoma: Bear Manor Media, 2017.

Basten, Fred. *Paradise by the Sea: Santa Monica Bay. A Pictorial History of Santa Monica, Venice, Marina Del Rey, Ocean Park, Pacific Palisades, Topanga, & Malibu.* Santa Monica, California: Hennessey+Ingalls, 1997.

Beauchamp, Cari. *My First Time in Hollywood.* Los Angeles: Asahina & Wallace, 2015.

Bingen, Stephen, Stephen X. Sylvester, and Michael Troyan. *MGM - Hollywood's Greatest Backlot.* Solana Beach, CA: Santa Monica Press, 2011.

Birchard, Robert S. *Early Universal City.* Charleston, South Carolina: Arcadia Publishing, 2009.

Brown, Karl. *Adventures with D.W. Griffith.* Toronto: Farar, Straus and Giroux, 1973.

Cerra, Julie Lugo and Marc Wanamaker. *Movie Studios of Culver City.* Charleston, SC: Arcadia Publishing, 2011.

Cherichetti, David. *Mitchell Leisen Hollywood Director.* Los Angeles: Photoventures Press, 1995.

Clymer, Floyd. *Cars of the Stars and Movie Memories.* Los Angeles: Floyd Clymer Publications, no date.

Dangcil, Tommy. *Postcard History Series: Hollywood Studios.* Charleston, SC: Arcadia Publishing, 2007.

Dawson, Jim. *Los Angeles's Bunker Hill. Pulp Fiction's Mean Streets and Film Noir's Ground Zero!* Charleston, SC: The History Press, 2012.

Delaney, Jeff. *Newport Beach's Balboa and Balboa Island.* Charleston, SC: Arcadia Publishing, 2007.

Dick, Bernard. *City of Dreams. The Making and Remaking of Universal Pictures.* Lexington, KY: University Press of Kentucky, 1997.

Diorio, Al. *Barbara Stanwyck: A Biography.* New York: Coward-McCann, Inc., 1980.

Drinkwater, John. *The Life and Adventures of Carl Laemmle.* New York: GP Putnam's and Sons, 1931.

Dumaux, Sally A. *King Baggot: A Biography and Filmography of the First King of the Movies.* Jefferson, NC and London: McFarland & Company, Inc., 2002.

Fleming, E.J. *The Fixers: Eddie Mannix, Howard Strickling and the MGM Publicity Machine.* Jefferson, NC: McFarland & Company, Inc. Publishers, 2005.

Golden, Eve. *John Gilbert: The Last of the Silent Film Stars.* Lexington, KY: University Press of Kentucky, 2013.

Golden, Eve. *Vamp: The Rise and Fall of Theda Bara.* Lanham, Maryland: Vestal Press, 1998.

Heimann, Jim. *Out With the Stars: Hollywood Nightlife in the Golden Era*. New York: Abbeville Press, 1985.

Kemper, Tom. *Hidden Talent: The Emergence of Hollywood Agents*. Berkeley, CA: University of California Press, 2010.

Lahue, Kalton and Terry Brewer. *Kops and Custards: The Legend of Keystone Films (A Book)*. Norman, OK: University of Oklahoma Press, 1968.

Schroeder, Barbara and Clark Fogg. *Beverly Hills Confidential: A Century of Stars, Scandals, and Murders*. Los Angeles: Angel City Press, 2012.

Sennett, Mack. *Father Goose: The Story of Mack Sennett*. New York: Covici-Friede Publishers, 1934.

Sennett, Mack with Cameron Shipp. *King of Comedy*. Lincoln, Nebraska: toExcel Press, an imprint of iUniverse, 1954, 2000.

Spoto, Donald. P*ossessed: The Life of Joan Crawford*. New York: William Morrow- Harper Collins, 2010.

Stanton, Jeffrey. *Venice of America 'Coney Island of the Pacific'.* Los Angeles: Donahue Publishing, 1987.

Thomas, Bob. *King Cohn: The Life and Times of Hollywood Mogul Harry Cohn*. 1967. Reprint. Beverly Hills, CA: New Millenium Press, 2000. Print.

Tornabene, Lynn. *Long Live the King: A Biography of Clark Gable*. New York: Pocket Books, 1976.

Vieira, Mark. *Irving Thalberg: Boy Wonder to Producer Prince*. Berkeley: University of California Press, 2010.

Walker, Brent E. *Mack Sennett's Fun Factory Volume 1*. Jefferson, NC: McFarland & Company, Inc. Publishers, 2010.

Walker, Brent E. *Mack Sennett's Fun Factory Volume 2*. Jefferson, NC: McFarland & Company, Inc. Publishers, 2010.

Wallis, Hal and Charles Higham. *Starmaker: The Autobiography of Hal Wallis*. New York: MacMillan Publishing Co., Inc., 1980.

Ward, Richard Lewis. *When the Cock Crows: A History of the Pathe' Exchange*. Carbondale, IL: Southern Illinois University Press, 2016.

Warner Sperling, Cass and Cork Milner. *Hollywood Be Thy Name: The Warner Brothers Story*. Rocklin, CA: Prima Publishing, 1994.

Watson, Jr., Coy. *The Keystone Kid - Tales of Early Hollywood*. Santa Monica: Santa Monica Press, 2001.

FILMS AND VIDEOS
Personal copies

- *Blonde for a Night*
- *The Marriage Circle*
- *The Flying Fool*
- *Party Girl*

UCLA Film Archives

- *Girl in the Pullman*
- *The Godless Girl*
- *It's a Wise Child*
- *Paid*

Online

- *Getting Gertie's Garter* <https://www.youtube.com/watch?v=P8NcAHPxpRw&t=195s>
- Jamon2112. "Hollywood - Ep 8: Comedy - A Serious Business" April 19, 2014. Online video clip. Youtube. Accessed April 20, 2014. <https://www.youtube.com/watch?v=qwfA7suKAng>
- *The Golden Age of Comedy* <https://www.youtube.com/watch?v=nVLyppnCOjA>
- *Ladies of Leisure* <https://www.youtube.com/watch?v=OJ8HmUcuJfU&t=2s>

ARCHIVES

Los Angeles Supreme Court Archives divorce records:

- Harlan vs. Harlan Record #D59479
- Taylor vs. Taylor Record #D19253

Margaret Herrick Library:

- Hollywood Museum Collection - Universal Film Manufacturing Co. Photograph album 1926

- Dwinelle Benthall and Rufus McCosh Scrapbook #1 1923-1928 Folder of removed material circa 1920s; contains: clippings and photographs, including sixteen 3x5 photos of Universal City [San Fernando Valley, New York street, Chinese temple, Monte Carlo sets for FOOLISH WIVES (Universal 1922), Austrian sets for MERRY GO-ROUND (Universal, 1923)], 1921-23. (1-OS)

- Mack Sennett papers- Prevost, Marie contains: contract, September 15, 1919, 2 pages; option, February 14, 1920, 1 page; option, July 1, 1920 (94.f-1444)

WEBSITES

Americans of Jewish Descent. <http://aojd-online.net/tng/getperson.php?personID=I25764&tree=aojd>

Arizona Memory Project <http://azmemory.azlibrary.gov/cdm/newspapers>

Bruce Long's Taylorology (Juanita Hansen, Part II) <http://www.taylorology.com/issues/Taylor27.txt>.

California Digital Newspaper Collection <https://cdnc.ucr.edu/cgi-bin/cdnc>

Colorado Historic Newspapers Collection <https://www.coloradohistoricnewspapers.org/>

Family Search. February 10, 2010 and subsequent visits. <www.familysearch.org>.

Fulton History <http://fultonhistory.com/Fulton.html>

GoogleNews Archives. January 13, 2011 and subsequent visits <https://news.google.com/newspapers?hl=en>.

Media History Project. February 13, 2012 and subsequent visits. <http://mediahistoryproject.org/fanmagazines/>.

Nevada Newspaper Archive <https://newspaperarchive.com/us/nevada>

newspapers.com <https://www.newspapers.com>

She Blogged By Night (Marie Prevost Project): <http://sheblogged-bynight.com/marie-prevost-project>

Utah Digital Newspapers <https://digitalnewspapers.org>

Water and Power Associates - Early Los Angeles Historical Buildings (1900-1925) (multiple pages) http://waterandpower.org/museum/Early_LA_Buildings%20(1900%20-%201925)_Page_1.html>

CONTACT

Want to know all the latest news from Laini?

Sign up for my newsletter at: www.lainigiles.com

Email me at: lainigiles@yahoo.com

Tweet me at: 4gottenflapper@twitter.com

See Pinterest boards on each book: pinterest.ca/lainigiles

Did you like this book? If so, writing a review at the website where you bought it (or at goodreads.com) will go a long way toward boosting its profile. A few words about what you liked with a star or two are most appreciated!

Want to see more books like these? It costs a lot to research and order records. Consider supporting me at Patreon:

https://www.patreon.com/lainigiles

www.ingramcontent.com/pod-product-compliance
Lightning Source LLC
Chambersburg PA
CBHW051209120726
47905CB00004B/1046